Before the Sun Goes Down

Clif Petty

10 - 30 -17

ISBN: 1543148646
ISBN 13: 9781543148640
Library of Congress Control Number: 2017902495
CreateSpace Independent Publishing Platform
North Charleston, South Carolina

For my father, Charles, and my nephew Justin.

Prologue

February 10
Alpha Cemetery, near Cascade, Idaho

REUBEN AXTELL FOUND it hard to concentrate on the preacher's words because his mind kept roaming back to that campfire and to the ghost story that Rains had told him.

Rains had been convinced that he had seen a spirit of some sort, a messenger from the other side. Reuben had been just as convinced that his cousin had seen a drunk white man, probably a lost hunter. The two of them had mulled it over around that campfire, Rains telling and retelling how he had first seen the man wandering aimlessly in the middle of a big stand of fir trees. It had been snowing, he said, light at first and then heavier about the time that he had encountered the stranger. Rains said he appeared from out of nowhere, looking a bit like one of the cowboys from the stockyards, who'd somehow wandered twenty miles into the wilderness. The man ran from him, in an odd jerky gait that Rains said was deceptively fast. Rains tracked him and called out, but the man never answered. The stranger only laughed, in a way that Rains said he could never quite describe, and moaned as though unable to talk. Then somehow Rains lost him. He said the man disappeared.

Reuben had teased his cousin, something he regretted now. Maybe if he'd taken the story more seriously, Rains wouldn't have kept going back to that forest, scratching around and looking for signs. Reuben had always had a hard time finding the right balance with the old ways and with stories of spirits in the forest.

Out of respect for Rains, he had gone out that next day, alone, and searched the area where Rains said he had seen the laughing man. It had been a decent day for tracking when he started out. The snow had stopped falling. But the sky had remained a heavy gray, and as he neared the spot, the wind had picked up. He had finally located Rains's trail. But he found no other human tracks. The wind had blown some of the snow around by then, and a single snowmobile had churned some of the ground. Reuben never told Rains that he had gone out that day. And now he didn't know why. Maybe it was spite.

The small group under the green canopy began singing a hymn, and Reuben cleared his throat and joined the chorus. When the song was over, a sudden gust of wind snapped a corner of the canopy, a single clap that was both sharp and unwelcome.

Reuben mumbled along with one of the traditional songs, his eyes wandering to the forests just beyond the snowy plain of the cemetery.

Chapter I

PROFESSOR DERRICK ANDERSON turned a key in one of the doors at the south entrance of Turner Hall, paused to take one last look at the beautiful May morning, and then yanked his key back and stepped inside. In spite of the bright May morning, it was dark inside the building. Turner Hall was one of the few buildings on the Idaho State University campus that had survived the 1918 fire. And so it had been repeatedly restored over the years, in spite of its Gothic gloom and narrow spaces. Anderson heaved his bulging briefcase into an ancient wooden chair by the outer door to his office and then walked back to turn on the interior lights.

He had that same old feeling as he walked toward the light switch—that he was retracing the steps of some long-gone professor who had opened up Turner Hall in 1894 or 1929. The fluorescent lights flickered a moment and then began to set. The white light tended to banish Turner's historical ghosts and to move time forward a hundred years or so. Derrick unlocked the outer door, walked the short distance to his office, and then unlocked his office door. After turning on his office lights and computer, he lugged the briefcase from the chair in the outer hallway to its usual resting place on the ancient credenza behind his desk. He withdrew two fat stacks of ungraded papers and set them on his desk. This would require coffee.

Anderson pocketed his keys and walked back out to the main hallway. Janice was just walking in the building. Her head was down, and a strand of dark brown hair covered her face as she worked to drop her keys in their proper spot in her massive black tote bag.

"Good morning, Janice," Derrick said.

Janice jumped and pulled her black tote close to her chest.

"Oh, Derrick. Whew, you scared me to death."

"So sorry! I thought you saw me. Here, can I help?"

"No, I'm fine. Good morning, by the way. Now that I'm breathing again." She smiled and ran a hand over her head to smooth her hair back. She was a petite woman, early sixties, with a pleasant smile and cheerful blue eyes. She was wearing a stylish navy-blue raincoat. Derrick hadn't heard a forecast of rain, but if Janice was wearing rain gear, there was a good chance that it would be raining by the time he left the office.

"Tell me you didn't sleep at your desk," she said.. She had recovered from the scare and was reaching her full office stride.

Derrick picked up the pace to stay alongside. "No, I'm not to that point yet. But I may get there soon. The grading is stacked up. How are things in the office?" Derrick asked.

"The usual crazy. But the end is near, huh?"

"Amen."

"After I unlock the main office, I plan to head down and get a pot of coffee on. Should be ready in about five minutes," Janice said.

"That sounds great. Thanks, Janice."

"You bet. Have a good morning."

"You too."

Derrick loitered around his mailbox and scanned a few journals while the coffee brewed. The coffee aroma filled the small workroom, and he felt himself gaining steam. Derrick poured himself a full cup and then headed back down the long hallway to his office. He passed Professors Aaron Jenson and Margaret Ellison on the way to his office and exchanged greetings. Anderson was grateful to reach his office corridor without encountering anyone else. He closed the outer door and took a seat at his desk.

8:45 a.m.
Windsor Arms Apartments
Two Blocks from Idaho State

Toby Davis took a quick gulp of coffee and was about to grab his backpack and keys when the apartment doorbell rang. *Crap. Who could that be?* He was already running late for class.

He was irritated and then confused when he swung the door open. It wasn't Cindy or Reuben. Some stranger. Great.

"Hey, listen," Toby began in a rush, "if you are selling something, I hate to be a jerk but I am running *so* late."

"Not selling anything, I promise." The stranger held up his palms in mock surrender. He didn't look like a college student—older and more like a guy who exercised a lot. Physical trainer? Were they going door-to-door these days?

"Jake. Name's Jake Turner. I'm a friend of Reuben's. Is he here?"

"Uh, no. Reuben's in class. But you can catch him after that if you want. He's at Turner Hall, room one oh two. If you go right—"

"You're Toby, right?" This guy was planted on the front step. Calm. Confident. Like Reuben, Toby thought. Must be an Indian thing. He dropped the arm that had been pointing out directions.

"That's right." Toby sighed.

"Reuben speaks highly of you. Listen, can I come in for just a minute? I don't think I've got time to track Reuben down after class. I'm just on my way through town, and my boss is on my tail, you know?" Jake said. "But one of my relatives made something special for Reuben, and I wanted to make sure and get it to him as quickly as possible."

"All right, sure, come on in," Toby said as he moved back slowly and opened the door wider.

Jake stepped inside and surveyed the apartment: one couch, one chair, a big flat-screen television—all the comforts of home.

"So no Federal Express, huh?" Toby asked.

"I'm sorry?" Jake gave Toby a quizzical look.

"The special gift…the one your relative made…I was just thinking that you might have shipped it or something."

"No, that wouldn't work. I wanted to deliver it personally." Jake smiled and took a seat on the couch.

"Have a seat," Toby muttered. "You want some coffee or something?" Toby asked and started toward the small kitchen.

"No, I'm good, bro. Thanks."

Toby turned back and took a seat in the green chair across from the couch.

"You and Reuben have a nice setup here. Just the two of you?"

"Yeah." Toby nodded toward the back of the apartment. "Place is set up for three, but Chris moved out last semester—grades."

"Oh." Jake nodded knowingly. "Happens."

For a moment there was silence. Toby cleared his throat. "So, are you Nez Percé?"

"Me? No." Jake shook his head. "Different tribe. Different school. But Reuben and I met through football. I was helping at Ridgecrest, and his uncle was an old army buddy of mine. So we all began hanging out and going hunting—that sort of thing."

"Oh, I just thought…" Toby motioned toward Jake's left arm.

"This?" Jake laughed and rolled up his sleeve so that the entire tattoo showed. "Oh yeah, I could see how you would think Nez

Percé—*NP*. But no, this one was for a girlfriend: Nancy Peters. What we do for women, huh?"

"Yeah, right?" Toby said. "So you're a coach?"

"No, I was just helping out in my spare time. Small-town rez stuff, you know. My job is equipment sales. I travel a lot."

"Oh."

A car backfired outside. Toby jumped. Jake didn't move and seemed not to notice. He drummed his fingers on the frayed arm of the couch and then looked down absently at his watch.

"Oh man, I need to text my boss!" Jake said suddenly. He began patting the pockets on his black cargo pants. "Shoot, I must have left my cell phone back at the hotel. Toby, would you mind if I borrowed your phone just to send a quick text. Then I can get out of your way and back on the road."

"Sure, no problem." Toby stood up and handed Jake his cell phone.

Jake turned away slightly and stooped over the phone. There was a moment of silence and then a light whoosh sound.

"Good. Perfect," Jake said. He stood up straight and stretched. Toby's phone was in his left hand. "Now just let me get that gift for Reuben." Jake rummaged in a coat pocket for a second, and then his right hand moved forward swiftly.

Toby only saw the barrel of the gun for a split second. He'd seen a silencer in a few movies. The gun hardly made a sound.

Jim Crowfoot slipped on latex gloves and locked the front door to the apartment. It was the first time he had used the alias Jake Turner, but he liked the sound of it. He took out Toby's cell phone and scanned his most recent texts. The emoticons made it pretty easy for Crowfoot to pick out Cindy as the girlfriend. He lifted Toby's hand and used the index finger to type: *Reuben has a gun. Acting strange.* He dropped

Toby's hand. Then Crowfoot took out a disposable phone from another pocket and typed: *All present and accounted for.* He hit send. Then he began cleaning up. He didn't have much time, and he couldn't afford any mistakes. He needed to be outside Turner Hall by 9:40 a.m.

9:30 a.m.

Turner Hall

The Turner Hall parking lot was filling up, but Tribal Police Officer Jim Crowfoot managed to find a spot in a back corner underneath a shade tree. After turning the key on the unmarked police cruiser, he took a long, slow sip of coffee. He checked his watch: 9:34 a.m. So far, so good.

Several students were gathered at the crosswalk, backpacks slung across their shoulders. One of them, a young guy in a St. Louis Cardinals jersey, bolted across the street toward the Do Not Walk signal. He was laughing and waving the others on, but the group held back as a Mustang roared past and the driver honked his horn. Crowfoot took another drink of coffee and scanned the parking lot. A couple dozen students were slowly migrating toward the intersection at the university's main entrance. Most were trudging along checking their cell phones or drinking their Starbucks. Here and there another car was sliding into the few open parking spaces.

Just another day at the U, Crowfoot thought. He downed the last sip of coffee and checked his service revolver one last time. His leather holster creaked as he shifted his weight and unfolded from the driver's seat. He was right at six foot, thickly built, with especially powerful forearms. In Afghanistan they had nicknamed him "Popeye." He ran a hand over his moderate crew cut of coal-black hair and then tossed his aviator shades back in the car and closed the door. He wouldn't need his shades today.

Crowfoot had locked up the black sedan and taken several steps when he spotted a disjointed-looking figure across the street. The young man mostly looked like a college student—tattered jeans, gray T-shirt, hiking boots. But he was carrying a bag like the one that baseball players carry. He was tall and thin, and the equipment bag gave him a seesaw gate. The kid looked up and nodded in Crowfoot's direction. *Nice try at casual*, Crowfoot thought.

Crowfoot had been against this plan at first, and now he was hoping that he hadn't made a serious mistake by approving it. This kid had strolled into one of their organization's chat rooms and talked up his desire to be a martyr for the tribal cause. Suicide agents weren't reliable, Crowfoot had argued, and anyway, if they were going to use them, then the Guardians should recruit their own. He didn't like the idea of taking on this eager volunteer.

But the other leaders had argued that the kid and his crazy plot could create a convenient smoke screen for taking out Reuben Axtell and his roommate. And they also thought that the story of a couple of Native school shooters could stir the pot of animosity between tribal people and Anglos. There was likely to be a backlash, and the Guardians could step in when the tribes got their backs up to defend themselves.

Crowfoot had proposed something less spectacular, like a botched burglary or an argument that got out of hand. All of the Guardian leaders believed that Reuben had shared some of what he knew with his roommate. So the roommate had to go, and he and Reuben had to be taken out at the same time. A double homicide would make news no matter the circumstances. But if they set it up right, Crowfoot believed, it wouldn't draw unusual attention, and nothing like the attention drawn by a school shooting. The kid was persistent though, and the other leaders became persuaded that investigators would see a school shooting and assume that they knew what to look for. They would see a troubled young loner acting out his revenge. The kid would make sure the classic signs were there in spades. It helped that the kid knew nothing about Rains's death, or about anything specific, for that matter. They could edit and steer his tribal rants so that they were too general to lead back in their direction.

Finally Crowfoot had suggested a compromise. He would take care of the roommate himself, and Crowfoot would follow the would-be martyr to make sure that he took out Reuben before plunging into the rest of his dark video-game fantasy. The gun Crowfoot used to kill the roommate would be planted with Reuben's body. The kid would get his two minutes of gory fame, and the Guardians would get rid of two potential problems in the all-too-familiar fog of a school-shooting incident.

Crowfoot could see now that the kid was quickening his pace as he headed toward the intersection. A city bus barreled through the intersection just as he arrived at the crossing. By the time it had passed him and the intersection was clear, the kid was gone. He must have already headed into Turner Hall. As Crowfoot had suspected, this kid was overanxious and lost in his own fantasies. He had better get inside and make sure that this operation didn't fall apart. Officer Crowfoot broke into a run and placed one hand on his holstered revolver.

9:40 a.m.

Reuben Axtel's cell phone buzzed and the light glowed through his cargo-pants pocket. Reuben slid the phone from his pocket and checked the text. It was from Lee. He was probably wanting Toby to help him get his old Chevelle SS started again. The text read: *Hey Chief—some big Indian dude parked on your doorstep when I drove by this morning. Maybe a cop trying not to look like a cop, so heads up. I got that money I owe you, so meet me at JJ's later.*

Reuben turned off the screen quickly and shoved the cell phone in his pocket.

Maybe it wasn't him. Reuben's mind raced. Pretty early for salesmen. Lee wasn't the sharpest on cultures—well, other than gang cultures. Maybe the guy was Hispanic or just a dark Anglo. Anyway, Officer Crowfoot wouldn't just show up on the doorstep in broad daylight. *"Hello, would Reuben happen to be home?"* Didn't make sense. Reuben's leg was bouncing, and he could feel his heart picking up the pace. Whatever the odds, he couldn't take any chances. "Big Indian dude" was just too close for comfort, even if it did come from his shady pal Lee. He couldn't go home after class. And he couldn't walk out the front door of Turner Hall with the rest of the crowd. He caught the professor's eye and made a few quick hand signals for not feeling well. The prof raised his eyebrows in a question and then nodded quickly. *Small benefit of being a good student*, Reuben thought as he slipped quietly out of class. A couple of students were loitering outside the student lounge, waiting for the change of classes. But he knew he didn't have much time. Class would end in a few minutes, and then the mad dash would be on. Reuben began loping past Anderson's office and toward the front doors.

But just as he was about to round the corner, Reuben heard some commotion at the doorway. He froze. To his right he noticed a recess, just under the stairs. He quietly wedged himself into the space, set down his backpack, and waited to make his escape.

9:52 a.m.

Professor Derrick Anderson glanced up at the wall clock in his office. An advisee was scheduled to drop by at 10:00 a.m., so he had just enough time to finish grading this paper. Mercifully it was a good paper. Adam Sterling. *Thank you, pal,* he thought. *Reading one of your papers always gets me through the next three.*

The halls outside his office were beginning to buzz with the change of morning classes. Like clockwork he could hear Reuben Axtell leaving the European History class down the hall. Derrick smiled to himself. *So much for Indians who are whisper quiet.* Reuben's departure from that classroom sounded like a rhino building up steam. Granted, the kid went at least 235. So Reuben wasn't going to go anywhere fast without making some noise.

Derrick had only had Reuben in one class, but he liked him. He carried his "great Red burden" gracefully, patiently dealing with those who fawned over his Nez Percé heritage and those who expected him to steal laptops and scalp his enemies. Mostly Derrick respected the young man for his depth and good nature. He could tell that Reuben carried some scars, but for someone so young, he also didn't seem to dwell on them. He was bright, wickedly funny, and comfortable with himself. He was also determined, and you didn't want to get between him and any goal. Right now Ray could hear that Reuben's goal was reaching the sunny outdoors.

Just as he was turning back to write "Great work" on Adam Sterling's last page, Derrick heard something that caught his attention. It sounded like a scuffle of some sort and then a thud. Something heavy had hit the floor near the doorway. More scuffling of feet, someone running now. And then, a few seconds later, a burst of gunfire.

Derrick turned off his desk light and paused a second to let his eyes adjust to the sunlight spilling into the hallway outside his office. The shooting had stopped, and he had caught a glimpse of the shooter moving north past his office door. It was only a glimpse, but Derrick guessed the guy was roughly his height but skinnier and right handed. He was dressed like a college student—no tactical garb or body armor that Derrick could see. Near the south wall, Derrick spotted an equipment bag lying on the floor. A weak moan came from the other side of the exit, in an area of shadow near the bottom of a stairwell. Screams and the sounds of chaos were echoing down the hallway. Another short burst, a crescendo of screams. Derrick tried to filter the sounds and to focus all his senses on the shooter. He heard a click and mechanical slide. By sound Derrick estimated the distance he needed to close at about fifteen feet.

The open hallway was a lousy place to confront a shooter. Derrick realized he would probably be shot before he covered two steps. It was the longest of long shots that he would have a chance to reach the shooter in any kind of shape to stop him. But then again, maybe the guy was a goofball. Heck, maybe he was blind in one eye. Derrick slid off his shoes and socks and then rushed out of his office and toward the shooter. He almost made it. But when the shooter turned toward him, Derrick lost a step. He knew this guy: a former student—Isaac Dupree.

In that split second, Isaac Dupree turned hard to his left and fired. Derrick was hit and spun around awkwardly. But then just as he began falling, his right hand caught hold of something solid—the barrel of an assault rifle.

Everything after that was a blur of black and red. A scream. A thud. He and Isaac were locked together and beginning to go down. Derrick's head hit the wall hard. Then it was quiet. And then everything faded to dark.

Chapter 2

JESSIE ANDERSON SAT slumped in the hospital version of a recliner. She hadn't slept all night, but now some of the adrenaline and fear was slowly evaporating. She could feel herself sinking into the chair. She batted her eyes wide and checked Derrick. He was OK. She couldn't stop saying that to herself. *He's OK.*

Derrick had been in and out all day, just enough to confirm what the doctors told her—that his body would need to rest but that he was going to be OK—but not enough to have anything close to a conversation. She shushed him when he tried too hard to talk, when he started explaining and then trailed off into exhaustion. She was simply content to know that he was alive, that he was still here with her.

Her head bobbed once, and then Jessie surrendered to sleep. She had no idea how long she was out, but suddenly she could clearly hear Derrick talking to her.

"Jessie…baby, you awake?"

"Derrick! Yes, um, yeah. I am now. Hello."

Jessie slid forward in the recliner and leaned toward her husband.

"Hi. Where am I?" Derrick turned his head slightly, and Jessie thought she caught him wince. But he covered quickly with a hazy smile.

"Well, you're in the hospital…Mercy Hospital."

"Why?"

"Um, that's sort of a long story. Are you really awake?"

"Maybe. I think so."

"You were at work. There was a school shooter. You stopped him, but not before he shot you. In the shoulder muscle mostly. Cracked a couple of ribs. A concussion—probably from hitting the wall. But thankfully the bullets missed the serious stuff—joints, nerves. The doctors say that you are going to be fine. Just some rest and recovery."

"Oh."

"I'm so sorry, Derrick. But you stopped him before it was much worse."

"Hmm. I'm getting tired again. You look beautiful."

"Aw. Is that the medicine talking or my hero husband?"

Jessie leaned over and kissed Derrick lightly on the forehead. He closed his eyes and sighed.

Jessie waited to make sure that Derrick was asleep again and then slipped quietly out into the hallway. The police officer was still sitting in a chair bolt upright near the door. Jessie startled and then caught herself.

"Oh, hi, Officer Brown. They still have you stationed here?"

"Yes, ma'am, Mrs. Anderson. It's procedure to maintain a watch for forty-eight hours. Not to worry. Just making double sure that you all don't have anything to worry about. How is your husband doing?"

"Good, fine—thanks. He just woke up and talked with me a bit."

"Oh, that's great to hear. Everyone is pulling for him. He saved those students."

"Yes, I know. It scares me to death to know what he did, but now I'm glad he did it."

"Yes, ma'am. Can I get you anything or help out in any way?"

"Thanks so much, but no. We are all good. I'm just going to walk down the hall and make a phone call."

"I'll be here."

The hallway was bright by comparison to the room, and Jessie felt herself waking up again. She remembered this sort of exhausted wakefulness from the time she had cared for her father a few years ago. Coffee always helped. The coffee station was mercifully quiet and empty. As she stirred in creamer, she began to prepare herself for the next step. She knew she had to call Ray, and sooner rather than later. But she also knew that she needed to have her wits about her. Ray would want to come charging through the phone connection. He would want to talk to Derrick. He would want to talk to the doctors. He would want to run through a brick wall. She smiled to herself. Even though she was dreading the call, Jessie knew that there was no one better to have on your side than "Crazy" Ray Anderson.

She stirred her coffee and considered the best way to break the news.

Hi, Ray; this is Jessie. How are you? Listen, here's the thing…

Hi, Ray; how are you? Derrick is OK, but there has been an accident…

After a few more run-throughs, she realized her approach was unlikely to matter. Better to take a couple of deep breaths and make the call.

Ray answered on the second ring.

"Hello?"

"Ray, hi. It's Jessie."

"Oh hey, Jessie! Good to hear from you! Sorry for the noise in the background, but I'm at work."

"Oh. Sorry to catch you at work."

"No worries. Is everything OK?"

"Well, everything is OK now. Derrick is fine, but he's in the hospital."

"What? He blow out a knee or something?"

"No, not exactly. I don't know if you saw it on the news, but there was a school shooter at the university. Derrick stopped him, but he got himself shot in the process."

"Jessie, I'm going to move into the shop office, so I can hear you better. Just a second…OK, now I'm good. Did I hear you say Derrick has been shot?"

"Yes. In the shoulder…some glancing off ribs. They operated to remove a few bone fragments and perform some vascular repair, but they were pretty clean wounds. Derrick is doing great. The doctors say that he will fully recover."

"I can't believe it. Of all the things…"

"Yes, I know. But, Ray, he is really doing well."

"Can I talk to him?"

"Not now. He's still in and out, you know. Loopy from the medicine and all. But soon."

There was a long pause. Jessie thought she could hear the clicks and whirs of Ray's brain processing information and planning his next moves. Ray's voice was quiet and a little ominous when he spoke next.

"What about the shooter?"

"He's dead," Jessie replied.

"Good. He messed with the wrong professor."

Suddenly Jessie began to cry. It was the last thing she wanted to do right now, but there was not much she could do about it.

"Are you OK, Jessie?"

"Yeah, sorry. Just kinda hit me there for a minute. But I'm fine."

"I'm so sorry. It's OK; it's perfectly OK. Listen to me—Derrick is going to be fine. We both know how tough he is—behind that brainy, mumbling professor routine of his. Right?"

Jessie smiled and wiped at her cheek. "Yeah, I know. The doctors say the same thing—that most people would have had a harder time with all this." She paused and gripped the counter. "I've just never seen him so hurt, you know…"

Jessie caught a breath and told herself to keep it together. Ray would run through two brick walls if she kept on blubbering like this. But when he spoke again, Ray's voice was softer and warmer than she expected. "Jessie, we're family. You cry and you feel what you feel—it's OK. Sorry I'm not there for you now, but I'm on my way as soon as I can get out of here. In the meantime is there anyone there with you?"

Ray's soothing tone had helped. She felt herself regaining her balance.

"Oh yeah, I have a new police officer friend and shadow. Officer Brown is guarding me and Derrick like we were his long-lost family."

Jessie chuckled and thought she heard a smile from Ray.

"Excellent," Ray responded. "You tell Officer Brown that Derrick's little brother, Ray, is on his way and that I will buy him a steak dinner when I get there. If you're OK, I'm going to let you go now, Jessie. I'm on my way, OK?"

"Thanks, Ray. Listen, be safe. I know it isn't an easy trip. No crazy rush, OK?"

"Don't worry about me. Talk soon."

"Love you, Ray."

"I love you, Sis."

Ray slid his cell phone in his pocket and walked out of the shop office. He needed to hit something. And then he needed to pack his kit and hit the road to Pocatello.

Chapter 3

DERRICK COULD SEE the stray steers peering dumbly through the mesquite break. They looked like little kids who thought they were easily winning at hide-and-seek.

Derrick wasn't amused. He and Ray were behind, and Dad was likely to be pissed. It was snowing pretty steadily now, small sandy flakes that bounced off his hat and saddle.

Where in the heck was Ray? Derrick hadn't seen him since noon. The day was getting away from them. They needed to get these runaways to the corral and loaded on the trailer before the snow set in harder or it got too dark to keep track of everyone.

Derrick eased Cisco toward the far end of the mesquite break. She was way ahead of these three goofballs. Derrick knew that he could drop the reins, and Cisco would plot strategy on her own. But it was getting late, and he was too tired to play it out. Once they had a good angle on the steers, he kicked Cisco in gear and hustled them out of their scrubby mesquite hideaway.

Suddenly lightning flashed on the northern horizon, and Derrick saw the silhouette of a man limping toward him. The man was still some distance away, and the snow was picking up, but Derrick knew that it was Ray. Derrick looked for Dakota, Ray's big paint, but no horse was tied up anywhere that he could see.

"Ray? Ray, you OK?" Derrick shouted.

Ray didn't look up at first. Derrick spurred Cisco and rode past the fugitive calves. As he got closer, it seemed that Ray was hunched over and holding one arm near his chest.

"Ray! Hey, it's Derrick. You hurt? Where's Dakota?"

Ray stopped and looked up. The lightning flashed again behind him, and Derrick shielded his eyes with one hand. He could barely make out the words when Ray began to speak.

"Scattered…They all scattered…"

Derrick could see the blood now, and he reined Cisco to an abrupt stop. He swung quickly out of the saddle and ran toward Ray. The snow was suddenly falling much harder. Derrick cursed the blizzard and leaned toward his brother. Ray was moaning and mumbling something that Derrick couldn't make out. The snow was swirling around his face now, and it was a mix of red and white flakes. Derrick wiped his eyes, and his glove came away streaked with red. Behind him Derrick heard Cisco rear and begin to bolt.

"Ray?"

"Yes, it looks worse than it is actually. But if he had been able to turn another six inches…"

Derrick was plowing through the snow and finally reaching Ray. He extended his hand through the driving snow. And then suddenly Ray was gone. The snow was a blanket now, a red and white weave swirling around him and cutting him off.

Derrick cried out. But the snow was filling his mouth and silencing his cry.

"Derrick! Derrick, it's me—Jessie. Derrick, can you hear me? You OK?"

The snow had stopped, and when Derrick opened his eyes, Jessie was looking down at him with a worried expression on her face. *How did she get here?*

"Yeah, I think so," Derrick replied slowly. Then his eyes sharpened suddenly. "Where's Ray? Is he OK?" "I just got off the phone with him, and he's fine." Jessie leaned close and placed her hand lightly on Derrick's good shoulder. "You were calling out just now, saying Ray's name."

"But Ray's OK? He's not hurt?"

"No, babe, I think you've got this turned around. *You* are hurt. Ray is just fine."

"We were at the ranch..." Derrick trailed off.

"Likely the lingering effects of anesthetic and the trauma."

Derrick was startled to hear another voice. He turned his head and saw the doctor at the foot of his bed.

"Oh. Hi, Doc."

"Derrick, this is Dr. Reynolds," Jessie said. "He performed your surgery."

"Hello, Derrick. Actually I'm one of the surgeons. Dr. Wendy Davis and I performed your surgery together. She's a vascular surgeon. I'm a trauma type."

"Thank you. I guess." Derrick smiled weakly.

"Yeah, I know. Right now you probably feel like we beat you up. But I promise the surgery helped. Gunshot wounds do a lot of damage, especially at close range. But in the grand scheme of things, you were quite fortunate. Nothing we couldn't repair. Some sore ribs and lots of stitching, as you can probably tell. But those will heal over time. You just need to rest and let us know how you are feeling."

Derrick was still trying to get his bearings. He felt like he was blowing on the wind, somehow moving back and forth between the ranch and this hospital room.

"Jessie."

"Yes?"

"Is Ray here?"

"No, but he's on his way."

Derrick closed his eyes.

Dr. Reynolds nodded to Jessie and whispered, as he was departing, "*If you need anything...*"

Just as Dr. Reynolds reached the door, Derrick spoke without opening his eyes. "Hey, Doc, do me a favor and find Dakota. He hates cold weather."

Jessie spoke up and waved Dr. Reynolds good-bye. "Don't worry about Dakota, Derrick. I'll bring him in. You just rest now."

Chapter 4

FBI AGENT LARRY Horton leaned down close and took a good look at the victim. As he was examining the head wound, Pocatello detective Erin Sheppard was reading off the profile:

"Toby Davis, white male, age twenty. University student and, obviously, Reuben Axtell's roommate. Shot twice at close range. Found one nine-millimeter casing by that chair. Still looking for the other one."

"Any signs of a struggle?" Horton asked.

"No. We found half a cup of coffee on the table in the kitchen. His backpack was there as well. Notebook open. We think Davis was sitting in this chair"—Sheppard nodded toward a ragged green lounge chair—"and that the shooter was sitting on the couch across from him. Then looks like Davis stood up. Maybe they started to argue. Anyway, that's when the shooter fired. Angles are consistent with firing at the same level."

"Yeah, and the position of his body looks like he crumpled," Horton added.

"Any signs that anyone else was here? I mean anyone besides Davis and Axtell."

"Still taking prints. But no signs of forced entry or anything," Sheppard answered.

"Adams?" Horton looked past Sheppard to his partner. "Take a look outside, would you, for any tracks or signs of a struggle. That OK with you, Detective Sheppard?"

Sheppard shrugged. "Knock yourselves out. Just keep it clear inside if you don't mind. We don't want to start stepping on each other."

Horton smiled to himself and turned back to the body. Sheppard was an old hand. She knew how to play nice and signal *back off* at the same time.

Adams headed slowly out the front door to check for tracks. Meanwhile Horton took out his pen and lifted the corner of Davis's pants pocket: a few dimes and nickels but otherwise empty. Davis had fallen on his right side, and Horton didn't want to roll the body.

"Excuse me, Detective Sheppard?"

"Yes, Agent Horton?"

Horton thought he detected an edge. Only so much longer that Sheppard would play nice.

"You find his cell phone?"

"The victim?"

"Yes."

Sheppard shot a glance around the room to check in with the other investigators. No one spoke up; one detective shrugged his shoulders.

"Guess not. Not yet anyway."

"I'm sure it will turn up. No college student is ever very far from his cell phone." Horton smiled his best *We're all one big team* at Sheppard and then headed out front to check in with Adams.

The sunlight was blinding, and Horton paused to put on his sunglasses. "See anything?" Horton called out to Adams.

Adams was kneeling in the parking lot about ten feet from the apartment door. He turned and squinted. "Nah, at least nothing that matters. Apartment parking lot is like a haystack full of needles. Cigarette butts, tracks, you name it. But nothing that catches my eye." Adams stood up and walked a few feet toward Horton, still surveying the asphalt but without much enthusiasm. "Why are we giving this such a comb-over, anyway? Looks pretty straightforward. Reuben Axtell and Isaac Dupree plan to do the Columbine thing. Axtell has a beef with his roommate. Or maybe figures his roommate is a loose end. Anyway, on the way to the big dance, he kills Davis. So why search around for tracks or forced entry?"

Horton took out a stick of chewing gum, shoved it in his mouth, and then smiled slyly at Adams. "Mostly because I like seeing you comb a parking lot for clues. You look happy when you are out here sniffing cigarette butts and roaming around."

Adams rolled his eyes.

"But also," Horton continued, "because I'm not sure that crew inside the house can find their way home at night. They haven't found Davis's cell phone yet."

"Davis's cell phone is probably in his car or something, but it won't matter," Adams said. "He just had the wrong roommate."

"Yeah, you're probably right. I think we've covered the bases here well enough for now. Let's go get some lunch. But on the way to my favorite restaurant, I want you to answer one riddle for me."

"What's the bet? You pay for lunch?" Adams began walking toward their car.

"Sure, why not." Horton shrugged.

"OK, what's the riddle?"

"Isaac Dupree brought a bag full of serious hardware to the scene, right?"

"Yeah, so? Pretty typical."

"Right, but with Dupree armed to the teeth, why is Axtell running around all morning armed only with a nine millimeter? What sort of school shooter was this guy?" Horton paused with his hand on the car door handle. "Oh, and after you buy me lunch"—he smiled over the car at Adams—"remind me we need to talk to this Officer Crowfoot. He's the one who had the scrap with Axtell. So maybe he has can answer my puzzler."

"I'm surprised the guy's alive to tell his tale," Adams said as he slid down into the car.

Officer Crowfoot was sporting a head bandage when Horton and Adams located him near the entrance of Turner Hall.

"Officer Crowfoot?"

"Yeah, can I help you?" Crowfoot looked up, smiled, and then winced.

"Ouch—you must have taken quite a knock," Horton said. Then, without waiting for a reply, he added, "Agents Horton and Adams, FBI. Wonder if we can ask you a few questions?"

"Sure, as long as it's not what day it is or how many fingers you are holding up. I'm pretty tired of those two."

"Concussion?" Adams asked.

"Mild. That means it wasn't the doctor's head that got whacked."

Horton and Adams both laughed politely at the joke.

"I'll be writing up my report later, but I suppose it won't hurt to give you guys a preview. So shoot," Crowfoot offered.

"OK," Horton began, "so you were the first on the scene. Is that right?"

"Far as I know. I didn't see anyone else."

"Were you called over here, or how did the timing work out?" Adams asked.

Crowfoot smiled again but more carefully. "I was scheduled to meet with the Native American Student Association this morning. Part community outreach, part recruiting for tribal police. We could always use sharp recruits. Anyway, my session was supposed to start up at nine forty-five in the building next door. I was heading that direction when I saw a strange character lugging an equipment bag into this building."

"The shooter—Isaac Dupree?" Horton asked.

"Yeah, that's the one. He looked suspicious, so I followed him in," Crowfoot said.

"What happened next?"

Crowfoot paused and rubbed his chin. "My attention was focused on Dupree. I was tailing him, you know? I entered the building, and it took a second for my eyes to adjust. And I had to take my sunglasses off. Wish now I had peeled them off outside. Anyway, I tried to follow Dupree and get acclimated. He had rounded the corner there." Crowfoot motioned toward a stairwell at the corner of the entryway and the hallway. "I moved along after him. But as I approached that corner, a big guy lunged from below the stairs. I don't know how a guy that big folded himself up in there, but he came out of nowhere. Strong dude too. That first blow to the head took a lot of the fight out of me."

"Did you get a good look at him?" Adams asked.

"Yeah, like I say, he whacked me good. But I turned and managed to tussle with him before my lights went out. This will all be in my report, but he was a good six feet three and maybe two fifty. Brown skin. Hispanic or Indian. Long black braids."

"And he was armed?" Horton asked.

"Yeah, handgun. I was a bit woozy, but I'm pretty sure it was a nine millimeter. My blood was on it, so that attracted my attention."

"He clubbed you with the gun?"

"Yeah. Twice actually."

"But he never fired it?" Horton asked.

"Not at me, not during our tussle. I don't know about later." Crowfoot nodded gingerly toward the hallway. "Crime lab folks still working on the ballistics and such. I figure maybe I walked in before the big guy—they tell me his name is Reuben Axtell—before he and Dupree had a chance to divvy out their weapons and set their ammunition. Only reason I can figure that a guy holding a nine millimeter doesn't use the business end of it."

Horton looked at Adams, and Adams nodded.

"Thanks, Detective Crowfoot," Horton said. "You know how these things are—everyone has paperwork. We appreciate you talking to us, so we can wrap up our part of the drill."

Adams added, "Say, one last thing: don't crows have claws?"

Crowfoot smiled good-naturedly. "Yeah, haven't heard that one before. Bit of Shoshone humor regarding how a person walks, but it's never funny when I explain the joke."

"Oh," Adams said. "You were a lucky man today, Officer Crowfoot. Glad you are OK, but you might want to take that doctor's advice and get some rest."

"Thanks, but I just feel stupid that I let him get away like that. Now we have a shooter on the loose."

"He won't last long on the run," Horton said as he and Adams turned to go.

Crowfoot watched the two FBI agents carefully as they walked back out the glass doors and toward their cruiser. His head ached, and his mouth tasted like copper. It was probably time to sign out. He had made enough of a show of the dedicated detective. Time to find Reuben Axtell and set things straight.

Chapter 5

RAY BURST THROUGH the hospital room door so suddenly that Jessie tossed her cell phone out of her lap.

"Big brother!" Ray whispered loud enough to hear three rooms away. "What are you doing lying around in bed?"

Jessie had recovered just enough to take a normal breath before Ray swept her up out of the hospital recliner and into a bear hug.

"Sis, all is well. Ray is on duty."

She smiled back tears and felt a surge of relief. If she had been holding a coffee when Ray burst in, she would have third-degree burns right now. But thankfully no burns this time, and she melted into Ray's hug.

"Let go of my wife, you big gorilla," Derrick said hoarsely. "I can still get out of this bed anytime I need to."

"Not seeing it," Ray said. "You look terrible. How bad do you hurt, old man?"

"No more than a bad rodeo," Derrick replied, "or maybe how you felt all those times after we fought."

"Yeah, right." Ray released his grip and grinned back at Jessie. "We'll see about all that when you get well enough. I know it takes older people longer to heal."

Derrick smiled. Really smiled, Jessie thought, the first time since the shooting. Ray was good medicine. She slid to Ray's side and wrapped one arm around his broad shoulders.

"I'm going to let you two cowboys catch up a bit while I run down the hall," she said. "Either of you need anything?"

"A No Visitors sign," Derrick replied, "but other than that I'm good."

"Nothing for me, Jess," Ray said, "thanks."

Jessie glanced back at the two of them as she closed the door. They were already picking up where they left off. She envied them that way. Distance or time didn't seem to affect those two at all.

Officer Brown was talking with a nurse named Sandy when Jessie stepped into the hallway. When he spotted Jessie, he excused himself quickly and headed her way.

"Mrs. Anderson, hi; good morning."

"Jessie, remember?"

"Oh, yes, ma'am. Sorry. Jessie, how are you doing?"

"We are good. Derrick's feeling better, and his brother, Ray, just arrived. They are visiting now." Jessie threw a thumb over her shoulder toward Derrick's room. "The two of them are catching up now."

"Right. I met Ray on his way in. He seems like a great guy."

"A character," Jessie added.

"That too." Officer Brown smiled. Then his face seemed to cloud over. "Listen, Mrs.—Jessie. I have a bit of an update for you."

"OK, what is it?" The transition to the hallway had been abrupt, and Jessie felt suddenly woozy.

"You OK, Jessie?" Officer Brown reached for her elbow. "Why don't we sit over here a second." He guided her toward a chair in a small waiting room.

"Sorry," Jessie began, "probably just late on my morning Diet Coke."

"Hey, you sit tight here. I'll be right back." Brown stepped out of the waiting room and reappeared a second later with a Diet Coke in one hand and a snack pack of trail mix in the other.

"Wow," Jessie said and smiled up at him, "I hope you didn't sprint all the way."

Brown grinned. "No, ma'am. A cop thing—we have a nose for vending machines."

"Thank you." Jessie took a long swig of Diet Coke and peeled open the trail mix. Had she eaten breakfast? She couldn't remember.

"Now, you were saying—an update about the investigation."

"Yes. Nothing major. I hope I didn't give you the wrong impression. It's just that the detectives are wrapping up their work on the scene. Forensics will take a bit longer, but the word I'm getting is that detectives are hoping to wrap things up soon, which all means that they are asking how Derrick is doing, wondering if they might be able to talk to him a little sooner than they had originally expected."

"How soon?" Jessie asked.

"As soon as Derrick is up to it: today or tomorrow would be good."

"Oh wow, that soon."

"I know. We just need his statement. It gets harder to remember details over time. And the detectives just want to make sure that they don't lose anything or miss something important. But look— everyone respects Derrick, and they will work with you to make this as fast and easy as possible. It was a school-shooting case. So they have to cover all the bases that way. But it's also pretty straightforward. So the questions will be routine, and you and your husband will be able to get this step behind you."

"OK, I understand. Will you let them know to set it up."

"Yes, ma'am, I'll take care of that. An Agent Horton of the FBI is heading up this phase, and he may bring along an Agent Adams. He and Horton are working the case together."

"Got it. Thank you. Oh, here's some money for the snacks. "

"No, ma'am." Brown waved his palms at her and smiled. "My treat."

"Thank you."

Jessie stayed in the waiting room for a few minutes after Brown went back to his post. She hadn't wanted to wolf down the trail mix in front of him. The queasy feeling was gone, replaced by early morning hunger.

Agents Horton and Adams caught the hospital elevator and punched the button for the sixth floor. Adams turned to Horton and acted like he'd forgotten something.

"I can't remember, Horton. Are we interviewing this guy or trying to recruit him for the tactical unit?"

"No joke. I can think of a few people he could replace before he even gets well."

"Yeah, I might nominate him to replace Hootch. Can you imagine entering a dark building with that guy covering your ass?"

"I can't imagine entering a street in broad daylight with Hootch covering any part of me."

Officer Brown was checking his cell phone when Horton and Anderson arrived at room 612. He stashed his phone and stood to greet the two agents.

Horton and Adams flashed their identification.

"So, Officer, how's he doing?" Horton nodded toward the hospital room.

"Good, from all I hear anyway. Mrs. Anderson is a vet, but between her calls about horses, I can tell that the reports have improved."

"Did you let her know we were coming today?" Horton looked past Brown to the door.

"Yes, sir, all set."

"OK, you can take a break. We'll give you a shout when we're done here."

Brown nodded and headed down the hallway toward the elevators.

Horton knocked lightly and was surprised when a thickset man with tousled brown hair answered the door. The man seemed planted in the doorway.

"Hello, sir; we're Agents Horton and Adams, FBI." Horton and Adams held their badges up longer than usual, as the man at the door was studying their faces and credentials. Horton began to wonder if he was going to let them in. "And you are...?" Horton asked.

"Ray Anderson. Derrick's brother. How about I see your driver's licenses?"

Adams gave Horton a quick look. "Sure." Both agents pulled out their wallets and held up their licenses for Ray's inspection.

Suddenly the sullen face broke into a smile. "Sorry, agents, just playing defense. Come on in. We've been expecting you."

"Hello, Detectives," Derrick called as Ray moved aside and let Horton and Adams enter. "Please excuse my brother the bouncer."

Horton and Adams moved to the foot of the bed and took their first look at Derrick Anderson. He was smaller than Horton had pictured him: maybe five eleven and around 185. Only the purple and red tip of his injured shoulder was showing through the bandages on his upper arm and side. The rib wrap was just visible through the hospital gown. A few IV lines snaked down from their hangers, and a small panel on the right kept track of vital signs. Horton glanced at the screen and noted with satisfaction that the vitals looked solid.

Anderson's head was wrapped in a broad white bandage. Horton could see the faint outline of blood underneath. The hair around the bandage was darker than his brother's and cut short. He had a broad and open face. Horton's first impression was that Derrick Anderson might make a good poker player. His face was friendly enough but not one that would be easy to read.

Derrick smiled weakly and lifted his uninjured arm to shake hands with Adams and Horton. Horton noticed some purple bruising along the knuckle line. The arm was wrapped in muscle, and the grip, firm.

"Mr. Anderson, thank you for seeing us so soon. We know that you need rest and recovery, so Agent Adams and I will make this as quick and painless as possible."

"Sure, I understand. I'm actually feeling pretty good today."

"That's good to hear. We've seen a lot of gunshot cases, and you look like you are doing great." Horton signaled to Adams, who drew a iPad mini from his overcoat pocket. "So, Mr. Anderson—"

"Derrick."

"Got it. So, Derrick, let's go back to that day and just have you walk us through it. Please tell us anything you remember—even if it doesn't seem like it matters. Why don't you start that morning when you left home and headed to work."

"OK. I was running a little late that morning. I had some trouble sleeping the night before, and I hit snooze a couple times. Jessie, my wife, had already gone. She had a horse she needed to check on, so she left around six thirty a.m. She's a veterinarian. I must have left the house around seven thirty. It's about a fifteen-minute drive from our house to the university. So I would say I arrived at the university around eight or so."

Adams looked up from his iPad to break in. "Derrick, this part could be really important for us. Did you notice anything on that drive, especially as you arrived on campus? Any unusual cars? Something in a place you didn't usually see it? Anything out of the ordinary."

Derrick closed his eyes and lay his head back on the pillow. "Man, I don't know. It was such an ordinary routine. And my head was probably somewhere else. I parked on the southwest side of lot B. It's across the street diagonally from my building. Only a couple of cars in the lot at that time—the usual early arrivals. No, I don't recall anything out of the ordinary."

"Sure, no problem. Go ahead," Adams said.

"I grabbed my briefcase and lunch bag and walked across the parking lot and then across the street. Usual scene: pretty quiet at that time of day, but here and there I probably passed a few students or faculty. Nothing stands out...Guess I was on morning autopilot. So I arrived at my office on the first floor around eight fifteen. Janice Lynn walked in the building a few minutes after me, and we said hello."

"A student?"

"No, sorry. Janice Lynn is our administrative assistant. She works in the main departmental office."

"Got it." Horton nodded. "Go on."

"So after that I walked down to the department mail room and grabbed a cup of coffee. Spoke to a few colleagues on the way back to my office." Derrick turned to face Adams. "The two colleagues' names are Aaron Jenson and Margaret Ellison.

"So I was back in the office and grading by eight thirty," Derrick said.

"Did you see or hear anything that you recall between eight thirty and the time when the shooting incident began?" Horton looked to see that Adams was ready to capture anything important about the timeline.

"No, just a usual day in the office until then."

"OK, that's fine. Then what happened?"

"I was finishing grading one student paper when I heard some noise outside my office in the hallway. It sounded like someone dropped something heavy. Startled me a bit. My office is just down from the south entrance, and the sound came from near there, close to the doors. Then I heard what sounded like scuffling, maybe a grunt or a moan. Then the shots started."

"Derrick, did it sound like the shots came from the same area as the heavy sound you heard or from somewhere else in the building?"

"No, farther in from the doorway, near the outer entrance to my office, maybe five feet to the south of it, and headed north in the hallway."

"OK, then what?"

"So I turned off my desk lamp and moved to the doorway where I could track the shooter. He passed by my outer doorway. Students were leaving class at that time, and most of them were pooled up in the north end. It sounded like chaos down there, lots of screaming and running, books and backpacks hitting the floor. The shooter seemed to be taking his time and firing in bursts. I listened for a bit to pinpoint his location in the hall. Then I slipped off my shoes and headed down the hall after him. I remember him turning, the shots hitting me, and I remember grabbing the rifle barrel. But everything else is pretty scrambled after that."

"That's good, Derrick. This is really helpful. Just a few more questions." Out of the corner of one eye, Horton could see Ray leaning to the edge of the hospital chair. Only so much longer baby brother would let their interview go on.

"We understand that you served in the military. Did you pick out any difference in the sound of the gunfire that morning? Dupree—um, that was the shooter's name—he brought multiple weapons to the scene, and we just want to make sure we don't miss any ballistic evidence."

"All automatic fire as I recall. Burst rounds." Derrick closed his eyes again. "Wait…I might have heard a few revolver rounds near the end—when I was tangling with the guy. But that must have been your guys arriving. Anyway, I'm not sure. But maybe a couple of duller pops coming from somewhere behind me. This was in that hazy part, so take it all with a grain of salt."

"Sure. Did the shooter say anything? Seems like a strange question, I know, but we will have to fill in whatever blanks we can regarding Dupree's behavior."

"I understand. There might have been some muffled talk around the same time that I heard that noise in the hall, like maybe the shooter surprised someone near those doors. But I couldn't make out any words. He screamed when I broke his arm, but nothing after that."

"Thanks, Derrick. You've been a huge help. Ray, thanks for letting us take the time."

Ray rose quickly and shook hands with Horton and Adams. The three of them began moving toward the door.

"Detective Horton," Derrick said.

"Yes?"

"How many casualties?"

Horton and Adams shared a brief look and then Horton answered. "Three dead and two wounded: one treated and released, the other in fair condition." Horton took a step toward the bed so that he could look Derrick in the eye. "Derrick, if you hadn't risked your life to stop this guy, there would have been a dozen casualties—maybe more. The students who walked out of that hallway alive have you to thank for it." Horton smiled at Derrick and then turned again toward the door to go.

"What about Reuben?" Derrick asked.

"I'm sorry…What?" Horton said.

"Reuben, a student I know—I heard him leaving his nine-o'clock class just before the shooting began. Big Indian kid. Hard to miss the sound of his footsteps in the hallway."

"Reuben Axtell. Yes, um, how well do you know him?"

"I'm his academic advisor, and he was a student in one of my classes. A good kid and bright—is he OK?"

Horton shifted his weight and crossed his arms. "Well, we don't know exactly. He was not one of the casualties."

"Oh, thank goodness." Derrick leaned his head back on the pillow.

35

"But he assaulted a police officer who was tracking the suspect into the building—knocked him unconscious. So at the moment we are hoping to talk to Mr. Axtell as soon as possible."

Derrick squinted. "You guys consider Reuben a suspect?"

Adams tagged in. "We haven't reached any conclusion. But we need to understand why he was on the scene and why he charged Officer Crowfoot. Unfortunately, he seems to have disappeared. And that makes things look worse for him right now."

"And he did have a connection to the shooter. When he was a freshman, we understand that Isaac Dupree and Reuben Axtell were roommates. Derrick, how well did you know Isaac Dupree?"

"He was a couple years ahead of Reuben—decent student most of the time. I heard whispers about cheating but never saw anything out of line when he was in my class. But he was in trouble with campus security pretty regularly for alcohol violations and practical jokes gone bad. He had a dark edge about him. When I saw that he was the shooter, I wasn't that shocked—maybe surprised that he would go the whole distance with something like this but not shocked that it was Isaac. Anyway, Reuben and Isaac had a falling out after one semester. Reuben moved out and has been a model student. Isaac stayed put and continued to get into trouble. I never saw them together after that first semester when they roomed together."

"Hmm." Horton signaled to Adams to close his notes. "Perhaps Reuben just panicked. Hopefully we can talk to him soon and clear things up. In the meantime, Derrick, Ray, thank you for taking the time and helping us with our investigation."

Ray shook hands. He walked them to the door and then nodded a greeting at Officer Brown before closing the door and resuming his post in the hospital recliner.

Derrick stared at the blank television screen mounted on the wall opposite his bed.

Ray shifted his weight, and the hospital chair creaked. "You want to watch a game or something?" Ray asked.

"Go ahead if you want," Derrick said absently, "maybe the Royals are playing."

"That's OK. I'm good," Ray said. He sensed that Derrick wasn't ready to focus on baseball. Derrick was competitive, and it was hard for him to watch casually.

Derrick breathed out heavily and seemed to be examining the ceiling. Then he turned his face toward Ray. "I never killed anyone that I knew," Derrick said slowly and deliberately.

"Derrick, this Isaac guy was a school shooter."

"I know," Derrick interrupted, "but it doesn't change the fact that I beat him to death."

"He was a threat, Derrick, a killer." Ray leaned forward and set his elbows on his knees. "Dupree may have been bullied in middle school; he may have had a terrible childhood. Maybe his whole life was one sad, sorry tale. I don't know. But here's the bottom line, Brother—on that one day he was planning on killing people. On that day he was a threat."

"I didn't have to kill him. Why didn't I knock him out? Take him down?" Derrick's jaw was tightening.

"Derrick, listen to me. It's our training. We didn't survive Afghanistan by using judo takedowns. It only works out that way in the movies. Isaac Dupree was a hostile. He meant to kill innocent people. You and me were trained to protect others against a threat like Dupree."

"Ray, I wasn't in your Delta team, remember? I was an intelligence officer."

"And a damn good one. But that's not my point. You were a Ranger before you were an intelligence officer. And you taught close combat at RASP. You guys didn't teach thumb holds, did you?"

"This wasn't Afghanistan, Ray. It was a university hallway."

"Roger that. Even more important in a place like that to stop a murderer dead in his tracks, don't you think?"

Derrick sighed. "I guess. I just keep seeing his face, you know?" Derrick's face loosened some, and Ray noticed that his eyes had calmed from that earlier, and wilder, look.

"Yeah, I know. Just remember when you see him that he gave you no choice."

Somewhere down the hall a patient's call button was sounding off. Derrick could hear the muffled sounds of conversation and the shuffle of steps along the hallway outside.

"Ray, I need you to do something for me," Derrick said. His voice sounded stronger suddenly, and Ray knew his brother was shifting gears.

"Anything," Ray said. "What do you need?"

"We need to find Reuben Axtell."

"The Native American kid? Sounds like the FBI has him pegged as a suspect."

"Yeah, I know. But that doesn't track for me. I think Reuben might be running scared. And I think he needs our help."

"Wait a minute—*our* help? Jessie will put your other arm in a sling if you so much as take one step from this room."

"Let's cross one bridge at a time. You are still a CI agent."

"Whoa, easy!" Ray whispered. "You want to broadcast that to Officer Brown?"

"Sorry," Derrick whispered. "But you are official. You know the drill, and you can flash a badge when it's needed."

"I was undercover in Missoula, Derrick. That might be blown now anyway, but I have to fly under the radar."

"Which is why I know you will be discrete. I don't want the FBI to know what we are up to either, but I do want to find Reuben before something bad happens to him," Derrick said.

"Derrick, what if you didn't know Reuben as well as you thought? What if Reuben is mixed up with the wrong people? He did pistol-whip a cop."

"We can be careful, play it as it comes. But either way Reuben is a dead man unless he has some help...and soon."

Chapter 6

RAY HURTLED INTO the Windsor Arms apartment parking lot and brought the Jeep to a sudden stop. A country singer was frozen mid-wail as he killed the engine and jumped out. The parking lines were barely visible, faded to a faint suggestion of yellow and ground away in places. Ray kicked absently at a flattened beer can relic. A mechanical pencil lay nearby, shattered by a footstep or car tire.

Ray began walking slowly toward the building. Yellow crime-scene tape snaked across the door of Reuben and Toby's apartment. A crime lab vehicle was parked out front, and Ray could hear the muffled conversation of the investigators inside. Locals, most likely. That was a good sign, as Ray hoped to avoid the FBI guys as long as possible.

It was a two-story rectangular building. Whoever'd built the place must have lived in New Orleans at one time or else dreamed of going. The brick was a haphazard patchwork, and the doors and windows were framed here and there by decorative ironwork painted a glossy black. The paint was worn and chipped, and the upstairs railing was missing several bars. The doors were also painted black and fitted with dark brass knockers. *Idaho meets Mardi Gras*, Ray thought.

He walked closer to the crime-scene boundary but not so close that he would be noticed. The investigators inside continued talking, and now and then Ray could see a lightning flash from their cameras.

He knelt down to get a look at the approach to the apartment from ground level. This was where he and Derrick began crossing the line. It was one thing to drop by a crime scene, maybe chat up the investigators, but quite another to be caught at ground level looking for evidence. It reminded Ray of the split second before he called for the gate man to open the chute. Once that gate swung open, nothing to do but ride the bull. Ray adjusted his sunglasses and began his sweep.

Sometime after Reuben shot his roommate, he would have walked out the front door of his apartment. Ray closed his eyes for a second and tried to picture Reuben coming out of that door. Derrick had said Reuben was a big guy and that he tended to barrel around wherever he went—a steamroller on the move. Asphalt was a lousy surface for tracking. Ray made a mental note to check the path from here to Turner Hall. Maybe some soft ground between here and there.

Did Reuben come bursting out of that door, sweating and all helter-skelter? Ray scanned for some small bit of newer debris. It was too much to hope for a shell casing or a lost round. But maybe Reuben had dropped a sign, a bit of his personal debris. *Are you really looking for Indian debris?* Ray chuckled to himself. *That's right. Maybe Reuben left an eagle feather behind as he rampaged toward Turner Hall.* Ray stood up. He expanded his scan but turned up nothing. Time to chat up the local police.

"Hello? Hello?" Ray called into the cavern behind the apartment door. "Hi, Officers. Can I talk to you just a second?" Ray took off his sunglasses and put on his best cowboy smile.

There was some movement inside, and then a tall black woman in a crime-scene windbreaker made her way to the tape. She was wearing reading glasses and looking over them at Ray with a gaze that was entirely unreadable.

"You a neighbor?" she said.

"No, actually, I'm Derrick Anderson's brother—Ray Anderson."

"I see. How's your brother doing?"

Ray smiled, this time a little less broadly. "Thank you for asking, um…"

"Sergeant Lavonne Johnson." Ray still couldn't tell if the garage door of this conversation was going up or down.

"Derrick is doing well, all things considered, of course. Hard to keep him down."

"Well, that's good to hear, Mr. Anderson. Was there something I could help you with? Because we are pretty stacked up here with everything that's happened." Johnson motioned back over her shoulder toward the half-open black apartment door.

"I understand, Sergeant. You all must be doing double-time."

"Roger that," she said, nodding her head.

"Sergeant, were you in the military by chance?" Ray asked, trying his best to look like it was the first time he had ever asked the question.

Sergeant Johnson studied Ray's face carefully and then sighed. She slowly shed her other glove and ducked deftly under the crime-scene tape. Ray thought she was even taller up close.

"Marines, Mr….Anderson, is it? But let's skip all the part where you chat me up about what unit I was in and where I served and you and me end up feeling like we had the same momma and daddy. I'm guessing you were army."

"How did you know?"

"Because my first husband was army—he liked to chat people up too."

Ray tried to find words, but she had caught him off balance. But before he could gather himself, her face began to soften into a smile.

"Now then, army man, why don't you just tell me who you *really* are and what you really want. Then we can go from there."

"I'm really Ray Anderson." Ray flipped out his wallet and showed his Montana driver's license. And then a crazy thought hit him. Ray's commanding officers had all, at one time or another, told him to count to ten before acting on these crazy thoughts. But he very rarely got past four. "But I'm also CI." Ray slipped a badge ID from his front jeans pocket and handed it to Johnson.

Johnson held Ray's ID like it was a snake and handed it back to him with barely a glance. He was about to speak, but she held up her hand toward him and then called over her shoulder, "Officer Jones, keep things moving in there for a few minutes. I need to take someone's statement."

She motioned for Ray to follow her to the crime-scene vehicle parked near the apartment. Ray took a seat on the passenger side, and Johnson slid in behind the steering wheel. She started it up, and they both took a second to enjoy the first brush of air conditioning. Johnson stared ahead toward the apartment building.

"US Army Counterintelligence—don't see that every day. In fact, you are about the first ghost I've seen in my life. And although I don't know much about ghosts, I know that if you showed me that badge, you are either crazy or desperate."

"A little of both...so I'm told," Ray said.

"No doubt. All right, CI Anderson. So now that we know a whole lot more about each other than I had in mind, why are you here? What does CI want with this investigation of a hometown murder?"

"Nothing, I'm not hear on CI business."

Johnson raised one eyebrow and gave Ray a chilling look of suspicion.

"Scout's honor," Ray said.

Johnson turned to look out the driver's side window for a second or two. Then she breathed deeply and turned back to face Ray. Her eyes were sharp but not unkind. She was a person to have on your side.

"So what is your business here?"

"Reuben Axtell."

"The shooter?"

"Yes, allegedly."

"What—was he in the military? Mighty young."

"No, nothing like that." Ray realized that he hadn't thought through his plan and that he was making this up as he went along. "My brother knew Axtell. He was his professor and advisor. So I came down here this morning as his scout, you know, to try and help him make some sense of what happened to Reuben."

"These things never make much sense."

"I know."

Johnson studied Ray carefully for a second or two. "OK, look. I'm not supposed to do this, but since you played it straight with me, I'm going to help you out. But you mess me around on this, and I'll hunt you down like I did that sorry first husband of mine. I don't care if you were in Delta. I'm *from the Delta*. We clear, army man?"

"Crystal clear, Sergeant."

Johnson lowered her voice and raised one hand to her chin. "I also want to save you and your brother some time and heartache. Been through enough." She swept a pen from her pocket. "All right, so that scene in there"—Johnson pointed the pen toward the apartment—"is about as clear as day. No forced entry. No struggle. The victim, Toby Davis, knew the shooter. And we think the two of them sat across from each other just before the shooting. Probably talked about something normal or maybe argued. Can't say. But what we do know is that they both stood up, and then the shooter fired two rounds from a nine millimeter: point-blank shots—one to the head and one to the heart. Victim was probably dead when he hit the ground."

"Pretty good shots for a crazed school shooter."

"Accurate, for sure. But they were maybe six feet apart."

"Right. No sign of another person in that scene."

"None. I run a tight crew, and with the FBI lurking around, we've been double-checking everything. No sign of anyone in there except Davis and Axtell."

"Was Axtell on foot when he left the apartment after the shooting?"

"Can't say. No bloody tracks, if that's what you mean. His car hasn't turned up last I knew. My best hunch would be he drove to Turner Hall and hit the road from there."

"Makes sense."

"Now here's the part where I could get fired. We found the victim's cell phone this morning. Must have gotten kicked or something, because it slid into a weird little recess. We missed it first couple of times through. Anyway, the victim sent a text just before he was killed. It was to a girl named Cindy, who was the victim's girlfriend. The text said, *Reuben has a gun. Acting strange.* Only prints on that phone belong to the victim."

Ray leaned back against the headrest and tapped the armrest. "Wow."

"Yeah, wow."

"My brother just couldn't believe that Reuben Axtell was a killer." Ray paused and looked toward the apartment door. "Guess he was wrong."

"Happens to the best of us." Johnson turned off the engine.

"Listen, Sergeant," Ray began, "about the—"

"Never saw it," Johnson interrupted. "And my verbal crime-scene report?"

"Never heard it." Ray turned and smiled.

"Two monkeys, army man, two monkeys." Sergeant Johnson stepped out of the car and headed back toward the apartment. Ray called out his thanks and began walking back to Jessie's jeep.

Ray hadn't seen a well-restored Chevy SS since his beach-bum days in California. And the one sitting across the street from the Windsor Arms was a beauty: glossy black with gray trim. Looked like a '68. Ray whistled softly and began walking across the street to get a closer look.

Whoever owned this car should park it in the garage, but Ray understood the temptation to display one's work. He and another Ranger had once restored a 1978 Camaro Z28. And because he and his pal Jim had finished their Camaro in stages as they awaited the next paycheck, he could see the boundary on this SS between *lovingly restored* and *awaiting the next paycheck*. The front bodywork could always wait until the engine was finished. The windows were rolled down, and Ray could see a tear or two that needed work on the interior roof. As he moved in closer, Ray began to duck down, so he could get a better look at the interior.

And then the interior of the SS was filled with huge white teeth and the snarling head of a pit bull in full rage.

"Jeez!" Ray shot back from the window and braced himself for the dog's charge.

The pit bull was frothing at the mouth and hammering his white teeth together. But something kept him from leaping out the window. Ray held his palms up toward the dog and took a few more steps backward just in case.

"Roscoe, that's enough!" a raspy voice shouted through an open door.

As quick as it had begun, the fury stopped. Roscoe closed his mouth and sat bolt upright in the passenger seat of the SS. The huge dog fell silent, but he seemed poised to tear Ray apart should he receive the go-ahead.

Ray heard a screen door slam and looked up to see a man emerging from the house where the SS was parked. He was tall and thin, with tousled black hair and pale skin. He was wearing dark green cargo shorts with ragged edges near the knees and flip-flops. As he twisted into a white T-shirt, Ray could see that the man's chest and arms were covered with a mural of tattoos, including a flaming skull across his chest. A cigarette was dangling from his lips. Once he settled his shirt, the man took the cigarette in one hand and blew smoke through pursed lips.

"Roscoe sort of considers that his car," the man said. He was smiling slyly at Ray and slipping a pair of dark shades in place from their perch on his head. "Sometimes he sleeps in the house, but when it's not too hot, he really likes napping in his car. You a cop?" the man said, nodding his chin upward at Ray.

"No, I'm not a cop. Just a fan of muscle cars who got a little too close," Ray replied. "Gorgeous SS. You do the work yourself?"

"Yeah, mostly. Some friends help me now and then." The man took another drag on his cigarette and walked around to the passenger side of the car. He scratched the dog's massive head and then opened the door. Just as Ray was about to jump on top of the car, he saw that Roscoe was on a chain that clipped to a shiny eyebolt rising out of the console.

"He's a big baby really, as long as nobody is messing with me or this place." The man waved his arm in a vague signal that seemed to take in the car and the house. Ray judged Roscoe would go ninety pounds. Pure muscle attached to shiny white teeth.

As if on cue, the big dog sat down beside the man and began panting placidly. The man held the chain—Ray thought a little too loosely—in one hand and extended his other to Ray. As the hand

47

came down, Ray noticed a blurred five-dot tattoo that he recognized. Roscoe's owner had done time.

"I'm Lee."

Ray shook the man's wiry and calloused hand. "Ray."

"So I guess you're a reporter then," Lee said. "A little late to the dance, but like I told the ones that came around earlier—I didn't see anything over there." Lee nodded toward the Windsor Arms.

Ray followed his gaze and then turned to face Lee.

"I'm not a reporter either," Ray replied. "My brother works at the university. Wounded in a scuffle with the shooter. He asked me to scout around for him. Just trying to get his head around what happened."

"That was your brother who dropped that guy? He's got some stroke. Shattered elbow, crushed—"

"Yeah," Ray said, thinking it a good time to get the conversation back on track, "Derrick's not a guy to mess with. Did you know either one of the guys across the street, Toby or Reuben?"

Lee leaned down and petted Roscoe. The big dog raised a slobbery tongue in appreciation. "Nope. Mighta said hi to the big fella once or twice. But that's it. I think the other one was scared of me and Roscoe."

"Why do you say that?"

"College boy. Wanted to keep his shirts pressed and avoid the riffraff." Lee smiled and shook his head. "Although it looks like he got himself sideways with somebody."

"*Somebody*? You don't think Reuben shot him?"

Lee brushed a hand at some flying insect that Ray couldn't see and then rubbed his cheek slowly with the cigarette hand. "Forgot the name for a second. Yeah, probably was Reuben. Likely some girl involved, or else the two of them fell out over who was going to do the dishes." Lee really laughed now, holding one hand to his mouth. He might have looked like a sixth grader who told a dirty joke, except for the prison tattoo on that hand and the sinister face behind it.

Ray knew instinctively that this joke was a sort of test and that if he turned defensive, he might show his hand or raise suspicions. Best to play along with Lee and then to leave him and Roscoe to their business. Ray grinned and shook his head. "Yeah, if it was like me and my brother, it would have started when one of us popped the other one with a wet dish towel."

Ray seemed to have passed, and Lee grinned as he leaned back comfortably against the SS. It was time for Ray to go.

"Lee, Roscoe, you guys take it easy. I better take off."

"OK, man, later on." Ray could see out of the corner of his eye that the big pit bull was watching him as long as possible, before Lee yanked his chain and Roscoe followed his master across the weedy front yard.

Later that afternoon Ray met Derrick at his house. The doctors had released him, and Jessie was getting Derrick settled in the couch when Ray arrived. Jessie fussed over the pillows for a minute, checked Derrick's bandages, and then headed back to their home office to call her clinic. Ray was pacing, and Jessie wasn't slow about taking hints.

Once Ray was sure that Jessie was back in the office and on the phone, he pulled up a chair near the couch and began reviewing what he had learned so far. The steak dinner with Officer Brown had served a double purpose. Ray had thanked him as he had promised, and in return Officer Brown had happily gossiped with Ray about the investigation of both shootings.

From all that Brown had heard, he thought that Isaac Dupree sounded like the classic case. A former student at the university, in and out of trouble, and finally washed out without graduating, no clear angle on his grudge but given the profile, it would probably turn out to be an alphabet soup of grievances. Dupree had done a study abroad in Egypt and had bummed around one semester out west somewhere. He might have been spurred on by rubbing elbows with some other drifters in one place or another. But Brown thought the detectives were only looking seriously at possible connections because the FBI has hanging around. Brown figured it would turn out to be the usual case of lone wolf, or of a lone wolf with an active Facebook page.

Reuben was a tougher nut, according to Brown. No priors and no black marks at university, in fact, Reuben was an honors student and had talked with a few of his professors about attending graduate school. But they had him cold on the killing of Toby Davis. Physical evidence all pointed to Reuben there. And as far as the school shooting went, the thinking was that a guy who had killed one person first thing in the morning looked pretty good for murder a few blocks away on the same morning. Maybe the kid just snapped. Or more likely Toby got wind of what Reuben and Dupree were planning.

Anyway, Brown was frustrated that Crowfoot ("and a tribal cop at that") had been the first guy on the scene. He told Ray that he thought Crowfoot botched that entrance somehow and that he wished he had been there to see it.

"He probably tripped and hit his head," Brown had told Ray, "then got up just in time to get clocked by Axtell." Ray thought some of this sounded like a twinge of jealousy. On the other hand, Brown seemed like a straight shooter with good instincts.

And then there was Ray's little recon visit to the Windsor Arms. Brown was right about the physical evidence in the apartment.

According to Sergeant Johnson, whom Ray described to Derrick as very much on top of her game, all signs led to Reuben on the murder of Toby Davis. But Ray still had a gut feeling that something was missing, especially after his near-death encounter with a pit bull. Roscoe was merely guarding his napping spot, but Ray sensed that his owner, Lee, was guarding a secret. He told Derrick about the prison tat and about Lee's attempt at lying while nonchalantly swatting bugs.

Derrick shifted up on his pillows and tried to cover a wince.

"So maybe Reuben got mixed up with this Lee character somehow, dealing meth or some sort of gang business."

"Maybe," Ray said slowly, leaning back in his chair. "But I didn't see any of the usual meth signs on this guy. He was smooth and deliberate. Gang business I wouldn't rule out. Maybe Toby saw something he wasn't supposed to see. If so, this Lee character could have been the shooter. He looks capable."

"But why let Reuben take the rap?" Derrick asked.

"Maybe Reuben screwed up somehow. Broke a gang code. Maybe this was Lee's way of killing two birds with one stone, so to speak." Ray smiled, but Derrick must have been too tired to catch the joke.

"Sounds logical, but your pal Lee would have to have ice in his veins to hang out across the street from a very active crime-scene investigation. He told you he had talked to reporters, and no doubt the cops have paid him a visit. Not every day you get to talk to the ex-con living across the street from a murder scene."

"I didn't say he was the brightest guy I ever met," Ray said.

"No, you didn't. But he would have to be as dumb as a fence post to make himself that obvious."

"So where does that leave us?" Ray's stomach growled. He had been on the run all day.

"What did you find out about Reuben's whereabouts?" Derrick asked.

"In the wind. No ATMs, no purchases. According to Brown, the latest thinking is that he might be heading to Boise. He has an uncle who lives there. Seems like a guess to me."

Derrick heard Jessie wrap up her phone conversation and begin to open the office door. He fell silent, and Ray followed suit.

Jessie slid her phone into her jeans pocket and smiled broadly as she entered the room. "Sorry, don't let me interrupt."

"No," Ray said, looking up and giving her a smile, "you didn't interrupt anything. Derrick was just telling me how he thought the Royals might win the Series this year."

"Uh-huh." Jessie rolled her eyes. "Two cats eating the canary. Now, would either of you boys like something more substantial to eat?"

Derrick started to shake his head, but Jessie cut him short with her *you have to eat something* look. Now he knew how it felt to be a horse under her care. You didn't dare not follow orders.

Ray didn't hesitate. "Wow, Jessie, you read my mind. Don't go to any trouble, but a sandwich or something would be great."

"No trouble at all—folks from church have brought enough food to keep all three of us set through the next month. I'll be right back with your sandwich and Derrick's…soup, was it, honey?" Jessie winked at him, and all resistance was futile.

Derrick shrugged. "Soup. Yes, dear, can't wait."

As soon as he was sure that Jessie was in the kitchen and humming to herself, Derrick turned to Ray. "I don't know how I'm going to pull it off yet, but I'm going to talk Jessie into releasing me from this veterinary hospital. You and me need to hit the road. We need to get to Reuben before it's too late. We can't wait around any longer playing the guessing game."

Just then Jessie walked back in with a tray of food. Ray thanked her, and when she turned her back, he signaled to Derrick. It was on.

Chapter 7

FRANK HIGHEAGLE AWOKE slowly, shifting his weight to relieve a numb arm. It was still too dark to see the chair in the corner of his hunting cabin. Around three o'clock, he guessed. What was he doing awake? He closed his eyes again, but it was no use.

Frank rose heavily and sat on the side of his bed. He turned on the lamp near his bed. Yep, 3:15 a.m. Too close to morning to try sleeping again. Frank worked his sleepy arm back and forth until he felt the blood reaching his hand. He slid a few bands off the nightstand and tied his hair back. Then he grunted as he heaved himself off the bed and began shuffling to the kitchen.

You sound like an old man, Frank, like your father sounded when you and your brother giggled behind his back.

Coffee would help. Frank stretched and then headed over to the small kitchen. He hit the brew button and walked to the nearby window. He could see just a tinge of frost around the corners. The weather was turning. But Idaho cold didn't let go easy. Frank stood at the window a moment gazing at the silhouette of the mountain range in the distance. The moon was only a thin, curved knife in the western sky.

The coffeemaker began hissing and gurgling, and the warm smell of coffee started to fill the small kitchen. Frank yawned loudly and readied a coffee mug. He studied his left hand for a moment. The swelling had gone down. No one but Frank would have known this, because his hands were normally massive. Bear paws. He smiled to himself remembering June picking out his wedding ring.

"Frank, at this ring size, we might as well start looking at bracelets."

The jeweler had frozen for a split second, unsure whether to laugh or brace for the start of an argument. But June had broken into that radiant smile of hers, and Frank had smiled at the jeweler and shrugged. On that happy day, he had been near the peak of his bear-like fitness, and his movements were smooth and quick. When he was interviewing with the Idaho State Police, the recruiter had made a few jokes about his height ("Not sure if we have a car to fit you, Chief!" Ha, ha, ha). *Anglo humor…always a riot.*

For twenty years Frank had surprised his partners with how smoothly he could fold his six-feet-five-inch frame into a police cruiser. He had also surprised many young suspects over the years with quickness that seemed at odds with his lumbering walk. Of course the years had caught up with him. His belt size had grown a few notches, and his speed had fallen to that merely expected of a big man. But he had never lost his command of situations or his vicelike grip. A few fast suspects may have outrun him over the years, but once collared no one could say that they had broken the grip of Frank Higheagle.

Frank pulled a jacket on and poured a cup of coffee. He walked carefully to the back door and out onto his small porch. After letting his eyes adjust to the darkness, he walked from the porch out to the closest spruce tree. Frank leaned back against the big tree and took a few deep draws of coffee. He hadn't been out this early in a while, and he had forgotten how quiet it could be at this time of the night. It was the in-between time—not yet morning, not fully night. *Nothing to see and nothing to do,* Frank thought absently, *so what the hell are you doing awake at this hour?*

Frank heard a twig snap nearby. Deer? He listened closely for a second. Then he heard the fussy scramble of ground squirrels. Frank took a few more sips of coffee and watched the squirrels. Then he shook the dregs out of his coffee cup and turned back toward the house. As he walked slowly back toward the light in his kitchen window, Frank's thoughts turned to his grandson Reuben.

He knew it made no sense, but he sometimes tensed up a bit when he thought of Reuben away at college. His grandson was doing so well. And every time he talked to him on the phone, Frank could hear the enthusiasm and sense of purpose. There was no reason to worry. These feelings probably boiled down to something as simple as missing his grandson. He and Reuben liked to fish and hunt. They both liked stories and the same goofy jokes. They were most comfortable in each other's presence. *Maybe that's why you can't sleep, old man,* Frank thought, *because you miss your camping partner.* Frank shook out the coffee cup one last time and headed back into his house.

Chapter 8

"THAT'S THE MOST ridiculous idea I've ever heard," Jessie said.

Derrick had hoped his argument might have been accepted a little better.

"OK, in a way it is ridiculous. I know that you think I need more time to recover. But, Jess, we aren't in charge of the timing here. Reuben is in trouble now."

"Now or never," Ray added.

"Shut up, Ray!"

Ray recoiled in mock shock and then shrugged his shoulders at Derrick.

Jessie was pacing now, and Derrick could see her gathering steam.

"Reuben is in serious trouble—no doubt. But that has precious little to do with you two." She wheeled momentarily on Derrick. "I know that he is one of your students, but he is not your responsibility, not in a situation like this. This is a problem between Reuben and the police."

And then Jessie turned back to Ray. She pointed at him like she was picking him out of a police lineup. "And don't you dare pull the CI card on me either. I've heard that one before. This has nothing to do with CI, and you know it!"

"Jessie," Ray began, "I wouldn't—"

"So what, Ray," she cut in, not missing a beat, "you think it would be great fun for you and Derrick to hit the road on some cowboy adventure? Wow—cowboys and Indians, come to think of it." Her green eyes were flashing white-hot now, and Ray knew it was best to leave well enough alone.

But Derrick wasn't ready to surrender. "Jessie, it was my idea. I sent Ray scouting around for me, and I'm the one that wanted to go after Reuben."

Jessie sat down suddenly in a leather chair at the end of the couch. Her anger was settling into a more sustained and moderate heat.

"Derrick, you've been shot. And it didn't happen out on some target range. You were in the big fat middle of a school shooting."

"Sweetheart, I know that," Derrick replied.

"No, I don't think you really do. I don't think either of you do. You are acting like there was a little accident at work. You two are talking about Reuben like he was just another guy who happened to be hanging around when the accident happened. Well, here's a news flash for you two: As far as anyone knows, Reuben Axtell was in that building for the same reason as Isaac Dupree—to kill people. He beat up a cop and made a run for it. What makes you think he wants your help or that he would even talk to you? What makes you so sure he wouldn't just start shooting again?"

"As far as we know, Reuben never fired a gun at anyone." Ray looked surprised, as though the words had slipped out of his mouth before he could stop them.

Jessie leveled a look at Ray. Derrick shifted positions on the couch and seemed about to speak. Just then Ray's phone began buzzing. It was on the right arm of his chair, between him and Jessie.

Jessie glanced down at the caller ID.

"Oh, look. Our friend Officer Brown. You two detectives will want to answer that one." Jessie's voice dripped with sarcasm, but Derrick sensed that her anger was beginning to subside and that he and Ray might survive after all.

"I can call him back later," Ray said.

"No, let's hear the latest," Jessie said, and before Ray could respond, she had swept his phone up and answered the call.

"Hello, Officer Brown," Jessie said. "Ray was working on something and asked me to pick up for him." Ray covered his face with one hand and then slid it away slowly and looked at Derrick. Derrick looked at the ceiling.

Jessie let Officer Brown do most of the talking, only interrupting now and then with a prompt or a note of response. Derrick was a little surprised that Brown was talking so much, but then again he had no way of knowing what he had interrupted. Jessie thanked him for calling and tossed Ray his phone.

"Well, boys, looks like your road trip is off. Reuben just turned himself in to Pocatello police. They are questioning him right now."

Derrick looked thoughtful for a moment and then turned to Jessie. Before he could say a word, Jessie smiled and began waving her hands in the air. "Go, you two, go! You might be better off getting yourselves arrested than hanging around here within my reach." She put up mock fists, and Ray ducked as he rose of his chair. The storm had passed, at least for now.

It was nearly nine p.m. when Derrick and Ray arrived at the main police station. But the station appeared to be doing a fairly brisk business. An older man in a shabby overcoat was talking to a guy who Derrick thought looked like he might be from one of the shelters. It was warmer this time of year, but the weather was maybe the least of the worries for an older guy living on the streets of Pocatello.

A couple of police officers came barreling out of the doors of the station just as Derrick and Ray were entering. Their cheeks looked red from exertion, and their expressions, stony. Derrick figured that they might have just delivered a particularly troublesome new tenant to the jail upstairs.

It took a while for Derrick and Ray to tell their story and persuade the police on duty to allow them back to the area where Reuben was being held. More than once they had to use their "Officer Brown" card, and Derrick hoped each time that Brown wouldn't take any hits for helping them out.

Finally they reached the end of the line. A detective named Libby Thomas guided them to a couple of chairs outside the offices where detectives questioned suspects and took down statements from witnesses. She was friendly but guarded and clearly a little suspicious about the professor-student connection.

"I can't say how long this will take, gentlemen," she said, "but you are welcome to wait here as long as you like. The detectives should be coming this way with Mr. Axtell when they're done." She waved at the two chairs, and Derrick and Ray took a seat.

"Do you happen to know if anyone from Reuben's family has arrived or if they have called ahead to set up an attorney?" Ray asked. He was mostly interested in the attorney part of his question but hoped that the family part was enough to cover his tracks a bit. Thomas wasn't buying.

"Can't say. It's been a revolving door around here today. Well, hope it works out for you. I'd better get back to my desk."

Derrick could hear Thomas's quick steps moving away from them, and he was reminded for a second of kids playing tag. Thomas had delivered Derrick and Ray to home base. And now—*tag*—they were someone else's problem.

If Thomas had only known how bad Ray was at sitting still, then she might not have worried so much about the two odd characters hanging around the police station. Ray fidgeted, made a few coffee runs, and then settled into a pattern of mostly pacing and occasionally sitting. In one of his sitting stretches, he turned to Derrick and grinned.

"Boy, you screwed that up with Jessie. Road trip—what were you thinking?"

"No joke. That went well, didn't it?"

The two brothers shuffled in their chairs and smiled. Derrick sensed that Ray was as happy to be crawling out of Jessie's doghouse as he was.

"It seemed like such a good idea at the time," Derrick said.

He took a sip of coffee and tried to listen for conversation or any sign that might indicate how long their vigil might last. But he could only make out the muffled sounds of footsteps and the occasional low rumble of conversation.

"Seems like a good sign that your student turned himself in," Ray said and stood again to start another round of pacing.

"Yeah, I think so too. No doubt he is getting the third degree in there." Derrick nodded over his uninjured shoulder, wincing slightly. "But he's safe for the moment. It could have ended very badly for him out there on the run."

"No doubt," Ray replied. As Ray was pacing away from Derrick, he saw three police officers enter the main door to the detectives' offices where he and Derrick were waiting. They were not dressed as detectives but in uniform. He couldn't see insignias from here, but he could tell that they were neither Pocatello nor state police. One of them was a stocky man with short black hair. He was smiling and seemed to be regaling the others with some exploit. Or maybe he had just won a bet.

"Why do you think Reuben turned himself in?" Ray asked as he pivoted and began walking back toward where Derrick was sitting.

Derrick had been eavesdropping on the three police officers who had just entered the offices, and it took him a second to catch up with Ray's question.

"Probably calmed down and started thinking more clearly. He's a college student, and not a guy who has been in trouble with the law. And I think he told me one time that his grandfather was a police officer...maybe state police. Reuben lived with his grandfather after his parents died. So maybe he started thinking that he didn't want to cause trouble or disappoint his grandfather."

Ray stopped pacing and sat down next to Derrick.

"What happened to his parents?"

"Car wreck, as I recall. Reuben was fifteen at the time."

A burst of laughter erupted from the bullpen area in the main office. Derrick and Ray couldn't see the three police officers from their seats in the nearby corridor, but the conversation was clearly picking up steam and volume. Ray could tell that the stocky officer was holding court now and that the other two officers were serving as his audience.

Derrick and Ray could now hear the stocky officer loud and clear.

"So I told her that she should just put everything in my hands. And she didn't slap me when I winked at her—you know what I'm saying?" More laughter.

Suddenly Derrick and Ray heard doors opening and more footsteps from down the corridor. A group was heading their way. As the final set of doors swung open, Derrick recognized Reuben walking between two detectives. A couple of uniformed police officers were following behind. Reuben was looking down as the group passed into the final hallway, watching his feet as though he didn't trust them to take him where he wanted to go. His braids hung down either side of his face, and the fluorescent lighting reflected sharply off his thick black hair. He was wearing jeans and a T-shirt. Derrick couldn't make out the lettering, but it looked like one of those giveaways from a campus event. Other than his formidable size, Derrick thought, a most unlikely criminal.

Reuben looked up as he caught sight of the two figures standing between the corridor and the bullpen area of the main office.

"Professor Anderson," Reuben said. "Are you OK?"

At first Derrick didn't understand his question, and then he remembered that his arm was in a sling.

"Oh yeah, I'm fine, Reuben, just fine. What about you?"

"I've had better days," Reuben said simply. As he approached them, Derrick could see the sadness and exhaustion in Reuben's face. And something else—defiance. That's good, Derrick thought, because he will need that.

The nearest detective stepped out of formation and greeted Ray and Derrick. "Detective Mark Henderson, Pocatello Police."

Ray and Derick introduced themselves and briefly explained Derrick's connection to Reuben.

"Yes, Detective Thomas let us know that you would be waiting here. We've tried to reach Reuben's grandfather, but it seems he is in the backcountry on a fishing trip. May take a while to reach him. Anyway, we've questioned Reuben, and we are satisfied that he is cooperating. He left the scene, and that's still a problem. But he also turned himself in, and, like I said, he's been cooperating with us tonight. So my partner put in a call to the DA, and she is prepared to hold off on any charges for now. We will likely need to talk with him again, so he needs to stay in Pocatello. But he is free to go for now."

"So he can leave with us?"

"Yeah, that's fine. Just let me walk out with you and get some basic contact information."

The detective nodded back at the other officers, and they dispersed. Reuben joined Ray and Derrick, and they walked with the detective toward the bullpen. The three police officers that Ray had seen earlier were lounging around one desk. The stocky one was seated on the desk, and the other two officers were leaning back in office chairs. As they got closer, Ray could make out insignias. Two of the men, including the stocky one, were tribal police from the Shoshone-Bannock reservation. The other officer was with the Pocatello force. Reuben had been talking quietly with Derrick on the way across the bullpen. But when they were a few desks away from the three police officers, Reuben suddenly slowed down and stiffened.

The Pocatello officer spoke up. "Hello, Detective. Reuben." The officer also nodded at Ray and Derrick. "I was just visiting with Jim and his partner from Fort Hall, and Jim was telling me that he's decided not to press charges for the assault."

The detective that was accompanying them introduced Ray and Derrick to the Pocatello officer, who in turn introduced the two tribal officers as Jim Crowfoot and Ted Nance.

With introductions out of the way, Detective Henderson responded. "Well, that's good to hear, Officer Crowfoot. That will probably simplify matters for Reuben and for us."

Jim Crowfoot took a step toward Reuben and looked him directly in the eyes.

"It was a scary situation. I can understand that Reuben just panicked—fight or flight, right, Reuben?"

Reuben looked over Crowfoot's shoulder, beyond him. "Mostly *fight* from the looks of those bandages on your head."

Crowfoot bristled but then seemed to catch himself. "Funny. But I wonder if your grandfather will think all this is so funny."

Reuben turned his gaze to meet Crowfoot's eyes directly.

Crowfoot seemed about to speak, but Ray suddenly stepped between Crowfoot and Reuben.

"Well, Officers, good to meet you all," Ray announced. "But I think this is probably a good time for us to take Reuben and go. Officer Crowfoot"—Ray looked at the stocky officer and smiled— "I've had a few knocks on the head in my time. Best to get some rest and let your head clear."

Ray had intended to move on quickly. It had been a long day, and he had no desire to get into a face-off in a police station. But something in Jim Crowfoot's face held him for a beat or two longer than he intended. It was hard to say what features caused the effect—whether the smoldering eyes or the set of the man's jaw. But Ray knew the overall impression all too well. It was the look of a man who had crossed a line somewhere in the past and who was never going back.

They drove away from the police station in silence. After solemnly thanking Derrick for coming to the police station, it seemed that Reuben was spent. He sagged in the back seat, only occasionally looking out the window at the passing lights.

Derrick could feel his own eyes drooping at times, but Ray's restless energy behind the wheel kept him from nodding off.

"So, did you know that policeman, Reuben…that Officer Crowfoot?" Ray was looking in the rearview mirror at Reuben, and Reuben turned slowly to return his gaze.

"Yes, he's Shoshone. Long story, but me and him don't get along."

"So I gathered." Ray smiled back at Reuben. "I don't think I get along with him very well either."

Reuben smiled faintly and turned back to the side window.

Jessie was waiting for them when they finally arrived home. It was nearly midnight, and she had changed into scrub pants and a long-sleeved sleep shirt. She greeted them and guided Reuben through the guest bedroom and back to the screened-in porch, where Ray and Derrick had already foraged snacks and taken a seat. After saying her good nights, Jessie slipped back inside, and the three men were left alone. The night was cool, and the sky, filled with stars. Reuben took a seat between Ray and Derrick, in one of the big, green outdoor furniture chairs arrayed around a wooden table. The sound of katydids and crickets ebbed and flowed, and somewhere in the distance an owl called in low hoots.

"Rain coming," Ray said as he passed along a snack tray to Reuben.

"Pay him no mind, Reuben," Derrick said. "He says that every time he is outdoors at night."

Ray laughed, and he thought he caught the faintest smile on Reuben's face.

"Thank you again for coming for me, Dr. Anderson," Reuben said.

"Glad to do it, Reuben," Derrick answered. "I'm glad you aren't out there on the run someplace. It was smart to come in and talk to the police."

A dog barked in the distance and was answered by other dogs farther off.

"I had nothing to do with Isaac and the shooting," Reuben said.

"I know," Derrick said. "So what did happen?"

"It's a crazy deal. But a friend sent me a text and told me that he had seen a 'big Indian dude' at my apartment door. Like I said before, me and Officer Crowfoot don't get along. So I slipped out of class and was heading out the door when I heard all the commotion. I hid under the stairs and then rushed Crowfoot when he came around the corner."

"So you weren't confused—you knew it was Crowfoot?" Ray asked.

"Yes," Reuben answered.

"Did you tell the police that?" Derrick asked.

"No."

"Jeez, Reuben," Derrick replied, "that could be a problem. But why did Officer Crowfoot back up your story and agree not to press charges?"

"That's the longer story," Reuben said. He looked down at his hands in his lap.

"Let's hear it," Ray said. "We're not going anywhere tonight."

Chapter 9

REUBEN AND RAINS had been more like friends than cousins. The two of them had grown up hunting and fishing together. Rains was skinny and lighter than Reuben, and many people mistakenly thought Rains was a little brother. But Rains was actually the older of the two by two years.

When Rains was in his senior year, he began hanging around with a rougher crowd, and for a time Reuben kept his distance. Now and then Reuben would call Rains up to go fishing or hunting. But Rains was often stoned. Even when Reuben happened to catch him on a sober day, it seemed that Rains was less interested in fishing or hunting.

Then, out of the blue, Rains had turned up one day at Reuben's grandfather's place. He seemed more like the old Rains—streetwise for sure and with additional tattoos, but otherwise intact. Reuben had begun hanging out with him again. They hiked into the backcountry and went fishing. Rains managed to get a job driving a cattle truck. He did some farming work as well, helping Reuben's grandfather haul hay on occasion.

Reuben and Rains had gone camping one time in the fall. The weather was perfect, and they stayed an extra day in the backcountry. The last night, they were sitting around the campfire when Rains asked Reuben if he could keep a secret. Then he began telling Reuben about some extra work he had picked up.

There was a cattle operation with gathering stations in a couple of remote areas of the Bitterroot and Sawtooth Mountain ranges. This operation made use of mountain meadows and some valley ranges. They paid Rains extremely well, nearly twice what he had made hauling for other cattle companies. They also paid in cash. Now and then they had Rains pick up cattle near Bonners Ferry within miles of the Canadian border. He wasn't one to ask questions or poke around, but he told Reuben that it was possible that some of the cattle were being smuggled in from Canada. This was only a now-and-then sort of thing, though, and Rains was mostly making ordinary cattle runs in the light of day.

But over time Rains had begun to notice a few odd things about the business. The men who met him didn't seem like the usual cattle wranglers. They were trying to look the part, but Rains didn't see the usual scars and callouses of men who worked with cattle day in and day out. All the equipment—feed troughs, squeeze chutes, and fencing—was expensive and mostly new. Rains had thought at first that the entire operation was probably a hobby of some billionaire from Boston or New York.

But then Rains had seen something really strange—something he couldn't shake. He told Reuben that he had been snowmobiling one day in an area not far from one of the collection stations where he had delivered cattle. Rains had been given strict instructions to stay out of this area and told that he would be fired on the spot if he ever broke the rule. But Rains told Reuben that he had seen trophy deer and elk in the area when making cattle runs. He had decided that day to take his snowmobile into the backcountry and see what he could find.

The snow picked up as Rains worked his way deeper into the mountain forests. About midafternoon Rains's snowmobile broke down. Rains was normally a whiz with machines, but he told Reuben that this repair took him longer because of the cold and the snow. He said at one point he grew frustrated and kicked a tread. That was when he first sensed that he wasn't alone.

Rains turned slowly and saw a man in a torn plaid shirt and dirty gray work pants. The pants were tucked into knee-high western boots, and the man was wearing a John Deere cap pulled to the side at a haphazard angle. He told Reuben that, after he got over the fright, he thought the man looked like a lost rodeo clown.

Rains made sure he could reach the pistol he kept aboard his snowmobile and then called out to the man and asked him where he was from and what he was doing. Rains said the man looked at him as though he understood. And then he began laughing. Rains grew angry and drew the pistol out of its case, just so the man could see it. He told him he wasn't fooling around. It was getting dark, and he needed to get home.

"Where are you from, and what are you doing out here?"

The man just laughed and then turned and began running. Rains took the pistol and followed the man, yelling the whole time for him to stop. Rains told Reuben that the man had a strange gait, almost as though he was flinging different parts of his body forward over the snowy ground. In spite of this, he was remarkably fast. Rains began to lose sight of him in the deeper forest. By that time it was snowing harder, and Rains was running out of daylight. He returned to the snowmobile, made the final repairs, and then fired it up.

Rains said that he drove the snowmobile along the man's tracks for about a half mile, and then suddenly the man's tracks ended. He circled a bit, but darkness was closing in, and Rains wasn't sure how much he could trust his machine. As he was turning around to head back, Rains said he heard a strange cry from deeper in the forest. He said it was a sort of laughing wail, some weird combination of the cry of a mountain lion and the chortle of a loon. Rains gunned the snowmobile and drove as fast as he could back to his truck.

Although Rains became increasingly convinced that he had encountered some sort of spirit, he kept going back to the area and looking for the one he called the "laughing man."

Reuben was pretty sure Rains had seen a drunk human being, likely a backwoods hunter who had strayed too far from camp. Either that or Rains had gotten too cold and started to see things that weren't there in the swirling snow.

And so they had argued. At first good-naturedly, talking over the possibilities and considering the evidence, but later the arguments had become sharper and Rains more distant. He was sure that he had seen a spirit and that it had a message for him. Reuben was just as certain Rains had seen a disoriented man, or maybe even nothing at all.

Reuben had gone out to the area once by himself. It hadn't been a smart thing to do, and he hadn't told his grandfather where he was going. But Reuben rode his snowmobile to the area Rains had described and then drove around a bit just to satisfy himself that there were no roaming spirits there. He had only seen a fox and a few deer.

Rains had always been more interested in the old ways and tribal history than Reuben. But after Rains had that strange encounter in the backcountry, he seemed to be jogging back in time. He started dressing more traditional and learning more of the language and customs. Rains thought that the spirit in the forest had been speaking to him and that he was calling him back to a better way of life. And in some ways, it seemed that Rains had found that better way, at least until he started adding drugs to the mix. He had sometimes sounded persuasive when he said it wasn't about getting high but about using the drugs as part of his spiritual quest. But they had argued about it, and more heatedly as time went on. Reuben had heard the spiritual argument before, but it usually worked out with another Indian dead or in prison.

Rains never got the chance to see how his own quest would play out over the longer haul. About six months ago, Rains had been working his day job, delivering a load of cattle to a meat processing plant in Pocatello. He was delivering a pretty full load. They said later that a bunch of cows must have packed in too tight around one of the mechanical chutes, probably rammed it with a horn or kicked it hard with a hoof. Anyway it was damaged, and Rains didn't know it. Rains was supposed to be on a catwalk, but for some reason he was down in the chute. Maybe he dropped something, or he was trying to fix the gate. Anyway, there was a terrible commotion, and when other workers got there, they found Rains being trampled by the cows in the chute. He was probably dead already. They said the defective gate hit him in the head before the cattle stormed into the chute.

"And so that's the longer story," Reuben said. He was staring toward the screen and the privacy fence beyond.

"Man," Ray said. He leaned back in his chair.

The katydids were in a low cycle, and it seemed especially quiet for a second or two before Derrick spoke. "Reuben, that is terrible what happened to your cousin. But I still don't see the connection to Jim Crowfoot."

"Oh yeah," Reuben said, "that part came after. I think I told you before that my grandfather is a retired state police officer?"

"Yes," Derrick answered.

"Well, I knew of Jim Crowfoot first from overhearing a conversation between my grandfather and one of his friends who is still active on the force. This friend was looking for advice. He worked the southeast, District Five, and he was having some trouble with the tribal police at Shoshone-Bannock. Jim Crowfoot's name was mentioned as the ringleader of the troublemakers. My grandfather seemed to know him and agreed that he could be difficult. But he told his friend that he thought Crowfoot was mostly just young and still adjusting to life after the military. My grandfather told his friend to tread carefully, because he thought Crowfoot was well connected among some businesspeople and tribal leaders. And he said that Crowfoot was hair trigger regarding tribal rights and turf. He was what my grandfather called a 'war bonnet'—someone quick to take offense on behalf of his tribe."

"But you hadn't met him?" Ray asked.

"Not until later, after Rains died. Me and some friends from ISU had gone to Fort Hall for a concert. We stopped at a local burger place on the way home, and while we were there, Jim Crowfoot and a couple of other police officers showed up. Crowfoot bantered with us a bit: *You guys aren't causing trouble down here tonight, are you? You look kind of rough, ha, ha, ha.* That sort of thing. No big deal. But then later, when we were getting ready to leave, Crowfoot called me aside. Told the other guys he just wanted to talk with me a second and that I would be right out. So he takes me aside and begins to act like he's my long-lost uncle or something. *You OK, Reuben? That was a rough business about Rains.* The words were respectful, but something about the way he carried himself put me off. I told him thanks and that I was fine. Then he started ranting about white people—sorry…"

"No problem," Ray said. He smiled at Derrick.

"So he took off talking about how white people had caused Rains so much trouble and how he had been so close to recovering his tribal roots. He said it was white ranchers that pushed Rains to work overtime and go without enough sleep and that they were responsible for the accident at the stockyard. He started to make me mad at that point, mostly because he was talking about Rains like he knew him so well. And the more he talked, the more it was about his own beef with whites, and not about the death of my cousin."

"So what happened?" Derrick asked.

"I cut him off. I said thanks for paying his respects but that I didn't want to leave my friends outside in the cold waiting on me. That didn't sit well with him, I guess. Because next thing I know, he was really pissed at me. He didn't yell or anything. But he got in my face. He said that I just didn't get it, that I was probably a lot like my grandfather...just another aw-shucks white Indian. I must have bowed up without really realizing it, because he taunted me to go ahead and hit him. Said he would love to see me locked up. I knew I had to get out of there before I did something I would regret. And I would never admit it to him, but he was scary that night. I wanted nothing to do with him."

"You did the right thing," Ray said. "The guy in the jail cell is the loser in that fight."

Derrick smiled to himself and thought about adding a comment, but he let it pass.

"What did he say he was doing there that day?" Reuben asked. "I mean at my apartment and at Turner Hall.

"At your apartment—no idea," Derrick answered. "This is the first I have heard about that. But he was at the university that morning because he had some meeting scheduled with the Native American Student Association. Outreach, I think," Derrick replied. "Anyway, he said he saw Dupree acting suspicious and followed him into Turner Hall."

Reuben leaned back in his chair and seemed to be studying the stars. A breeze was beginning to stir, and the first cold of the night was making its presence felt. Derrick called an end to the conversation and guided Reuben back to the guest room. He hung around the kitchen to make sure Reuben was settled. In minutes he could hear Reuben's breathing stretch into a heavy sleep. He returned to the screened-in porch to find Ray mumbling to himself.

"Solve the world's problems?" Derrick asked. Ray jumped.

"Jeez, you should wear a bell!" Ray scowled. "And yes, for your information, I have most of it worked out."

"Good, then you can set me straight in the morning. I'm calling it a day." Derrick shuffled out of the porch, and his footsteps faded away inside.

Ray stayed put for a while longer, listening to the night sounds and making plans.

Chapter 10

DERRICK OPENED ONE eye and checked the red numbers of the alarm clock on his nightstand: 6:03 a.m. He felt stiff and like it should be much later. But he gave himself a shove and sat upright on the bed. He could hear the shower running. Jessie was humming lightly to herself and singing a stray word now and then. She had a nice voice but was notorious for garbling the lyrics. He smiled to himself remembering the time she had belted out, *"I can see clearly now Lorraine is gone,"* to the song about disappearing rain and vanishing gray clouds.

His shoulder throbbed more than it had in a few days. It was beginning to move better, and he was working it as hard as Jessie would allow. But it was definitely talking to him this morning and mostly saying that Jessie had been right that it was too early for him and Ray to be heading off on any road trips.

Ray was sitting at the kitchen table when Derrick managed to shuffle down the hall and take a seat beside him.

"You don't look so good," Ray said. As usual, Ray looked rested and ready to sling a rucksack over his shoulder. He had always been a morning person.

"Thanks, and good morning to you too," Derrick muttered.

Just to rub it in, Derrick thought, Ray bounced up and poured Derrick a cup of coffee.

"Reuben's sawing some serious logs," Ray said. "The life of a fugitive can take it out of a guy."

"Yeah, I figured he might sleep like the dead." Derrick yawned and worked his shoulder one ginger turn. "Weird business between him and that Crowfoot character, huh?" Derrick took a sip of coffee and recoiled. He had forgotten how strong coffee could be when Ray brewed it.

"Pretty strange, but I think I recognize the type—lots of talk and lots of pawing the ground. Now that Reuben is standing his ground, I imagine this Crowfoot guy will move on down the road to pick on someone else."

"I hope so. Reuben's a good student and a hard worker."

Jessie swept into the room at a fast walk and bearing her usual morning smile. *I'm surrounded by morning people*, Derrick thought, smiling to himself.

"So what's for breakfast?" Jessie was wearing a light blue work shirt under a brightly patterned clinical coat, jeans, and old calf-high boots. Derrick imagined her for a moment at the stockyards, a songbird moving purposefully amid lazy cattle and grumpy cowboys. And woe to either one that got in her way.

"Coffee," Ray announced. "Freshly brewed."

"And strong enough to wake the neighbors," Derrick added.

"You two are worthless. But never fear, Jessie is here." Jessie breezed by the kitchen table and disappeared into the pantry. She came back a second later with a box of cinnamon rolls.

"Freshly made of course, yesterday at the pastry shop," Jessie said. She brought plates and forks, and the three of them settled in to their impromptu breakfast.

After Ray had inhaled his first one, he swept the crumbs from his thick reddish-brown beard. "I need to run back toward home for a few days. Take care of some things there if that's OK," Ray said. "Then I could run back when you two start missing me again."

Jessie looked at Derrick. "You OK around here on your own for a few days? I've got the stockyards today, but after that I should be able to check in on you during the day."

"Sure, I'm fine," Derrick said. "I will probably enjoy the quiet, and I can make myself some coffee that is worth drinking."

The sun was just clearing the horizon when Ray turned north on I-15 toward Blackfoot, Idaho. He often took the southern route when traveling from Hailey to Derrick and Jessie's place. Ray liked the longer run of Interstate 86. It was one of those flat stretches of western highway that opened a man's mind and gave him room to work things out.

But today he was heading north. Ray had already made a phone call to an old army buddy, one well placed to return favors. And while he waited for a return call, he figured it made sense to head toward Fort Hall, Idaho, the headquarters of the Shoshone-Bannock reservation. Maybe his buddy would help him get a better bead on Jim Crowfoot. But if not, he would do his own digging. One way or another, Ray wanted to find out what lay behind that distinctive burn in Jim Crowfoot's eyes.

Jessie might have wondered what Ray was doing on I-15 that morning if she had happened to see him behind the wheel of his black Jeep. But Jessie was only on the interstate for the short run from Pocatello to Blackfoot, and she had other things on her mind.

Livestock sales had been brisk lately, and the Blackfoot operation was likely to be in full gear when she arrived this morning. Cattle prices had bounced here and there as usual, but mostly they had been trading in a healthy range. Ranchers were happy, and meat-packers were happy. Or at least they had all been happy until the first signs of listeriosis began to appear.

A few steers had started showing signs yesterday. They appeared otherwise healthy, but a few of the workers at Blackfoot had noticed them wobbling and turning in circles. Dexter Hamilton, from the main office, had taken a look and was concerned enough to quarantine the steers and call Jessie. Listeriosis wasn't the worst thing that could happen, at least so long as they had caught it early, and Dexter had done a decent job of isolating all the infected animals. Jessie could treat the infected steers with antibiotics and then perform spot tests on the various cattle lots to isolate the cause. She had to make sure that it was indeed listeriosis first, but if this hunch was correct, then Jessie already suspected that the ultimate source would turn out to be some spoiled silage back at the ranch where those steers were raised. If she was right, the rancher might already know he had a problem, or he might be about to find out. Either way, after making sure that Blackfoot was taken care of, she would need to get in touch with the rancher and check his cattle. She hoped Derrick was doing OK at home, because she might be busier the next two days than she had hoped.

Jessie pulled into the parking lot at Blackfoot, grabbed her gear, and began walking toward the office.

The Blackfoot Livestock Auction was a complex of low-slung white buildings on either side of the Union Pacific railroad tracks. Jessie preferred the ranch work, but as sale barns went, the Blackfoot was a solid operation. On days when Jessie had driven all over southern Idaho making a stop here and a stop there, especially in bad weather, she had come to appreciate the opportunity now and then to park in one place and let the cattle come to her. Livestock auction managers were generally more businesslike about the role of a veterinarian as well, so at least on her days at Blackfoot, she could skip the routine hassle of listening to a rancher drone on about the costs of veterinary care and drop hints that maybe he could have handled the whole thing himself without calling her.

But the biggest reason for working the livestock auctions was to maintain her network of relationships in the regional cattle business. Jessie learned bits and pieces from buzzing around from ranch to ranch. But seeing the whole puzzle meant hanging around the beehive. She could learn more about patterns and problems in a day at the Blackfoot than she might learn in a week of calling on individual ranches.

Of course in addition to solid information about cattle and their health, she also picked up a fair amount of gossip and tall tales. Jessie moved too fast to stay up-to-date with the most long-winded storytellers. Now and then she was trapped at some task while an auctioneer or wrangler tried to catch her up from the beginning of time. But she was fairly adept at displaying disinterest and an absolute master of strategic silence. Over the years Jessie had recognized a few of the downsides of growing up on an isolated ranch in central Texas. But two of the positives she had inherited were a casual indifference toward gossip and roughly equal contentment with conversation and silence. And so Jessie tended to receive gossip in tight bundles. Mostly she heard chatter involving cattle, business deals, and fights over one or the other. Storytellers who specialized in darker tales of human misery or misconduct had no shortage of audience elsewhere. Blowhards generally avoided Jessie like the plague.

And so that was why it was a shock to the system that the first person she encountered that morning was Ralph Jones. Ralph could talk the ears off a mule.

"Well, hello there, Dr. Anderson. What a pleasure!"

Jessie smiled and greeted Jones. Over his shoulder she could see her assistant, Chris, gathering his gear from his car and walking away from her toward the main office. If he had looked this way, she would have waved at him like a long-lost friend, but he was on a mission and of no help to her in her present predicament.

Jones was a heavyset man in his late sixties. He had been a bank president at one time, and then had retired to the life of a gentleman farmer. This was all fine except that in his own mind Jones was a major player in the cattle business. He dropped names relentlessly and garbled common cattle language with amazing consistency. Jessie reminded herself that Jones was a child of God too and tried to offer enough concentration to be courteous without offering the slightest encouragement for the conversation to continue any longer than necessary.

"And so I simply told them that broken machinery is the responsibility of the workers. You know how these people are, Jessie. Why, they could break a ball bearing! So it's little wonder that a man gets killed because these derelicts don't pay attention to the most basic maintenance chores. I sympathize with management who..."

Jessie's concentration suddenly looped back from the workday ahead to the present moment.

"Killed? Did someone die in an accident here at Blackfoot?" Jessie shielded her eyes from the morning sun and looked steadily at Jones.

"What?" Jones seemed to have been caught off guard by a question in the middle of his soliloquy.

"You said someone was killed in some sort of accident?" Jessie asked again, slower, as she might ask a child.

"Yes, but not here," Jones replied. "Over at the meat-packing plant. It happened back in December or January sometime. I thought surely you would have heard about it."

"Oh, the accident involving that Rains fellow. I thought you were talking about something that happened in the last day or two."

"No, sorry. The Rains case is the one I was talking about. It's just that now the family is making some noise about a lawsuit. And so there's some posturing and digging around. You know how that goes." Jones flapped one arm toward her in what Jessie guessed was supposed to be a conspiratorial gesture, like the two of them were in the know on something. Jessie thought it made him look like a heavy-set rooster.

"Anyway," Jones went on, "I just heard from a reliable source that the gate was broken somehow before the poor Rains man was killed. Seems some of the mechanical parts had been sheared off. Cattle machinery can be so tricky sometimes."

Jessie fought the urge to roll her eyes. She knew that Jones wouldn't know cattle machinery from a toaster oven.

"And all I'm saying is that where such machinery has been mistreated to the point it malfunctions—if indeed that turns out to be the case—then the blame ought to fall on the workers who use that machinery day in and day out. The managers of an operation can't be expected to know the current condition of every nut and bolt on their place!"

"I see what you mean." She did, but she also thought Jones had no idea what he was talking about. Jessie knew there was no point arguing with him. "Well, Ralph, good to see you. But I imagine Dexter Hamilton is inside the office over there wondering where I am. So I better get moving."

"Right, well stop by the ranch sometime. Adios!"

Jessie hustled across the tracks toward the main office. Jones might not know much about the workings of a cattle operation. But Jessie knew it by heart. And as she approached the door of the Blackfoot office, she wondered what had really gone wrong with that chute and how an experienced handler like Rains had ended up dead.

Dexter Hamilton was studying some papers attached to a clipboard when Jessie entered the Blackfoot main office. The ubiquitous toothpick was perched in the far corner of his mouth, and a white straw hat was cocked a little back on his head. He wore a crisp, white cowboy shirt, and his faded jeans were tucked into knee-length work boots. Dexter was in his fifties, and the hair around his hat was thinning gray with touches of brown. He was a wiry and somewhat nervous man and walked with the distinctive gait of a lifelong cowboy. It was not unusual to catch him talking to himself, usually muttering, as he walked alone through the maze of the Blackfoot complex.

As Jessie drew closer, Dexter looked up and smiled broadly. He stuck the pencil he had been holding behind one ear and extended a hand. The skin on his arm and hand was a deep copper, the only contrast a simple turquoise ring.

"Jessie Anderson! Good to see you, Doc! How are you? And how is Derrick doing?"

"Good morning, Dexter! Good to see you too. I'm fine, and Derrick is doing well. He'll need some downtime, but so far he is cooperating about as well as I can expect." Jessie smiled.

"Better than a Brahma bull, I expect?" Dexter replied with a wink.

"I don't know, Dexter. Most of the time Brahma bulls go where I want them to and do what they are told."

Dexter smiled, and his blue eyes twinkled between deep creases around his eyes.

"Well, please tell Derrick that we are praying for a full and speedy recovery. I hated to hear he had to deal with that nonsense, but sure glad he was able to stop it."

Jessie nodded. Dexter reached one hand toward her elbow and pointed with his other out toward the lots. Jessie felt relieved by this sign that they would be getting to work.

"So I've got those sick steers in the isolation lot if you want to take a look."

As they walked toward the isolation lot, Jessie scanned the cattle in the other pens. The pens were maybe half full, which was about typical for a weekday. By the Saturday sales, the pens would be nearer capacity. It was important to make sure that she and Dexter had a handle on the listeriosis before all those other cattle arrived.

A Hereford cow munching hay turned and looked at Jessie and Dexter and then contentedly turned back to her feed. Jessie smiled and turned to Dexter. "I see a few more Herefords than usual. These all from the Bar T, or are you seeing more of them in general these days?"

Dexter pulled his hat brim down a notch and glanced at the nearby pen. "All from the Bar T. Still about the same mix in general. Well, maybe a few more Simmental. They seem to be the flavor of the month." Dexter thumped the remains of his toothpick into a nearby trash can.

Jessie smiled and looked down at her boots. She knew that Dexter loved Angus cattle and that with any prompting he would debate their advantages over other breeds, the popular Simmental included. But Dexter was a man on a mission today, and she didn't want to distract him. One of the reasons that she liked working the Blackfoot so much was that Dexter was one of the few people she knew who loved cattle as much as she did. It was impossible to imagine Dexter without picturing him among cattle. And, like Jessie, he hated cattle diseases and parasites. To Dexter the appearance of a parasite was a personal affront, and an outbreak of disease, a direct assault on his caretaking. And although he hid it expertly behind hat and handkerchief, Jessie knew that now and then Dexter personally grieved the loss of a sick animal.

"Here they are." Dexter stopped and put one boot on the first rail of the small isolation pen. He leaned a hand on another.

"These the only ones? No other signs?" Jessie asked.

"Nope. Just these. I've got a listing here on the clipboard." Dexter handed Jessie the clipboard. "Two different operations involved for sure, maybe a third. I've put some buffer around all three just to be on the safe side. Right now we can afford the space."

Jessie scanned the short list of animals and ranches.

"I recognize these two. I doubt that the Simmons place is the source. They are particular about their feed and run about the cleanest operation I've seen. But Randy Adams likes a bargain...So he might have bought some grain on clearance sale for the Rocking M. Of course you don't have to run a sloppy operation to get an occasional case of listeriosis. So I'll have to touch base with all of them." Jessie furrowed her brows and looked up at Dexter. "I'm not familiar with this one—Circle T. They from outside the area?"

Dexter snagged his pencil and pointed at the name. "No, but they are a fairly new operation. Small outfit, best I can tell, and very particular about what they buy. At least as far as weight and age goes. They've bought different breeds. From what I understand, they are one of those specialty operations that are providing range-fed beef for California restaurants. Must be slowly building up their herd, because they only buy and haven't posted any sales."

"So they are on the list because they bought an animal that's suspicious for listeriosis?" Jessie asked.

"That's right. Asked me to hold her a day or two while they arranged to have her picked up. Like I say, a small outfit. But one of the three heifers they purchased had some exposure to these suspects."

"Got it," Jessie replied. "Well, I'll get to work here and then begin working the list. I know you are on top of this anyway, but in the meantime you might also remind all your hands to keep a sharp eye out for wobbly animals—and to practice their hygiene extra sharp."

Dexter nodded and touched the brim of his hat. He thanked Jessie and began walking back along the dirt path between the pens.

Jessie checked her kit bag and then walked to the gate of the pen. She paused for a second to observe the three black steers. Angus, she thought briefly, an especially bad blow for Dexter. Two of the steers stood within a few feet of each other, but their stance together was off a bit—not the usual comfort that herd animals draw from being near one another. The two were standing almost perpendicular to one another, and their heads hung down below their shoulders. She noticed muscle twitches in their haunches. The other steer was much more clearly ill. He was leaning a bit against the outer railing of the pen. His head drooped nearly to the ground, and both nose and mouth were trailing strings of milky fluid. The animal's front leg was trembling, and he seemed near collapse. His eyes had the dull, flat cast that Jessie had learned to recognize all too well. This one might be beyond rescue. But she would treat him along with the others and hope for the best.

Jessie opened the gate and moved slowly into the pen. She wanted to cause as little stir as possible, especially since the one steer had little reserve strength left. Hopefully she could run her tests quickly and get the treatments going in time to make a difference. Just as she was wondering where he might be, her assistant, Chris, arrived and followed her into the pen. Working together they managed to conduct the tests with little fuss from the two stronger steers. They seemed reconciled to the handling and mostly oblivious to the needles.

But the sickly steer was a different matter altogether. Jessie had hoped that he was willing to go along, but she had experienced enough outbursts from sick animals to know that it was a mistake to underestimate their remaining power or willingness to fight. This one wanted to play rodeo. And so by the time Jessie and Chris left the isolation pen, they were both heaving and covered in muck. As she left the pen,

Jessie mouthed a silent combination of prayer and curse on the wild-eyed steer. *After all that trouble, you better live. But if you don't, I may not be all that sad that you died.*

Dexter walked up just as Jessie was examining the changing colors in a test vial. She had set up shop in her usual spot in an unused supply closet a few doors down from Dexter's office.

"Well, Doc, what does it look like?" Dexter asked.

"Sorry, Dexter, but it's definitely listeriosis," Jessie replied. "I think we can save those two that don't look so bad. But I'm not so optimistic about the other one, your tag number one eighty-five. He gave us quite a kick out there just now, but that doesn't always mean much."

"No," Dexter said. He looked down at the floor for a second and then at Jessie. "Well, what do you think of the quarantine so far? Think we've got a handle on this thing?"

"I do," Jessie replied. "We ran spot checks, and they all came back negative. That number one eighty-five might have been sick a little longer, but probably in transport. I think you caught this early. I'll go to work on the ranches involved and check in with you tomorrow. Call me in the meantime if anything changes or you think I need to come back out."

Jessie gathered her gear and had Chris take it to her truck. She took out her cell phone and called the first rancher on the list. It was one of the parts of her job that Jessie didn't like. No one liked to hear that they might have an outbreak on their hands.

Chapter 11

DERRICK WAS DOZING off when he heard the knock at the door. He was disoriented for a second and took in a quick breath. Then he was home and all was well. And he knew who was at the door.

"Mr. Higheagle, please come in," Derrick said as he swung the front door open.

Given Reuben's size Derrick hadn't expected a small man. But the man stepping slowly into his house was even bigger than he'd imagined.

"Sorry if I am disturbing you," Higheagle said and turned to shake Derrick's hand. "I really appreciate you taking care of Reuben until I could get down here."

"Happy to do it," Derrick replied. "I'll let Reuben know you are here."

Derrick ran his hands over his face and padded toward the hallway. Reuben met him coming the other way. As Derrick headed to the kitchen to gather coffee, he could see that Reuben and his grandfather were greeting each other and sharing their relief in each other's presence. The three men took a seat around the kitchen table, and Derrick served coffee and offered the remains of yesterday's box of cinnamon rolls.

"Don't go to any more trouble, Dr. Anderson. We can't stay long," Frank Higheagle said between sips of coffee. "I want to get back to Cascade."

Derrick paused a beat to consider his words. "Please, call me Derrick. You know, the detective who released Reuben to me said that he needed to stay around. I think they expected to do some more questioning."

"And call me Frank. Yes, they didn't want Reuben out of pocket. But I stopped by the Pocatello station on the way over here. Things are pretty well straight now. Officer Crowfoot isn't filing charges against Reuben. They wouldn't have amounted to much anyway, but it could have been a hassle. The main thing is that the investigation has made some good progress, and they know now that Reuben wasn't mixed up with Isaac Dupree and his assault at the university. And the more progress they make on Toby's murder, the more things there point away from Reuben as well."

"Oh, that's great to hear," Derrick said.

Frank shifted forward in his chair and leaned his arms on the kitchen table. He folded his massive hands in front of him, and Derrick noticed that a couple of the fingers pointed a bit more east and west, and that there were small scar lines here and there on both hands. *Been in his share of scrapes*, Derrick thought.

"It was a brave thing you did, stopping Dupree like that. I was talking with some of my friends down at the station, and they said that he was armed like a Navy SEAL, carrying one of those shorter-barreled modified M16s."

"The M4A1?" Derrick asked. He frowned at his half-eaten cinnamon roll.

"Yeah, that's it—commando gun. It's ridiculous what sort of firepower is floating around these days. Knucklehead like Isaac Dupree can get his hands on a military weapon and enough ammunition to start an invasion. Not a fair fight for cops—or professors, for that matter." Frank had been building up steam on what must have been a longtime sore topic of his, but when he mentioned "professors," his face softened into a wide smile. He studied Derrick's shoulder for a second and then asked, "How are you getting along?"

"Good, I'm doing well, thanks," Derrick replied. "Ribs are sore, but otherwise I think I'm all good."

"Take it slow." Frank was looking directly at him, and his black eyes were searching and intense. "Gunshot wounds take longer to heal than you think. Especially ribs. Ribs are pretty close to the heart you know." The black eyes gradually melted into a smile, and laugh lines began crisscrossing Frank's face. Derrick smiled, and Frank broke into a baritone laugh. "Yep, pretty close to important stuff." He looked over at Reuben and laughed again, and Reuben rolled his eyes.

"Sorry, Dr. Anderson," Reuben said. "My grandfather is known for really bad jokes. He just told one there, but it was hard to tell."

Derrick smiled and looked toward Frank, who shrugged and then playfully swatted Reuben on the back of the head.

"Well, I'd better get this one back to Cascade and put him to work," Frank said, eyeing Reuben. "I have been saving up chores for him for months now."

"Can't wait," Reuben said. He shuffled off from the table to check the guest room for anything he might have left behind.

Derrick took advantage of his absence to talk with Frank alone.

"Reuben told us about Rains. He also told us about a past run-in with Jim Crowfoot."

Frank sighed and looked for a second down the hallway. Then he turned back to Derrick.

"You have been a great help to Reuben. He talks of you often. So thank you for your concern. But don't be worried about what Reuben told you. He and Rains were close, and it was tragic what happened to him. But Rains was also a dreamer and a storyteller. He had trouble sometimes telling truth from nonsense.

"And as far as Jim Crowfoot goes, well…It's tribal. Sort of hard to explain. But I'm not worried about him. He's got his turf, and we've got no plans to visit."

They could hear Reuben lumbering back down the hallway in their direction. Derrick walked them to the door, and then Frank turned back toward Derrick.

"Oh, almost forgot." Frank reached in a pocket on his cargo pants and recovered a slightly crumpled gift bag. "This is for you. Thank you again for helping Reuben."

Derrick began to protest, but Frank waved him off. "It's a small gift, but when I've been hurt, for some reason I always craved those things. Hope you enjoy them. Thanks again, Professor."

Reuben waved at him, and then he and Frank lumbered toward the Dodge truck parked in the driveway. Grandpa bear and baby bear, Derrick thought to himself as he closed the door.

Once inside he opened the gift bag to discover a large box of Whoppers. Well, he and Frank Higheagle had at least one thing in common. Derrick opened the box and popped a couple of the candies in his mouth.

As he walked back to the kitchen, Derrick wondered about Frank's morning visit to the Pocatello police station. He wished he could have been a fly on the wall. Maybe the investigation had moved swiftly overnight, but not that swiftly. Frank had either lowered the boom on someone or else used all his charm and connections—maybe a little bit of both. It was great to see him taking Reuben home, but Derrick hoped that the old man wasn't underestimating Jim Crowfoot or the trouble that Reuben might be facing in the days ahead.

As Frank Higheagle and Reuben Axtell were heading west on Interstate 84 toward Cascade, Officer Jim Crowfoot was heading out of MacKay driving north on State Highway 93. It had been a crisp, clear morning, but as Crowfoot had driven from Arco to MacKay, he had noticed gray clouds gathering to the northwest. It looked increasingly like they might be in for an afternoon shower. He hoped it held off. He would need to be on the trails this afternoon, and anything more than a mountain shower would slow his progress.

He had left suitable excuses back at the reservation, but Crowfoot didn't like being called out so urgently without warning. Dr. Nasim had sent word through runners that Crowfoot needed to make way to the main facility as quickly as possible. A "security issue" was all the information that had been given to the messenger.

The narrow strips of grassland were green along either side of Highway 93. It had been a snowy winter followed by healthy spring runoffs. Low hills bordered the two-lane road to the west, and mountains pressed in close to the east of the road. Crowfoot was leaning on the unmarked black cruiser, and occasionally he zipped by a run-down trailer or small farmhouse. As he sped along, he began mulling over some of the possibilities.

Dr. Nasim had been increasing the size and scale of their testing program. He had complained bitterly about the pace, maintaining a running argument with Crowfoot that he needed another year to make sure that their plan worked perfectly. Nasim was dedicated to the cause, but he was also a scientist by nature. He was a slow and deliberate man, and one who was easily unnerved by any change in schedule or routine. Crowfoot thought it most likely that this urgent call was a tactic on Nasim's part. The good doctor had probably run into a glitch of some sort and had decided that this would be a good opportunity to show Crowfoot firsthand why the project could not possibly be completed this summer.

Well, what Nasim didn't know could get him killed. This project was a train on the tracks. The train was scheduled to arrive in June, come hell or high water. Crowfoot was personally committed to that schedule, but he was not Dr. Nasim's only problem. Other Guardian leaders were also fully invested to this timing. And anyway they were past the point when they had needed Dr. Nasim's unique abilities. The Guardians had made contingency plans for replacing Nasim if the need arose.

It was also possible that the operation had been rattled by Reuben's escape from the trap they had set for him in Pocatello recently. But that was really none of their concern. Crowfoot was responsible for security, and he would see that Reuben Axtell caused them no problems. If they yanked Crowfoot's chain over something related to Axtell, he might just terminate Nasim's appointment on the spot. Most of the other members of Guardian leadership were aware of Nasim's nervous behavior recently, and they were also aware of the progress that had been made in large part because Crowfoot had kept all of the teams on schedule. He could weather a controversy and call in a chip or two if needed.

The gray clouds were beginning to dig deeper into the valley and looking more like the hulls of ships than fleeting spring sailboats. Their shadows began covering the western mountains, and he could see rain falling in the high country. Crowfoot eyed the mountains and whispered a curse.

As he turned his attention back to the road, Crowfoot turned to the worst case. The one thing he didn't want to hear when he arrived at the facility was something to do with a perimeter breach or a newly emerging threat. They were so close, and they had managed to tie up all loose ends to this point. It was such a complicated project, and they had managed to thread the needle so far. He could almost feel himself celebrating victory. So this was no time for some nosy rancher or hippie kayaker to throw a wrench in their plans. If there was something new, then Crowfoot would have to make sure that it had no opportunity to spread, to compromise everything they had worked for, for so long.

A ray of sunlight spotlighted a pasture on his left, and the light and wind played over the grass in waves of tan and dark green. Crowfoot's mind drifted, and he could see her then, coming across the field toward him. She was laughing and holding her arms close to her body in a girlish and irresistible pose. She was wrapped in a traditional dress of sky-blue silk with intricate patterns in red and yellow. The scarf was a shimmering material that seemed to radiate many colors at once like fine cloth woven from opal stones. Her dark eyes were shimmering with laughter and mischief. As she got closer, she gradually stopped laughing and brushed aside a strand of hair dark as night. And then she smiled at him. Her smile always took his breath away, and even now, so many years later, he realized he had stopped breathing for a moment. And then she was gone.

Crowfoot turned his attention back to the long road ahead. His dark eyes narrowed, and his jaw tightened. He glanced once more at the mountains and cursed the gathering storm.

Just before he reached Challis, Idaho, Crowfoot had turned south on Idaho 75. He left behind the arid plains and low, rocky mesas along Interstate 93 and drove south through increasingly deep pine forests. The Salmon River ran alongside the road much of the way. The river was boisterous this time of year, and in places the snowmelt had banged out new curves and cutbacks. Crowfoot drove on to a smaller feeder road and then finally to a rutted dirt and gravel track in the national forest. He finally parked the cruiser in a bank of trees and opened the trunk. He gathered up his backpack and tossed in a bag of energy bars. He also lifted out a Beretta shotgun and made sure that he had packed adequate ammunition for both his nine-millimeter pistol and the shotgun. The latter was more for bears than humans, but it wasn't a bad gun to have along for any situation. Crowfoot slammed the trunk and began walking down a barely visible trail. As he headed out, he noted with some relief that the rain seemed to have blown east for the time being.

After what for him was a leisurely hike Crowfoot arrived in the camouflaged camp deep in the backcountry. A sentry popped up to confront him but quickly dropped his weapon and greeted Crowfoot. He shouldered his shotgun and headed to a ramshackle building made from aged lumber. Crowfoot briefly admired the work again, as he had helped to identify and harvest the discarded lumber that was the skin of an otherwise state-of-the-art facility. He turned the nineteenth-century doorknob and entered a twenty-first-century laboratory.

A lab assistant spotted him immediately and disappeared down a hallway. If not that one, another of the nervous lab workers would run for their master soon enough. Crowfoot slung his backpack to the floor and unloaded the shotgun. He dropped the shells in a pocket and leaned the long gun against a wall nearby. He had just begun to unwrap an energy bar when Dr. Nasim appeared, striding purposefully across the testing laboratory in his direction. Nasim removed safety glasses as he walked and ran a hand through his graying hair.

"Crowfoot, so glad you are here. We must talk."

Nasim stood for a moment blinking up at Crowfoot. His dark eyes were circled with darker half-moons underneath. His breath smelled of coffee and cigarettes. He had a hawkish nose and large front teeth. "In my office?"

"Lead the way," Crowfoot said without offering a greeting.

Nasim shuffled down a narrow corridor, glancing now and then over his shoulder. His glances reminded Crowfoot of some badly treated dog, conditioned to look out for the next kick.

They reached a small office in a corner of the building, and when Nasim entered, he turned on the fluorescent lights. Even though the mountain sunshine was ample outside, the building had only faux windows and no natural light. Nasim swept a few papers off the center of his desk and into a drawer and then waved a floppy hand for Crowfoot to have a seat.

Crowfoot took a large bite of energy bar and munched slowly while at the same time studying Nasim's face. Nasim cleared his throat a few times and then seemed to be gathering himself for his next step. Crowfoot noticed as Nasim lit a cigarette that his hands were shaking—not good for a man handling sensitive materials.

"We may have a situation," Nasim blurted out.

"What sort of situation?" Crowfoot's voice was low and even.

"That fellow Rains had some contact with various cattle dealers, and well, it seems that one of these dealers—or maybe more, I'm not sure. Anyway, the point is that some of the cattle he purchased for us may have been compromised."

"Nasim, you aren't making any sense. What is the problem?" Crowfoot's voice was still quiet, but the menace in it was growing.

"Cattle were purchased on behalf of the operation. Some of them we were able to disguise well. No one would ever be able to trace them back to our operation, much less to this facility. But some of the people you—I mean, some of the people involved made mistakes. They carelessly signed documents and used contact information that is only a few steps removed from us. So the problem is that today we received a call from a veterinarian who works for one of those cattle auctions—I believe in Blackfoot. She made contact with someone in our outer ring."

"What did she want?" Crowfoot took the final bite of his energy bar and tossed the wrapper toward Nasim's empty trash can. He missed, and Nasim studied the wrapper for a moment, as though he expected it to move.

"She thought we were some Idaho cattle ranch. Rains had signed the Circle T or some such. She wanted to come out to our ranch and do some follow-up testing, make sure the listeriosis wasn't spreading any further."

"This is the big problem?" Crowfoot's eyes narrowed. Nasim shrank back in his chair and waited. Finally Crowfoot blew out a breath and shook his head. "You used the emergency protocol and dragged me all the way out here over a phone call from a veterinarian? Over some routine cattle bug?"

Nasim tapped his cigarette on an ashtray and shrugged. "You are head of security. The protocol calls for me to report all potential security breaches." Nasim started to smile as though pleased with his answer, but the smile faded quickly when he looked up to face Crowfoot.

"For such a well-educated man, you have a lot of trouble using your brain," Crowfoot said flatly. "What you have described is not a potential security breach. Granted, Rains shouldn't have given out contact information. But we took care of that situation. This vet got in touch through that dated contact information, but there is no breach."

"What do we do about her request—her desire to visit our ranch?" Nasim said.

"We let her visit a ranch. That's not so hard, is it? You know that we have easy cover in our outer rings. So set a time and let her visit the ranch. She can meet one of our wranglers, who will be ranch owner for a day. Let her poke some healthy cows and get a look at a healthy cattle operation, and then she can be on her way."

"Your overconfidence is going to get us in trouble one day," Nasim said.

Crowfoot rose to his feet and towered over Nasim's desk. Nasim recoiled and brought one arm up toward his face in reflex.

"And your cowardice is going to get you killed even sooner." Crowfoot seemed to catch himself and gradually lifted his hands off the desk and stood up straight. "Now, Dr. Nasim, I know what you are really up to here—and it won't work. The target and the schedule are fixed. Creating emergencies won't change either one. So even if aliens are landing on the roof of this place, I suggest that you stick to your work and meet your deadline. I will take care of the harmless veterinarian. But don't play games with me again, or you will pay dearly. Do you understand?"

"Crowfoot, my only concern—"

"Do you understand?" Crowfoot growled.

"Yes, completely," Nasim said as he tapped out his cigarette.

"Good, glad we had this little chat. Now back to work." Crowfoot turned and walked slowly out of the office and down the hallway. At the door he recovered his backpack and drew the shotgun shells from his pocket. As Nasim walked down the hallway and back toward the laboratory, Crowfoot slowly loaded each shell in the Beretta. Then he stepped out of the building into the blinding mountain sunlight. Crowfoot pondered the veterinarian and the phone call as he slid a pair of sunglasses from his shirt pocket. It was maybe more of a problem than he had let on to Nasim. But in any case, he wouldn't know until he checked it out himself. The Guardian rings were pretty resilient, but Crowfoot couldn't afford to let something come apart this late in the game.

Officer Crowfoot made his way down the trail to his cruiser and began the drive back to Idaho City. Nasim had caused him to waste a day, but the time would come when he could settle up with Dr. Nasim. In the meantime he was relieved that the problem was not a serious one. Any delay at this point could have been a fatal blow. Crowfoot dug around in a messenger bag and recovered a disposable cell phone. He dialed the number that Nasim had given him.

"Hello, this is Dr. Anderson."

"Dr. Anderson, hello. This is Amos Greene from the Circle T. Dexter Hamilton tells me that you needed to touch base with us… something about listeriosis?" Crowfoot smiled at the sound of his own voice. He was a natural mimic, and his ranch boss impersonation was a dead ringer for the real thing.

"Yes, thanks for getting back to me, Mr. Greene. I left a message with someone in your operation. Did you get that one?"

"Oh no, sorry. But I have been burning up the roads lately, and sometimes my messages have a dickens of a time staying up with me."

Crowfoot listened absently as the veterinarian explained what he already knew; he then drew more alert as she reached her conclusion and requested to visit their operation. He readily agreed and directed her to a location that he knew they could stage in twenty-four hours. Once the meeting was set, Crowfoot hung up and then called a Guardian crew boss to make the arrangements for Dr. Anderson's visit.

"Make her visit perfectly pleasant," Crowfoot instructed him. "And give her every reason to forget about us and move on with her other business."

After Crowfoot hung up, he placed the cell phone in an outer pocket of the messenger bag. He would burn it later. Problem solved. Dr. Anderson would make her visit to a perfectly forgettable little cattle operation. And Crowfoot would get back to focusing on what really mattered. It was time to begin closing in on their target.

Chapter 12

RAY SLID INTO one of the small seating areas at the Snakebite Restaurant in Idaho Falls and quickly retrieved his vibrating cell phone.

"Batman, hey, buddy. That didn't take long."

"Hi, Ray. Well turns out your man has a pretty interesting file. You in a place where you can talk?"

"Mostly good. So what's the scoop?"

"Jim Crowfoot is marine. Served three tours in Afghanistan. Two in combat and a third as a chemical and biological specialist. Platoon leader. Cited for exemplary service and a couple times for distinctive bravery. Somewhere near the end of that second tour, he requested the transfer to hazmat duty. Not a usual move for a combat guy, but his reviews there were clean."

"Sounds like a real gung-ho."

"Yeah, mostly. The only black mark on his record is a pretty big one though. Seems he got into a nasty fight with another marine at base. Broke the guy's jaw. Shouted down an officer who ordered him to stand down and then tussled with the base police when they showed up."

"What happened?"

"Crowfoot lost a stripe and was given a nice little timeout in the brig. Could have been a lot worse if the officer involved hadn't cut him slack."

"Sounds like this fight was more than blowing off steam. Any idea what it was about?"

"Nothing in the official record. But I made a call. There was some scuttle about Crowfoot taking up with a young Afghan woman."

"Wow, this guy is more nuts than I thought."

"Roger that. Some places those love stories work out just fine. But unless the girl has no living male relatives, the Afghan tribal region isn't one of those places. Apparently Sergeant Crowfoot didn't get the memo or chose to ignore it. Didn't matter as it turned out."

"Why?" Ray asked.

"The woman was killed in a drone attack. She was in a house that was targeted as a terrorist hangout."

"Jeez. So she was mixed up with Tangos?"

"No, at least not that day. Drone strike was a screw-up. The people were there for a family celebration. Not one of those gray cases either: an official apology was issued, and the families were compensated. *Case of mistaken identity, fog of war, blah, blah, blah.*"

Ray turned to make sure that no one was listening in on his conversation. He paused another beat to scan the restaurant window.

"You there, Ray?"

"Yeah, just thinking. So Crowfoot comes back to base, and another marine pops off about the woman or the drone attack. And that triggers the brawl, right?"

"The guy I talked to didn't know all the particulars, but he did tell me that the fight was related to the drone strike. Chances are good that the other marine didn't know the bird went astray. Probably started barking about it being a win for our side."

"I can picture that. What I can't picture is an experienced marine sergeant trying to date a tribal Afghan woman—at least not straight up. Any sign of rape or harassment?"

"Again, this is Afghanistan we are talking about. You know the territory, Ray. I don't think Crowfoot would have lived through another tour if this was about something like that."

"Right, I just don't see his end game."

"Agreed. Oh, and one more thing, Ray…"

"Yeah?"

"There's a scribble in his file about an incident when he was out bug hunting. Seems a marine recon team came up on a site investigated by Crowfoot and his bunch. They found signs that somebody had tried out some anthrax on a few local animals. Then they ran across the body of an Afghan teenager who showed signs of anthrax poisoning. He had apparently been tending sheep, and the animals were milling about the body. The recon leader called it in, and he mentioned that Crowfoot and his team were already onsite and available to investigate. Command checked it out, and Crowfoot and his crew were supposed to be at another village nearby working a different case. They claimed a mix-up or bad directions or something, but reading the reports, I gather that the recon guys thought things were a little fishy."

"You think they suspected our guys of the anthrax poisoning?"

"They never said that. Recon team probably thought the Taliban were responsible. But they hung around until their leader heard back from command, and that makes me think they didn't like the feel of things. Those guys aren't big on phoning home."

"No. So did anything come of it?"

"A few pings of initial interest at command, but then Crowfoot found some clues that led to his group capturing a mad scientist who was cooking up dirty bugs. The suspicion about that anthrax incident disappeared, and Crowfoot never looked back."

Ray suddenly took a small notebook and pen from his pocket.

"What was the name of this scientist that Crowfoot captured?"

"Let's see. Oh, here it is—Dr. Abdul Nasim."

Ray jotted the name and closed the small notebook just as the waitress arrived at his table.

"Batman, you're the best. You wrapped up that vivid report just as my burger arrived at my table. You still have that uncanny sixth sense."

"And you are still full of it. So, Ray, remember where you didn't hear all this."

"Roger that. Will be in touch. Keep your head down."

"You too, Ray."

Ray prayed silently and then took a bite of his Snake River burger. Batman's report wasn't conclusive. Crowfoot was an experienced combat marine, and that alone might account for what Ray had seen in his face that day in the police station. The switch from combat to hunting dirty bombs and bugs was a bit odd. But it was the story of the Afghan woman that snagged Ray's attention. It wasn't the idea of a soldier and a local woman falling in love. His own father had married a Vietnamese woman. And ironically, now that he thought about it, she had died shortly after Ray's father had brought her home to the United States. But all the soldier and civilian love stories happened somewhere else—France, Vietnam, Spain, Australia. Afghanistan was an entirely different story. In addition to dodging murderous fathers and brothers, any US soldier crazy enough to pursue such a relationship would face a maze of resistance from the woman's tribe, from Afghan officials and police, and from the US military. So Crowfoot was either crazy in love or just crazy or some combination of the two.

And then he had lost this woman in a drone strike. Ray set his burger down and tried to feel, for just a second, what that might have been like—to arrive on scene. Sometimes Ray could picture things vividly from another perspective. This ability had served him well as an operator and an investigator. He had seen the aftermath of missile strikes before. The news media liked to use the term "surgical" when describing these strikes. But Ray was looking at the scene the way he had seen them on the ground. At ground level the only surgery done by a missile was the sort performed by a drunken and angry doctor. They tore a ragged gash in buildings and vehicles, and scattered body parts in all directions. Car horns and the cries of the wounded blended with a devastating ringing in the ears, a mixed soundtrack of this cacophony and an enlarged sense of silence, as though the missile had warped the air around the hit.

Ray swept a hand over the top of his head. He had just seen that line that Crowfoot had walked across that day. He didn't want to walk across it in his own mind. Ray knew what lay on the other side of that line, and he had too many memories of his own losses. But if Crowfoot had stepped over the line that Ray had seen in his mind, then there were only two ways a man could go. He could break for the daylight and find release over time, or he could break for the darkness and go hunting. The look he had seen that day on Crowfoot's face convinced Ray that he knew which path the man had taken.

Now that he knew more about Jim Crowfoot's history, he was ready to begin digging around in the present. There was more to this man than tribal police officer and perhaps more than a disillusioned soldier with a general beef against white ranchers.

One thing he had learned from Batman seemed a good place to start. He needed to know more about this Dr. Nasim and about his capture. Ray hadn't worked around the chemicals and bugs when he was a Ranger. But in the unit, every Delta operator had been trained on the basics. He knew enough to know that he had a natural fear—perhaps a phobia—of biological and chemical weapons. This he knew because it stood out from his naturally low level of fear in general. Between ranch, rodeo, and the military, Ray had been given ample opportunity to test himself against the common causes of phobias. He respected snakes, bulls, and dangerous men, but he felt confident dealing with them. He had noticed a low-grade fear of heights in jump school, but experience and training had lessened it over time.

But danger that he couldn't see gave Ray the creeps. He had lost a rodeo friend to meningitis. Jimmy was one of the toughest bull riders he had known. But one day he had complained of a headache and of feeling out of sorts. A week later Ray had attended his funeral. Bacteria, they said. One doctor thought that maybe a mosquito had been responsible for infecting Jimmy. Even though he was riding in a closed car, Ray couldn't help checking his arms for rogue mosquitoes. Yeah, he hated bugs and goo. If Dr. Nasim was one of the characters that worked to weaponize such things, then Ray already didn't like him either.

Although Ray only knew the basics about chemical and biological weapons, he knew most everything there was to know about capturing bad guys. And based on both experience and knowledge, Ray thought that there was more to the story of Nasim's capture than the official account. If he had been a valuable asset for the Taliban or some other terrorist outfit, then Nasim would have been heavily guarded. Ray had fought against some of these protective details. They didn't have any weak links. To get your target, you usually had to lay them all down. Crowfoot was a battle-tested platoon leader. But it still seemed far-fetched that he and his hazmat crew had captured such a strategic target. There were only two ways Ray could see that happening. One possibility was a shootout at the OK Corral. Crowfoot's team and the terrorist guardians would have squared off, and when the dust settled, there would have been many casualties. Almost certainly one of them would have been Dr. Nasim, because his guards would have been instructed to execute him if they were unable to defend him from capture. Batman could not have resisted telling Ray about such an exciting conclusion if one had existed. So that left the other possibility—an inside job. Crowfoot was on the ropes with command when he made the capture. Grabbing Dr. Nasim had wiped Crowfoot's slate clean and, at the same time, distracted attention from that odd incident involving anthrax. If Crowfoot was dirty, he might have made some kind of deal with the devil that involved the easy capture of Nasim.

Well, the theory was easy enough to test. If Crowfoot and his team had somehow pulled off a clean capture, Dr. Nasim would be in the system. The marines at Gitmo probably had a special soundtrack that they saved just for mad scientists. Ray smiled to himself as he began thinking of country and western songs that he would recommend. *Tell us the formula, Dr. Jekyll, or you are going to listen to* Redneck Yacht Club *another hundred times!*

Ray left the Snakebite and emerged into bright summer sunshine. As his eyes adjusted and he made his way to his car, he settled on a plan. Thus far he had been scratching around on his own. He was still officially on leave. And he wasn't ready to call the cavalry. All he had so far were a handful of hunches. Make this an official army CI thing at this point, and he ran the risk of overplaying his hand. Of course, if he waited too long to get back on the grid, it could complicate things or even take the case out of his hands. It was a familiar razor's edge. And as usual Ray leaned toward trusting his own instincts and sense of timing. He would continue to work as the lone scout until he had more information. And right now he needed to gather more information on the whereabouts of Dr. Abdul Nasim.

Chapter 13

CROWFOOT IS AN *idiot—a loose cannon.* Nasim fumbled with the large ring of keys and mumbled to himself. A drop of sweat fell from his forehead on to the keys. He wiped his brow and glanced over his shoulder before opening the next steel door. The brightly lit passageway was empty and silent. Once through the door, he heard the comforting whoosh as the door resealed. Nasim dabbed his forehead with a handkerchief. He took a few deep breaths and absorbed the silence of the transitional room. The image of the hulking Crowfoot was beginning to evaporate. Nasim could feel his heart rate slowing and his respiration growing steadier. For now Nasim was leaving behind the kingdom of idiots, including its Prince Crowfoot.

The next door was the entrance to the Kingdom of Nasim. It was his own private world, of his own magical creation. Dr. Nasim had chosen all his subjects carefully. Only a handful of the most loyal and committed crossed through this door, and only then with Nasim's blessing. He had handpicked the best scientists and technicians from around the world. Only two of them were from his tribe. But they had another bond now, one that was even stronger than their clan or homeland. And all of them owed their selection to Dr. Abdul Nasim. In the orderly world on the other side of that door, he was the supreme leader. As far as Nasim's scientific tribe was concerned, the Guardians were mostly an abstraction, a banner flying over the ramparts.

They were all here as scientist-warriors. *The purest type*, Nasim thought to himself as he selected the next key and approached the last external barrier. For now Nasim tolerated Crowfoot and his noisy band of knights. But one day soon, Nasim and his tribe would no longer have need of them. Then they would simply unlock the last door. The two kingdoms would soon be one.

As Nasim was donning his protective gear and entering the heart of the laboratory, two technicians emerged into a back passageway on the far side of the laboratory. Although they were nowhere near the heart of the laboratory, they wore complete protective gear. Mobile breathing equipment hummed and clicked as they made their way down the hallway. They were pushing a gurney between them. They might have been orderlies in some International Space Station hospital, transporting a fellow astronaut from hospital room down to radiology. The gurney's wheels rolled silently along the hallway, in spite of what appeared to be a heavy load on top. Two black bags were stacked one on top of the other and strapped down to the gurney. The black load was chest high to the technicians, and they seemed to strain and lean out to make the corner at the end of the hallway. One of them swiped a card at a reader near a set of double doors, and then they heaved and strained to move their load out of the hallway and through the doors. On the other side, their suits registered a significant increase in temperature. They still had one more passageway to clear, but they were getting close to their destination.

As night enveloped the pastures of the Circle T cattle operation, one lone cow grazed apart from the rest of the herd. Cows were funny animals, as Jessie might have told anyone who had not had so much experience with them. They were herd animals, for sure, and sought the comfort of other animals in rough weather or when threatened by predators. In such times they tended to move and act according to ancient instincts. The stronger cows protected their own calves and the weaker members of the herd. And the bulls, otherwise more prone to loitering about on their own, became fearsome battering rams in protection of the entire herd. Those with horns used them, and those without simply stomped their way through any threat.

In spite of their size and strength, cattle were vulnerable to both clever predators and their own fear response. Wolves and dogs were notorious enemies. Working in packs, they identified a vulnerable calf and then worked to create distractions and distress. A harried cow might eventually seem to give up or lose heart. A bull could sometimes be led away from the herd by his fury at a single dog. And an otherwise protected calf might suddenly panic and run straight from the circle of the herd into the middle of a wolf pack.

Cattle could learn to identify friendly humans and to recognize friendly dogs. They associated certain sounds and smells with good things. Jessie's father had owned a Chevy pickup that his cattle could hear coming from a mile away. By the time she and her father pulled into a particular pasture, the cows would be lined up three deep at the feed troughs, bawling expectantly in the direction of the gate. One time her father had borrowed a friend's Ford pickup—same color and about the same model year. When they entered the pasture that day, the cows were scattered around the pasture, paying little attention to the unfamiliar truck. And then her father had stepped out and waved his hat. His cows came running and made them both smile.

Mostly cows were dependable and docile. They could generally be counted upon to gather and move along familiar trails. Familiar animals would enter a trailer or a corral without too much fuss, especially if it seemed that others were doing the same. Pawing or stamping the ground was common, especially among younger steers and apex bulls. Cows often shook their heads up and down or kicked haphazardly in the direction of anything or anyone who happened to irritate them. Mother cows could be dangerous in defense of their calf. Most bulls reserved their energy for rivals or tenacious predators. In spite of their rodeo reputation, bulls generally got along well with humans—except, of course, when they didn't. Mature bulls were like large sharks—it was the rare exceptions that one had to take into account.

That night the exception was not a raging bull, but a young cow. She was meandering on the far edges of a pasture leased by an operation known as the Circle T. She waggled her ears as she grazed, and one of them bore a yellow tag and the number 209. She suddenly turned her head and stomped a back leg. The flies were bad this time of year.

Her herd was bedded down far away, in a meadow beside a small creek. The moon was bright overhead. Ragged clouds, stragglers left by the earlier storms, drifted across the night sky. In spite of the danger of predators and the distance from her herd, cow 209 grazed contentedly as she worked her way toward the remains of a large tree. If she had come this way the previous night, she would have been frightened away by the lightning and the smell of fire. But tonight there was only the hulk of the tree sprawled over the ground like a sleeping giant. The tree had fallen over the expensive metal tube fence that circled the pasture. It seemed intact on both sides, running straight and true into the darkness on either side of the fallen tree. But where it'd fallen, the giant trunk had smashed the fence into the ground.

As cow 209 approached the tree, she hesitated for a moment, sniffing the air and then the leaves of the fallen tree. Muscles in her front shoulders twitched. She blew out a breath suddenly and began to take another step forward. Then she kicked a back leg, as if at an unseen threat. Her eyes widened and white slivers like crescent moons shown behind her dark pupils. She blew out her breath in a quick gust and then moved on toward the grass near where the tree trunk and the fence met.

The Guardians only intended to use the Circle T operation for a few more days. There had been little time to establish security in preparation for the veterinarian's visit. They had also needed to use a light touch in order to avoid spooking the landowner or nearby ranchers. And so the lightning strike had overloaded the rather basic perimeter security system. The small breach in the fence had gone unnoticed.

Cow 209 noticed a large clump of green grass on the other side of the fence. The breech was just large enough for her to squeeze through and reach the other side. As she nosed the tender grass on the other side of the breach, cow 209 suddenly shivered all over. Her head pulled to one side as if she had heard a noise behind her. But the night was quiet and warm.

Cow 209 was no longer in the pastures of the Circle T. And she was beginning to show the first signs of the sickness.

Chapter 14

BY THE TIME Jessie arrived at the Circle T, she could see that it was shaping up to be one of those spectacular spring days. The sky was a robin's-egg blue, and the sun shone down warm and friendly. It was just the sort of day when Jessie enjoyed walking a pasture, the kind of day she had imagined when she was a girl and had pictured herself being a veterinarian. As Jessie grabbed her gear and headed toward the small ranch office, she thought to herself that visiting a small ranch and examining a new herd was the perfect sort of work for this kind of day.

The Circle T manager was a heavyset man named Tom Smith. He spoke with a bit of Colorado accent. Tom had made apologies for his boss, Mr. Greene, who was apparently still on the road. And then he quickly introduced Jessie to a few of the ranch hands and began his tour. The Circle T was a small outfit, he said, and so the tour shouldn't take long. Jessie briefly explained the situation at Blackfoot and the need for preventing listeriosis from spreading among the area's cattle.

"How many head?" Jessie asked as Tom closed one of the pasture gates behind them.

"Two hundred."

"Planning to grow this herd out?"

"Slowly, if at all." Tom reached out a hand as if to take Jessie's elbow but then hesitated and let the hand drop to his side. "Not my daddy's cattle operation."

"I'm sorry?" Jessie shielded her eyes with one hand and gave Tom a puzzled look.

"Oh, I just mean that things are changing. My dad tried to grow his herd and build up bloodlines at the same time. Couldn't afford to be this small." Tom swept a hand out ahead of them in the direction of where Circle T cattle were grazing. "But today it seems like there's a new market opening up every day: range fed, organic feed...Yep, a new day."

"Right. Got it. And you all are slicing the onion even thinner, right? California restaurants?"

"Primarily. But that part of the business is more Mr. Greene's bailiwick. I just tend the cattle."

"So where is your family ranch?" Jessie asked.

Tom turned suddenly to study the side of Jessie's face. She was looking ahead at the cattle but sensed the change in his gaze.

"Eastern Colorado. But we sold out a long time ago."

As they drew closer to the herd, Jessie began to survey the animals. They were good stock and appeared healthy. It was a rather odd mix of breeds, but Dexter had told her that the Circle T was crossing lines and trying to thread the needle of some particular customer requirements. They were mostly Red Angus but with a smattering of Hereford and a few Simmental. A young steer eyed her for a moment too long and received a protective shove from its mother. Jessie smiled. *Boys...always getting in trouble.* As Jessie moved through the herd, she patted hindquarters and surveyed back lines: muscular animals and backs straight as arrows, no runny noses and no signs of tremor or unsteady gait.

"They look good—excellent, in fact."

"Thanks," Tom said as he moved closer to where Jessie stood in the middle of the herd. "We do our best." A mother cow kicked half-heartedly at Tom as he passed by.

Jessie laughed. "Always one, huh?"

"Always several in my experience—especially the Red Angus." Tom was smiling, but Jessie thought his expression seemed a little forced. And that maybe he wasn't as comfortable among this herd as she might have expected.

"So where's the bull in this pasture? Is he a problem?" Jessie scanned over the cows and toward a cove of trees near a fence line. Maybe the bull was resting in the shade.

"Nah, nice fella." Tom followed Jessie's gaze. "You're looking in the right spot. Probably asleep over there in the shade. He doesn't like to work more than to keep up appearances. A Simmental—we call him Moses, but that's a joke. He doesn't seem to lead and not many follow."

"You just seemed a little nervous, and I like a little warning before the start of a rodeo." Jessie smiled at Tom.

He smiled back, but his jawline tightened. "Sorry, Doc, but I let my mind wander sometimes. These cows are all right, and Old Moses—wherever he is—would only follow us if he thought we had a feedbag."

"So any signs of disease that you've noticed? Wobbly gait, runny nose—any of that sort of thing?"

"No, nothing like that. All good here."

Jessie took samples of the feed and grain used by Circle T. She also took a few blood samples from the cattle, although she didn't expect to find anything. Every animal she examined was sleek, well fed, and alert. In fact, by the time she left the Circle T, Jessie was challenging herself to find anything—even a stray parasite. As she put her gear away and fired up the truck, Jessie watched Tom walk briskly back toward the Circle T office. If there was a tick hiding anywhere on the Circle T ranch, Jessie hadn't been able to find it.

She wondered if Tom would be able to find it either. Maybe he had really grown up on a ranch in eastern Colorado. But if so, Jessie thought, Tom must have had other chores than caring for the cattle. He had tried to cover it well, but Jessie could often sense when someone wasn't comfortable with particular animals. Either Tom wasn't the cowhand he claimed to be, or he hadn't spent as much time with this particular herd as he let on. Maybe there was no listeriosis problem here, but Jessie wondered about this perfect ranch and its green manager. She decided to take the long way home and drive a back road on the west side of the Circle T.

Jessie almost hit the cow. She hit the brakes hard and sent a cloud of dust and gravel up to encircle cow 209. She was a Simmental, and Jessie thought she had probably once been a prized cow. But now she looked wild and unhinged. Her legs were splayed at odd angles, and her eyes were bloodshot and crazed. She had barely responded to the pickup barreling in her direction: a nod of the head just before the truck came to a stop, a stumbled half step back. Something was terribly wrong with this animal. Jessie turned on her hazard lights, grabbed her kit, and slowly opened the truck door.

"Easy, girl." Jessie calmed herself and tried to calm the terrified cow. "Easy now. I'm not going to hurt you. Just want to see if I can help."

Jessie slid out slowly from behind the pickup door and began walking toward the cow. The road was little used and mostly known to locals. So she had some time here. But it was important for Jessie to move the cow back to pasture, or better yet, to a trailer. She slid her cell phone from her pocket and made a quick call. For once Chris answered the clinic phone promptly. Jessie gave him directions and told him to bring the trailer as quickly as possible. She would try to move the cow off the road and then hold it until he arrived.

As Jessie moved closer, the cow ducked its head and wobbled in place. The eyes seemed to soften a bit, and Jessie thought her plan might just work. She took out some items from her kit and laid them on the hood of the truck. The cow's eyes were dull, and mucus dripped from her mouth. Her muscles rippled now and then like waves stirred by an unseen wind.

Jessie administered a mild sedative before slipping the lead rope around the cow's neck. The animal gave no sign of protest. After a few minutes, the cow seemed to be growing calmer and her sides were heaving less than before. Jessie decided it was time to lead the animal off the road. There was a gate entrance about twenty feet away. The ground was clear and shaded. It would be a good spot to wait for Chris.

The cow had difficulty walking, but otherwise she gave Jessie no trouble, and the two of them reached the shady spot. Jessie talked softly to the cow and began a casual examination. Was this listeriosis? It didn't look like any case that Jessie had ever seen. This animal hadn't been sick very long. She was still muscular and showed none of the usual signs of longer-term illness. The illness might be neurological. It certainly caused muscular tremors and spasms. The cow's gait was compromised. But beyond that it was hard to tell outside the clinic.

Where was Chris, anyway? Could he have taken a wrong turn?

Jessie wasn't sure later how the idea had first popped into her head. She would admit then that it was a bad idea. But at the time, it seemed to make sense to her. She and the cow had nothing else to do, and Chris was nowhere in sight.

So Jessie decided to take a few blood samples. The cow was being so docile. And she could be that much ahead of the curve if it was still possible to save this cow's life.

She had just slipped the last sample into the container in her kit and turned back to the cow when she noticed a change. The cow's eyes no longer appeared dull. They seemed instead to sparkle with fear. Jessie noticed that the cow's shoulder muscle was remarkably tense. And then came the charge.

The last thing Jessie remembered seeing was the cow's forehead heading toward her own. And then the beautiful spring day turned instantly to night.

"Dr. Anderson, can you hear me? Dr. Anderson, it's Chris! The ambulance is on its way. Just hang in there, OK."

The words seemed to be coming from a distant hallway. Jessie couldn't tell if they were meant for her or if she was sitting outside a room where someone was calling a person named Jessie. Her name.

"Chris?" Jessie's eyes fluttered open and then closed again. The light was painfully bright, and everything seemed out of focus.

"Oh, thank God. Dr. Anderson, just relax. I can hear the ambulance now."

By the time the ambulance arrived, some of the cobwebs were beginning to clear, and Jessie was starting to feel just well enough to argue with EMTs. She assured them that she was a doctor herself and that she was used to taking knocks from her animal patients. Speaking of patients, hers was missing, and she needed to locate the cow before it was too late. But the blood streaking from her forehead and occasional garbled word made the EMTs equally stubborn. After giving Chris strict and detailed instructions, Jessie was finally loaded into the ambulance and driven to the hospital.

Chris drove by the Anderson home and picked up Derrick for the ride to the hospital. On the way there, he explained about the sick cow and the accident. After he drove Derrick to the hospital and received an update that Dr. Anderson would be OK, Chris drove back to the dusty ranch road and began searching for the sick cow. He had picked up his ATV on the way from the hospital and used it to drive all the trails and back roads in the area. He did not want to report to Dr. Anderson that he was unable to find the cow. So Chris used his spotlight and kept searching long after dark. But finally it was no use. He was exhausted, and the cow was in none of the expected places. Dr. Anderson had said that the cow was very sick. By now it was probably too late anyway.

Chris loaded up the ATV in the trailer and headed for home.

Cow 209 was gone.

Derrick winced as he walked through the hospital room door.

"Ouch. What did the cow look like after your fight?"

"Very funny."

Derrick walked to the bed and took Jessie's hand. "You OK?"

"Head hurts. Took a pretty good knock. But I'm not staying more than one night. And you can tell that pinhead doctor that I'm not having any more tests either."

Derrick smiled and kissed Jessie on the cheek. Jessie smiled and then winced.

"You don't know how good it is to hear you raising Cain. Chris isn't the best messenger in the world, so I wasn't entirely clear whether you had been run over by a cow or taken hostage by aliens. He was pretty shook up. So what did the pinhead doctor say?"

"Concussion. Gash on my forehead. He reassured me that the scar wouldn't show and didn't believe me that I like having a scar or two. Adds character, don't you think?"

"Most definitely. A good cow fighter should be proud of her scars. So what happened out there?"

"I made a rookie mistake. Assumed an animal was too sick to fight. Only saw her coming just before the head butt."

"Where did this cow come from? Chris said you were out on a ranch road west of the Circle T."

"That's right...at least I think so. Kind of fuzzy. But I remember I was driving on a ranch road when this cow just appeared in the middle of the road. I almost hit it."

"Looking back, it might have been better if you had."

"We were friends at first. Things only turned ugly there at the end."

The trauma doctor came in and introduced himself to Derrick. He reviewed Jessie's condition and made the case for keeping her one night for observation. Jessie was growing tired, and she didn't feel like arguing anymore. Derrick thanked the doctor and pulled up a chair. He would wait for Chris to return with news about the cow. And then he would take his turn at sleeping in the chair next to the hospital bed.

Chapter 15

A COLD FRONT had moved through overnight, and the morning dawned crisp and clear. Jessie had agreed to take it easy at home for the day on the condition that Derrick and Chris make another sweep to look for the stray cow. Although Derrick thought it was a bit optimistic at this point, they connected the clinic's trailer to Chris's truck and struck out early for the area west of the Circle T.

Gray clouds were draped along the northern horizon. The wind had howled overnight, but now it was reduced to the occasional gust. Patches of mist brushed over the windshield of Chris's old Ford pickup and grew heavier as they drove on north. There was a rattle in the door on Derrick's side, and he had made a few subtle attempts to hold his weight against it. But the rattle persisted. Derrick shifted his weight and started a conversation in hopes of ignoring the noise.

"So, no luck tracking this stray when you came out before?"

"No, sir, I could see where she charged and some scattered tracks along the road. But just off the road, it turns to brush and rocky ground."

"Blood trail?" Derrick asked.

"Some from the collision, and I picked up color here and there in the brush near the road but not enough to pick up her trail coming or going."

Derrick leaned forward and studied the sky. He was partly interested in the weather and partly covering his reaction to Chris's report. Chris was a good vet tech, but he was also a suburban guy whose trail experiences revolved around mountain bikes.

"This rain won't help. Looks like it might settle in later."

"Does look that way. I hate to wish someone a dead animal, but I keep thinking this cow couldn't have gotten far. The way Dr. Anderson described this stray sounded like she was on her last leg."

"Yeah, must have appeared that way at first, but funny how a dead cow can catch her second wind. Jessie tells me this one still packed quite a punch."

"There is that. Crazy Simmental." Chris checked a landmark and made the last turn onto the old ranch road.

The gravel and dirt road was damp and a few shades darker than it had been the day that the stray cow had appeared out of nowhere. It still looked like a dusty road but one with the dust trapped and blanketed to the primitive strip of road. There was one clear and level patch of ground near the end of the tracks made by Jessie's truck. It was an old gate entrance, and the ground had been worn smooth in a funnel shape leading to the gate. Derrick could see why Jessie had chosen to lead the cow to this spot. It was shaded and just small enough to comfort the cow and provide Jessie a bit of room to maneuver.

The bad news was that other than this one smooth patch, the old ranch road was bordered by thick brush and rocky outcroppings. It was the sort of ground that caused an animal to leave signs as it bumped along and raked through snags. But it was also the sort of ground that made those signs difficult for a tracker to find. Derrick kneeled down on his haunches to study the track that led away from the collision between the cow and Jessie. In spite of the recent weather, it was not hard to pick up some blood around the gate entrance.

Derrick shivered as he examined the chaotic pattern. Most of this blood was probably Jessie's. He moved on from the site of the collision and tried to pick up signs of the sick animal. At first it wasn't hard to follow, even though Chris had muddled some of the tracks with that ATV toy of his.

Derrick had tracked enough strays in his time to know something about the patterns. It was important to follow the particular signs, but experience taught a tracker that most of the time cattle responded in similar ways. Now and then Derrick had tracked the eccentric and unpredictable cow. But mostly the behavior of a stray animal fit into a handful of categories. A calf, or a mother with a nursing calf, was the easiest to follow. They might panic when separated, and sometimes that panic led them into strange places. But mostly a calf would try to return to its mother. And a mother cow would break down the gates of hell to be reunited with its calf. Bulls wandered off in search of a female cow in season. Find her and you found him. Occasionally a bull either sought out a rival or encountered one as he chased his romantic interest. Bulls were destructive but not complicated. A mature bull might tear through a section of fence as easily as a football player tearing through a paper sign on game day. But the *reason* the bull walked through the fence boiled down to only one or two possibilities.

Solo cows were the trickiest cases. They mostly stuck to the herd, and a healthy cow would generally find her way home. But a panicked cow had the strength and endurance to carry her farther afield. Sometimes dehydration and exhaustion befuddled a healthy cow and made it impossible for her to find the way back home. And if anything went wrong with a cow—and a hundred things could go wrong with them—they might wander in a way that fit none of the usual patterns.

Derrick told Chris to check the road for signs that someone might have come by and trailered the stray cow. In his initial scan, Derrick saw only tire tracks from Jessie's truck and the ATV. It was possible that this road was so rarely used that they might luck out and pick up signs that the owner of the cow had recovered her.

Meanwhile, Derrick began following the cow's tracks off the road. At first the trail was fairly easy to follow. The cow had bolted from her encounter with Jessie and crashed ahead for twenty yards or so. Beyond the right of way, the grade steepened and the brush grew thicker. Derrick could see broken limbs with bits of reddish hair on them. The blood trail was easy to follow here too. The cow was heaving with the effort and throwing a light spray onto nearby bushes and rocks. She wasn't bleeding badly and mostly, it appeared, from wounds suffered when she knocked against rocks and stumbled over the broken ground. Her gait was jerky, and it was clear to Derrick that her path was wider than normal. But in spite of her illness, this was a powerful cow. Her stumbles appeared to be more from frenzy than weakness. And when she went down, she came charging back up, digging furrows in the softer ground and pawing scratches in the rock. She wasn't circling like the usual listeriosis case, but now and then there were signs that her back legs were locking up on her. The drag marks carried on for about five yards and then abruptly shifted back to the jerky four-legged gait. This cow had heart, Derrick thought, and was not one to lie down and die easily.

Chris had completed his scan of the road and hustled up to join Derrick on the trail.

"No sign of a trailer on the road."

"I was afraid you were going to say that. She's rocked along on the same line here. After her encounter with Jessie, it seems that she wanted nothing to do with the road."

The two walked along deeper into the brush. The ground grew steeper, and thick tangles of hawthorn and sage slowed their progress to a crawl. The sky had continued to cloud over, and Derrick had to reach for a penlight to make out the trail. He briefly thought that this would make great cover for a bear or mountain lion, especially if the predators happened to be stalking the same sick cow that he and Chris were hunting. But instead of being afraid of pressing farther into the dense brush, Derrick found the idea of encountering a bear or lion strangely amusing. Maybe it had to do with him and Jessie surviving their recent battles, but anyway he felt pretty bulletproof. Derrick glanced back over his shoulder. Chris, on the other hand, looked like he might take any excuse to sprint out of the brush and back to the truck.

And then, abruptly, the trail ended. They had reached a small patch of ground that was less steep. Up ahead the trail turned up sharply and on over to a rise that fell away to pastures. Somewhere over that rise, Derrick knew, the land was fenced, although from here he couldn't see any fences and had no idea who might own the pastureland on the other side of the rise.

Wherever this cow considered home, it was likely trying to get there. And home had probably been somewhere on the other side of that rise. If they were lucky, maybe one ranch owned all the land on the other side.

But that didn't help Derrick with his immediate puzzle. How could the trail stop so suddenly? By this point the cow would have been winded and probably looking for shelter. It might have been why she plowed so deeply into this brush in the first place. She might be the exception to the pattern. If she had been growing weaker, the cow might have shifted gears from searching for home to seeking immediate shelter from predators. She hadn't chosen a great location if that was her aim, but then sick cattle weren't usually good at avoiding large predators.

So where did she bed down?

Derrick asked Chris to expand the circle and to look carefully for any sign that the cow had wallowed out the brush. He thought about mentioning to look for signs of predators but then thought better of it. Chris was unlikely to forget about that possibility. And if a predator had attacked the cow anywhere in this area, they would have known about it by now. That tussle would have left signs everywhere, including an unmistakable blood trail. But the area around where the trail ended was undisturbed. Derrick saw no signs of bear, cat, or dogs.

Where had she gone? There were no signs of ATV traffic or hunters on foot. Derrick saw no way that even the best driver could get a Jeep, much less a truck and trailer, in here to load a cow. And even if by some miracle a wrangler had managed to pull that off, where were the tracks in and out?

Derrick realized Chris was staring at him, and at the same time trying not to make it obvious.

"Any ideas?" Derrick asked.

"Not a clue." Chris shook his head. "Unless you consider aliens a possibility."

Derrick grinned. "One step ahead of you. But I don't see any place to land the spaceship."

"Good point."

"OK, let's try to work this out. Unless you want to try out our alien theory on your boss?" Derrick raised an eyebrow and glanced up at Chris.

"You have my full attention."

"So this cow thrashes hard on her way from the road into the brush. She's sick, and she bangs herself up here and there on the brush and the rocks. But she's still barreling along for a time. Has some gas left in the tank. Then her gait worsens; she shows some signs of paralysis in the back legs. The going is much harder up here, and she begins to fade."

Derrick pauses and glances up to the ridge and then waves a hand in that direction. "I'm guessing she was a couple hundred yards from pasture. Likely fenced, but maybe she came through a break. About the only way she's out here to begin with, unless she broke from a trailer. Can't see her running hard enough to get away from wranglers at a trailer or corral.

"Anyway, she's on her way to pasture, maybe on her way to the home herd. She stops here—not a bad place to stop but not great either. She's more exposed than she might be if she pressed on closer to the ridge or if she backed down into that heavy brush there."

"Maybe she sensed a cat," Chris said as he glanced up to the few larger trees clinging to the hill. "We didn't find tracks, but maybe we missed them or the rain washed them away. Cat might have come downhill toward her."

"I can see that," Derrick said. "But what happened next? I mean, either the cat broke off its hunt, or we are lousy trackers. I see no signs of a struggle anywhere. If we were looking for a favorite hunting dog, I would say that the cat might have killed it and taken it to the trees. But this is a thousand-pound cow we are talking about."

"You're right. She would have either been spooked or fighting, and I don't see any signs of a panic or a struggle. What's your best guess?"

Derrick paused and rubbed his chin. He was especially careful with his guesses, something that had been appreciated by his dad and his commanding officers. It had always driven Ray crazy.

"I have no guess."

Chris nodded. "I have one more idea. But let me check it out. Probably a dead end and no sense both of us getting scratched to pieces. Be right back."

And with that Chris disappeared into the heavy brush just along the bottom flank of the ridge. Derrick found a flathead rock nearby and took a seat. A mosquito buzzed down to land on his forearm. Derrick deftly smacked it before he remembered that it was his injured arm. He winced and coughed away a yelp. The clouds were breaking here and there, creating a patchwork of shadows among the rocks and brush. The cow's last prints fell into deeper shadows and then opened back into a miniature of the light and shadow on the ridgeline above. Derrick took his phone out of his pocket and checked for messages—no bars. This cow had managed to locate the absolute middle of nowhere.

Derrick thought of Jessie suddenly, and for the first time since the accident, he was truly worried about her. It was an odd feeling, both because he now felt worried and because he realized that he hadn't been so worried earlier. They had both grown up on ranches, he told himself, and had seen plenty of accidents with cattle and equipment. Most of them were minor, and it was part of the culture to make them the subject of jokes and tall tales. He had been tossed off a green horse and broken three ribs when he was fifteen. And he remembered more teasing about his riding skills than expressions of concern about his injury. Jessie was the prettiest woman he had ever met. And she was also the toughest ranch hand, male or female, that he had ever known. So in a sense, it was culturally ingrained in both of them to make light of injuries that other people might not consider so funny.

He had been truly concerned when he first heard that she was in an accident and on her way to the hospital. But Chris had quickly informed him that the accident involved a cow and that Jessie was arguing with the EMTs about taking that ride. He had slid so quickly from deep concern to mild concern and admiration. But now, in maybe the first quiet moments since the accident, he realized that for all her toughness Jessie was human and vulnerable. She might have been hurt seriously by that cow or even killed. Derrick couldn't imagine a day of life without her.

"Hey, Derrick! Over here!" Derrick was startled by the sudden call. He jumped to his feet and made his way toward the sound of Chris's voice. The brush was thick at first, but then it cleared some and Derrick began jogging. He broke past a few large trees and then saw Chris standing nearby. And at his feet were the remains of cow 209.

Mystery solved, or so it seemed. She was a good-looking cow, a mousy gray with straight back and muscular body. She hadn't been dead very long. Other than the tongue lolling from her mouth and a slight stiffness in her back legs, she looked like she might get up at any moment. She hadn't made it to the ridge and had actually wandered parallel to it in her last moments. Derrick walked around to the head and bent down to examine the ear tag. It was a bright yellow tag, or had been before it had become smeared with blood and dirt. Removing a bandana from his back pocket, Derrick wiped off the tag. *Number 209*. Well, it was definitely the stray. Jessie had reminded him and Chris to be on the lookout for this ear tag.

Derrick stood up and stepped back a few paces from the cow. He removed his cell phone and began taking pictures of the cow.

"What are you doing?" Chris asked. "She's two oh nine for sure."

"Yes, but I know your boss better than you do. And as much fun as we have had this morning, I would rather not hike back out here to let Jessie see the body for herself."

"Good call." Chris swatted at a mosquito. "But let's not take too long with it. I'm about to be carried off here."

Derrick snapped one more photo and then put away his cell phone. He looked about for a simpler route to the road, but finding none they began trudging back down the way they had come. Derrick was relieved to be heading back and especially relieved that he could report the outcome. He knew that Jessie would be disappointed about the cow's death. For all her toughness, she had a soft spot for nearly every cow she encountered. He smiled at the memory of a Brahma bull she had wanted to euthanize once, but that was after he had torn through a fence and killed a beloved Hereford bull she had nicknamed

"Jake" because he followed her around like their golden retriever of the same name.

Derrick's toe caught a rock, and the stumble broke him out of his reverie. He gasped at the thought of falling on his bum shoulder. Now more alert, he studied the ground carefully as he walked along behind Chris on the trail. There was no trail really, just a matter of following Chris's lead. Suddenly Derrick realized that he had seen no tracks or signs since they had left the spot where cow 209 died. He started to examine the brush and rocks more carefully as he walked along. No blood. No signs of broken limbs or hair. Derrick's pace slowed further, and he began scanning a wider path on either side of where he and Chris were walking.

"You OK?" Chris asked.

Derrick looked up and realized that the gap had widened between them. "Yeah, I'm fine. Say, what was that hunch you had? You said you thought of something before you took off in the direction where that cow ended up dead."

Chris leaned against a pine tree and absently peeled at a piece of bark. "Oh, it was a crazy idea really. Can't believe it worked out. But I had heard Jessie—I mean, Dr. Anderson—say that sometimes sick cows made a last quick bolt before they died. 'Death sprint,' I think she called it. Anyway I just looked at the direction of clearing and thought if that cow took off fast, maybe her tracks would be loose and light. Rain might have softened up the ground enough that they would be invisible later."

"Oh," Derrick said, nodding his head. He was puzzling over what Chris had just said and trying to imagine Jessie saying it. Chris seemed to be studying Derrick carefully for a moment. Then he slowly turned and continued walking.

Derrick followed Chris and continued examining the path. A running cow, especially one with partial paralysis in her hind legs, would land with considerable force on her front hoofs. A running cow would leave distinctive prints, deeper at the front of the hoof and sloping up sharply to ground level. There would also be kicking and scratching marks. An animal on the run also tended to leave more hair snags behind in the brush. Derrick couldn't find any of these tracks or signs.

If cow 209 was on a death sprint, she must have been flying so fast she hardly touched the ground.

Chapter 16

"THAT'S NOT HER." Jessie handed Derrick's phone back to him and put her hands on her hips.

"Jessie, take another look at these photos. It's got to be her."

Jessie took the phone and studied each of the photos again. She paused over the last one and then handed the phone back to Derrick. "I'm sorry, Derrick. I know you want me to say it's her and be done with it, but the cow in those photos is not the one I encountered on the road that day."

"No, because she's dead—I know, she looks different."

"That's not funny, if you were trying to be funny."

"Jessie, I'm not joking around. Look, let's think this through together. You encountered a stray cow on a deserted ranch road. You recognized her as a Simmental and noticed that she had a yellow ear tag numbered two zero nine. She was very sick but then mustered enough energy to charge you. Now, twenty-four hours later Chris and I return to this same ranch road. We trail the cow into the brush and up the rocky ground on the north side of that road. After some searching we locate a dead Simmental cow with a yellow ear tag marked two zero nine. What are the odds that the sick cow number two oh nine that you saw yesterday is the same sick cow number two zero nine that me and Chris found today?"

"Thank you, Detective Anderson." Jessie's tone was growing icy. "But I'm not crazy, and that's not the cow I saw yesterday."

"No one is saying you are crazy. But, come on, Jessie, give yourself a break…You did have a concussion."

"I know cows."

"You can pick any cow out of a lineup. I'm just trying to make sense of what seems like a real long shot in this case."

Jessie folded her arms over her chest and lowered her head. When she spoke next, her voice was quiet and distant.

"Me too. Maybe I *am* a little off." Jessie didn't like going to bed angry. But she also knew that it took her some time to cool off. She decided to start now. "So did Chris pretend that he could track, or did he just sit in the truck and eat donuts?" Jessie managed a weak smile.

"He mostly pretended. But I can't say too much because he's the one that found her."

"You've got to be kidding?"

"No, I trailed her to a point where she just seemed to vanish from the earth. And then Chris suddenly had a hunch and walked straight into the woods and right to the spot."

"Go figure. And I thought you were the tracker." Jessie smiled more fully now as Derrick moved closer and hugged her. He seemed to have decided it was safe.

Derrick held her for a moment and then spoke over her shoulder. "Chris did give you credit, by the way. Said that his hunch came from something you had taught him about a *death sprint*…a sudden sprint that cows make sometimes before they die. I had never heard of that."

Jessie stiffened. She hadn't heard of it either. Now she wondered if she really was losing her mind, if maybe that knock on the head had been worse than she thought. Tonight she would rest, but tomorrow she needed to start looking for some answers. Either Derrick was right about this cow and she was not thinking clearly, or else something suspicious was going on with respect to this wandering cow.

Ray drummed his fingers on the table to the loud beat of a Kenny Chesney tune. The waitress brought him his Coke and asked if he wanted to order for his friend, but Ray waved at the empty side of the booth and told her he would wait for his friend to arrive.

It hadn't taken Ray long to determine that Dr. Abdul Nasim was not occupying a cell at Guantanamo. In fact, Ray couldn't locate Nasim anywhere in the vast system of US military and intelligence. Ray was an insider, a counterintelligence officer, and short of the CIA, he probably had access to the best information available. Nasim's disappearance had been papered over in places. It was an embarrassment to everyone from the army Rangers who had aided the capture in Afghanistan to the senior brass who had added his capture to their tally of blows against terrorism. Ray hadn't worked all the way through the maze that was constructed after Nasim vanished. He knew the whole idea was to keep any curious party scurrying around long enough that they would either lose interest or else begin to believe all the mind-numbing explanations. And all Ray needed was to establish that the maze existed. Once you had seen one, you had seen them all.

So now he was hoping for help from an expert maze buster. "Deacon" Henderson and Ray had served together in the Rangers and had come close to serving together in the unit. But instead of opting for Delta, Deacon had decided to double down as a combat Ranger. When Ray asked Deacon why he wanted to stay in the heart of the chaos that was Afghanistan at the time, Deacon shrugged and said, "Reminds me of home." Home for Deacon had been the toughest single neighborhood in Detroit. He had a scar under one eye courtesy of a crack dealer who'd been hassling his mother. The dealer had taken a lucky swipe at him. But one swipe was all he got. Deacon had been fourteen at the time.

When he had decided to stick with the Rangers instead of following Ray to Delta, Ray had also suspected that Deacon had been recruited for CIA duty. It wasn't supposed to work that way, and Deacon would die before admitting to it, but Ray had picked up clues now and then. In a sense Deacon had been a CIA "type" long before he entered the military. He worked magic with computers and communication systems, picked up languages easily, and observed every detail of people and situations. No doubt these skills—especially his talents of observation and language—had helped him survive his deadly Detroit neighborhood. But his capabilities also seemed imprinted on his personality and demeanor. Deacon was simply one of those "go-to" people, a natural.

Ray was checking his watch when Deacon suddenly plopped down in the booth across from him. It was always a shock to see Deacon if he hadn't been around for some time. He was the most intimidating-looking man Ray had ever seen. He was a bit shorter than Ray, around six feet. But he was probably thirty pounds heavier, and all of that difference seemed to be concentrated in Deacon's chest and arms. His skin was a midrange brown, except the dark ragged line of that knife scar. His cheekbones were prominent, and his jawline appeared cut from bronze. In some ways Ray could imagine him on the streets of Detroit. His face would have turned heads but not suggested anything other than a hometown case. But it was Deacon's eyes that made him stand out, that completed the face that was able to stare down even the saltiest of the bad boys in the army. His eyes were a remarkable shade of the lightest brown, almost yellow, and flecked with green. Ray had heard it said of some person that their eyes "blazed." But Deacon was the only person he had known whose eyes truly blazed whenever he became angry—or when he was defending others. In those moments Deacon could look like some terrifying combination of Caribbean pirate and middle linebacker for the Detroit Lions.

Ray could still remember the expression of every guy paired with Deacon for any army combat drill: sheer terror. And most of them, even the Rangers, couldn't easily hide their fear. It wasn't so much that Deacon was so strong or aggressive. He was both of those things, but so were most of the army Rangers Ray had known. It was his utter calm and sense of absolute confidence. Deacon was going to dominate any threat and any hostile situation he encountered. It was not so much a question as a conclusion, and everyone who met him under those circumstances could read that conclusion on his face.

And then he would smile. For such a fearsome man, Deacon had the warmest smile imaginable. And now he flashed the full sunshine.

"What's up, Redneck?"

"Deacon! His blackness."

Deacon took off his shades and set them on the table. "Been a while, Ray. How's life on the Ponderosa?"

"You know, same old roping and riding. How's the life of a Motown celebrity?"

"Can't complain. Me and JD started our own security company. We're not the players, but at least we are guarding the players. Not a bad gig. I would try to recruit you except for your sorry temperament and questionable work history. Maybe you could check if Derrick would be interested?" Deacon flashed that million-dollar smile, and Ray had to laugh.

"Yeah, I'll ask him if he has any interest in joining the Detroit mafia. In the meantime, I have a favor to ask."

Deacon shifted to settle into his side of the booth. "So what can I do for my cowboy friend? Need me to help you meet a nice girl?"

"I would call Batman for that sort of help. No, I need your underworld talents to help me locate someone who has disappeared."

"I see. Stateside or abroad?"

"Don't know. Disappeared in Afghanistan but could be anywhere."

"Lovely Afghanistan! So my next question: did this person disappear on their own, or are we talking about someone who may have taken a ride in the trunk of the car?"

"Don't know."

Deacon shifted back against the booth and rubbed a massive hand over his shaved head. He fixed his gaze on Ray.

"OK, this sounds dark. Perfect case for a brother from Detroit. So why don't I order a beverage, and you tell old Uncle Deacon the whole sorry tale."

Deacon signaled for the waitress. After she had left the table, Ray began to tell what little he knew. He explained the connection to Crowfoot but stopped short of going as far back as Reuben's tale about Rains. And Ray reviewed what he had learned so far about the disappearance of Dr. Nasim and the signs of cover-up. Deacon listened patiently, occasionally turning his head to one side as though he were considering something Ray had just said. When Ray finished, Deacon folded his hands together and placed them on the table.

"I don't want to disappoint you before we jump on our horses and ride, but are you sure this whole thing isn't just grunt gossip? Spooky doctor disappears from tribal region. Sounds a little like something that might be shared around the campfire."

"I trust my sources on this one. I know the story sounds a little weird. But my gut tells me that it sounds so weird because it would have taken so much juice to pull off. This Nasim guy was a high-value target, and yet he managed to vanish from custody and from the army paper trail."

"CIA sandbox?"

"Maybe. But the guy never landed in Gitmo or in any of our other garden-view villas, so far as I can tell."

"Or maybe he exists, but he wasn't the threat your sources make out. Maybe he was making rat poison for friends and neighbors."

"Possibly. But anthrax isn't rat poison."

"You can tie Nasim directly to anthrax?"

"No, but he was captured shortly after an anthrax report—and by the same unit."

Deacon took a sip from his drink and rubbed his chin. "All right, Ray, so let's say that this guy is the real deal. Then this sounds like a case that should be handled by army CI and the FBI. But here you are shooting the breeze with Brother Deacon. What's up with that?"

"I believe Dr. Nasim vanished with a great deal of help, and some of that likely came from people with military and political clout. Before I go rattling cages and stirring up trouble, I would like to know more about what I am up against. Nasim's helpers have already provided him some deep cover, but I imagine he could burrow deeper if I set off any alarms in official channels. And there's something else."

"What's that?"

"You have a nose for these things, Deacon, and I could use some ideas about what to look for on this side of things. If Nasim is operating in the United States, we could be sitting on a ticking time bomb. You are good at isolating those things that someone should look for in order to locate someone. So while you are scouting, I thought maybe you could be kicking over those kinds of rocks."

"Hmm, well there are a few obvious things. Setting up a bug lab requires major funding. Somebody's moving cash around. Specialized equipment, but I doubt they bought it retail. Most likely picked up things here and there from hospitals and research facilities. Might have stolen some of what they need. They need technicians, and they might have taken the risk of bringing in a few of Nasim's best help from overseas. Probably your best bet until we know more is tracking the cash and the animals."

"Animals?"

"Yeah, laboratory animals. They need to run experiments, and they might be setting a profile that would lead to specialized purchases—rabbits of a certain type, or some such thing. And as long as we are talking about mad scientists, they would need human subjects at some point. For those they would target vulnerable populations—homeless persons, the mentally ill—so I would look for any pattern of disappearances."

"Anything else?" Ray asked.

"Yeah, accidents. Using bugs for weapons is a two-edged sword. If they are scaling up research, they are bound to make mistakes. I would be on the lookout for deaths among technicians, scientists, or people who might be working for their suppliers." Deacon leaned back to wave off the waitress. "OK, so suppose between the two of us, we locate some things that look promising. Then what?"

"Then I make it official. Hunt down the bad guys."

"Which raises a question. I always assumed that you guys and maybe the CIA were keeping a close eye on these bug terrorists and their science experiments."

"Counterterrorism is a patchwork, Deacon. You know that. Better than it used to be but still a crazy quilt. But you may be right—there may be some CIA operative tracking Nasim's every move. All I want to do is get close enough to find out."

"If he is the high-value resource you think he is, getting even that close could get us both killed."

"I know. If I were you, I would seriously consider taking a pass on this one."

"No, you wouldn't. And neither would the Black Knight of Detroit. It'll be just like that Stevie Wonder song man." Deacon began to sing softly, "*Ebony and ivory…*"

"Please stop," Ray said. "I might take anthrax instead of listening to you sing."

"Don't know a velvety voice when you hear one, cowboy. Been listening to Willie Nelson too long."

"Compared to you, Willie Nelson sounds like Nat King Cole. So how much do I owe you to run this down?"

Deacon stood and stretched. "On the house for now. I can't let you slop around and make a mess of things. But I'll let you know if you need to sell any cows and send me some of that ranch money."

Deacon scanned the area around their table for a moment and then looked back at Ray. His gaze was level, and his voice more quiet when he spoke next.

"All joking aside, Ray, I'm going to scout light and careful on this one. We're brothers and all, but I got a nice new business going. I don't want to get sideways with the CIA, much less the spooks on the other team. So I will put my ear to the ground, and as long as I can stay invisible, I will see what I can find out. But I'm not poking my head up even a little bit, and I'm not wearing a badge or joining the posse."

"So we aren't going to take a selfie before you go?" Ray feigned a hurt look.

"Only if you want to see your cell phone go flying into that fish tank over there."

Ray shook Deacon's hand and watched him walk toward the front door. If he was ever on the run, Ray thought to himself, he hoped that no one else would have the idea to contact Deacon and put him on the hunt. Derrick was the best tracker of animals that Ray knew, but Deacon Henderson was a genius at tracking down a single human being.

Chapter 17

WHEN SHE FIRST woke up, she thought that maybe she'd dodged the bullet. Everyone said that day two was the worst. But her headache was better at first, and she felt a bit less like she was underwater. The day before, she had felt like she was a diver trying to move through her day at a depth of about twenty feet below the surface. This morning the sunlight had not seemed nearly as sharp, and she had managed to drag herself from bed only an hour behind her usual start time.

But on the way to the shower, Jessie decided that she might not be the exception to rule about day two after all. Everything from her waist up felt like she had lost a boxing match with an iron-fisted opponent. Her legs were better overall, but the few places where the cow had stepped on her legs produced sharp pain and muscle cramps.

Shower water never felt so good, and Jessie adjusted the dial to the pulsing massage.

What a wild ride the past few weeks had been—and now this. Jessie made her own cursory examination. Her skull wasn't fractured, or if it was, the crack was so slight that it wouldn't matter. The swelling around her forehead and eyes was pretty gruesome, but she hadn't developed any of the other signs of more serious concussion. The fact that her head seemed to be clearing this soon was a good sign.

She had been hit harder in the chest than it had seemed that day. The EMTs had thought she might have broken ribs. Jessie didn't find any signs of fractures, but she understood now why they had been worried about thoracic or abdominal injuries. She and the cow had certainly met head-to-head, and that was what she had felt in the time just after their encounter. But a cow was built like a compact train car. The cow's knees and chest had barreled through Jessie's upper body. She would need to let those bruises heal and avoid reinjury. She hadn't really been listening when the doctors had told her and Derrick that she was not to be working with large animals for at least a couple of weeks. But now her body was talking directly to her, and Jessie was listening. She couldn't risk another rodeo any time soon.

The bright purple hoofprints were too sensitive to touch. The prints were so distinct that Jessie thought investigators could take prints from this cow and match them to the marks on her thigh. Although the muscle cramps were painful, she was glad that the cow had stepped on these larger muscles. Otherwise she would have certainly broken one or both of Jessie's legs.

That was some cow. How had Jessie missed the signs? Usually she could read an animal pretty well. She remembered getting out of the truck and looking at the stray cow. She had seemed pretty sick, and Jessie remembered her taking some faltering steps. Her gait was compromised, likely sliding toward paralysis. Jessie had managed to get the cow to the side of the road somehow. Oh yes, the rope lead. She had walked the cow to that clear spot. And she had given her a mild sedative, just something to calm her down, so she could...what? Why had she wanted to calm the cow down? Think, Jessie. What did you do next?

The water was swirling at the drain, the start of little water tornadoes. She had been waiting for something or someone. Oh yeah, Chris. He was coming with the trailer. Maybe that was why she had wanted to calm the cow. They would need her calm for loading. But there was something else. What was it?

After a few more minutes of fruitless meditation, Jessie shoved the shower dial to off and buried her face in a towel. Maybe her head wasn't as clear as she had thought. She couldn't remember telling Chris anything about a *death sprint*, and now she couldn't shake loose what had happened in the time just before the cow had charged her. Jessie dried off, slid into a light satin robe, and walked gingerly back to a chair in one corner of the bedroom.

She sat down and by habit began drying her hair until the pain persuaded her to let her hair air-dry. The morning sun was spilling through the curtains now and brightening the room. Jessie thought ahead to the clinic. It might take her another hour to gain steam, but then she could put in at least part of a day in the office. She had some billing to catch up on and a few phone calls to make. She needed to follow up on the Blackfoot quarantine. And there was some lab work awaiting her attention. Maybe she could send Chris to the field if she needed to collect anything from the field. He couldn't run some of the tests, but...

Jessie leaned back in the chair and closed her eyes. There had been a flicker of something. *Tests.* What did it mean? Had she planned to conduct some test on the cow when they trailered it back to the clinic? Maybe before the accident she had been trying to remember a test she wanted to perform. Listeriosis—was that it? Jessie let her mind drift back to the ranch road and the encounter with the stray cow. She had left the truck and then come back for a lead rope. Now she could feel the lead rope in her hand. The cow had been submissive at first. She had talked to it, calmed it.

A thought interrupted. *What does it matter? The cow is dead.*

Jessie refused to give up. She went back to the road and to the sound of her calming the cow. Jessie began speaking out loud.

"That's it, girl. It's OK now. I'm here to help. Easy now. Easy."

Jessie moved her arms out to deliver the shot of sedative.

"That should help. Easy does it. Just be still now for a minute longer, girl. Just hold still while I—"

Jessie dropped the towel and opened her eyes wide.

Tests. She had taken samples. The "tests" that snagged somewhere in her memory were blood samples drawn from cow 209.

Jessie stood up—too quickly—and braced herself against the back of the chair. Forget waiting an hour. It was time to get dressed and make her way to the clinic.

When Jessie arrived at the clinic, Chris was already there. She could see that he had completed one or two helpful chores and then run out of initiative. She wasn't sure how long he had been adrift, but sometime after she triggered the chime on the front door, she could hear Chris whistling loudly and working a little too vigorously at some task in the back room of the clinic. Jessie smiled as she imagined him trying to imitate productive labor in that nearly empty space and then winced as his whistling reached a high note.

"Chris, why don't you come up here for a second."

"Oh hey, Dr. Anderson." Chris peaked around the corner and wiped the back of his hand across a perfectly dry forehead. "I was just straightening up in back. Didn't know if you would be in the office today."

"Yeah, thought I would try to get some clinic work done. If you are finished out back"—Jessie looked over Chris's shoulder—"then I have some field errands for you."

"Um, sure. I was wrapping up."

"Good. I think that's how we'll work it for the next day or two. I will do what I can here, and you can do the fieldwork. You can pick up supplies and maybe later make a few follow-up visits."

Jessie gave Chris a full list of errands and happily sent him on his way. Sometimes Chris's chatter was a pleasant distraction, especially his wide-eyed recounting of thoroughly bogus tales that he heard around the cattle barns or read somewhere on social media. And on a really good day, she could tolerate spells of his cheerful whistling. But today silence sounded great, and Jessie would probably make better progress on the lab work without Chris around.

The first test of the day might be the most difficult. Jessie picked up her dusty kit bag from the counter where Derrick had placed it for her.

What if the samples weren't there? What if her mind was playing tricks on her again? Jessie took a deep breath and released the top strap on the black leather bag. She released a drawstring and opened the bag wide. The sample kit was there, and it was closed. That was a good sign. Jessie withdrew the kit and brought it over to her lab bench. If she had managed to collect the samples and store them correctly, the blood vials would be inside and kept at the appropriate temperature. She flipped the latch and breathed a huge sigh of relief. There they were—two vials filled with blood, resting in a bright white protective cocoon. So she hadn't lost her marbles—or at least not all of them anyway.

Jessie turned down the bright lab lights a few notches. Today she would trade laser vision for a bit less throbbing at her temples. She began firing up the necessary pieces of laboratory equipment, including a battered laptop. She drew some instruments from nearby drawers and set them on the counter. Jessie was preparing the first vial when she heard the front door chime. She should have locked the door after Chris left, Jessie thought. They sometimes had drop-ins looking for help with their house cat. Jessie removed her lab glasses and began to stand up.

"Dr. Anderson."

Jessie jumped and then almost fainted. She sank back into the lab chair.

"Chris—not quite so loud."

"Oh, sorry. Didn't know if you would hear the door chime."

"Yeah, I did."

"My bad. I just forgot something. I always take those milk carts when I pick up supplies. Keeps the stuff from sliding around in the truck."

"Good call. I believe they are stacked up in the back room." Jessie was still recovering from being startled. Her vision was a bit wavy.

"You OK?" Chris asked.

"Sure, yes. Just a bit foggy now and then."

"Working on some blood tests, huh?" It took a beat or two for Chris to notice the awkward silence, but then he headed for the back room to retrieve the plastic milk crates.

As he passed back through the lab, Chris seemed to slow down. Jessie hustled him along with an instruction to lock the front door on his way back out.

Jessie turned her attention back to the vial of blood collected from cow 209. The equipment was warmed up and ready, and she began working through her procedures. It was a relief to be alone again, and the laboratory was one of Jessie's favorite places. As the blood analyzer worked its magic, Jessie poured herself a cup of coffee. She knew it was taking a risk of worsening her headache, but she was such a coffee hound that going without wasn't likely to improve her condition either. If nothing else, the smell was a tonic. Coffee was always a comforting aroma, one that ran like a ribbon from her childhood memories of barn and ranch-house kitchen through the slog of veterinary school, and the comforting routines of her work today, and finally to early-morning laughter shared with Derrick. Jessie was so lost in pleasant memories that she thought for a moment the chime had something to do with a fresh pot of coffee. Instead she looked over to see a green light flashing on the blood analyzer. The first sample was ready.

Jessie set down her coffee cup and rolled her lab chair over to examine the results. What she saw made her glad she had set the cup down. She might have dropped it otherwise. Cow 209's blood was certainly abnormal. The analyzer seemed to be lighting up like a Christmas tree. And yet the pattern was unclear. Jessie knew as much about common patterns of disease as any large-animal veterinarian. Actually she knew more than most. Jessie had completed two research fellowships after her graduation from veterinary school. For a time she had even considered a career in veterinary research. One of her fellowships had been completed at the US Army Medical Research Institute of Infectious Diseases. USAMRIID, or simply "the institute," as it was known in military circles, was a fabulous place to conduct advanced veterinary research. It was among the best places in the world to study the possible intersections between animal disease and human disease. It was also a great place to meet other sharp people. Jessie had been introduced to a handsome Army Ranger named Derrick Anderson by one of her fellow scientists at the institute. They had begun dating, and before long it seemed like they had known each other forever. They had shared so much in common, including the ability to love what the other loved. Derrick had put up with Jessie's excited monologues about disease vectors and the dynamics of epidemic. Jessie had eaten Chinese food and nodded along as Derrick gave animated presentations on military conflict and its role in world history. Sometimes they carried on nerdy dialogues on ten-mile runs or hair-raising mountain-bike rides. Their friends thought they were both pretty odd—and perfectly matched for one another. They had been right on both counts.

Most of the other scientists at the institute had focused on primate research, and for good reason. USAMRIID's mission involved protecting soldiers from biological threats. The most immediate and dangerous of such threats were likely to emerge along the boundary between human beings and other primates. The terrifying case of Ebola was just one of the many "monkey" diseases that drew attention at the time. Chickens and ducks were not neglected, of course, as influenza crossed back and forth among humans and these domesticated birds. Even though it was commonplace, influenza could be a mass killer and also notoriously difficult to outrun with vaccines. In this pecking order of apocalyptic cases, cattle were not among the hottest research subjects. So Jessie had mostly concentrated on garden-variety disease transmission and left the doomsday scenarios to others. She couldn't escape the gloom entirely, however, as her colleagues would now and again remind her that a single mutation could make Angus cows the next Ebola monkeys. They were a cheery lot.

Jessie looked back at the test results and began making notes. Then she remembered the photos that Derrick had taken. After rustling in her bag for a moment, she located her cell phone and pulled up the photos. She needed larger copies. Jessie hit print and sent the photos of the dead cow to the nearby wireless printer. As they rolled off the printer, she lined up the photos on the laboratory bench alongside her notes.

The cow's body showed few or no signs of bloating. A cool front had moved through between the accident and when Derrick and Chris had located the body. But Jessie thought it was still a bit odd that the body showed so few signs of decay. No signs of predation or postmortem assaults on the body either. Jessie's aching head bore witness that the cow had been strong and aggressive enough to fend off coyotes or other nuisance predators. But as she lay dying, she would have been a tempting target for larger and stronger animals. Even stray dogs were often attracted to such a corpse. Buzzards usually showed up pretty quickly. But Jessie examined the photos one at a time and saw nothing but a perfectly intact body.

Well, not perfectly intact. The back legs showed signs of stiffening consistent with a neuromuscular problem. This was consistent with the gait that Jessie had noticed when she encountered cow 209 on the road that day. But the defect was not nearly as pronounced as it should have been hours after she had encountered the cow. And *nothing* else about the body seemed consistent with her earlier impressions. The dead cow's haunches were full, and the muscles appeared normal. The back was less impressive than she remembered, with a slight dip in the middle and a bigger paunch. But the head and neck were the dead giveaway. Jessie glanced up at the blood analyzer results and then turned again to scan the line of photos. *There was no way.* The photos showed a cow with beautiful neck and fully intact head. The tongue was lolling, but it showed no signs of progressive disease. Otherwise the head and neck area looked like they could belong to a cow that was simply lying down in a field and taking a nap. The test results, on the other hand, indicated something on the order of plague. A cow with a raging illness would not enter death in such peaceful repose. Finally there were the eyes. To Jessie, the faces of cows were as recognizable as those of humans. Over the years both cowboys and veterinary colleagues had dismissed this capability she had. Any of them who had cared to wager against it had consistently lost. Even Derrick had had his doubts about it at first. But she had convinced herself long ago, and Derrick not long after they began dating, that with a single glance she could distinguish one cow from another. And the cow she had seen on the ranch road that day was not the cow in these photos. For Jessie that realization answered two questions at once. The cow in the photos was not the same cow, not the cow 209 she had encountered. And wherever the true cow 209 was, she was certainly dead by now.

Jessie took off her lab glasses and rested her forearms on the table in front of her. She knew it didn't make much sense to grieve now, and Derrick would tell her so if he were here. But she grieved anyway, for just a few moments. Then she picked up her cell phone and cleared her throat. She needed to find out what this blood pattern meant. Jessie scrolled through her directory until she located the entry for the friend who had introduced her and Derrick.

Dr. Francine Booker had moved up the ranks to become one of the most senior military researchers at USAMRIID. She had chased level-three and level-four killer bugs all over the world. If anyone could help Jessie identify the bug that had killed this mystery cow, it was Francine.

Chapter 18

SENIOR SCIENTIST FRANCINE Booker was sitting in her office under the faint glow of her small desk lamp. The lab work part of her day was over, and for this evening at least, Booker was happy to be shed of the lab. Her most recent series of experiments were not turning out as well as she had hoped they might. The disease was a tough one, an emerging strain of malaria with potent resistance to drug treatment. Booker had been testing a new line of attack on the illness. But so far the results were not encouraging. No US soldiers were in danger yet. But Booker knew that USAMRIID command was concerned about the possibility that the new strain would begin to spread more rapidly before they had developed a means of combatting it.

Dr. Booker would regroup and redouble her efforts tomorrow. But for now she looked forward to some quiet time reading at her desk. It wasn't everyone's cup of tea, but Francine Booker was quite content to pick up the latest bound volume of the *Assessment of Risk: Worldwide Survey of Infectious Diseases*. She had just completed the first chapter when her cell phone began buzzing. She was about to silence the alarm and keep reading before she read the caller ID.

"Well, hello, stranger! How are you, Jessie?"

Jessie and Francine caught up briefly and shared some small talk. Then Jessie turned to the point of her call.

"Francine, I could use your help. I know about the demands on your time, so I thought about not calling. But I've got a problem here I can't solve, and I have a sense that it might be important that I find a solution. I thought of you and called before I could talk myself out of it."

"I'm glad you did, Jessie. What sort of problem?" Francine marked her place and pushed the heavy book to the side of her desk. By habit she took out a pen and slid a notepad into place.

"OK, this is going to sound a little crazy. And I'll leave the craziest parts out for now. But my basic problem is that I have blood-test results from a missing cow, from a cow I now presume dead but cannot locate. And this blood pattern is wild, like nothing I've ever seen before."

"Any cases of emergent illness recently in that area? You're still in Idaho, right?"

"Yes, Idaho. And just a few routine cases of listeriosis. Seems we caught it early. Quarantine set at the livestock auction barn where the first few cases were reported. Nothing on follow-up tests at area ranches so far."

"When did this break?"

"Um, about a week ago."

"And you're sure that your sample isn't some strain of listeriosis?"

"Yes. Not even close."

"Hmm. Because I tried to recruit you to stay on with the institute, I know that you are great in the lab. But any chance you've contaminated the sample somehow?"

Jessie cleared her throat and fidgeted with a lab instrument. "I don't think so, Francine, but I butted heads with the cow that provided these samples. That's a bit of that crazy piece of the story. Anyway, I had secured the samples before all that, and they looked good to me when I recovered them for testing."

"I take it you have a blood analyzer in your clinic there?"

"Yes."

"I'm impressed—living in Idaho but using state-of-the-art tools."

"It's not the middle of nowhere, you know. You should visit sometime."

"Sounds nice, but you know I'm a city girl. Why don't you download the test results from your analyzer and e-mail them to me here. Will that work?"

"Francine, you're the best. Don't let it take too much time, OK? But I will send them right away."

"Relax, I like working on puzzles. And I get tired of monkeys sometimes. Might be nice to try a cow puzzle."

Jessie could picture Francine's expression. She did love puzzles, and Jessie was relieved that she had made it so easy to ask for this favor. She said good-bye for now and then turned her attention to downloading the test results. Once they were ready, Jessie typed a brief note and sent the e-mail and attachment to Francine.

Although Francine had been so gracious about it all, Jessie knew that the life of senior scientist at the institute was hectic. Each scientist carried more than her or his share of projects, and an emergent threat could require around-the-clock attention at any moment. So Jessie was surprised when Francine called her back only thirty minutes later.

"Jessie, this is Francine. I think I'll take you up on that offer to visit Idaho."

"What's going on?"

"You alone?"

"Yes."

"All right, well what I'm about to tell you needs to be kept between you and me. Don't even tell Derrick until I get there. We clear?"

"Sure, OK. But what is it?"

"Well, the pattern you sent is in the same ballpark as BSE—only worse."

"What can be worse than mad cow disease?"

Jessie's brain seemed to be slipping gears. She was trying to stay focused and to stay up with Francine. "Francine, wait a second. BSE lives in nervous-system tissue. How could you make that read from the test results from blood?"

"I couldn't have seen classic BSE from a blood test. But this is something different, something new. We've added some fancy new gear since you were last out here, and it is a big help with cases like this one. Listen, we'll talk specifics when I get there—which will be as soon as I can get a flight. In the meantime, take every possible precaution with those samples. Jessie, do you remember the protocols we use out here?"

"Yes."

"OK, well follow them with these two samples. Use a bleach bath. Don't unseal the second one until I get there. Don't let anyone else in your lab. Whatever protective gear you have available, put it on now. Lock up the place and scrub down well when you leave."

"Francine, what have I been exposed to?"

"Nothing. I'm being extra cautious. I shouldn't have said 'worse' earlier—that sounded too scary. What I meant was in terms of possible change from the classic form. I don't think these samples contain infectious agents, but I just want to make double sure we play it safe. I'm still trying to recruit you, you know."

"This is not a great pitch."

"Right, I'll work on that. Jessie, listen to me—you are safe. OK? I'll be there soon. I'm glad you called me when you did."

"Yeah, me too. See you soon."

"Oh, Jessie—I almost forgot something important. We really need to locate that cow. And secure the corpse when you do."

"OK, Francine, will do."

Jessie's voice was hollow. She noticed that her hand was shaking and then upbraided herself. *No time for that, cowgirl.* Jessie proceeded to follow Francine's checklist to the letter, imagining all the time that she would be reporting to her as if she were a member of her USAMRIID unit. When she was done, she turned out all the lights and walked outside. She called Chris and used her own condition as an excuse to give him a couple of days off. Then she put out the closed sign and locked up the veterinary clinic. She stopped at the medical apparel store on her way home and bought some new scrubs. Derrick had told her that he was running a few errands that afternoon. She was relieved that he wasn't home yet when she pulled into their drive. They had a shower in the barn, used to clean up after mucking stalls. Jessie went straight to the barn and removed her clothes. She took a good long shower and then dressed in the new scrubs. By the time she had burned her old clothes and returned to the house, Jessie was spent. She stretched out on their living-room couch and fell into a fitful sleep.

Later when Derrick gently touched her shoulder, she was disoriented for a moment. She had been dreaming that she was in a research monkey house and that it was time to go home. But when Jessie had tried to leave, she found that all the doors were locked. She was trapped.

She had been so relieved when her eyes opened and she saw Derrick. But the relief had been short-lived.

Chapter 19

REUBEN AXTELL WAS lounging on the couch and reading a spy thriller. It had been almost a week since the school shooting at ISU. So far it hadn't felt much like summer, and certainly not like a break. His grandfather had taken it easy on him with respect to chores and daily routine. Grandfather was generally a stickler for early starts and a balanced routine of work and play. But in his decades of service as an Idaho State Police officer, Frank Higheagle had seen more than his share of violence. He understood better than most people that it took time to recover, even if you had been blessed to walk away without any physical wounds. And so Reuben sensed that his grandfather was giving him a bit more space than usual. He had also held off pressing Reuben to head for the backcountry. Reuben knew that the first thing his grandfather would want them to do upon their return to Cascade was to drop everything and pack deep into the mountain country for some fishing and camping. Frank Higheagle loved nothing better than a summer camping trip. And usually Reuben loved it at least as much.

But so far Reuben hadn't wanted to get far from home base. It was comforting to be back here, in Cascade, and around people whom he knew and trusted. His grandfather seemed to sense Reuben's desire to stay close to home. He had mentioned summer camping as something that they might do later, when they both thought the time was right. And now and then, he had provided handy excuses.

"Awfully dry," Frank had said one day as he studied a cloudless sky. "It'd be better to camp when the fire danger is lower."

Reuben smiled to himself at the time, knowing that his grandfather was ignoring the soaking rain they had received a few days before.

Reuben looked up from his reading and thought to himself that this was the first day that felt close to normal. He was lounging more than usual, but otherwise the simple joy of reading on a summer day seemed as close to normal as anything had in weeks. Maybe he *would* be ready to go camping in the backcountry soon.

Just then Reuben heard a scratching noise outside the front door. He put his book down and listened. Nothing. Must have been the wind. A second later he heard what sounded like shuffling noises moving away from the front of the house. Must be the pack of squirrels that were raiding his grandfather's bird feeders. Reuben smiled and thought it was too bad that his grandfather wasn't here to catch them at their crimes. He loved watching the old man shuffle fast to the front door and hiss the squirrels away from his feeders. Best Reuben could tell, the only thing this accomplished was to drop more feed on the ground for the deer and ground birds. But it was always a treat to watch the show. Reuben heard a car fire up down the road. His grandfather's house was on a gravel road that branched off Warm Lake Road just east of Little Pearsol Creek. Most of the people along this rather remote stretch were either relatives or longtime friends. So when Reuben heard the car fire up, he decided to take a look out the front door and see who might have arrived just in time to scatter the band of squirrel bandits.

At first Reuben didn't see the car. The sunlight was bright, and Reuben raised a hand to cover his eyes as he surveyed the porch and front yard. He saw some scattered seed, for sure, but no squirrels. As his eyes panned the front yard, something caught his eye. It was swinging from a kite string at the corner of the porch. It looked like someone had tied a stick to the string and left it dangling there at eye level. Reuben moved closer, and the wind blew the object closer to him. When he caught it in his hand, Reuben realized that it wasn't a stick. It was a crow's foot. Reuben felt a cold chill run up his spine. And then, the current inside shifted, and Reuben felt a surge of hot anger. He yanked the string down and stormed down the front steps. Reuben scanned the road in both directions. Nothing to his left, but when Reuben turned to the right, he spotted a dark sedan parked in the shade about fifty yards from where he was standing. A man slowly got out from the driver's side and stood behind the car door. He was wearing shades, but Reuben knew immediately that it was Jim Crowfoot. He raised a hand and waved at Reuben and smiled. Reuben clenched his fists so tight that he could feel the claws beginning to dig into his right hand.

Crowfoot slid back down into the car and closed the door. He made a leisurely U-turn, and then he was gone.

Reuben stood for a moment watching the sedan kick up dust as it drove away. He yelled after the car—jumbled words, mostly bellows of rage and frustration. And then Reuben turned and made his way back to the house.

What is this guy's problem? Reuben wondered. Why would he drive all the way out here just to leave some...what...warning? A taunt? A curse?

One thing was for sure. This went beyond some argument over tribal pride, or even the fact that Reuben had gotten a punch in on him at the university that day. This was about something deeper and more dangerous. Reuben needed to protect his grandfather and to keep his guard up.

When he reached the porch, Reuben made sure to remove the remaining string and scan for any other signs that Crowfoot had visited. He wrapped the string around the crow's foot and put it in his pocket. Then Reuben went back inside and scavenged in the kitchen. His anger had played itself out; now he was as hungry as a bear.

After consuming a substantial midmorning snack, Reuben returned to his reading on the couch. He wasn't going to let some wacked-out tribal police thug intimidate him. Crowfoot could put up all the creepy signs and curses he wanted, but Reuben was determined to get back to his life and to enjoy this summer with his grandfather. He settled back into his book.

Sometime later Reuben heard his grandfather's old truck pull into the drive. He recognized the creak of the driver's door but was then surprised to hear another door slam. Maybe he needed help with groceries. Reuben was just beginning to sit up when he heard an unfamiliar commotion. His grandfather was talking to someone—or *something*. He could hear grunts and heavy breathing. *What now?*

The door burst open before Reuben could get to his feet, and a giant dog came pouring in ahead of his grandfather. Frank Higheagle was holding a leash that looked about the size one might use to hold an ocean liner to the dock. But Reuben only hoped it was big enough, because the dog at the end of it was the size of a pony.

"What in the hell?" Reuben blurted, as he stood up on the couch. "Do you have a good hold on that thing!"

Frank Higheagle was panting and laughing at the same time. He began waving Reuben off his perch on the couch.

"You should have seen your face. I wish I had taken a picture."

"Very funny, Grandfather. Now what are you doing with that monster?"

"You remind me of your mother when she used to get scared by a spider. Priceless to see you jump up on that couch. Now get your feet off there, and come meet our new dog."

Reuben climbed down cautiously and kept a close eye on the dog. He wasn't entirely sure that his grandfather knew what he was doing. He could be spontaneous at times, and this might just be one of his very bad ideas.

"What is it?"

"Neapolitan mastiff—a male, and I haven't decided on a name yet. *Tiny* might be good…What do you think?"

"I think you've lost your mind—maybe dementia or something. Where did you get him?"

"Lewis Tanner—he's a friend from the state police. Trains K-9s. Me and Lewis were having coffee the other day, and he told me about a little experiment of his that didn't work out so well."

"Let me guess—this beast was the experiment."

"Good guess. Lewis wanted to see if he could train a Neapolitan for police work. Smart dogs, but this one didn't work out."

"Who did he eat?"

"Funny. No, actually the opposite problem—he was a little on the gentle side for police work. At the same time, he looked a little too intimidating. So basically he scared little kids and didn't show enough enthusiasm for attacking criminals."

"Great, sounds like the perfect pet. Does this Lewis guy hate Indians?"

Reuben walked closer and examined the dog. He was an unusual and silky bluish-black color, something like a polished gun barrel. His eyes were also distinctive, a wheat color that made a striking contrast with the dark, shiny coat. He was incredibly muscular and seemed less clumsy than most giant dogs. But what struck Reuben most was the distinctive head. The dog's ears were cropped, and his head was broad and the jaws immense. The tongue lolling out of the dog's mouth reminded Reuben of a red carpet rolled out for some celebrity. A few wrinkles were draped over the massive dog's face, and the unusual eyes and deep folds gave the impression that he was deeply contemplating something. At the moment the big dog seemed to be contemplating Reuben.

"Go ahead, it's OK. Let him smell you first." Frank was smiling and clearly enjoying his grandson's trepidation.

Reuben held out the back of his hand near the big dog's face and immediately got a giant lick on the back of the hand. The dog's tail was wagging, and he came closer. Reuben scratched him behind the ears. The head was even bigger up close than it had seemed from across the room.

Reuben looked up at his grandfather and shook his head. "You are nuts. You know that, right?"

Frank Higheagle was smiling broadly and shaking his head in agreement. "Nutty as a loon. So…Can we keep him?" Frank chuckled at his own joke and then tugged the leash. "Come on, big boy; let's get you some food and water. You can slobber on Reuben later. Hey, Reuben, while I get him set up, will you grab the stuff out of my truck. I got him a bed and some toys and such."

Reuben shook his head and headed out to his grandfather's truck. He hadn't seen the old man so happy about anything in a long time. If he had known that getting a pony-sized dog would make his grandfather feel like a little kid again, Reuben might have been on the lookout for such a beast. He had to make three trips to get all the dog accessories in the house, if only because the giant dog bed was all he could carry on the first round, and the second round was taken up with a seventy-five-pound bag of food. Reuben noticed that the food was a premium variety. His grandfather was sparing no expense on their new roommate.

When Reuben arrived with the food bag, Frank cut it open with his pocketknife and scooped some of the food into a deep dish as big around as a pizza pan. He looked on approvingly as the big dog gulped water and then began eating the food.

"Good to see he likes food other than people," Reuben said.

"Yeah, he's a good eater. Aren't you, Bear?"

"Bear?" Reuben studied his grandfather's beaming face.

"Yeah, Bear. Don't you think? Tiny...I think that joke would get old after a while."

"Bear. Yeah, that fits. *Literally.*"

The big dog stopped eating when Reuben spoke and looked up at him for a moment. Those light colored eyes almost looked friendly, in a terrifying sort of way.

"See, he's already beginning to recognize his name." Frank pointed down at the dog and winked at Reuben.

"Yeah, he's a genius. So where do you want me to put Einstein's king-sized bed, or is he just going to sleep on the bed with you, Grandfather?"

"Nah, put it in the living room. We'll give him plenty of space to stretch out."

Frank smiled as he watched Reuben lug the huge dog bed away from the kitchen and down the hall to the living room. When he could no longer see his grandson's back, Frank looked down at the dog. He had played up his excitement a bit and felt a twinge of guilt that he wasn't telling Reuben the whole story about the dog. The big dog recognized his name because he had been named Bear months ago, just before Frank began working with him. It had been a pastime back then, helping Lewis with his latest K-9 experiment. But Frank had known all along that he would take the big dog if things didn't work out the way Lewis hoped. Now it seemed like an even better fit. And he hadn't stretched the results of Lewis's experiment all that much. It was true that Bear had appeared too intimidating for community policing in a small town like Cascade. But Frank had only told his grandson half the truth about the dog's gentle nature. He was a gentle dog by nature and absolutely steady. But Bear was also fiercely protective. He was a natural guard dog.

Frank didn't expect any trouble here in Cascade. But Lewis had taught him how to handle Bear and how to make sure that the big dog adopted Reuben as well. Frank hoped that neither one of them would ever have to see the big guard dog in action.

About the time Bear was settling in to his new home, Dr. Francine Booker was arriving at the airport in Salt Lake City, Utah. Francine usually traveled light. Her parents were both career army, and she had learned early that anything she packed was something she would lug all over the world. Her role as an army scientist sometimes required her to be more of a pack mule, but she still preferred to work around some missing item than to carry any more than she absolutely needed. So she felt an odd sense of embarrassment as she located the signs for baggage claim.

But for this particular journey, Francine had decided that she needed to cover most of the bases and to be prepared to move with as much speed as possible. She might be overreacting, proceeding here with an "abundance of caution," as she had told Jessie in their phone conversation. Francine sure hoped so. And the probabilities were still in their favor. She was a disciplined scientist, and she knew that there were several alternative explanations of those preliminary test results. The worst-case scenarios carried some very low probabilities at this point. But the fact that there was at least one doomsday scenario in the mix meant that Francine had to pack heavier than usual.

Francine watched as the first bags began rolling onto the luggage carousel. Hers would be hard to miss. Two monster bags, one stuffed with equipment and the other carefully packed for a variety of contingencies. As she stood with the others waiting for their bags, her mind drifted back to probabilities and scenarios. She recalled an illustration she had used when teaching a graduate course on research methods and analysis. The students had been asked to estimate the probabilities of seeing a shark while at the beach and then of being attacked by a shark at the beach. Simply asking the students to cue up that image of a shark sighting almost always resulted in overestimates of the probability of shark attack. The shark scenario was a good one to use in class because it highlighted the tendency to overestimate certain risks. Some terrifying events are quite rare. But Francine knew that our fear of them, like our fear of shark attack, could lead us to overestimate the risk. Francine hoped that this trip worked out that way, like reading the book *Jaws* before enjoying a perfectly safe weekend of playing in the water at the beach.

Francine suddenly had a feeling of being watched and took a glance over her shoulder. She thought of that music from the *Jaws* movie and laughed at herself for being so nervous. Her bags came rolling out of the chute about that time, and Francine gathered her gear and headed to the exit.

As Francine Booker headed out to meet Derrick and Jessie, a pale young man with blond hair and gray eyes slipped on a pair of sunglasses and followed her through the crowded airport.

Chapter 20

AFTER HE HAD moved her luggage from his truck to their guest room, Derrick returned to the hearth room and took a seat. "We have rocks in Idaho, Francine. You didn't need to bring us any more."

Francine raised an eyebrow and looked toward Jessie, who was leaning back in her chair and smiling. "Well, Derrick, a city girl has to cover her bases. I thought I should bring my own English saddle."

At USAMRIID Jessie and Francine had been known as "city girl" and "country girl." Their backgrounds could not have been more different, and yet they found so much in common.

Jessie laughed along with Francine and then attempted a British accent. "Darling, we simply must call out the hounds tomorrow."

Derrick rolled his eyes and shook his head.

"Actually, dear," Francine responded, "I believe that a serious shopping safari is in order. Nothing more therapeutic than roaming a few boutiques."

Derrick turned to Jessie. "Have you given city girl here any preview of Pocatello, Idaho? Her shopping safari might take all of a morning if you two go nice and slow."

"As we shall, dear Derrick, as we shall."

Francine and Jessie broke down laughing again; then Jessie signaled to Francine, and the two of them headed to the kitchen for another glass of wine. Derrick leaned back in his chair and watched them go. It was good to see Jessie laughing and having a good time. Francine was good medicine. He wasn't sure yet what all the two of them were really up to, but for now he was simply content to see them together and enjoying one another's company.

Once they were in the kitchen, Jessie and Francine kept up a simmer of kitchen noises to cover their whispered conversation.

"So what does Derrick know?" Francine asked.

"Precious little. He knows that I don't think the cows matched, that I don't believe he and Chris found the body of the cow that I encountered, but nothing about tests or blood samples and certainly nothing about mad cow disease."

"And my visit?" Francine couldn't help a quick glance over her shoulder.

"Nothing really. I told him that I called you about some research that we are both interested in and that one thing led to another, and you agreed to come out for a visit."

"Think he bought that? You are a terrible liar."

"Thanks, I think. I hope he bought it for now. He thinks the world of you, and I'm sure he also thinks that your visit will be good for me…which it will be, of course, unless you came here to tell me I'm dying of some plague."

"Stop it! No plague deaths will ruin my first visit to Idaho."

"If you say so. So what's the plan, city girl?"

"We continue the city and country reunion tonight; then tomorrow morning I would like to get down to your lab and run all this through the drill. I brought the gear, and I'll be ready as soon as you think we can pull off our 'leaving to go shopping' ploy."

"OK, sounds good. We better get back in there."

Francine and Jessie picked up the conversation where they left off and then began reminiscing about their time together USAMRIID.

Derrick initially joined in, especially to correct the record when Jessie or Francine strayed into exaggeration or outright fabrication. They both knew how serious Derrick was and that he was easily baited by incorrect facts or garbled recollections. But eventually Jessie and Francine settled into mellower conversations about their lives after USAMRIID and about their mutual interests in veterinary research. Although he was gaining his strength quickly now, Derrick still found it tough to hang in past nine o'clock most nights. When the two friends reached a lull in the conversation, they realized that Derrick had drifted off to sleep.

Jessie looked at Francine and smiled. It was a pleasant scene. She was so glad to see Francine sitting on her couch here in Idaho. They were good friends, of the rare type that can pick back up right where they left off. And it was the first night that Derrick had fallen asleep in his chair since the shooting. He was gradually unwinding, feeling safe enough to drop off to sleep without checking doors or outdoor lights.

As she helped Francine to the guest room, Jessie said a silent prayer that nothing that she and Francine learned tomorrow would shatter the peace they had all known tonight.

Jessie and Francine stood in the open back room of the veterinary clinic. They were just about to don their biosafety suits when Francine spoke up.

"Jessie, before we suit up, I need to tell you a couple of things."

"OK, what's up?"

"First, I'm not here alone. I mean, I'm not in Pocatello alone. Two members of USAMRIID's Emergency Response Team are here. I put them up at a hotel nearby."

"What? Why would you do that? Francine, I thought I made it clear on the phone that I was looking to you for help sorting this out.

I don't even know if there is anything to it or if this is just a wild-goose chase."

"I know, I get it."

"So you made this official already? We are already on the institute's radar?" Jessie began pacing in front of the white biosafety suit draped on a folding chair.

"Not exactly. This is a half step. The two people I brought with me are colleagues and good friends. I told them that I had a friend with a hunch and a weird blood sample, and nothing more. They agreed to come out here off the radar, but only if *I agreed* to make it all official if anything we find out here trips an alarm."

"Wow, Francine. This is different than what I imagined. I feel pretty foolish dragging three Institute people out here just to hold my hand."

"And both of us will feel worse than that if we have a problem here and we aren't prepared to deal with it properly." Francine's gaze was level and her jaw tight.

Jessie remembered one of the reasons she liked her so much. Francine was one of the few people Jessie considered as tough as she was. "I suppose you are right about that. But a heads-up would have been nice."

"Would you have said OK to them coming out with me?"

"No."

"Didn't think so. Thus I went for asking forgiveness instead of permission."

"Touché. I hate to ask, but you said a 'couple of things.' What other fun fact have you been waiting to tell me about?"

"We've been concerned for over a year now about the possibility that some dark labs are tinkering with prion illnesses—trying to weaponize them. Part of the reason that I'm here—other than your friendship and the fabulous shopping opportunities—is that your sample looked like a few others that have turned up in terrorist channels. Thankfully your sample wasn't consistent with weaponized prion disease. But some markers were consistent with intermediary development—a bug along the path toward weaponization."

"I know about mad cow, or I should say BSE, but I'm not remembering the other prion illnesses."

"Yeah well, they are a nasty family. Kuru—that ring any bells?"

"The disease that struck tribal villagers in Papua New Guinea? Laughing disease?"

"That's it. Some of the victims laughed at odd or inappropriate moments, at least in the early stages of the disease. But that stage is pretty brief. Once the symptoms start, kuru steadily destroys brain tissue, and the patient lapses into paralysis and stupor."

"This is cheering me up. But on a brighter note, aren't the prion diseases extremely slow burning? It takes years, sometimes more than a decade, for a person infected with the human variant of mad cow to develop symptoms. Why would terrorists want to infect their victims with an illness that takes so long to strike?"

"They wouldn't. We've mostly considered prion illnesses a back-burner risk. They have features—like that long lag between infection and illness—that we've considered quirky and tough to manipulate. They are a case of shark attack—a very low risk of an absolutely catastrophic event."

"So why the concern?"

"We think someone may be getting close to making a shark. Prion illnesses are not natural candidates for weaponization. But if someone can manipulate those natural features, say, by dramatically shortening the time from infection to onset, well then..."

"Suddenly a fin's in the water."

"Yes. And worse yet, if a dark lab can manipulate both disease progression *and* ease of transmission, then the shark begins swimming toward the crowded beach."

"Creepy. I hated that movie."

"You kidding? I thought Richard Dreyfuss was hot in that movie."

"You would." Jessie began slipping her feet into her biosafety suit. "So is the air all clear now, city girl? Or do you have any other confessions you would like to make before we go check out the monster lab?"

"No, I think I'm all good now. I'll be right behind you, country girl."

Two hours later Jessie and Francine were drenched in sweat and peeling out of their bulky suits. A few moments of quiet passed between them while they gained their equilibrium. They each took water bottles from the refrigerator in the back room and guzzled the cold water. Finally, Jessie turned to Francine and spoke.

"Well, how bad is it?"

"You are safe. And your lab is safe. I have some procedures I want you to follow tomorrow just to make triple sure that there is no contamination risk. But the abnormal patterns in your sample are not consistent with fully weaponized prion agents."

"Thank God."

"Yes indeed."

"Any bad news?"

"Well, there's some not-so-good news. You and your lab are safe. But your samples also contain compelling evidence that someone out there is working on that shark we were talking about earlier. Any chance we might still locate the corpse of the cow that these samples came from?"

Jessie ran a hand through her hair and then rested it on her chin. Francine thought she reminded her for a second of that statue of the thinker.

"Doubt it," Jessie finally said. "Derrick is a good tracker. But someone went to a great deal of trouble to throw him off, to leave a corpse that they hoped we would see as the cow that gave us those samples."

"And you're sure that's the case? You couldn't be mistaken about cow two oh nine and the whole switching-bodies conspiracy?"

"If you colored your hair, I might have trouble recognizing you for a moment. I might walk right past a friend from high school without recognizing her, especially if she had made some changes over the years. But cows? No, for some very odd reason, I never forget a cow's face. Two different cows involved here."

"That's too bad." Francine studied the clear face shield of her suit for a moment and then set it down beside her. "Because I sure would like to have access to that cow's cerebrospinal material."

"I know. And if I thought we could find the corpse, I would be the first one in the truck. But I figure if someone went to all that trouble to throw us off the track, then that person has also made sure by now that the body of the diseased cow is long gone and beyond reach—probably cremated."

Jessie stood and stretched slowly. Her ribs were still sore, and she was trying to work out some of the stiffness.

"So," she asked, "how far along do you think the bad guys might be with this little science experiment?"

Francine shrugged. "Hard to say. So far we have a few puzzle pieces and not the whole picture. But honestly your sample leads me to believe that they may be farther along than we thought."

"I thought you said I was safe, all clear?"

"You are. Some interim steps on the path to weaponization result in harmless agents. But a harmless agent can sometimes be produced in the final step before crossing the threshold. One day the agent is harmless; the next day it is a doomsday disease."

"How many steps remain on this prion path?"

"Impossible to say with confidence. But what I am seeing worries me that they are closer than we thought."

Jessie and Francine ran through the final decontamination drills and then packed their gear. The bags containing the biohazard suits were bulky, and Francine and Jessie decided to load them in the truck first and then come back for their other gear.

They lugged the load along to the back door of the clinic and then flung it open to bright western sunshine—and to the sight of Derrick leaning against his truck.

Jessie sucked in a breath suddenly and dropped the huge duffel bag. "Oh hey, babe, what are you doing here?"

Derrick had sunglasses on, and his arms were crossed over his chest. He was smiling. Jessie thought it was the smile of a security guard who'd just caught two cat burglars.

"Hey there, Jessie. Francine. Funny-looking shopping bags."

Francine chuckled, a bit too loudly. Jessie shot her a look and then turned back to Derrick.

"Yeah, well, we decided not to go shopping after all. Thought we would do some lab work—you know, just like old times."

"Right." Derrick heaved himself off the side of his truck and walked over to the bag beside Jessie. He slipped his sunglasses in a shirt pocket and then bent down and unzipped the bag. He stood up and put his hands on his hips.

"OK, Jessie, I've been polite and played dumb so far. I see now that was a mistake, but I thought you two were up to something harmless. Now that I know that isn't the case, I want you two to tell me what is really going on here!"

"We're busted. And yes, we'll tell you everything." Jessie waved a hand back toward the clinic. "But not here. Let's load this stuff and head back home. The three of us can talk there."

Thunderheads were building on the horizon by the time they arrived home. Jessie made coffee, and the three of them took their seats on the screened-in porch. A cool breeze blew now and then, and the trees rustled softly around them. The front was slow moving, and the rain arrived gradually, in fits and starts that barely dampened the ground.

Francine tried to take the lead and to take responsibility for going back to the clinic to test for contamination. But Jessie cut her off and made it clear that she had been the one who'd contacted Francine in the first place and that she would have insisted on testing the lab herself, whether or not Francine was there to help her. The two scientists then worked together to help Derrick understand what had initially triggered the concern and what they had together discovered so far. Francine reviewed what she knew about the potential for weaponizing a prion illness and about the evidence USAMRIID had collected regarding such a possibility.

While Derrick was listening to Francine and Jessie explain the technical challenges of manipulating a prion disease, a man in a jeep parked nearby was setting down a pair of tactical binoculars and picking up his cell phone.

"Looks like we have a problem."

Jim Crowfoot set his drink on the black coffee table. "What sort of problem?"

"The bags I told you about—from the airport. She brought a couple of moon suits with her. She and the cow doc took them to her clinic today."

"Where are you now?"

"Staking out their house. The two docs are having a nice chat with Rambo as we speak."

Crowfoot took a long drink and then leaned back and rubbed his forehead.

"Hey, boss—you there?"

"Yeah, dammit, I'm here. Any chance they know that you have been tailing them?"

"No chance. I'm a ghost."

"OK, then stay put. I want to know the second they move. And keep a sharp eye on Anderson. He's dangerous."

"So I'm told. What do you want me to do about that?"

"Nothing—at least for now. Keep watch there as long as you have good cover. If Anderson hasn't moved by first light, then put a tracer on him and get back here. We need to be prepared to move fast now."

"Roger that."

The man put his cell phone away and scanned his surroundings. The storm seemed to be breaking apart, and the rain was not as heavy as he had expected earlier. He checked the location of the jeep and the shadows around him to make sure that he still had adequate cover. From the house he was invisible. Anderson would only have been able to see him if he was looking for him and only then if he was lucky. Part of him hoped that Anderson was lucky somehow, even though Crowfoot would kill him if he knew that he was having such thoughts.

That was the problem with boredom, the man thought, and with easy assignments. A bored man's mind wandered, and he ran the risk of losing his edge. Most of the work he did now was far too easy, far too predictable. He missed *the games* in Bosnia and Chechnya. What was the good of being a ghost if you couldn't leap from the shadows now and then? Why follow a warrior like Anderson if you couldn't really test yourself against him?

He closed his eyes for a moment and imagined this night as he dreamed it might be if it weren't for the Guardians and their plans. He could even picture Anderson's brother here. "Thunder" and "Lightning" they called them. *How perfect!* It would be just like the good old days, a mercenary's paradise. He lingered in his fantasy for a moment and then opened his eyes and picked up his night-vision gear. Back to the desk job. But as he moved a long strand of blond hair aside and slid on the headset, the man vowed to himself that someday soon he was going to leave the Guardians and return to the life of a lone hunter. He was not a man who was content to daydream.

Chapter 21

RAY ANDERSON SCRATCHED the XT Supply Company off his list. For the past few days, Ray had been working hard to follow Deacon's tips and to locate a possible supplier to the kind of laboratory that Dr. Nasim might be running. The work was tedious and frustrating. Some suppliers were easy to identify, but others were secretive and guarded. XT Supply was a case in point, as Ray had to run through a maze to nail down whether or not the company supplied animals to research laboratories. Maybe the shadowy supplier network was getting to him, because Ray was also beginning to wonder if they were searching for Bigfoot. Maybe Nasim hadn't opened a dark lab after all. He might not even be in the United States. In fact, given his line of business, there was a fair chance that Nasim was either locked away somewhere or dead.

He was about to pull out of the parking lot when his phone buzzed. Ray glanced down and saw the call listed as *No Caller ID*. Probably nothing. He almost let it go but then, at the last second, snatched up the phone and answered.

"Well howdy, Hoss Cartwright! I was beginning to think that you were riding the fence line somewhere out of cell-phone range."

"Deacon—no ID. I thought you were someone wanting to sell me a time-share."

"You would want to buy one from me. But no, not selling anything today. I'm calling without ID to let you know that I think we should have coffee and follow up on that conversation we had not long ago. You know the one I'm talking about, right?"

"Roger that. Where are you?"

"About a block away watching you try to talk on the phone and fiddle with your sunglasses at the same time. You never were very coordinated."

"Cute. I'm going to put my sunglasses on now and start driving. Why don't you follow me, and I'll buy you that cup of coffee."

"And a piece of pie. You lead, I'll follow."

Deacon and Ray took more than a casual look around the little coffee shop. A bald man with a single earring was behind the counter, absently scrolling through some sort of listing on his iPad. An older couple was seated in a corner booth, each absorbed in a section of what looked like a local paper. A TV was on in the opposite corner, set to CNN and a droning volume.

Ray ordered at the counter and paid the bald man for the coffees and a slice of apple pie. He gave a generous tip and hinted that he and Deacon worked for a chemical company. If the man overheard bits and pieces of talk about research labs, he wanted the guy to consider it background noise. As Ray studied the man's face, he realized that this bit of cover was probably unnecessary. The barista seemed thoroughly distracted, and Ray might have just as well told him that he and Deacon were hit men.

They settled in the corner booth opposite the older couple and near the TV.

"I hope you enjoy that slice of pie. He charges for it like his grandma made it from scratch."

"Pie making is a fine art, Ray. Don't begrudge the man his commissions."

"So what's up? Why the burner phone and stalker routine?"

"Your man is in the neighborhood."

"What? Here?"

"Not this square block." Deacon took his first bite of pie and waved the fork in a circle. "More like central Idaho neighborhood."

"How do you know? Never mind, don't answer that. Does our new neighbor know that we are looking to meet him?"

"Nope. Someday I will tell you the whole story of the brilliant methods I used, but for today the main thing to know is that this was a clean search—no trail and no followers. Man, this is good pie. Ray, go give that man another five bucks."

"Funny. So what are my next steps in order to get our business started?"

"First thing, don't mess up the work I've done. Clean so far, but if you make a big enough mess, it might somehow spill back on me. Clear?"

"Crystal. Now that we have taken care of your personal safety, what about the business we've been talking about?"

"I think the best location might be somewhere near Sun Valley but not right in the town—too expensive in Sun Valley or Ketchum and too much traffic. But if someone wanted to set up a lab nearby—you know, within striking distance of Sun Valley—now I think that's the ticket."

Ray glanced over his shoulder to see if the man working the counter was paying any attention to their conversation. The man was sitting on a stool and appeared to be absorbed in a YouTube video.

Ray turned back to Deacon. "Any ideas about time frame and target market?"

"I think this is a hot market, one that requires immediate action. Several suppliers are already signed on, and I believe the time to go to market is this summer. There are a few good target markets in this region, but my money is on Sun Valley. It's sort of a gathering spot, especially for people interested in this sort of technology."

Suddenly Ray felt like it was ten degrees cooler in the little coffee shop. *The Allen & Company Sun Valley Conference*: held each year in Sun Valley during one week in July, it was one of the largest gatherings of influential business and political leaders in the world. Warren Buffet attended some years. Tony Blair, Larry Paige, Bill and Melinda Gates—the guest list was a Who's Who of the wealthiest and most powerful people in the world.

Ray watched Deacon nonchalantly savoring a bite of apple pie and then washing it down with a sip of coffee. He had just given Ray the coded message that Nasim and some band of terrorists were cooking up a biological weapon to be unleashed this July on an unsuspecting group of world leaders, and yet Deacon looked for all the world like he was just shooting the breeze and enjoying the best pie he had ever eaten. No wonder he was so good at tracking people. He could be telling your darkest secrets, and you would think he was talking to someone in his fantasy football league.

"Deacon, am I understanding you that our information is solid? We can move forward?"

"Rock solid. I know that you and your partner like to review the numbers yourselves, but in this case that's probably not necessary. The key is to start it up and stay on track until the job is done."

"We will do that. You have done amazing groundwork. Thanks for getting back to me so quickly."

"My pleasure. Keep me posted, and call me when you feel that you should buy me another cup of coffee and piece of pie."

Ray and Deacon parted as though they were wrapping up a routine business conversation. And just like that Deacon was gone. Ray waited until he was in his Jeep before checking his key ring. He didn't know how Deacon had pulled it off, but sure enough there was a tiny flash drive attached to his key ring. *The key is to start it up...*

Ray made a few switchbacks just to be sure that no one was tailing him. He knew that Deacon was the consummate pro, but he also knew that his friend had been swimming in some dangerous waters. One could never be too careful.

Once he was certain that no one was following him, Ray made his way back to his hotel room. He closed the blinds and pulled his laptop from his backpack. Ray inserted the small flash drive and paced the room while the computer came to life. Once it was fired up, Ray sat down to work. He spent the next hour pouring over the puzzle pieces that Deacon had assembled for him, at the same time marveling at the man's ability to convey information without leaving breadcrumbs.

It was clear that Nasim was in the United States. And he was not the only one. At least a half dozen scientists and technicians with links to Dr. Nasim had ducked across the Canadian-US border and then made their way to central Idaho. Their supply chain and logistical support was being managed from abroad and funneled through a spider's web of routes and organizations. They had moved items in small packets, routed them to couriers in the organization scattered about the country, and then used the courier system to assemble the operation in Idaho. As he studied Deacon's notes, Ray realized why he had turned up nothing so far with the research-animal angle. Someone had designed this network to be off the grid and without pattern.

Can Nasim be that good at logistics and operations? Or does he have a partner, perhaps one of these overseas handlers, covering that part of the operation? Ray hoped that it was all Nasim. But he was pretty sure he was looking at the work of more than one evil genius.

Ray was also frustrated to learn that he had visited a few monkey houses for no good reason. Nasim and his crew weren't using monkeys. Deacon had tracked some odd movements of cattle, and the connections seemed to fit when they were overlaid with the other supply routes and the movement of key couriers. Of all the places to look, Deacon's cattle data came from the good old US Department of Agriculture. They had run a survey on regular pattern for years, and Deacon checked it for anomalies. He caught a signal and followed it to the transportation routes. The group seemed to be working with both legitimate operators and some cattle rustlers, so the pattern was ragged. But it was enough to persuade Ray that cattle were being used for research.

Since when has anyone used cows for this sort of research? Ray wished he could talk to Jessie about this data and the possibilities.

Deacon had neatly solved one mystery. As far as the US military and intelligence networks were concerned, Dr. Nasim was dead. According to what Deacon had uncovered, Nasim had been transferred from Afghanistan to Egypt. There he had purportedly been under the watchful eye of the CIA and protected by a mix of Delta Force operators and members of Egypt's counterterrorism unit known as Task Force 777. But somehow the Egyptian operation had fallen apart.

Nasim was under regular questioning by both the CIA and Egyptian officials investigating a related case of bioterror. He was being transferred between an interrogation location and a safe house when his transport detail was attacked. The gunmen used motorcycles and an armored vehicle. All the evidence pointed to a professional hit, and Egyptian authorities identified the assault team as militant members of the Muslim Brotherhood. All but two of the attackers were killed, but unfortunately Nasim was also mortally wounded. It was a wild shootout, even by Middle Eastern standards. According to the report, two civilians were wounded, and the area where the attack took place was thoroughly strafed. It was unclear whether Nasim was wounded by the terrorists or by a stray bullet from one of his defenders. In either case, he was rushed to the hospital. The surviving terrorists were treated and released to Egyptian custody. Not surprisingly, both later died in jail. The official cause for one was listed as "suicide," and for the other, "complications from injuries suffered in the attack." Ray could picture the sort of complications that might have developed for this man while he was undergoing Egyptian interrogation.

The official record also listed Nasim as a casualty. Deacon's notes mentioned that an official death report was filed. According to this report, Nasim suffered three gunshot wounds, one to the lower abdomen and two to the chest. Time of death was 8:38 p.m., some three hours after the attack. The body was processed out from there, with Egyptian authorities coordinating with the Afghans regarding burial and family notification.

But several things about the report didn't add up. Deacon had easily recognized that someone had sterilized the report of the attack and Nasim's death. Certain CIA files had been left open, and it was clear that at least a few people in the agency were not convinced that Nasim had been killed in the attack. The records were oddly silent on what Deacon (and later Ray) considered a most important element. No one in Delta Force or the CIA had signed off on the Egyptian version of events. And Deacon had not been able to locate any sign that anyone in the US military or the CIA had officially verified Dr. Nasim's injuries and subsequent death. Unofficially, one of Deacon's better sources had expressed strong doubts about the entire episode.

Ray could see why both Deacon and his source were skeptical. Delta operators didn't fire off their guns like Wild West cowboys. They aimed with deliberation and fired with precision. Terrorists might like to shoot up the town on occasion, but they wouldn't have much of an opportunity if they picked a fight with members of Delta and Task Force 777. Once the shooting began, terrorists would be falling quickly. And the report said the attack force was small—a couple of motorcycles and one heavy vehicle. Two Delta operators could knock out a group like that before they had much time to spray ammo. Ray knew that Egyptian counterterrorist forces were highly trained as well. They also benefited from regular bouts of engagement. Such a lightweight attack would be simply another day at the office for Egyptian Special Forces.

If indeed they had all been Egyptian Special Forces...Ray doubted it. Nasim's detail had been compromised. If, as Ray now suspected, Nasim was knee-deep in a major bioterror plot, then his handlers would consider him both a valuable asset and a dangerous liability. The attack had been staged and someone had managed to arrange the defense detail so that a high value prisoner could disappear into Egyptian hands. Delta Force leaders would have been suspicious of any arrangement that transferred Nasim out of US custody, even for a moment, and even if he was bleeding profusely. The CIA was also generally good at making arrangements to maintain continuous absolute control, or at the very least continuous shared control, over such a prisoner, which to Ray meant one thing—someone powerful in Egyptian politics had demanded control for his Special Forces. Then that same person, or people with whom he had conspired, compromised the defensive detail and whisked Nasim off to points unknown.

Well, unknown to most of the world—Deacon had picked up the trail. Nasim wasn't dead. His shooting had mostly likely been staged. The Egyptians who were posing as Special Forces troops had come prepared to make it appear that Nasim had been hit. His only real gunshot wound was accidental, the result of Nasim panicking and attempting to grab a weapon from one of his rescuers. He was shot in the foot, and Deacon had learned that the injury left him with permanent nerve damage and a noticeable limp.

The small attack squad was a group of young men who'd volunteered for martyrdom. The men who infiltrated the Special Forces detail had been given orders to abduct Nasim if possible, and failing that to make sure that he did not survive to answer any questions from Egyptian or US authorities. Their vehicle peeled off from the Delta Force unit when the attack was neutralized, and they radioed that Nasim had been hit and they were rushing to a secure location where he could receive medical treatment. Several hours later Egyptian authorities contacted their US counterparts to inform them that Nasim had died, providing "verification" with a poor quality photo of a body alleged to be Dr. Nasim.

Nasim turned up next in Morocco. He used the alias Dr. Achmed Salim and shuttled among a network of hideouts and safe houses. He also began to meet with recruits and to reassemble his bioterror team for the next big push.

Deacon picked up only traces over the next couple of years. It was possible that Nasim was lying low during this period, but Ray suspected that it was more likely the case that he was being spirited wherever he needed to go on the wings of forged identities and over routes created by a sophisticated terrorist operation. On two occasions Deacon had encountered a nickname for the group—the Guardians. They were not on anyone's radar and, as far as Deacon could tell, Nasim had managed to stay almost completely off the grid. This pattern would have been a grave concern if it involved a high-value terrorist who had gone to ground in some remote corner of Afghanistan or Pakistan. But this pattern was even more troubling if it was connected to a genius bioterrorist who was assembling a sophisticated bioterror operation.

The trail was sketchy after Nasim left North Africa. Deacon suspected that he had spent some time in Canada, including at least a few months in Montreal and a few more somewhere in the province of Alberta. If Deacon was correct, Ray thought that southern Canada might have been the staging area for the operation. They might have attracted attention if they had concentrated in major cities, but instead they had spread out across more remote areas and communicated with one another primarily through trusted couriers. Maybe they gathered briefly in Canada before crossing over to the United States. But Ray could also picture them spreading out and crossing the Canadian border before gathering somewhere in the wilderness of central Idaho.

The remaining pieces of the puzzle that Deacon had assembled involved the cattle records and some bits and pieces related to scientific equipment. It wasn't much—debris mostly. They could be off base. But Ray trusted Deacon's nose and his judgment. If Deacon thought a trail was worth pursuing, that was enough for Ray.

Deacon had taken care to use a code known only to him and Ray for the notes and then to use a layer of standard encryption. Ray reversed the process to inoculate the flash drive and then scrubbed his laptop clean. He wanted no trace of Deacon's involvement left behind. His friend had earned more than a good piece of pie and bottomless cup of coffee. Now it was time for Ray to go back on the clock and to earn his keep.

Ray contacted his commanding officer and arranged a meeting. Colonel Doug Harkin had assumed that Ray Anderson was helping his brother recuperate from his injuries and perhaps enjoying a day or two of R & R. It was hard to get Anderson to slow down, and Harkin had been concerned at times that he had not adequately processed out from the unit. Some former operators had had a hard time with the transition to other roles that involved anything less than full-on intensity. Army counterintelligence work was no cakewalk, and Anderson had seen his share of dangerous cases. But CI excitement was rarely anything like Delta Force excitement. Harkin thought Anderson was sometimes overcompensating by taking on more work and by maintaining a training regimen that would wear out most Special Forces soldiers.

So the colonel wasn't altogether surprised that Ray Anderson was calling a case meeting during his leave. He only hoped that Derrick Anderson had backup help. Ray Anderson was not exactly the best person for bedside duty.

But Colonel Harkin was surprised by Ray Anderson's report. And he was more than mildly irritated by the dodge he was getting with respect to sources.

"Damn it, Anderson, I want to know how you obtained this information! Some of this looks like CIA, some of it looks like compromised unit information, and some of it looks dirty."

"Sir, I did some digging through anonymous contacts. I will personally vouch for them, but I feel honor bound to maintain their anonymity."

"Bullshit—*honor bound*." Harkin shook his head and seemed to be chewing on each word. Suddenly his index finger pointed across the desk at Ray, and his gaze narrowed. "Don't try to feed me a line, Special Agent Anderson! I didn't get to this position by playing a mean game of golf. If you have been running around behind my back to CIA sources, or otherwise running rogue, I *will* find out about it! And so help me, I will have your—"

Ray held up his hands in surrender, and Harkin paused in midsentence and then said, "Well?"

"All right, sir, let me clear the air." Ray looked Harkin straight in the eye. "I have not gone behind your back to CIA. I don't know many people over there, and the ones I do know well I wouldn't trust for this sort of help. I had only a few bits and pieces to go on, and I needed some quick information to know if it was even worth pursuing. With all due respect, sir, sometimes phoning in with a hunch can result in alarm bells and needless delays. If my hunch was even close to the mark, I knew that we would lose some time with protocol. If my hunch was bogus, which I half expected to be true, I wanted to know that before I called anything in. I have a friend who has all the right experience to do some checking on things like this. He is an honest man and a patriot. Other than that I would very much like to request that we keep his identity protected."

"That's all very sweet, Anderson. But we aren't talking about some minor breach of security here. You are bringing me information about a possible case of bioterrorism, a plot to harm US citizens. What am I supposed to say when the president wants to know where we received this information? 'Well, you see, Mr. President, Special Agent Anderson has a good buddy, and he would prefer not to name this buddy, but he is an excellent and thoroughly reliable source of anonymous intel regarding international terrorism.'"

"Sir, I believe the information is credible. I think it warrants investigation."

"Suppose your mystery man is a terrorist himself. Suppose you were fed this information as part of a ruse, a means of distracting us from real plots and real targets."

"He isn't a terrorist. I would bet my life on it."

"What if he is an unwitting accomplice? He might think this information is solid, but how do we know this mysterious source isn't being used by the terrorists? That's why we check people out! That's why we vet sources!"

185

"My friend is not a terrorist, and he is not a dupe. He would know if he was being played. He mostly works in the shadows and by reading patterns that other people miss."

"Real Sherlock Holmes—this friend of yours." Harkin pushed away from his desk and studied Ray for a moment. Before he spoke next, he rested his chin in one hand.

"Did you even go to Idaho? Have you seen your brother at all?"

"Yes, sir. Thank you for asking, sir. Derrick is strong and recuperating well."

"Give Derrick my regards next time you see him. Outstanding soldier. Excellent record of following orders and respecting command."

"Yes, sir, he always had a knack for that sort of thing."

A thin smile worked the edges of Harkin's mouth, in what Ray thought were the first signs that he might survive this meeting without being booted out of the army.

"I should probably let you go so that I can begin writing a disciplinary letter."

"Yes, sir." Ray began to rise from his seat.

"Sit down, Anderson!" Harkin waved a hand absently in his direction. Then he stood up and walked to a window near his desk. He seemed to be scanning the sky for signs of changing weather. Ray tapped his finger on the chair's armrest for a few beats and then caught himself and placed his hands in his lap. He had learned over the years that his fidgeting irritated some officers, and Harkin was one of them.

Without turning around again, Harkin began to speak in a subdued voice.

"Let's say this source of yours is legitimate. You were still guessing about the target, right? We don't know where they are right now or where they plan to strike?"

"That's correct, sir. I would assume that they need their operation to be fairly close to their target. But that's all I know at the moment."

"And we don't have confirmation on the ground of a laboratory or any other bioterror facility."

"No, sir."

"So I don't have anything solid to run up the chain of command—nothing actionable. Wouldn't you agree, Special Agent Anderson?"

"But, sir…" Ray started to object, but then Harkin turned from the window to face him. Ray studied Harkin's face, and he saw what he thought looked like an opening. "Yes, sir, I would agree, sir."

Harkin seemed to relax, and he walked calmly back to his seat behind the desk. "Here's how we are going to play this, Special Agent Anderson. You are going to return to Idaho. You are *not* going to speak to any friends or any mystery persons. But you *are* going to follow up on these scattered bits of information. We are acting out of an abundance of caution—probably nothing—in which case I will try to forget that we had this little chat, and you will never again bring me information born on the wind. Do we understand each other so far?"

"Yes, sir. All clear, sir."

"You skated in here on very thin ice. Go to Idaho and shore it up. If your brother is up to it, you might want him to go along and make sure that you don't do something else that might result in you being court-martialed. Derrick knows his way around this sort of investigation, and you can tell him for me that I would personally love to see him return to the agency. In any case, I want you to chase these spooky leads to ground. I'm going to leave your friend in the shadows for now, but if any of this turns out to be the real thing, I imagine the president of the United States will not be so understanding. Got it?"

"Yes, sir. Thank you, sir."

"Get back to Idaho on the next plane. You are on duty, so keep that in mind before you run roughshod over anyone."

Ray was relieved to be dismissed, although it hadn't gone as long or as badly as he had anticipated. Colonel Harkin wasn't sold, and he certainly wasn't sticking his neck out. But he had left the door open just a bit, and he had allowed Ray to follow up without lighting up the grid. All in all, the meeting went far better than Ray had expected. Now his only problems were explaining all this to Derrick and then locating a group of deadly international terrorists before it was too late.

Chapter 22

At about the same time that Ray was leaving the colonel's office, Derrick was peppering Francine and Jessie with questions both scientific and practical. *How might the terrorists attempt to manipulate a prion disease like mad cow? Had such a thing been done in other labs, or had others gotten close to such manipulation? How certain were they about the safety of Jessie's veterinarian clinic? What if they were wrong, and how would they know?*

Francine and Jessie did their best, but their explanations were often reduced to educated guesses. It was one thing to sequence something in the lab and quite another to speculate about the sequence that someone else might have followed. Prions were a tough nut, and neither Francine nor Jessie saw an easy way to convert misfolded prions into a bioweapon.

"So have either of you modeled the possible pathways?" Derrick asked. He was rubbing his head and seemed to be growing calmer but at the same time concentrating more intensely. Jessie had seen this look before and knew that once it started she might as well become comfortable with seeing it for days or weeks on end.

"Yes," Francine replied quietly, "I gave that a run before I left the institute. And I also quietly checked around for modeling work done in the past by others. I think you are on the right track, Derrick, because I believe that's how a rogue scientist might tackle the problem."

"What do you mean, Francine? Why do you say that?" Jessie walked over to fetch a carafe and began to refill their coffee.

"Thanks, Jess. Well, the problem is so hard that I think it defies finesse. No one that I know has laid down a clear theoretical path to prion manipulation, at least any that pushes toward the frontier of weaponization. That might be the case because it is simply impossible to weaponize this sort of illness. But it might also be the case because of the limitations of human brainpower and time. Theory work and laboratory testing take a great deal of time and money, and at the end of the trail, there is a good chance of coming up empty."

"So you attack it with supercomputing," Jessie said.

"Yes. At least that's what *I* would do if I were the evil scientist trying to create a monster illness. I would carpet-bomb the possibilities and then pursue the models that showed the most promise. If I was lucky, I might shave decades off the time required for development. If I was superlucky, I might stumble on a clean solution."

"Let's hope no one is that lucky," Derrick said quietly. "Francine, I'm confused about something. Usually bioterror involves pretty classic illnesses—smallpox, anthrax, the plague. Terrorists who work with those older diseases know quite a bit about vaccines and treatments, right?"

"Sure. Not that it makes them bulletproof—people die every year handling these agents or even some precursor bugs."

"Right, but they make plans to protect themselves. And the fact that they have some disease history to work with makes that easier, right? So if these terrorists are working with entirely new stuff, Frankenstein-type creations, then aren't they exposing themselves to a high risk that their weapon will backfire and kill off their friends, as well as their enemies?"

"I've been wondering about that myself. Thankfully that blowback hazard is one of the things that reduces the risk of catastrophic bioterrorism. The bad guys have to know that they can control the monster and that they can get ahead of it enough to protect those whom they want to shield from the illness. Those things aren't easy to do. The disease may behave badly once it is out of your hands. It may change rapidly or suddenly, as we often see with influenza. And even if it remains stable, you still have the problem of shielding some people and destroying others."

"They might plan to vaccinate their people or to use some sort of quarantine strategy," Jessie said.

"Yes, but those moves would also raise the risk that they tip their hand about the existence of their weapon. Governments and disease trackers would likely catch wind of something like that."

The three were quiet for a moment. Derrick took a sip of coffee and then turned back to Francine.

"I don't get it. Who would be making this stuff, and why would they be doing it out here?"

"No clue," Francine responded. "And keep in mind, Derrick, we are still talking about long-shot risks here. Someone is fooling around with prions. What you all found was apparently a cow infected with a possible precursor. That's all we really know. For all we know, that cow was the last one used in a failed experiment."

"And you two are sure about the precursor thing?"

Jessie smiled at Francine and then walked over to Derrick and placed her hands on his shoulders and drew her face close to his.

"For the eight hundredth time, Francine and I do here solemnly pledge that we never exposed ourselves to the plague. We worked in the suits, and we followed strict protocols. And, yes, what we found was a precursor."

Derrick stared back at her without breaking a smile. "It made the cow pretty sick."

"We've been over this already."

"You are still in the doghouse." Derrick smiled and turned toward Francine. "You too."

"Oh, I'm well aware of my status at the moment—coconspirator, among other charges. I should get some sleep so that I am ready to walk the plank in the morning."

"That's navy."

"Oh yeah."

Jessie kissed Derrick lightly on the forehead. "I think we could all use some sleep. Each day has enough trouble of its own." She stretched and turned to gather some papers where she had left them earlier in the day.

Just then Derrick's cell phone began buzzing.

"Hey, Ray." Derrick's smile faded as Ray began talking. Ray was too concerned about the security of communication to give Derrick any more than coded notice that something was up, that it was related to things they had been pondering recently, and that he needed to see Derrick as soon as possible. Derrick nodded and let Ray know that he understood. The conversation was over in seconds, and Derrick quietly set his cell phone down on the arm of the chair.

"Ray's on his way over. Looks like I better make some more coffee."

Chapter 23

REUBEN AXTELL OPENED his eyes slowly and checked the alarm clock on his bedside table: 5:30 a.m. Reuben groaned and started to turn his back on the clock when he heard a noise that sounded like the soft shuffling of feet.

Suddenly awake, Reuben shook into a pair of cargo shorts and walked quietly out of his bedroom. It was still dark, but he knew his way around the small house by heart. He had reached the entrance to the front room before Reuben remembered the big dog. Bear was seated facing the front door, but his head was turned in Reuben's direction. In the half-light Reuben could just make out the ghostly amber eyes and the tip of the dog's wide tongue.

"Great. It's you, huh?" Bear closed his mouth and looked at Reuben intently. It seemed to Reuben that the big dog had been sitting at the door for some time. Bear turned his big head back to the door and cocked his ears.

"Hopefully you woke me up because you need to go out, and not because you wanted to lure me out here by myself." Reuben turned on a nearby lamp and stepped cautiously over to the big dog. Bear stood and began wagging his tail. Reuben thought the tail was another odd feature of his grandfather's new pet. It had very little taper and was only about half as long as the dog's back legs. Reuben thought it looked like yet another bit of weaponry, a police baton bringing up the rear.

Reuben managed to located the enormous leash and led Bear down the front steps and around to the side of the house. He was surprised that the mastiff moved so smoothly alongside him. He had half expected a tussle. But Bear glided along beside Reuben. The big dog's ears were cocked, and he frequently turned his head to sniff the wind. Bear seemed alert, and as Reuben walked the dog to a bare patch of ground, he wondered how long the dog had been sitting there silently at the front door.

"Hurry it up, dog. It's too early." As if on cue, Bear relieved himself. When he was finished, he walked to Reuben's side and sat down.

"Nice. Back to bed." Reuben began walking back toward the front steps, and Bear fell back into step alongside him. He had just turned the corner back to the front of the house when Reuben felt the leash tighten suddenly. When he looked down at Bear, he was surprised by the transformation. The big dog was standing perfectly still and fully alert. His feet were squared as though dug in, and the hair on the big dog's neck was bristled. At first Reuben didn't recognize the deep rumbling sound as Bear's growl. It was so low and soft that he thought maybe he was hearing his grandfather's snoring through the wall of his corner bedroom. But then Reuben felt it, the low rumble radiating from the dog's throat.

Reuben scanned the yard and the road beyond. It was too dark to make things out clearly, but everything he could see appeared perfectly normal. There were no cars on the road, and Reuben heard the familiar morning sounds of a few distant cars on the state road and the usual band of crickets and songbirds.

"What is it, boy? What do you see?" Reuben stood completely still and listened. Then he leaned down and rubbed his hand over Bear's head and neck. It felt like rubbing his hand across a hairbrush at first, but by the third stroke the dog had begun to relax, and his coat was smooth again. Bear looked up at Reuben and then sat down. Reuben scanned the yard and the road one last time and then headed back into the house.

Frank Higheagle poured himself another cup of coffee and passed a plate of eggs and bacon to Reuben. He smiled as he studied Reuben's face.

"Don't let your face fall into your plate."

Reuben eyed his grandfather and spooned a scoop of eggs onto his plate. "Very funny. I would have slept a little better last night except I had to take care of your little buddy over there." Reuben lifted his chin in the direction of the big dog lying on his bed. Bear's head was resting on his front paws, but his eyes seemed to be tracking the breakfast conversation.

"I think it is a good thing that you two are getting to know each other better. You must have gone for a long walk, or maybe watched a movie together." Frank kept his head down and took a bite of toast. But then he couldn't contain a chuckle, followed by a spasm of coughing.

"Serves you right, old man. Does your dog know how to help you out if you start choking?"

Their banter fell away as the two men became more serious about their breakfast. Reuben and his grandfather were not big eaters, especially for their size. But they enjoyed good food, and they were both good cooks. Frank's breakfasts were especially good. When they finished, both men sat together in silence for a time. The morning light was beginning to spill through the windows and warm the kitchen and front room. At the sound of a car moving down the road out front, Frank stood and began gathering up his dishes.

"I need to run over to Hailey today. They've asked me to help again this year with security at the Sawtooth Rangers' rodeo. Do you want to go with me or stay here with your new best friend, Bear?" At the sound of his name, the big dog raised his head off his paws and looked at Frank.

"I thought that rodeo was on July Fourth?"

"It is. But we need to do some planning, and I may need to recruit another helper or two."

"I better go with you, so I can pick out my job. I'll leave the worst stuff for the other helper you recruit."

"I knew I could count on my devoted grandson."

It was early afternoon by the time Frank and Reuben arrived at the Snow Bunny burger joint in Hailey, Idaho. The route through Boise was usually faster, but both Frank and Reuben preferred driving the scenic route through the Sawtooth National Forest. Even though it was near the peak of the summer tourist season, two-lane Highway 75 had been mostly free of cars until they dropped into Sun Valley and approached the outskirts of Ketchum. Frank and Reuben were accustomed to crossing this border between the high-country wilderness and the wealthy enclaves of the valley, and the two of them hardly noticed the gaggles of summer residents sipping coffee at sidewalk cafés or the occasional Maserati purring alongside Frank's old pickup at one of the many intersections.

They had chugged through Ketchum and Sun Valley at the usual crawl before making the final sprint to the satellite community of Hailey, Idaho. While it was connected to the other towns of the valley by tradition and commerce, Hailey was in some ways quite distinct from its more famous neighbors. It was the town where people lived who worked in Sun Valley or Ketchum and the place where year-round residents settled to raise their children and enjoy the area's stunning beauty. Hailey had the feel of a comfortable cross between the hardy western town and the pleasant northwestern suburb.

As Frank and Reuben unfolded themselves from the pickup and headed toward the front door of the Snow Bunny, they were within a stone's throw of Hailey's hip skate park and its classic rodeo arena. Frank noticed as he entered that two old cowboys occupied one corner booth and four young hipsters were at the booth just behind them. Frank smiled to himself. He had always appreciated the town of Hailey, almost as much as Cascade.

Henry Johnson and two other members of the rodeo planning committee were already seated at a booth near the counter when Frank and Reuben arrived. They greeted the three men, and then Frank took a seat while Reuben headed to the counter to place their lunch order. Johnson was anxious to get started, and before Reuben had returned, he had been assigned his first task. He would be responsible for helping the rodeo hands unload gear and move it to the arena staging area. The meeting rolled on for another hour, and then the small group left the Snow Bunny and took a walk to the nearby fairgrounds and rodeo arena. Reuben enjoyed being with his grandfather when he was at work. His grandfather loved to clown around and banter at home, but when he was working, Frank was all business. And Reuben knew that he was very good at his work.

He could spot a security weakness from a mile away, and he could head off trouble with the best of them. Frank used his disarming manner and keen sense of humor to encourage good behavior from the mild cases. And for those who failed to take the hint or who were determined to cause trouble, he was perfectly comfortable playing the part of human barricade. The Fourth of July rodeo in Hailey was a friendly and low-key event. But Frank was committed to anticipation and preparation. Henry Johnson's initial enthusiasm had waned somewhat by the time Frank was satisfied that they had completed the initial security review.

It was nearly midafternoon when Bear suddenly woke up from a deep sleep. He breathed a soft woof as he left his bed, but otherwise the big dog moved quietly. He stood in the middle of the front room for a moment with his ears cocked. Then he padded around the house, his head erect and his eyes alert. Something wasn't right. Bear made two full laps through the small house, checking each room and standing on his back legs to peer out bedroom windows. He finally returned to the front room, but he didn't go back to sleep. Instead, Bear sat down by the front door and waited.

Frank and Reuben left Hailey in the middle of the afternoon, hoping to get back to Cascade before dark. The Sawtooth National Forest was a scenic drive on a summer day, but at night it could be a different matter altogether.

When they arrived in Sun Valley, they encountered several blacked-out SUVs. The drivers wore dark aviator sunglasses, and Reuben could see a few phone lines snaking from one ear.

"What's with the entourage? Drug lord or celebrity?"

Frank grunted. "You never know around here. But it's probably tied to the Allen & Company Conference."

"Never heard of it."

"You should read a newspaper once in a while. It's only one of the most important gatherings of technology and media people in the world—Bill Gates, Google guys, the whole crew. Even LeBron James has been known to show up."

"Boy, that's what Sun Valley needs—a greater concentration of wealthy people and high-tech gear."

"Careful, you might be asking one of those people for a job one day. Anyway, the valley's not such a bad place for these folks to gather. Security is already good, given who owns the homes here."

"So you think all these black Suburbans are one person's detail?"

"No, they look like they are all part of the same team—probably hired by the conference hosts to oversee security. Most likely they are running initial sweeps and identifying potential problems."

"Can they secure the entire town?"

"More or less. It's not such a big place, and Sun Valley people know the drill."

Frank slowly made his way through the thicker afternoon traffic. Finally they were leaving Ketchum behind and heading into the exclusive ranch country just to the north. And then they crossed into the national forest and the familiar terrain of broken forests and jagged peaks. Clouds were gathering on the northern horizon as they turned off on Highway 21 at Stanley and headed west toward Cascade. And by the time they had reached the cutoff to the Bonneville Campground, a pelting rain was beginning to fall. Lightning snaked across the northern sky and backlit the mountains as they drove on toward home.

The truck's wiper blades had a squeak, and Frank was trying to distract himself. He gazed out his side window at the streaks of rain brushing the mountain peaks. Just as he turned his attention back toward the road, Frank noticed a dark sedan heading their way. Decades of highway-patrol work made it second nature to recognize an unmarked police car, even in a gathering rain. Frank was just preparing a hearty wave to the fellow trooper when the windshield cleared and he saw a snapshot of the face behind the wheel of the oncoming car. Frank's hand froze before it came level with the side window. The driver was Jim Crowfoot.

And then he was gone, heading east with the storm. Frank hadn't been able to tell if Crowfoot had seen him or recognized his truck. Pretty hard to miss out here in the middle of nowhere, but perhaps the rain had provided just enough cover.

What was Crowfoot doing out here anyway? This was a long way from his reservation beat. And the only place out here to make one of his community outreach calls was in Stanley. That town's population was sixty-three last Frank checked, and he doubted that even one among that number had the slightest interest in police work or the latest news from the Shoshone-Bannock reservation.

"You OK?"

Frank had forgotten about Reuben for a second, and the sound of his voice startled him. "Sure. Why?"

"You jerked like you feel asleep or something."

"Oh. Just avoiding a bad spot in the road. I'm fine."

Reuben studied his grandfather's face for another second. Then he turned back and looked out his side window at the grassy meadow and the forests beyond. The rain was coming down harder now, and the forests and meadows were blurring together in dark streaks.

Meantime Frank was thinking that it might be time to get more serious about Crowfoot. There must be more to that story than he had originally thought. He had said his peace the last time they had met, but that was based on what Frank knew at the time. He couldn't rely on Crowfoot to keep his word, or on the business in Pocatello to simply fade away. When they reached the house, he would make a few calls and get the ball rolling.

As Frank was forming a plan, a herd of deer was moving northeast from the junction of the Cascade Reservoir and the Payette River. The old buck had picked up a troubling scent. He stamped and ducked his head to move the herd forward. They would graze fitfully at times but, at the old buck's prompting, continue their march toward the east. Their route would lead them away from the river and just south of Frank's house. They would graze one last meadow before the buck hustled them across Highway 55. By then daylight would be running out, and the rain would be falling harder. Just as their hooves hit the pavement, an old truck would be heading their way.

Frank and Reuben were riding along in silence and looking forward to being home. They had no idea that the deer would be crossing their path soon or that an unmarked cruiser was following them on their last stretch toward home.

It was nearly midnight by the time Ray sprinted through the rain and knocked on the front door. Jessie hustled him in and took his jacket. A bright lightning flash struck just before they closed the door, but Ray and Jessie were too focused on getting inside to notice anything beyond the porch.

"Senior Scientist Booker—well, hello. Didn't know you were here." Ray shook water from his hair and at the same time managed a salute.

"Hello there, Special Agent Anderson. Yeah, I'm in the doghouse at the moment. Saving a place for you." Francine smiled and waved away his salute.

Ray had planned to talk with Derrick alone, but Derrick quickly caught him up. It was time to share their notes and work together, so Derrick encouraged Ray to share his news with the group.

"I'm back on the grid. This is official army CI business now, just so you know. A scientist named Dr. Abdul Nasim escaped from Egyptian custody and made his way to the United States. He's Pashtun and affiliated with some bad actors known as the Guardians."

"I haven't heard of that group." Derrick looked at Francine, but she shrugged.

"Low-key bunch. Apparently these Guardians are not as interested in publicity as some of their terrorist brethren. But they seem to have big plans. It appears that several scientists and technicians affiliated with Dr. Nasim managed to make their way to Canada and then cross into Idaho. They are working on some sort of biological weapon. They've used a system of couriers and front organizations, and they appear to be well funded."

Jessie shook her head. "Why Idaho? I mean usually terrorists are focused on big targets: major cities or military installations."

Ray nodded. "Right. But this group picked Idaho so that they could build their superbug in a remote location. And they had another good reason—their target is the summer conference in Sun Valley."

"That technology and entertainment thing…the…um…" Derrick snapped his fingers and tried to come up with the name.

"Allen & Company Conference," Ray said.

"That's it—Allen & Company—a big event for the technology crowd."

"Yeah, and I think that makes it an attractive target."

"I thought that was in Jackson Hole?" Jessie asked.

"Similar idea but different resort venue," Ray responded.

"We sure Jackson Hole isn't the target?"

Ray turned to Francine. "Not sure of anything, but so far the timing and evidence points to Sun Valley. One could be used as a decoy for the other, of course, or they could plan to hit both of them. The Jackson Hole event draws central bankers and major players in finance."

The group sat in silence for a few seconds. Thunder rumbled in the distance.

"Oh yeah, I almost forgot the main reason I raced over here," Ray said suddenly. "And, Francine, I'm glad you are here for this one. I needed to ask you and Jessie something. According to my information,

Nasim and his crew are using cows for some purpose. Any chance that might help us narrow down their location or what type of monster bug they are working on?"

Jessie and Francine looked at one another, and then Francine turned to Ray. "Yes, Ray, I believe we have some ideas about that cow connection."

Chapter 24

As he walked down the hallway to the testing chambers, Nasim replayed the latest round of argument with Crowfoot. As usual Crowfoot had blamed the most serious security problems on Nasim's team. Nasim found the man's imagination impressive, even as he found his deflection of responsibility so utterly exasperating. Crowfoot had argued that the curious veterinarian had located a wandering cow 209 not because, as Nasim firmly maintained, Crowfoot bungled the impromptu ranching operation, but rather because Nasim's group had used too many test subjects. According to Crowfoot it was simply a matter of time before they let one of their infected subjects slip through the cracks.

It had been harder for Crowfoot to dodge responsibility for the two stray humans. Nasim had simply been stating the obvious when he pointed out that Crowfoot was given an assignment back in May. And because he left a loose end that day at the university, now there were at least two loose ends and likely a few more. Crowfoot had better access to the latest surveillance than Nasim, but it didn't take a brilliant scientist to connect the dots between Reuben; the hero-professor, Derrick Anderson; and Anderson's wife, Jessie. Nasim summed his case against Crowfoot by pointing out all their troubles with the veterinarian and cow 209 could be traced back to the failure to take care of Reuben Axtell.

Of course the chief Guardian was not willing to let go of his support for Crowfoot, even if he seemed to agree with Nasim on some points. Crowfoot may have made mistakes, but he was viewed as the fiery core of the Guardian movement. None of his errors had yet been proven to compromise the mission. And so another round had ended in a draw. Crowfoot had fumed and growled and then sworn to Nasim and the chief Guardian that he would ensure security. He staked his own life to the success of the project, offering to give himself up to the chief Guardian for execution in the event that the plan was compromised in any way.

Nasim had never been particularly impressed by such gestures. The life of every Guardian was already committed to the coming battle. What difference did it make if one slashed an arm and wrote out the contract in blood? Such pledges were mere theater. But the chief Guardian was a man of symbolism and drama, so he accepted Crowfoot's pledge as a solemn oath. The two of them conducted some miniature theater around the point, but Nasim had not waited around for the show. He had work to do and little time for drama or excuses.

When Nasim reached the entrance to the honeycomb of testing chambers, he drew a ring of keys from his lab-coat pocket and slipped the correct one in the lock. The door was heavy and fixed with an airtight seal. Nasim heaved it open with a slight whoosh and then slipped inside the entrance chamber. The door swept back and fell into place with a final metallic click. The entrance chamber was silent and snowy white. The lighting system was linked to the door mechanism, and the fluorescent bulbs flickered for a moment after Nasim entered. Nasim savored the transition into this silent space while he waited for the lights to lock into midday brilliance. For him this place represented a sort of inner sanctuary. Here all of the promise and power of the laboratory was concentrated in this silent white refuge.

Once his eyes adjusted to the light, Nasim drew a biohazard suit from the line of hooks on the far wall of the entrance chamber. He usually brought a fellow scientist along to make these rounds, but today he wanted to be alone. Encounters with Crowfoot always left him on edge with other people. Having someone along today might increase his chances of making a mistake, and the operation could not afford for him to make a mistake at this point. Working alone he had always been a model of precision and protocol, but at times when accompanied by others, he had been known to become distracted. And this was no time for distraction. The agents were now expressing themselves in their full bioweapon glory. Even though the prion killers were not designed as airborne agents, one could never be too careful with something so novel. As the senior Guardian scientist, Nasim knew that his life would not be a long one. But he had no intention of dying by the sword that he had especially designed for their enemies.

When he had checked his suit for the final time, Nasim passed through the heavily sealed doorway into Testing and Observation Wing A2. This wing contained eight rooms, four on each side of the hallway. Each room was brightly lit and contained a bed, a small cart, and, in the far corner of each room, a steel pathology table. A mechanical arm reached out from the cart toward the ceiling and held a tablet computer screen at eye level above the bed. The computer screen in each room linked to a screen in the hallway near the door of each room. Technicians who monitored the rooms could read vital testing information from beside the bed. From where Nasim was standing in the hallway, he could scan the same information on the screen by the door of each room. Perched in the corners of the eight rooms were tiny camera eyes and microphone buds. Every detail of the tests and their results was recorded and examined.

Nasim smiled when he noticed that the first bed was empty. One technician was spraying down the metal pathology table, and another was resetting the bed for the next test subject. The screen in the hallway reported that the last test had been completed at 10:20 a.m., and the duration from initiation to completion was twenty hours and sixteen minutes. This was almost two hours ahead of schedule. It was only one subject, and Nasim knew that it might be an outlier. But it was still a positive sign. They were marching in the right direction and might reach their median target of eighteen hours in time to make at least some of the final refinements Nasim had originally planned. Nasim had set the target by the time required for all the victims to leave Sun Valley and scatter back to their respective homes.

But even under the best of circumstances, he would only have time to narrow the duration so much. Some targets might fall ill after as little as twelve hours, and others might require twenty-four hours or even longer. It would not be the precise wave that he had always imagined. Crowfoot and the chief Guardian were determined to strike the earlier summer gathering, and it was unlikely that either of them could be convinced by scientific evidence to wait for the second meeting instead. Nasim believed only in perfection, and he was confident that he could provide perfection if they held back the few weeks required to strike at Jackson Hole. But Crowfoot was an idiot, and the chief Guardian, a man of action. Nasim was the brilliant minority.

He tapped on the screen at the Profile link. The last test subject had been close to profile, only slightly younger than the median and a bit lighter. Nothing in his scan pointed to an obvious contaminating factor. Perhaps the gap *was* closing a bit ahead of schedule.

Nasim walked down the hallway to a point just past the second branches of test rooms. From this vantage point, he could scan all the rooms and the available test information. The rooms on his left were testing their latest version, and those on his left the previous version, labeled on the screens as "minus one condition." Test subjects occupied each of the remaining beds, and a technician was assigned to each of the rooms. The hallway was soundproofed. If he liked, Nasim could tap a button on any one of the room screens, and the sound from the test room would be sent directly from the microphones in the test room to headphones in his biohazard suit. But Nasim was content with the absolute silence. He almost always preferred silence to the sounds made by other human beings.

One of the other subjects in the latest-version group was fading fast. Nasim noted the glassy eyes and deep stillness. He moved closer to examine the computer screen for this test subject. The vitals were smoothing out, losing the whitecap intensity of the baseline condition and sliding toward low tide. Nasim checked the timer function. This one might come in under sixteen hours—another good result.

The two other subjects in the minus-one condition were mostly still, although the last one was occasionally swept by the lightest of tremors. Like being tickled by a feather, Nasim thought, as he had tickled his younger brother on the ear with a hawk's feather when they were small boys. The eyes of the last two subjects were not yet fixed, but they were beginning to glaze over. Perhaps two more hours. Perhaps less.

Nasim reluctantly turned to face the four subjects in the control condition. He did not like to look back or to contemplate the short-comings of his previous work. But perfection was gained by patient construction. These were the necessary building blocks. The four sub-jects in the minus-one condition were all still in heavy constraints. They could not risk damage to equipment or lost results at this point. All four were feverish. Nasim could see that two of them were shout-ing or screaming, and the other two seemed to be laughing. Their eyes were wild and darting. They seemed to be seized by various dreams or nightmares. Now and then their eyes would fix on some point in the room or in one case on a technician. At these moments their gaze took on a dark and intense aspect. Nasim's team had noticed spasms of aggression among the cattle in earlier tests. Although not a feature that Nasim had designed, he was more than happy to take credit for it now. If some of those infected became violent in the middle stages of their illness, well, so much the better for Guardian purposes. Of course, Nasim knew that it was also possible that the aggression was a transitory feature that, like the laughter, would disappear as the agent was refined. It was also possible that features would reassert themselves. Nasim smiled at this thought, imagining a gang of laughing killers wandering the streets of Silicon Valley.

As Nasim was reviewing the latest results of his experiments, a pair of Guardian hunters were prowling the streets of Seattle for more subjects. The man they called Ghost was paired up with one of the old-timers, a massive Samoan named Tupe. Ghost had been disappointed at first when he was called off from following Derrick and Jessie Anderson. He still hoped to finish that business sometime soon. But in the meantime, Crowfoot had assigned him and Tupe back to hunting duty. Supposedly this was the last batch of subjects that Dr. Jekyll would need for his mountain laboratory, but Ghost wasn't holding his breath. He had met Nasim and thought that behind the scientist exterior lurked a sadist who simply enjoyed the process.

Whatever. There was worse duty than hunting stray individuals in an urban setting. And there were probably worse partners than Tupe. Ghost didn't like the man's looks. Those fearsome tattoos and massive arms tended to scare people off from about a mile away. But the big fella was handy for the manual labor.

Ghost and Tupe parked across from the pristine tech firm campus and began unpacking their Chinese food takeout. These tech types played havoc with their schedule. Their target might come strolling out of the building like a normal worker bee at 6:00 p.m., or might just as well come sauntering out at 3:00 a.m. like that was a normal time to be knocking off a day's work. Ghost tried to snag a shrimp with his chopsticks but missed on his first attempt. With the sticks poised over the red takeout box, he turned to look at Tupe, who was shoveling a heaping forkful of noodles from the box just under his chin into his mouth. Ghost motioned toward the gleaming building with his chopsticks and then spoke.

"Tech slaves—that's what they are, just a bunch of tech slaves. Might just as well be rowing a galley ship as sitting up there in a cubicle for twenty hours at a pop."

Tupe swallowed his noodles and glanced up at the building. He shrugged his enormous shoulders and then spoke through stray noodles.

"Who's free anyway, man? Me and you?" Tupe swiped a napkin across his chin and chuckled to himself. "Yeah, bro, me and you are a couple of free birds."

Ghost stabbed the shrimp and shoved it in his mouth. Then he pointed his chopsticks at Tupe. "I go where I want, Tupe, and I choose my bosses. No one tells me what to do unless I want to do it."

"If you say so Ghost." Tupe crushed the empty box and dug another out of the brown paper sack on the floorboard. "But me and you ain't sitting here eating Chinese food together because we're best friends. We got a boss, and those geeks in there got a boss. Our boss sent us to pick up one of them, and here we are. No difference I can see. Are you gonna eat your other rice?"

"Knock yourself out, you big dumb Samoan."

"Careful, Ghost, I might begin to feel insulted and decide to deliver two new subjects to Nasim's lab."

Ghost turned back to his food, and the two men ate in silence. Office lights occasionally winked off, but they didn't see anyone leaving the building. And for every light that went out, it seemed that another flared to life. The people inside were moving around as they worked or snaking through the building in some tech worker conga line. Either way, Ghost was growing irritable. This was shaping up to be a long night. He had hoped that they could make the grab early and that he could get home to his own party. But it was beginning to look like he was stuck on patrol with Tupe. The Samoan had finished his dinner and promptly fallen asleep against the passenger door.

Ghost pondered the possibility of slitting the Samoan's broad throat. That would be something to see, the big fella blubbering and gurgling in surprise. He knew he could make the cut in time and deeply enough that Tupe would have no chance to fight back. He doubted he really needed Tupe in order to overtake an exhausted software programmer. But then again there would be all the mess and logistics—and hell to pay with Crowfoot. The big Samoan was right about one thing. They all had a boss.

Ghost turned away from Tupe and scanned the building. Just then he saw a solitary figure making his way down the stairs toward the front door. He lifted his binoculars and examined the face carefully. It was him. Time to roll.

Crowfoot had made the U-turn on impulse. Sure, he had planned to go after Reuben and Frank in the next day or two. But then they had simply presented themselves, the old truck flying past Crowfoot's cruiser. And a few beats later, Crowfoot had banked the cruiser around and begun following the old truck as it headed west toward the town of Cascade. As he tailed the old truck under the shield of the driving rain, Crowfoot began to form a plan. His turnaround made perfect sense now. It was one of those moves that one understood better in hindsight.

When he'd first spotted Frank's old truck, he had been replaying his earlier argument with Nasim. He was so tired of the same old second-guessing, of Nasim's endless whining to the chief Guardian. The closer they came to executing their plan, the more anxious Dr. Nasim became. When Crowfoot pointed this out, Nasim quickly countered that his anxiety was driven by security concerns, by mounting evidence that Crowfoot had failed to protect the mission. But Crowfoot suspected that the true source of Nasim's anxiety lay closer to home. The scientist was growing fretful that his creation would fail. All of Nasim's theories would soon be tested, and his life work, evaluated. If there was a breach in security, Crowfoot suspected that the fatal gap would be the Guardian's light hand with Nasim. Their chief scientist reported what he chose to report, and Crowfoot suspected that his scientific minions were more loyal to Dr. Nasim than to the Guardian cause. Some of them were not even tribal people, and many were chosen on the basis of their scientific expertise alone.

If he was right about Nasim, Crowfoot's single reassurance was an ironic one. Nasim's operation was not airtight. And Crowfoot doubted that he'd received a full accounting of the testing and its results. But he hoped that the same paranoia and ego that fueled their clashes would also drive Nasim to make the mission a success. Nasim could not fail. If for no other reason, to do so would be to admit that Crowfoot had been right all along. But there was another reason. Nasim could not fail because he saw this mission as the sum total of his life. In order to be chief scientist of the Guardians, Nasim must daily convince others that he believed in a victory born by the merger of science and the Guardian cause. Perhaps Crowfoot alone saw that underneath this loyalist exterior beat the true heart of Nasim's cause—using science to create the perfect weapon. The Guardians gave Nasim the cause and the resources needed to fuel his program. But if it had not been for them, Crowfoot believed that Nasim would have gladly built his weapon for others. It was the weapon itself that mattered to Nasim, even more than the weapon's ultimate target.

Most of their argument earlier that day was the same tired replay. But one thing Nasim had said was new, and it floated to the surface of Crowfoot's thoughts after he had turned the cruiser and begun following Frank's old truck. Nasim had said that they were short of test subjects. The durations had been closing more rapidly, Nasim had said, and they would need perhaps another six subjects to complete the final rounds of testing before launch. And so, Crowfoot realized, his spontaneous turnaround presented an opportunity to kill two birds with one stone. He would take care of the old man and his grandson, and at the same time fill a few of open slots in Nasim's final round of testing.

Chapter 25

Sofia DeClair pinched an errant bud from a flower arrangement and surveyed the entryway. Everything was falling into place. Just then a technician who looked more like a lost skateboarder crossed in front of her. Well, *almost* everything was falling into place. She would need to alert all the contractors to begin sprucing up their staffs and pulling all the headbangers to the background.

She had been working on this project for two years now and on nothing else for almost six weeks. It was hard to believe it was almost show time. Soon the entryway would look like the hive of some rare type of well-tended bees. The invited guests were a relatively small number; two hundred fifty was the official number. But every one of those invited to this "billionaire's summer camp" would bring along at least a handful of worker bees. Some of the guests would bring a much larger entourage. The security personnel alone constituted a small army. Sofia had spent a good deal of time over the past several months negotiating with heads of staff in a mostly vain attempt to pare down their rosters of attending staff members. Although she had avoided using terms like *essential staff*, the subtext was unavoidable. All the worker bees wanted to stay close to the hive, and all the billionaires preferred lots of buzz. The best she had been able to achieve was something close to the line between humming and chaotic.

Sun Valley Resort had been remodeled and recast any number of times. *The old girl is holding up pretty well*, Sofia thought as she moved from the entryway to the dining space. Lodges were not her thing, but she could see the charm of this place. It was a lodge of the old-school Swiss type, at least as interpreted by US railroad barons and bored East Coast socialites. A few of the revisions had been rather earnest for Sofia's taste. She had once joked to an associate that Bob Iger should be comfortable here, since this place reminded her of how Disney might build a classic mountain resort. It had been a close call for her career when both Bob Iger and a longtime Sun Valley resident had heard about her offhand joke. Sofia had only been spared by Iger's good sense of humor and a personal apology to the octogenarian Sun Valley native.

Although it was easy for Sofia to criticize certain features in isolation or to point out the tiny scars left behind by reconstructive surgery, the overall effect was one of a resolute and dignified beauty. Sofia respected the place and its people, scars and all. She could think of any number of European lodges with grander design and more breathtaking scenery. But Sun Valley Resort was a comfortable eccentric, it's "own special sort of odd" as one of her design teachers used to say. In fact, if Sofia had given her Disney joke more thought, she would probably have used a different punch line. Sun Valley was more like a quirky Swiss lodge designed by the Google guys.

"Sofia, where do you want these?" Amelia Benton had appeared out of nowhere. Her hipster glasses were sliding on her nose a bit, and she was lifting her head back to keep her green eyes trained on Sofia. Amelia was holding a box of gunmetal pens at eye level.

Sofia took out a pen and examined the script, swiped the stylus end on her iPad, and then flipped the pen and wrote her name on a box flap. Satisfied, she dropped the pen back in the box and waved Amelia toward the entryway.

"Check with Tony to get the holders for these. They are black with a fine line of gunmetal along the rim—a handful of pens in each holder and then a holder in all the places on the placement grid."

Amelia nodded and turned to go.

"Oh—and, Amelia, remind Angie to keep these filled throughout the conference. All of our guests would swear that they never use pens anymore, but at a meeting like this I've seen them burn through pens like firewood."

The last front in Sofia's campaign was the kitchen. Earlier in the day she had caught wind that there might be trouble brewing over menu and service logistics. Sofia was relieved that this conflict was surfacing now. Major conflict in the kitchen was a fact of life for an event like this one. Sofia preferred that her crew have some kitchen battles under their belt before the conference opened. She felt comfortable when the knives were out and the personality conflicts visible. Guerilla warfare was much tougher to manage.

In this case she would not have to worry about secret warfare. She began hearing the shouting long before she reached the staff entrance to the kitchen. As she closed in on the battleground, Sofia noted that the lodge was making good progress in hiring a diverse workforce. She could make out at least three different languages sparring in colorful terms, as well as a number of dialects and styles of cursing. Sofia took a deep breath, leaned against the kitchen door, and entered the fray.

If anyone inside the kitchen noticed her entrance, Sofia could not tell from the reactions of any of the kitchen staff. If anything, their volume and venom seemed to pick up a notch. She had learned over her career that attempting to shout down a chef, even a relatively inexperienced and low-ranking chef, was a lost cause. So she breezed past the knot of gesturing and shouting men and women dressed in white to a rack of pots hanging over a cutting board.

She selected a nondescript looking pan and a battle-hardened ladle and then began banging them together. In prior experiments with this method, she had noticed that the kitchen staff grew quiet in order of rank, the lowly first and the senior chefs only after her hands began to ache.

"You know nothing at all. Nothing!" This summary statement rang amid the last echoes from Sofia's pan and spoon. The senior chef's face turned from a scowl to a smile as he turned his attention to Sofia. He seemed pleased with his closing argument.

"Ladies, gentlemen, so I take it everything is going well in here, right?" Sofia scanned her audience and was met with glares from most and sheepish expressions from the others. It was usually the sheepish ones she kept a closer eye on. "Right. So, let's everyone put down the sharp instruments and take a few deep breaths. We are going to hear from you one at a time, and I am going to stay here with you until we can work this out and agree on a plan to serve amazing food to our guests who will be arriving oh so soon.

"A few ground rules: Let's try to steer clear of deeper philosophical commitments. We don't really have time to debate the merits of one school of thought over another. We may also want to dial down the character attacks a wee bit. Whatever our differences at the moment, we all know that in the end we are going to need to work well together and pull this thing off. And finally, if anyone in this room is stirring up trouble simply because you don't like being here or because you have some personal issue with this conference or any of our guests, please, do us all a favor and turn in your apron now. Throwing a fit or starting a fight is a lousy cover for wanting to be somewhere else, and we would all appreciate you for helping us out and making it just a little easier to negotiate our peace treaty.

"OK, boys and girls, who wants to go first? Amelio, how about you?"

Sofia had no idea when she opened her preconference in the kitchen that it would take two and a half hours to negotiate a resolution—not a record in her book but within fifteen minutes or so of that mark. Some translation had been required, and the two Greeks on the staff disagreed hotly over the translation of certain key words. Some of the workers seemed to be talking around the problems, and a few didn't speak at all. Sofia hoped that these reluctant participants would not keep the conflict simmering. Two of the quiet ones had held a brief sidebar in a language she didn't recognize. She had asked one of them if there was a translation issue, but he had responded in perfect English that they were tracking the conversation. He said the other worker had simply asked him about the schedule of preparation for an item on the evening menu.

She had moved on but not without some reservation. Sidebars in a kitchen were almost always a bad sign. Sofia briefly wished that she had learned more than the two languages she had mastered so far. She made a mental note to continue her language studies until she gained mastery of most of the major languages spoken in the best kitchens. And then Sofia had forgotten about the two less vocal kitchen workers and continued negotiating with the others.

Sofia couldn't have known that even her most aggressive language study was unlikely to cover the one spoken by the two men in the kitchen that day. It was a Chechen dialect only spoken in the highlands and mostly by older people and by warriors. The two men could have conversed in Russian, French, or Arabic, as the need arose. They had also studied English since childhood. It had been a small risk that day to whisper in the language of their homeland, but the message was urgent, and when it came to communicating across languages, they were confident of covering their tracks. The two Guardians felt especially confident at the end of the meeting, when they were sure that the kitchen staff had returned to work and that preparations for the conference were back on track.

Aaron Thompson slipped on his ear bud and checked his appearance in the hotel room mirror. Even though he had been working private security for more than three years now, he was always surprised to see himself as a well-dressed civilian. He had been a British commando and special-operations leader for twenty years. The ghost of that soldier was always there in the mirror for a moment, staring back at him and puzzled by the sports coat and wool slacks.

But Thompson shook off the sensation and brushed the shoulder of his coat with the back of one hand. He had a mission. That much hadn't changed. And as was the case in Bosnia and Iraq, he worked in a context of hidden and dangerous opponents. Billionaires were attractive targets for terrorists and assassins. And his employer was not one to shy away from any spotlight or to forgo any opportunity to needle his enemies. He was what Thompson's commando unit had referred to as a "parrot." They had often been tasked with rescuing hostages. Most of these hostages were grateful and compliant. But now and then, they had rescued a hostage who was loud, belligerent, and prone to ignore their instructions. On one occasion such a parrot had triggered an ambush, and one of Thompson's best mates had been badly wounded. And another had nearly gotten Thompson killed when he pulled out a hidden butane torch and lit a cigarette. The sniper's bullet had sailed so close to Thompson's ear that he could feel the rush of air as it passed.

Oh well. Even parrots shouldn't be gunned down in the street. So Thompson loaded his nine millimeter and slipped it into the holster inside his coat. He knelt for a moment and checked the knife strapped to his left ankle. Thompson knew that the knife was as much

219

a security blanket as anything else. But since that single time when it had proven useful, the knife had become part of suiting up.

Thompson stood and smoothed his clothes—time to take the field. He threw his leather duffel over one shoulder and left the hotel room behind.

As Aaron Thompson was entering the elevator on the ninth floor, Leonard Davis was drumming his fingers on a leather armrest and occasionally checking his diamond-encrusted watch. He was anxious to get this little chore over with and move on to more important matters. His security man, Aaron Thompson, had insisted on a live walk-through of the Sun Valley Resort before the Allen Conference opened. And Davis had finally agreed to come along, even though he thought the entire exercise was more about making the security man feel important than about keeping him safe.

Who the hell was going to attack him at Sun Valley? This place was so laid back that even the Starbucks crowd was sedate.

Davis was certain that he had nothing to worry about from the crowd of nerds in Sun Valley this week. Everyone who wanted to gun him down lived in a city and wore a suit. They might fly over Sun Valley sometime without realizing it. But they didn't hate Davis enough to pay whatever the going rate might be for a Chicago hitter to come out here and mingle with this crowd.

He saw Thompson approach and rose to begin his morning growl.

"Where the hell you been? I was waiting."

"Good morning, Mr. Davis. Straight-up nine a.m. Our car is waiting outside."

"No, my car is waiting outside. Your car is probably parked under a carport beside your dingy little house. People like you who specialize in wasting other people's time don't have cars parked outside waiting for them."

Thompson turned to Davis's personal assistant, the stunning and ever-present Ms. Elliot. "Ms. Elliott, could we have a second in private?" Nancy Elliot nodded with a cold smile and drew her cell phone as she turned back toward the main lobby. Thompson waited until he was certain she was out of earshot and then moved in close to Leonard Davis and began to speak.

"Maybe I should just shoot you here in the lobby of this hotel and save us all the trouble of trying to protect you at the conference."

Davis tried a laugh, but it came out more like a nervous cough. "I might be the only one hiring washed-up soldiers like you these days, Thompson, so if I were you, I would tread a bit more carefully."

Thompson's face hardened, and he leaned in a few inches closer. "Oh, I think we are about even, Mr. Davis. You are the biggest pain in the ass among billionaires, and I am the only former operator crazy enough to take this job."

"You can't talk to me like that!"

"Yes, I can. And one more thing: I have these flashbacks sometimes. Mostly they happen at night. But lately I notice them during the day. They seem to come on when some jerk is giving me a hard time or making sarcastic remarks. And snap"—Thompson snapped his fingers in front of Davis's nose—"just like that I'm back in close combat."

"You are a disturbed man." Davis leaned back away from Thompson's hand.

"Maybe you should keep that in mind. That will help keep you safe—from the bad guys and from me."

Nancy Elliott could only stand to be dismissed for so long, and she rejoined Thompson and Davis in time for the three of them to head to the waiting limousine. Thompson wouldn't have admitted it to Davis, but he liked this working arrangement. He felt more comfortable in confrontational relationships. And he knew that Davis really didn't have much choice when it came to security. Leonard Davis had already run through most of the high-caliber security contractors. Unlike Davis, Thompson was good at reading just how far he could get away with pushing someone. Davis was bad-tempered and obnoxious. But he had a pretty good tolerance for pushback, especially when he considered someone the best in their field. And Thompson was the best in his field.

Chapter 26

THE RAIN HAD mostly subsided and was running down in rivulets beside Idaho Highway 55 just north of Cascade. The big buck paused to drink and to nibble the tender grass along the side of the highway. Several does and a few fawns were strung out along the shoulder of the highway and into the edge of the forest behind him. The only sounds were the dripping of the rain off the trees and the low rumble of thunder. The storm was moving off, and the night would be clear and cooler.

Just then the buck heard a higher-pitched rumble. He lifted his head and pointed his nose toward the sound. He cupped his ears and stood frozen for a few seconds at the edge of the highway. And then he heard the sound again. It was danger. He blew a warning and bolted back toward the group of deer at the edge of the forest. The fawns and younger does raised their heads and twitched their ears for the briefest of seconds and then bounded deeper into the forest. But two big does and a young fawn were farther out ahead of the old buck, and they hesitated. The smaller group on the road could feel the slightest vibration in their hooves and see a light suddenly topping the nearest hill.

When the light burst over the hill, the deer all froze. They could no longer see their way back to the forest. It was too late to go back anyway. The oldest doe bleated and jumped to cross the highway. She made it across just in time.

Frank didn't see the deer until he was on top of them. The flash of a white tail alerted him to the danger but not in time to miss the second big doe leaping across the highway. The truck slammed into her at near full speed. As Frank hit the brakes, the truck began to slide sideways and careened into another deer. The windshield shattered amid the squeal of tires on the wet pavement. Frank lost control, and the truck slid off the road, hit a shallow culvert, went airborne for a second or two, and then smashed into the young spruce trees at the edge of the forest.

Smoke rose from the crumpled hood and curled through the cabin. The sharp smell brought Reuben back from the white haze of the exploding airbag. He began swimming up to the surface of full consciousness, struggling to get his bearings and to locate his grandfather. His head felt thick and cottony, except for his right temple, where he felt a slick of something cold and wet. He called for his grandfather, but he didn't hear any sound. Reuben couldn't tell if the words were not getting out or if his hearing had been damaged in the crash. Slowly he put his left arm into motion and reached toward the driver's seat. But his hand fell over the seat and landed on broken bits of glass and metal. He reached again, farther this time, and his hand brushed the rough cotton of his grandfather's work shirt.

He heard a groan and then a faint voice, "Reuben...Reuben, you there?"

Reuben answered that he was, and this time he could just make out his own voice.

His grandfather's voice was calm, but he seemed to be struggling to gather his words. "My leg is busted...or pinned. Tough to see."

Reuben heard a sizzle like bacon frying. He was rising faster now, and his senses were beginning to connect the dots. They had hit the deer and then the trees. The truck was busted up bad. He needed to get them out before the wreck caught fire. Reuben shifted his weight and used his left arm to free himself from the tangled seat belt and deflated airbag. When Reuben lifted his right arm to search for the door latch, a bolt of pain shot from his upper elbow into his lower arm and hand. Reuben winced and leaned back into the seat.

"Smoke." His grandfather seemed to be sliding in and out of awareness now, and the single word was barely audible. Reuben needed to move now. He reached across his body with his left hand and unlatched the door. The truck was tipped at an angle, and the door flew open faster than Reuben was expecting. He toppled out of the truck and into a tangle of brush. A second wave of pain shot through his right arm. He scrambled in the brush to gain his feet but was finally able to catch a low branch with his left hand and pull himself free. When standing, his body felt oddly disconnected, as though he were standing beside himself and watching his own movements. But the pain was less sharp, and his head was gradually clearing enough to see the situation and to recognize his next step. He moved through the tangle of brush and debris to the other side of the truck.

His grandfather was more tangled in the seat belt and in various strands of metal and debris. His left foot had become pinned under the brake pedal, and his pants leg was wrapped around some of the tangled wreckage. Reuben fished a large pocketknife from his right pocket and had the fleeting thought that he was grateful for its one-handed mechanism. He cut away the seat belt and other tangles and then knelt to examine the floorboard. The leg was only pinned lightly. Reuben was able to push the wreckage aside with his good arm and to hook his injured arm over his grandfather's leg and slide it free. It was a costly maneuver, and Reuben thought for a moment that he might pass out from the pain. But he willed himself to hold on. He still needed to move his grandfather from the smoldering truck.

Except that it was no longer smoldering. Reuben saw a flash of light reflected in the raindrops on the side mirror, and then an orange tongue of flame curled up from the engine toward the shattered windshield. Reuben wrapped his left arm around his grandfather's chest and lifted him onto his back and out of the truck. His grandfather grunted but did not cry out. He shifted his weight as he could and ducked so that Reuben could clear the crumpled doorframe. Reuben felt a sharp stab of pain radiating from his right forehead and saw little pins and wheels of light amid the rainy evening gloom. The flames were growing now, and the orange light was making crazy patterns across the shattered windshield. Reuben focused his sights on a clearing some distance from the back of the burning truck. He steadied his feet underneath the load and shuffled forward, testing each footstep. The fire behind him was growing by the second. He could feel the heat at his back and a panic rising up inside him. But Reuben couldn't afford to run or to stumble. He was not sure that he would be able to lift his grandfather a second time or to muster the strength to drag him to safety.

The ground near the clearing was broken and slick. Reuben bent lower and used their combined weight to plant each step. Finally he made it to the edge of the clearing and straightened up a bit to locate a good place to lay his grandfather down. Suddenly an explosion tore through the truck behind him and sent a blast of hot wind and debris into Reuben's back. The last thing he remembered was a sudden weightless feeling and then the sensation of flying.

Reuben landed just behind his grandfather, and the two of them lay sprawled out in the clearing like two scarecrows battered by a storm. Not far away, the flames from the truck were already dying down. Here and there sparks flew into the trees. But the explosion had broken the fire, and the sparks fizzled in the rain-soaked trees.

Soon the forest was quiet, and the only sign of the wreck were the skid marks and the blackened husk of the pickup.

Bear had perked up when he heard the distant drone of the familiar truck. His body tensed, and he whined softly. A few seconds later, he heard a sharp and unfamiliar sound. Bear stood up and listened. He could no longer hear the low drone of the truck. He stood motionless for a moment and then began working to break out of the house.

Ray and Francine drove past the clearing and the wrecked pickup on their way to Frank's house. After hitting the deer, the truck had slid at fifty miles an hour over the rain-soaked ground and down the embankment. If they had been looking for a wreck that day, they might have noticed the skid marks and wounded trees near a slight bend in the road. Instead they rounded the slight bend and drove on the remaining half mile to Frank's house.

As he turned the Jeep into Frank's driveway, Ray noticed that the front window was knocked out. He signaled Francine and then slipped out of the Jeep and drew his nine millimeter from a shoulder holster. Francine drew her own weapon and signaled to Ray that she would check the back of the house. After a quick search, the two met in the front room and stood staring at the open window and scattered debris.

"What on earth? Busted from the inside…You see that?" Ray rubbed his chin and turned to Francine.

"Yeah, I see it. Pushed out from the inside. Maybe we startled whoever was in here."

"Maybe. Look like a robbery to you?"

Francine surveyed the front room, walked a few steps down the hallway to look in a bedroom, and then walked back to the front room.

"Doesn't look like anything tossed around or obviously missing. If it was a burglar, I don't think he had a chance to take anything."

"Francine, check this out." Ray pointed at scratch marks in the dining table. Francine moved closer and then knelt down to examine the floor around the table. A strewn saltshaker was in one corner and a pepper shaker lay on its side under one table leg. Francine spotted something else. At first she thought it was the remains of a spilled drink. Maybe the robber had bumped the table on his way out and turned over a glass of water or orange juice. But there were no glasses on the table or the floor. And as Francine studied the stains, she also noticed scratch marks near the window frame.

"Dog. *Big* dog." Francine stood up and smiled.

"What?"

Francine pointed, and Ray knelt down to get a closer look.

"See the scratches? Same as the ones on the table. And those spill marks there and there—well, I thought at first they were spills. But no sign of any drinks on the table."

"So what is it?"

"Drool," Francine said. "Like I said—a *big* dog."

"He jumped through the window?" Ray ran a hand along the scratches on the table.

"I think it's more likely that he pushed the window out of the frame. Probably took a look outside from up there." Francine nodded toward the table. "But then I think he jumped down and stood here barking for some time. At some point when he put his front paws on this window, he must have felt it give way a bit. Any dog that can reach that window with his front paws is likely to weigh enough to exert some leverage. Either he fell through on his first attempt, or he pushed it a couple times. *Then* he jumped through the window."

Ray and Francine stood for a moment looking out through the tattered window frame at the debris left on the porch. Then Ray walked out the front door and down the front steps. He studied the pattern of debris and then knelt down at a spot just beyond the front porch.

"I've got tracks. And you are right—that is one big dog." Francine came out of the house and down the steps.

"Maybe we should track down Frank's truck first. He and Reuben could have driven to Cascade for all we know. Might not even know that their dog took a holiday."

"Yeah, you're probably right." Ray bent over and followed the tracks for a few more paces. "He was in a hurry to go somewhere. Maybe a rabbit or cat wandered through the yard." Ray stood with his hands on his hips and looked down the road in the direction of the tracks. Francine watched him for a moment and then began walking toward the Jeep.

"Better get going, Ray. We need to locate Frank and Reuben."

Ray glanced back at the house. Then he turned and headed to the Jeep. Frank and Reuben could be anywhere. The two of them enjoyed being outdoors, and after the recent rain, the weather had cleared. It was a gorgeous summer day, and Ray thought that under any other circumstances he would like to join Reuben and Frank at their backcountry campsite. But Francine was right: the best shot they had of locating them easily was checking in at Cascade. Hopefully Frank and Reuben were running an errand in town.

Ray and Francine rounded the bend past Frank's house and drove on toward Cascade. Reuben might have heard the Jeep pass by on the highway not far from where he and his grandfather lay in a clearing. But it was hard to say what he was really hearing and what might be a dream. Reuben heard buzzing noises that grew more intense from time to time and a distant sound of wind or cars on a highway. Everything seemed to be muted and running together.

And then a face loomed into view. Reuben wished at that instant that he was dreaming, but he knew that the face was real. Jim Crowfoot smiled back at him.

"Well, good morning, Reuben! You and Grandpa camping out in the open, huh?"

Reuben struggled to push himself up. Pain shot through his left side, and his vision faded in and out.

"Oh, I wouldn't jump right up if I were you. Looks like that arm is a wreck. And I'm guessing he has some other internal injuries, wouldn't you say, Ghost?"

The face of a tall, pale man appeared over Crowfoot's shoulder. "Yeah, he don't look so good. Should probably see a doctor."

Crowfoot grinned up at the man and then stood looking down at Reuben. "You know, you're right, Ghost. We should get these two to a doctor as soon as possible. And we happen to know a good one. Reuben, you and your grandpa are a couple of lucky white Indians. No telling what might have happened if we hadn't come along."

Reuben heard a commotion behind him, but he couldn't turn far enough to see what was happening. He realized his feet had been tied together, and his arms felt pinned to his side.

"Take it easy, old man. You look a little worse for wear."

Reuben didn't recognize the deep voice, but he realized that the man was talking to his grandfather.

"Leave him alone!" Reuben yelled. "Do what you want with me, but leave my grandfather alone."

Crowfoot smiled. "Can't do that, Reuben. What sort of men would we be if we left an old man out here alone in the wilderness? No, we have a duty to see that your grandpa is taken care of just right...and your dog for that matter." Crowfoot nodded toward the truck. "Yeah, that's some impressive dog. Almost took Ghost's arm off before we could get him in that cage. But don't you worry; we'll find him a good home."

Reuben heard more scuffling behind him, the sound of a punch, and then a grunt followed by a low moan.

"Grandfather, you OK?"

"I'm OK, Reuben. How about you?" His grandfather's voice sounded surprisingly strong and clear.

"Yeah, I'm fine. Just waiting until my hands are free, so I can pick up where I left off with Crowfoot."

In a flash Crowfoot drew a tactical knife and dropped to the ground. He pressed the black blade to Reuben's throat. "If I were you, white Indian, I would keep my big fat mouth shut. Otherwise, I might just turn Ghost and Tupe loose on the old man over there. And then I might just slit your Anglo throat."

The man called Ghost jerked Reuben to his feet and grabbed his injured elbow. Reuben screamed.

"Oh, sorry." Ghost leaned in close and laughed. "Forgot about that sore spot on your arm."

Suddenly Reuben was lifted off the ground and dropped on his back into the bed of the truck. Hovering over him was an enormous man with elaborate tattoos covering half of his face. Tupe stared back at him for an instant and then pulled a heavy tarp over him. It was too dark under the tarp to see his grandfather, but Reuben could sense his presence beside him. The two men were silent until they were sure that their captors had closed the truck doors and begun to drive away from the clearing. Then they whispered to one another about the state of their injuries and their restraints. They didn't need to tell each other that they should fight as soon as they were given the slightest opportunity. Frank and Reuben concerned themselves instead with planning for the fight they hoped would come soon.

Now and then they could hear Bear's heavy breathing and muffled growls. The cage was under the tarp near the cab of the truck. He must be muzzled, Reuben thought, and that must have been at least a three-man job.

"You should have stayed home, Bear. What did you do anyway, chew through our front door?" Reuben could barely see the outline of the big dog's head. Bear whined and scratched at the cage. The metal cage rattled, and the truck bed shook. Tupe glanced back and knocked the back of his fist against the truck's back window.

"Cool it back there, dog. Don't make us stop."

"Bear, down." Frank listened as the dog quickly settled himself. "Good boy."

"Nice," Reuben whispered. "Have you two worked on anything yet like 'escape' or 'take out those three psychopaths'?"

Frank smiled to himself in spite of the pain. His grandson's sarcasm was a good sign under the circumstances.

"Me and Bear will be ready when the time is right—won't we, boy?" Frank clinched his teeth and began the painful process of working his huge hands free. The Samoan who had tied him up was a big man too, so he probably assumed that Frank's hands would not be a problem. His captor may have forgotten, or never been told, that Frank was a veteran police officer. In any case, Frank had been through dozens of drills over the years. And he had learned in a few of the kidnapping drills that he was quite flexible for such a large man.

"You head that direction, and I'll go this way." Ray motioned over his shoulder toward the south end of the street. "We'll meet back at the Jeep."

Ray and Francine had made a few laps through the town of Cascade without spotting Frank's truck. Now they were hoping to hit some of the most likely looking places and see if anyone had seen the two men recently. It was probably a long shot, but Ray was beginning to have a bad feeling about the situation. He and Derrick had checked in with Frank and Reuben now and then since the school shooting. Every time they called Frank, he had answered his phone before the third ring. They had left messages for Reuben, but only because he was listening to music or outside working. Both Frank and Reuben talked about the camping and fishing trips they were planning to make together, but in the time since the shooting, they had mostly been homebodies. Maybe they had finally pulled the trigger and headed into the mountains. But for some reason, Ray thought it was unlikely that Frank would head for the backcountry without letting someone know.

Frank's house hadn't shown signs of being buttoned down either. Surely they would have taken that big dog with them or taken him to a kennel. The whole business with the dog breaking out of the house still seemed odd. Ray had known of coonhounds breaking out of a pen to chase a raccoon, but most dogs would simply whine and bark. And Ray never knew a big do—or, judging by its tracks, a *giant* dog—to stir itself enough to break out a window and jump through the opening.

Ray ducked into the dim light of a sports bar named Across the Tracks, but no one inside had seen Frank or Reuben in several days. At a coffee shop a little farther on, he talked with a man who had seen Frank two days ago. The man eyed Ray a few seconds before responding.

"Now, how did you say you know Frank again?"

Ray ran down a short version of the story.

"Frank didn't say anything about a camping or fishing trip."

"Think he would tell you if he was planning one?"

"Most likely." The man's eyes twinkled. "Unless he's found a good fishing spot and doesn't want me to know about it. I'm a better fisherman than Frank."

"Do you think he and Reuben might have taken a trip somewhere?"

"Doubt it. The boy's been staying around home. Repairing fence and such."

"Do you have any idea where they might be? I need to talk to them as soon as possible."

"Is everything all right? I mean is Reuben in some kind of trouble?"

"No, no, nothing like that. I just have some more information about the investigation, and I'm sure he would want to hear it as soon as possible."

"Hmm. I can't think of anything Frank said about going camping or fishing. He had that job coming up in Hailey anyway, so I doubt he would want to plan anything until that was finished."

"What job in Hailey?"

"Oh, it's something Frank does most every year. Helps out the town of Hailey with security for their annual Fourth of July parade and rodeo."

"That's still weeks away. Does he go to Hailey before that?"

"Yeah, now that you mention it, he does. Usually takes a few trips over to check things out and meet with the folks planning the event. He might have even mentioned to me that he was going to Hailey sometime soon...But I just can't remember when."

Ray hustled out of the coffee shop and headed back to the Jeep. Francine was already there, sitting on a bench near the Jeep and checking her phone.

"I struck out. How about you?" Francine said as Ray approached.

"Possible lead. I'm calling someone in Hailey."

Ray turned aside and spoke briefly with the Hailey city manager. Then he hung up and turned back to Francine.

"Frank and Reuben were in Hailey yesterday, visiting with a group planning their annual Fourth of July event. They left Hailey midafternoon headed this way. The city manager was certain that Frank said he was driving straight home from Hailey. He remembered that Frank said they were taking the scenic route home, through the Sawtooth Wilderness. Frank had said that they needed to make a beeline home so that they would get off the backcountry roads and safely home before dark."

"They should have arrived home by eight last night, or nine at the latest. Where are they?"

"I don't know. But we need to find them. Let's backtrack their route from Cascade to Frank's house again, only more slowly. You can call the forest service and let them know to check the road through Stanley and on out this direction."

Chapter 27

DERRICK AND JESSIE arrived at Sun Valley Resort just as Aaron Thompson was completing his initial security sweep. They were not alone. By the time they were making their way through the lobby, Derrick had spotted several security and protection contractors. He recognized a few of them as ex-military. They wore the suit and tie as well as anyone, but something in their posture or manner usually gave away the soldier underneath.

He and Jessie made their way to the main office of the resort. After a few redirections, they were told where they could locate Sofia DeClair. She was overseeing preparations, their guide had offered, and she was the one to see regarding any aspect of the upcoming conference. They could find her in one of the old drawing rooms off the main hallway.

Derrick didn't have to be told that they had located the right person. He would have picked Sofia DeClair from any lineup as the consummate conference orchestrator. She was a tall and striking woman, with elegant black hair and sharp green eyes. A yellow pencil was perched behind one ear. She was sharply dressed and tightly wound. When Sofia turned to greet Derrick and Jessie, her face was at once welcoming and aloof.

Jessie extended a hand as she approached. "Sofia DeClair?"

"Yes. What can I do for you Ms....?" Sofia closed the cover over her iPad and returned Jessie's handshake.

"Dr. Jessie Anderson. Good to meet you. This is my husband, Dr. Derrick Anderson."

"Yes, personal physicians, welcome. I trust that Angie has helped you settle in."

"Actually I'm a veterinarian," Jessie replied. She was about to explain Derrick's credentials, but Sofia spoke first.

"Oh, I see. Excellent. Certainly the animals need the same level of care as their owners. Do both of you work on the same staff?"

Derrick thought he would give it a try. Jessie could only tolerate so much confused chitchat.

"We aren't here for the conference, Ms. DeClair. I'm a professor, and Jessie is a veterinarian in private practice. We have something rather urgent to discuss with you regarding the conference. Is there somewhere we might visit in private?"

Sofia studied Derrick for a moment and then turned back to Jessie. "Are you from one of the activist organizations? Because we have a process for registering your organization and—"

"Have you ever heard of mad cow disease, Ms. DeClair?" Jessie's smile had been replaced by a determined glare. "And now that I have your attention—no, we aren't protestors or members of any activist organization."

"Perhaps you could follow me to the office just down the hall." DeClair turned on a dime and marched down a wide hallway to an unoccupied office. She took a seat in a club chair and motioned for Derrick and Jessie to take a seat on a small sofa.

"OK, I'm listening. What is all this about?"

Jessie took a deep breath and began to tell a short version of their story. When she reached the point where she identified the Allen & Company Conference as the target, DeClair spoke up.

"How did you come by the information that our conference is the target of this alleged plot?"

Derrick leaned forward and rested his elbows on his knees. "Ms. DeClair, would it be possible to speak to your head of security? Time is of the essence here."

Sofia had been tapping a pen on the arm of the leather club chair. She suddenly stopped. "Yes, I think that would be a great idea. I'll just step out in the hallway and give him a call."

Moments later DeClair rejoined them, accompanied by Bill Sanders, a stocky man in his midfifties. He had a shaved head and alert gray eyes. Sanders unbuttoned his coat and took a seat in a chair opposite the couch. He seemed to be making sure that Derrick and Jessie got a good look at the holstered .38 pistol. Once he was settled in his chair, Sanders looked directly at them with a most concerned and attentive expression.

He's been tipped off, Derrick thought. *DeClair made the call from the hallway so that she could use whatever code language this group employs for "We have a couple of nutcases down here."* Sanders might listen politely, even make a show of taking a few notes, but they were being given the polite blowoff.

Derrick tested his theory with a few pretty obvious stray points. When Sanders didn't show the slightest curiosity, Derrick knew it was time to wrap this up and move on. They didn't have time to waste with the tea-and-biscuits routine.

"Well, Dr. Anderson, Professor Anderson, thank you so much for coming by and alerting us to this potential hazard. We will pass this along to our security team and make sure that we keep a sharp lookout." Sanders stood and shook their hands. Sofia DeClair added her breezy appreciation and then dismissed herself with a helpless gesture toward her cell phone. Bill Sanders buttoned his coat over his sidearm and escorted them the full distance to their truck.

"Such nice people," Jessie said as Derrick started the truck. "How obvious was it that I might want to strangle dear Sofia?"

Derrick smiled. "I thought you two girls were hitting it off just fine until she realized you were a *cow* doctor."

"What now?"

"Well, we know for sure that they weren't listening to us. I count that as a win of sorts. If those two had been better actors, they might have persuaded us that they were taking us seriously. At least they made it obvious that we can expect no help from them."

"True. But those are the very people whose help we need right now. Queen Sofia's kingdom is the one under threat."

Derrick eased the truck out of the parking lot and turned south on Sun Valley Road. "How would they deliver a weaponized version of this bug?"

"What?"

"The terrorists—how would they deliver a weaponized form of this disease to their targets?"

"Francine's the expert on that sort of thing."

"If you were guessing, how might they do it?"

"OK, if I were guessing, I would say that they would probably spray it on their food. They might also mix it in beverages. Prions are tough, so they wouldn't be affected by extremes of temperature, or alcohol for that matter."

"They wouldn't need to inject it or spray it directly on the person?"

"No, I don't think so anyway. If this stuff works anything like Creutzfeldt-Jakob disease—the human form of mad cow—then it wouldn't require injection or direct contact. In all the CJD cases I'm familiar with, the means of transmission was eating something contaminated by the brain or spinal material of an infected cow."

Derrick pondered Jessie's response as he arrived at the intersection of Saddle Road and North Main Street. If Jessie's hunch was correct, the terrorists might have already compromised the conference. Much of the foodstuffs for the Allen & Company Conference would have been delivered days or even weeks ago. According to what Francine and Jessie had told him about prions, there was no risk of the stuff going bad or losing its potency. It could be in baking soda or sugar or any of a dozen other basic ingredients. It might be arriving along with the stream of fresh items pouring into the Sun Valley Resort, especially the dozen or so varieties of fresh meat.

Derrick pulled into the parking lot of the Java on Fourth coffee shop. He turned off the engine and stared ahead at a cloudless sky.

"We need to get in touch with Ray and Francine. It may be time for them to call out the cavalry."

"I think so. The worst that can happen is that the terrorists disappear into the woodwork."

"Well, almost—the worst that can happen is that we drive them to ground, and they resurface to attack somewhere else, like Jackson Hole or even some White House event a year from now."

"What other choice do we have? The crowd is already arriving at Sun Valley Resort."

Ray and Francine had been working their way carefully along the highway leading to Frank's house. There was only a mile left, and Ray was frustrated that they had covered so much ground without learning any more about the whereabouts of Frank and Reuben. They were almost to the house, and he had no idea where to search next.

Just then Francine grabbed his arm. "Ray, right there!"

Francine was pointing at a spruce tree just off the highway. He hadn't seen it before, likely because it had been in shadow when they passed by that morning. But now the sun was shining bright on a deep gash in the tree. Ray thought he could see a few sparkles at the lower edge of the gash. Fresh sap would mean a fresh wound.

He quickly pulled the Jeep off the highway and parked at the edge of the trees. He and Francine jumped out and walked toward the wounded tree. The sudden thunderstorm had softened the ground and combed over part of the tire tracks. But now that they were close, Ray could make out the twin tracks of a pickup. It had been in a fast slide, careening off the wet highway and down into the underbrush of the forest below. He and Francine followed the tracks and the marks in the young trees on either side. Now and then a brush of red paint was visible on one of the trees. Despite the speed and rough ground, Frank had managed to keep the truck on a fairly straight line into a section of younger trees and heavy brush. The old truck had hurtled within a foot of some of the more mature trees. But it had hit only two, and these were glancing blows. The tree they had first spotted was one of these close calls, and they found another down the incline and near the place where the truck had come to rest.

Whatever optimism Ray had felt as they had followed the truck's path evaporated as he and Francine emerged into a small clearing and saw the burned-out wreck of Frank's truck.

The fire had sparked suddenly, perhaps from an explosion. It had burned hot but not lasted long. Ray could see that the cabin was only singed, and the back of the truck had been mostly spared. Frank must have been low on gas, likely coasting home near empty. The doors were hanging open, and the driver's seat belt was cut. A tangle of seat belt and airbag dropped from the opening. The smell of smoky debris and wet forest hung heavy over the clearing, and Francine began to cough. Ray followed a blood trail from the driver's side of the truck to a small piece of open ground not far away. There were drag marks and backward-facing footprints. Reuben had dragged Frank from the vehicle. This was good news. Reuben must have weathered the crash in decent shape if he was able to disentangle Frank and drag him from the wreck. The extent of the blood trail was a good sign too. One or both men were injured. But the wounds didn't look life threatening.

Reuben had dragged Frank to the small open space and lay down beside him. Ray knelt down in the depressions in the grass and soft ground and then looked back toward the wreck. This was probably what Reuben had considered a safe distance. Or maybe it was simply as far as he could go before running out of strength or losing consciousness. They had been lucky. The explosion had been a mild one, and the wet trees had not caught fire. Otherwise the two of them might have escaped the wreck only to die in the ensuing brush fire.

But where were they now?

Francine came over and sat on a rock nearby. Her cough had grown worse, and she had come to the clearing to get some fresh air and take a few draws from a water bottle.

"You OK?" Ray asked.

"I will be. A little asthma." Francine smiled weakly. "Find anything?"

"Yeah, looks like they made it out of the wreck OK. That's saying quite a bit. Reuben cut Frank lose from the driver's side. Don't know if that means Frank was unconscious or just banged up, but a few of the later drag marks suggest he was moving one foot pretty good. So I think he was awake but hurt. There is a blood trail, but it doesn't look too bad. Looks like they landed here, either because they were far enough away from the fire or because Reuben ran out of gas. They lay here awhile—maybe hours."

"Then what?" Francine squinted up at Ray.

"Good question. I'm working on it." Ray bent at the waist and began walking in a circular pattern outward from the spots where Frank and Reuben had lain.

"Well, our giant dog has reappeared. His prints are not hard to spot." Ray pointed the tip of one boot at a large print in a patch of sandy soil. Francine stood and walked over to inspect.

Ray continued to work the clearing. At first the signs were few and far between, but then they were everywhere. Someone had driven another vehicle down here to this clearing. It looked like the prints of three men, one of them very large. Ray guessed that the big one wore a size 16 boot. There had been some shuffling of feet and some lifting. It looked to Ray like the men had spotted the wreck—or maybe the fire—and come to help. They had apparently lifted Reuben and Frank off the ground and loaded them into the vehicle—maybe the dog too, because Ray could find none of the big dog's prints beyond the small clearing. They had driven back the way they came. In all likelihood they had taken Frank and Reuben to the hospital. The dog may have insisted on going along. All they had to do now was find out where the men had taken Frank, Reuben, and their dog.

"Ray must be tracking." Derrick slid his cell phone back in his jeans pocket.

"How do you know that?" Jessie asked.

"Not that Ray is a great fan of cell phones, but he generally keeps his on, except when he's tracking. He hates distractions when he's on a trail."

"So I guess that means he and Francine are working on foot? I thought they were just driving to catch up with Frank and Reuben."

"Yeah, me too. Maybe we should head out that way. There's no way we'll miss them on that route."

"True, but it isn't exactly in the neighborhood. Let me try Francine first."

Derrick could hear the rings and the start of Francine's voice-mail message. Jessie left a message and then sat still for a moment with her phone in her lap. Then she turned to Derrick and pointed back toward the highway.

"Francine's no tracker, and she *always* answers. Maybe we head that way and see if we can catch up with them."

As they drove west and then north on Highway 75, Derrick tried to imagine what was going on with Ray and Francine. They might be searching for Frank and Reuben in the area around their house. Frank's house was part of a tiny line of residences that was surrounded by vast spaces of uninhabited mountain country. Derrick hoped that Frank and Reuben had decided to take a day trip in the area and that Ray was tracking them to a nearby campsite or fishing spot. If so, he and Jessie might be able to make contact before long and arrange to meet somewhere closer to Sun Valley. They all knew that the start of the conference marked a hard deadline. But Derrick sensed another clock ticking—and one with a much closer deadline. Heading off the terrorists would require taking the right steps in the time *before* the opening moments of the Allen & Company Conference. Well-designed terrorist plots were a bit like the cartoon snowball rolling down the hill. They grew infinitely more difficult to stop as they gathered momentum and closed in on their target. Derrick sensed the terrorists gathering steam toward Sun Valley. What he couldn't see yet was the best way to head off their attack.

Sun Valley Resort was focused on the happiness and comfort of some of its most prized guests. Bringing a mad cow message had made him and Jessie about as welcome as a pair of skunks visiting an outdoor wedding reception. They could have rung official bells and brought out law enforcement to shut down the party. But law enforcement leaders, even army CI brass for that matter, would be reluctant to act in this case unless they were provided with rock-solid evidence. Acting to protect Sun Valley and the conference attendees would be a fine motive so long as there was no mistake or gap in their intelligence. But shutting down a conference like this one on the basis of what might turn out to be bad information would be the end of a few dozen promising careers. No one in their right mind would take that risk on the basis of the information that the four of them had gathered so far, suggestive though it was. They needed to nail down loose ends—and the sooner the better.

If Ray and Francine were not searching the area near Frank's house, it would mean that they had left the road somewhere along the way. Perhaps someone in Cascade had guided them to a location where the two men might be camping or fishing. Frank and Reuben were old hands in the backcountry, and they would likely move deeper into the forest rather than staying at a recognized campsite. The campsite could serve as a handy address, a location to discuss with an old fishing buddy in Cascade. But Frank and Reuben might easily stray a mile or more from such an anchor point without giving it much thought. Anyone who needed to find them would know where to look or could easily track them down. Ray would make short order of a search from a known anchor point and then would hopefully remember to begin answering his phone.

Derrick didn't like to think of the remaining scenarios, if only because they would mean more time lost and less chance to coordinate their next steps. Anything beyond the searches around Frank's house or a known campsite would likely mean that Frank and Reuben were truly missing or that Ray and Francine were tracking them on a longer camp trail. Derrick hoped that he and Ray were hearing the same clock ticking in their heads. They couldn't afford to be wandering the backcountry right now.

Chapter 28

THE TRUCK WAS banging along on a rutted and rocky track. Frank groaned now and then, and Reuben could almost feel his grandfather wince at the deepest ruts. But Frank was fully conscious now, and Reuben could sense that he was rolling with the bucking truck and doing his best to shield his injuries. Now and then the bumps sent a jolt of pain through Reuben's right arm. But mostly he noticed the burns on his left side. He hadn't noticed them before, but now his face and left arm seemed to be radiating heat. The fire hadn't seared his skin. He hadn't been that close to the flames. This was more like the microwave version of deep sunburn. Reuben turned his face more to the right, and as he did he noticed that the tarp had slipped one tie. He could make out a patch of clear blue and, when the truck dipped, the outline of mountains in the distance. He could also catch flashes of the forest and rock formations as the truck passed close by them.

Reuben whispered to Frank, and his grandfather turned his head in the direction of the gap. A faint shaft of light was shining under the tarp now, and Reuben could just make out Frank's outline. He could also see Bear. The light reflected off the big dog's shoulders, and Reuben could see that his muscles were tense as piano wires. The big dog was eyeing him and looking like he might whine. But Bear remained quiet.

He didn't risk any more whispering. It was enough for Reuben to know that both he and his grandfather were watching the gap. The truck had not gone far from the clearing when it turned off onto this backcountry road. So they were still in familiar territory. Reuben and Frank knew most every backcountry road and trail for miles around. They weren't going to get many puzzle pieces. The opening was small, and most of the view was sky and distant mountains. But at every dip, they caught a glimpse of the terrain around them. Reuben wasn't sure what difference it would make to know their location. They were tied up and heading into the backcountry with a truckload of lunatics. But he had always prided himself on knowing where he was at any given time. His father and grandfather had taken him to the backcountry as a child and used games to teach him the basics of finding his way and following a track. By the time he was twelve years old, his grandfather could drop him off most anywhere, and Reuben could find his way to a fixed meeting spot. He might lose his bearings for a short time, especially when he was fly-fishing and the bite was good. But when Reuben took a few deep breaths and relied on what he had been taught, the wilderness transformed into a friendly neighborhood. He simply started walking to the place he needed to go. And he never failed to arrive.

Except maybe this time. Reuben caught a glimpse of a few trees and realized that they were moving into higher terrain. The nearest range was around Warm Lake, but Reuben thought Crowfoot would probably want to steer clear of that area. Vacation homes and fishing docks dotted the shore around Warm Lake. Besides, if they had been heading through the Warm Lake area, they could have made better time on a few roads that circled the area and were traveled mostly by distracted vacationers. The other possibilities lay mostly north of Warm Lake. They might be heading to the north into the Payette

National Forest. Or was it possible that they were already farther east, beyond Warm Lake, and heading into the Salmon or Sawtooth Mountains?

The truck lurched to a sudden stop. Bear slammed into his crate and barked his annoyance. Frank groaned. Reuben could hear the men talking inside the truck cabin, and then the doors opened, and they piled out of the truck. Their boots were scuffling on hard ground—worn rock with a few loose slates. Reuben braced himself. He expected the men to walk to the back of the truck and untie the tarp. He hadn't fixed a location yet, but he knew from the bits and pieces he had seen that they were far enough into the mountain backcountry to be completely alone. Most of this country was remote, so any remote stopping place was likely to work as well for their captors as any other.

But the tarp remained in place, and the men seemed to be standing still beside the truck. Reuben could only make out the sound of the wind and the distant call of a hawk. Finally one of the men began to walk out ahead, beyond the front of the truck. The others followed without a word. They walked out far enough that their footfalls became faint scratches and then turned off the road and uphill. Reuben could make out the faint grunts of men covering steeper ground, along with an occasional slide. They were moving up to a rise maybe fifty feet from the parked truck.

"Reuben, you hear all three of them?"

His grandfather's whisper startled him at first. He had been so intent on listening and interpreting the sounds that for a moment he had forgotten about his fellow captives. "Yes, all three, up ahead and climbing ground on this side."

"Maybe they are confused about what to do next."

"Or maybe they are just making sure that this is the location where they want to dump us."

Reuben suddenly felt a hand on his shoulder. He started, and he barely caught himself before yelping in pain. His grandfather's huge hand was resting on his shoulder, and Reuben turned to see his grandfather smiling at him.

"Sorry, I should have given you more warning."

"How did you…"

"The big one is lazy," his grandfather interrupted, "and lousy with ropes for a Samoan."

"Now, help me get us both out of these ties—smooth and quiet. Their talk won't last too long, and they will be watching for the tarp to move."

Frank quickly untied Reuben's hands, and then Reuben slid down to work on the restraints around their legs. Frank's body tensed when Reuben untied the rope around his injured leg. But he patted Reuben's shoulder to continue, and Reuben cleared all their ties. He slid back to his starting position and caught his breath. It was growing hot under the tarp, and Reuben was sweating and breathing hard. Frank encouraged him to slowly work his hands and feet. They needed to get their blood flowing, even if it made their injuries flare. In fact, Frank whispered, they needed to channel their pain and prepare to fight their way free.

"What about the beast there?" Reuben asked.

"Is there a lock on the crate?"

"No, just a pin."

"Good. But don't pull it just yet. We all need to make our move at the same time."

Ghost blew out a last stream of smoke and crushed the cigarette butt with an absent twisting motion of his hiking boot. "So will they still be of any use in your friend's laboratory? They are pretty banged up after all."

Crowfoot studied Ghost's light gray eyes. They were as cold and distant as the man's Finnish homeland. "Since when do you care about what happens in Nasim's laboratory?"

Ghost smiled and rubbed one hand over his mouth. "I couldn't care less about your mad scientist and his experiments, Crowfoot. But I care very much about avoiding loose ends. I care about finishing a job and moving on."

"Ah, the mercenary's code—the Samoan and the Laplander just want to get paid."

"Please don't start up with all that Guardian nonsense about uniting the tribes in victory. You want to play the part of a folk hero, war-chief? This is fine with me. I will enjoy the show and even applaud when I feel like it. But don't delude yourself that I am truly expecting you to save me—much less my Sami people."

"No one can save you from yourself, Ghost."

Tupe moved closer and spoke with a deliberate calm. "Look—none of us has any claim to the other. I'm not doing any of this for the sake of tribal people in Idaho or Finland. I'm a mercenary, Crowfoot, and not ashamed to admit it. But I am a practical mercenary. So I'm not ruling out the possibility that the Guardians will succeed. And I will work for tribal people when I have the chance—even crazy tribal people.

"But I'm with Ghost on the methods. You have a problem with those two Indians." Tupe motioned toward the truck below. "So let's take care of your problem, here and now. I don't see the point of torturing them in this way. Such things can buy a person more trouble than they bargained for."

"You are afraid, aren't you?" Crowfoot was smiling, and his dark eyes shone. "You are afraid of their spirits." Crowfoot shook his head and chuckled to himself. "Ghost's partner is afraid of *ghosts*. What a pair."

"Look, Crowfoot," Ghost said, "I'm not afraid of anyone, living or dead. But this little expedition of yours is taking too much time and exposing us all to too much risk. Tupe and me didn't sign on to this." Crowfoot moved so fast that neither Ghost nor Tupe had a chance to react. Neither one saw the knife either, until it was pressed against Ghost's throat.

"You signed on to do a job. And the job isn't finished yet."

Ghost leaned back away from the knife, but a trickle of blood had already started to run down his neck. Tupe took a step toward Crowfoot. Just then Crowfoot released his grip and shoved Ghost in Tupe's direction. Ghost heaved and reached a hand to the shallow cut on his neck.

"What the hell? Are you *insane?*" Ghost reached a hand behind his back.

Crowfoot drew his nine-millimeter pistol and pointed it at Ghost's forehead. "I wouldn't if I were you."

Crowfoot motioned with the pistol, and Ghost raised his hands. Tupe stood silent with his hands at his sides. His eyes were fixed on Crowfoot's face. They stood frozen for a moment, and then Crowfoot lowered the pistol and spoke in a calm and even voice.

"Now then...This area is patrolled by the Guardians. There is no risk of encountering a park ranger or a group of Boy Scouts. If I send up the slightest signal, help is nearby."

Crowfoot whistled a birdcall and pointed over his shoulder. A sniper appeared on the ridge above them, outfitted to match the rocky outcropping. Ghost and Tupe exchanged a quick glance, and then Ghost took a handkerchief from a pocket in his cargo pants. He wiped the blood from his neck and then waved the cloth at the sniper on the ridge.

"All right, Crowfoot, you've made your point. Me and Tupe got to see your scalping knife. You have friends in high places. So now what?"

"Now I want you to help me with something."

"You're kidding, right? Or you really are insane. I just felt a blade on my neck."

"That was for show. For them—up on the ridge. I don't want anyone thinking we are on friendly terms."

"No danger there," Tupe said.

"I only have a few minutes to explain this before one of them might get the idea to come down here and check things out. So listen close. I want you to help me kill Nasim. That's the reason we are going to the lab."

"What about our hostages?" Ghost eyed Crowfoot.

"They are cover. I will use the same story on Nasim that I used on you. We brought him some test subjects. You came along to help. I want to make sure that Nasim has completed his work and that everything is in place for the attack. But once I know that the scientific part of the mission is completed, I want Nasim eliminated."

"Why do you need us? You have the guy on the hill"—Ghost nodded over his shoulder—"and I'm sure a few other Guardian comrades."

"Some Guardians are loyal to Nasim, especially in the lab. I have all the support I need elsewhere, but you two can help me tip the balance at Nasim's home base."

"I don't like it," Tupe said. "I don't want to get mixed up in Guardian business. And besides, I don't trust you."

"Trust doesn't have much to do with it, Tupe. If I make the wrong birdcall right now, that sniper puts a bullet in your brain. If you go with me now and help me take out Nasim, you live to fight another day. But just to show you that I place some value on your cooperation, I will agree to kill our hostages before Nasim gets his hands on them. Oh yeah—and I will double your pay."

"Let's make it triple," Ghost said. "And since we are sharing so openly with one another, Crowfoot, I should probably let you know that Tupe and me have a little black box."

"You are lying, but nice try."

"OK, you can ignore me if you want. But if me and Tupe don't appear at a certain location by a certain time, then you are going to find yourself tailed by someone you may know. His Norwegian name is rather hard for Americans to pronounce, but you probably know him better by his nickname anyway. The Dane has also been given instructions about where to find certain information related to your cause and your plans. He is a most helpful person when he wants to be but an absolute terror when it comes to disrupting plans. Some sort of childhood trauma at the root of it all I suppose. Funny, huh? A Danish Terror as insurance against terrorists!"

Ghost smiled up at Crowfoot. His gray eyes were cold and vacant. "Shall we go now? It seems we are all on a schedule."

"No, we camp here. The scouts are expecting us to act like bait." Crowfoot turned back to wave off the sniper.

"Bait? If you led us into a trap…" Ghost took a step forward.

"Relax, will you? The trap is for anyone who might be looking for one of us…or for those two." Crowfoot motioned toward the truck. "It's a standard security procedure, and I'm the one that set it up. If we break that protocol now, alarms will go off at the laboratory. So, Ghost, why don't you and the giant go find us some good firewood. I will check our prisoners and begin setting up our camp."

Francine ended the cell-phone call and turned back toward Ray. "Not there and haven't been there—that's the last one in the immediate area. It's possible they would have flown them on to a bigger trauma unit if they were hurt badly."

Ray was driving south again on Highway 55. They had headed south on the gamble that the hospital would be in this direction.

"Boise? But wouldn't someone around here know about it?"

"Yes, yes, they would. And I asked them all about medical flights in the past twenty-four hours."

"So where does that leave us?"

"I don't know, Ray. But I'm concerned. Based on that wreckage, I'm thinking that one or both of them are hurt pretty badly. It doesn't make any sense that Good Samaritans would drive past any of the hospitals in this area, even if they aren't full-scale trauma units."

Francine studied the map on her cell-phone screen. Boise was nearly two hours away from the crash site. But maybe these particular Good Samaritans had reasons for continuing on to Boise. Maybe they had a medical background and felt confident that Frank and Reuben were stable and would be OK making the trip. Francine was looking up the number of Saint Alphonsus Regional Medical Center in Boise when Ray flinched and then banged his hand on the steering wheel.

"You OK?"

Ray told Francine to hang on and then began executing a rapid U-turn.

"What's going on?" Francine asked, at the same time swinging a hand up for the grab handle.

Ray straightened the truck and began speeding north. Then he turned to look at Francine.

"Good Samaritans," Ray said. Francine waited, and Ray realized that she hadn't made the connection. "What if our three Samaritans are not so *good* after all?"

"Oh my God," Francine responded. "Crowfoot."

Chapter 29

DERRICK AND JESSIE were walking the crash site when Ray and Francine arrived.

"There you are. These things are handy." Jessie held up here cell phone.

"Oh yeah." Ray fumbled in his pocket.

"You find Frank and Reuben?" Derrick looked up from the ground and shielded his eyes with one hand.

"We think Crowfoot may have taken them hostage. I got side-tracked at first thinking that the other tracks out here were made by rescuers. But they haven't shown up at any hospitals. We came back here to see if we could pick up the correct trail."

"It starts over there." Derrick pointed to the tire tracks leading out of the clearing. "But they went back to the road. They could be anywhere by now."

"Maybe Crowfoot would head back to his home stomping grounds. The Shoshone-Bannock Reservation is a long drive, but he would certainly know where to hide out there." Jessie looked first to Derrick and then Ray.

"Maybe," Derrick said, "but I don't think he would risk it. Too much ground to cover, and they would be on open roads much of the time."

"So where do you think he might go?" Francine asked.

Ray looked at Francine and then at the forests surrounding the clearing where they were standing. "To their base camp," Ray said.

Derrick turned and studied Ray's face for a moment. "That wouldn't be very smart, Ray."

"I know. If these guys intended to do Frank and Reuben harm, why not just end it out here someplace—or leave them to die for that matter. But my gut tells me that if Crowfoot went to all the trouble to come out here and take Frank and Reuben—and maybe even that monster dog of theirs—that he had something more in mind."

"Like what?"

"No idea. But I looked this guy in the eyes once, and I think he might do anything to prove a point."

Derrick began walking alongside the tracks, and Ray followed. Jessie and Francine stayed behind and watched them.

"You OK?" Jessie asked.

"Yeah, I guess. Not my usual day in the lab. But I suppose I am due for some field training. You?"

"I've been better. The Sun Valley folks blew off our warning. That kitchen is like Grand Central Station anyway. I don't see how it could be protected without locking it down."

"Then we need to make sure it gets locked down. The institute has contacts with CDC, and I'm sure that between us we could figure out a way to force a closure."

"You willing to stick your neck out like that on the basis of what we know now?"

Francine kicked at a pebble. "Good point. I've been hanging around with you so much lately that I forget that all this would make no sense to anyone else. We only have hunches to connect these dots."

"And no government agency is going to risk shutting this thing down on our hunches."

"You are probably right. So what are we going to do?"

"I don't know. But we need to figure it out soon."

Derrick and Ray began walking back toward them. They were moving faster and appeared to have located something out near the road. They joined Jessie and Francine, and then Derrick pointed back toward the road.

"They turned north. We'll need to drive that direction and then see if we can locate where they might have turned into the backcountry."

Jessie noticed that Derrick was speaking a bit louder, and she thought he might be trying to boost his own confidence. His plan sounded like hunting for a needle in a field of haystacks, and Jessie was sure that Derrick knew the odds.

"We need horses," Jessie said. "It's going to be hard to spot their track from the road."

"No time," Derrick said. "Our horses are a day away from here."

"Frank had horses at his place," Francine said. "I saw them in a field when Ray and I were searching the house."

Ray smiled. "I saw them too—not horses exactly, but three or four fine-looking mules."

"Even better," Jessie responded, "they will be more surefooted over broken ground. Francine and I can ride the mules alongside while you guys drive the jeep along the road."

It only took a few minutes for them to drive back to Frank's house. After briefly catching Derrick and Jessie up on the story of the empty window frame and the big dog, the four of them walked around to the back of the house. Just past the rough boundary of Frank's backyard was a small field surrounded by a wooden rail fence. A small wooden shed occupied one corner of the field nearest the house. Two big mules were grazing in the midday sun, along with a miniature donkey and a single Appaloosa gelding. One of the mules looked up from grazing and brayed loudly. The Appaloosa ran to the fence and reached his head over the railings.

"Look like pets," Jessie said. "Probably feeding time."

"Pets that may not recognize a saddle," Ray said. "How do we know these guys haven't all gone to seed?"

"One way to find out, rodeo cowboy." Jessie smiled at him and then at Francine.

They found saddles and tack in the small shed, along with feed. Jessie put out feed and matched up saddles and tack. From the look of things, she guessed that the mules were ridden fairly regularly. Frank probably used them for his hunting and fishing trips. The Appaloosa was a wild card. The gelding seemed more skittish and less comfortable around saddle and tack. He might be an old friend, one that Frank kept around but no longer rode much. Jessie saddled the two big mules. They eyed Jessie throughout this process, now and then shaking their heads and flinching. Neither mule seemed entirely convinced that these strangers had proper authority to saddle them up. But they came bearing feed, which was no doubt the only reason they were able to get this far. The Appaloosa left some feed behind, content to move off to one corner of the field and watch from a distance.

"Want me to go first?" Ray reached out to take the reins from Jessie.

"No, I think I've got this," Jessie replied. "If I don't make my eight seconds, then you can give it a try."

"Jessie..." Derrick was hustling to the fence and pointing at the top of his skull. "Your last rodeo didn't go so well. Maybe you should let me or Ray tangle with these two."

"What are you three talking about?" Francine asked. She had been a decent hunt seat rider at one time, but these animals looked nothing like her family's Thoroughbreds. "Is there something I should know?"

Jessie laughed. "Derrick, I'll be safe. Francine, if there is something you should know, I won't have to tell you what it is. You'll be able to watch me and reach your own conclusions. In the meantime you all may want to stand on the other side of the rail fence." Once the three of them had ducked between the rails and were safely on the other side, Jessie slid up onto the back of the mule in one fluid motion. The mule's eyes widened for a moment, and he snorted once, but otherwise he showed no reaction. Jessie clucked her tongue and moved the reins gently to the left. The mule turned and moved ahead a few steps. Jessie settled fully upright and moved the mule through a few turns and one lap around the trampled area near the feeding troughs.

"Gentle as a lamb: Frank has trained this one well." Jessie walked the mule through the nearby gate and handed the reins to Francine. "You won't need as much steering as you used on Thoroughbreds," Jessie said. "He's a trail animal and probably accustomed to mostly making his own way. Let him know you are in charge, but don't make it a contest. Make sense?"

"Yes, just do everything the opposite of all my equestrian training—got it." Francine took the reins with a bit of hesitation. She reached a hand out and patted the mule's neck and then slid easily into the saddle.

"Oh yeah," Jessie said over her shoulder, "stay away from the mouth and back hooves. I'm guessing that Frank wouldn't tolerate nonsense from these two, but they might try to sneak in a bite or kick on a stranger."

"Great," Francine said as she began adjusting her position in the saddle.

The second mule was a bit more skittish, as Jessie had anticipated. This was clearly the protector of the field, the leader of this motley-looking herd. But Jessie was usually better with the hard cases, and after a few minutes of work, she had the big mule well in hand. She rode to catch up with Francine, and the two of them made their way across the yard and back to the road. Derrick backed the jeep out of the driveway, and the search party began making its way north.

Jessie and Francine rode along the two-lane highway on its eastern side, searching along the way for tracks leaving the road or for a promising backcountry ranch or logging road. Meantime Derrick and Ray scouted farther ahead in the jeep, searching for anything that looked like a promising route. When they encountered one, Derrick would stop the jeep, and Ray would hop out to examine the ground in search of tracks. It was slow going, and they both grew impatient. Crowfoot had a big lead at this point, and he knew the terrain better than they did.

It was midafternoon when the mule that Jessie was riding turned off the road and began walking through low brush and down a slight incline. Jessie tried to turn the mule away from the tangle of low rabbit bush and hawthorn, but to no avail. Francine's mount followed the lead mule, and both riders were soon struggling to turn their mounts out of the low thicket. But before they could regain control, they had burst through the brush and into a narrow open space. A logging track was barely visible snaking through the scattered trees ahead. The slope was gradual and broken here and there by fallen rocks and shallow cuts made by spring runoff.

"Well, that was fun." Francine picked a small thorn from her jeans. "What's with these two?"

"I don't know. Maybe this leads to one of Frank's secret fishing spots." Jessie slid down from the saddle and tied her mule to a nearby hawthorn tree. She looked back toward the road and then walked a few steps ahead down the logging track. "Someone's been down here recently," Jessie said.

Francine nudged her mule ahead and looked down at the ground where Jessie was standing. "Think it's our guys?"

"I'm not sure. Could be fishermen or campers. But this doesn't get any traffic, and it's practically invisible from the main road up there." Jessie nodded back toward the paved road, and Francine followed her gaze. The tangle of brush that the mules had carried them through under protest formed a dense screen. The roadway was barely visible and only in patches here and there.

"These tire tracks look fresh to me—certainly made after the rain," Jessie said.

They called Ray and Derrick, and soon the four of them were studying the tracks and making their way slowly down the old logging road. Derrick agreed with Jessie's read of the tracks. They were fresh, and they appeared to match those of the truck that left the clearing. It wasn't a sure thing. Old trucks like this one were popular in the backcountry. But the clearing near the wreck had been softer ground, and Derrick had gotten a good look at the track of this particular truck. He had noticed a small scar in the tread on one side. The logging road was mostly hardscrabble and drier than the clearing. But now and then Derrick noticed a mark that he thought might be the same one. Derrick also thought the road matched what he would look for if he were in Crowfoot's position—an abandoned backcountry road that was not visible from the main road. It made sense, the trail was fresh, and anyway it looked like their best option.

"What do you think?" Ray was standing with his hands on his hips and examining the dusty ground.

Derrick looked up at him and then stood up from where he had been crouching over the tire tracks. "It looks right. The tracks seem to match, and it is certainly the sort of road I would pick."

"Yeah, I was thinking that too," Ray said. "Only downside for their team is I don't think they can cover it so well from above. But they get points for forest and broken ground on either side, not to mention a lousy road with no room for us to maneuver."

"As though our little jeep and mule team is highly maneuverable to begin with?" Derrick said.

"Good point. I'm pulling up a topo map." Ray moved to a shady spot and studied the screen on his cell phone. Derrick followed, and the two studied the emerging topographical view of the valley. Ray swatted at a gnat and then looked up from the map to the mountains beyond.

Derrick sighed and then broke the silence. "Well, little brother, what would a Delta team do?"

Ray blew out a long breath. "Well, for starters a team of operators would have about five times the firepower we now have in our possession, night vision, air support. Probably wouldn't use a soft-top jeep for anything but suicide missions."

Derrick smiled. "Yeah, but I bet you wouldn't have mountain-ready mules. So seriously, how do you think we should play this?"

"First of all, we can't just keep heading down this road. The topo makes it clear that this road leads into a natural funnel. The bad guys outnumber us, and those ridges are probably well covered by scouts and maybe a sniper or two. Our jeep won't do more than twenty miles an hour anywhere on that road without breaking an axle or slamming into a tree. And the mules, in spite of their obvious talents, aren't so useful down here in the valley. They come in handy up there." Ray pointed to the nearest ridge. "But we don't have enough players on our team to work the high country."

"We could rig the jeep as a decoy."

"On flat ground maybe...But we would need some high-tech gear to make that work here."

The two brothers stood for a moment surveying the road and the mountains beyond. The shadows were falling into a late-afternoon pattern, and the air in the shade was growing cooler.

Derrick turned back to Ray. "We need to come up with our best move and get started. Not much daylight left."

"Yeah. All right, I have an idea. It's not great, but under the circumstances, I think it reduces the risk of the four of us dying while still giving us some shot at rescuing Reuben and his grandfather."

"I'm listening, Ray."

"We need to try a leapfrog—get ahead of these guys and cut them off near their base. I would like the decoy idea if we had the manpower to work the ridges. We could take out a scout or two, and we would be able to infiltrate their communication system. That might even the odds some. But four of us aren't enough, and I'm not liking the idea of picking decoys among the four of us. So I say we go for broke. Take the mules back home and load up in the jeep. The highway runs along the western ridge to this point." Derrick followed Ray's finger to the snaky line of the highway on the cell-phone screen. "And then it cuts pretty sharp to the east here—an elbow into the wilderness area. We can cut off the road from the point of that elbow and make our way over the western ridge and back into the valley down here. Their base camp has to be within a circle of a couple of miles of this point."

"How do you know?"

"About thirty percent is lay of the land and natural barriers. The other seventy percent is my gut. When I first opened this topo, that's the place that caught my eye. That's where I would put it."

"Your gut, huh?" Derrick smiled and shook his head.

"Never misses."

"Except with Darlene Thompson."

"Not my fault. Got bad intel from my brother."

"OK, OK. It sounds as crazy as most of your plans, but I don't have anything better. What happens when the two of us mutts catch this car we are chasing? We can't extract Reuben and his grandfather without some backup."

"Yeah, I know. I was thinking about that too, but you may not like my idea."

"Try me."

"We head back to Frank's to return the mules and load up. But we set up Jessie and Francine there at Frank's house."

"No way. We don't know where these guys are, Ray! For all we know, they might loop back to that house."

"Hear me out. Jessie and Francine won't be alone. When we go back to Frank's house, I will make a call to CI brass. We'll tell Francine to get the whole USAMRIID ball rolling. They'll be inside the base camp, with help on the way. We work reconnaissance and phone back in locations when we make contact with Crowfoot and locate the laboratory."

"The army doesn't turn on a dime, Ray. It will take some time for them to get out here. If we leave Jessie and Francine behind, I also want to call the state police. Let them cover Frank's house until your friends from CI hit the ground."

"That sounds risky to me, Derrick. How do you know that Crowfoot doesn't have someone working for him inside the state police force? After all he is holding a former state trooper hostage right now."

Derrick sighed heavily. "You are probably right. The Guardians wouldn't go into something like this if they were blind on the local level." Derrick turned back and looked at Jessie and Francine. They were leaning against the jeep and holding the reins of the mules, looking like two friends on a camping trip. *What in the world are the four of us doing out here hunting a rogue cop and a crew of bioterrorists?* Slowly Derrick turned back to Ray.

"Can you arm Jessie and Francine—just in case?"

"To the teeth. They'll have the baddest command post in Idaho." Ray smiled.

"We'd better get going. We have a lot of work to do."

Chapter 30

WHEN JESSIE RELEASED the mules, they trotted to the far end of the pasture and joined the wary Appaloosa. One of them brayed his annoyance at being roused to duty by a couple of strangers. The spotted horse shook his head as if in agreement that it had all been a bad idea from the start. Jessie smiled to herself and lingered a few seconds at the fence. The little pasture was pretty, and the animals were well tended. An "I told you so" conversation between horse and mules was just the sort of thing that she found funny and relaxing. She could usually tell something about people by their animals, and these three suggested to Jessie that Frank was quite a character. Jessie turned and began walking back to Frank's house.

The little house was crackling with activity when Jessie returned. Francine and Ray were on their cell phones, each speaking in their own tribal language of army terms and acronyms. Derrick was kneeling near a couch and surveying a floor full of weapons and gear. Three large duffel bags lay crumpled behind him. Ray had apparently packed for the invasion of a small country. When she entered, Derrick looked up, a bit sheepish.

"Oh, hey baby. The mules glad to be home?"

"Pretty tickled. So when does the battalion arrive?"

"No kidding. Ray tends to overpack."

Jessie glanced toward Ray and Francine, who were each lost to their respective conversations. "Can I talk with you a second?" she asked.

"Sure, what's up?"

"In the kitchen?"

Derrick first pointed to the floor as if to say that he was awfully busy, but then he saw Jessie's expression and realized she would not be waved off. He followed Jessie into the small kitchen and leaned against a counter.

"Derrick, I know that we are doing something necessary here. We've all sort of been pulled along in this thing without giving it too much thought. But now you and Ray are talking about going out on some sort of recon against…against, well, who knows? I just want to remind you that it hasn't been that long since I was sitting by your side in the hospital and waiting for you to wake up."

"What are you saying? I didn't ask for this, Jessie—none of us did. But here we are, and Frank and Reuben are in grave danger."

"If they are still alive."

"And a group of terrorists are planning to hurt many more people."

"Which is not exactly a professor's job to stop."

Derrick sighed and looked down at his feet.

"OK, that was a low blow," Jessie whispered. She could hear Francine wrapping up her call. "I'm well aware that your background prepares you for more than grading papers. But you had a close call at the university. It scared me to nearly lose you then, but it scares me more now to think that you might take off on this mission before you are fully recovered. You know how important it is to have your head in the right place."

"I do, Jessie. Really, I do." He pushed off the counter and walked toward Jessie, taking her in his arms. "I get it. And I don't want to miss out on a moment with you either." He held her tight, and Jessie began to soften.

"This has just come up too fast," she whispered.

"I know. Life is crazy that way sometimes. But for some reason, God has us on duty here. We can't walk away from this right now."

"I know."

"But I promise you, Jessie, I am a professor for a reason. I'm long past trying to prove anything to anyone. We simply need to do what we can to help. Also, I promise you that I will take whatever backup Ray and Francine can arrange—no Lone Ranger here, OK?"

"OK. But if you get hurt again, I swear..."

"I know. Listen, you concentrate on taking care of yourself and Francine. Now that I have been pinned to the wall, I want you to promise me that you will stick with the plan and keep your head down. None of your ninja foolishness, OK?"

Jessie smiled up at him. "I promise not to kill anyone—except you if you break any of your promises to me."

"Deal." Derrick kissed her lightly on the forehead just as Francine came bolting into the kitchen.

"Oh, sorry, guys, but Commander Ray requests our presence in the main armory." Francine shot Jessie a wink. Jessie smiled, but Francine could see the worry in her eyes. This was becoming more serious all the time. And although Francine was certain that Ray and Derrick knew the shooting risks that they faced, she and Jessie were the ones who best understood what might happen if the terrorists had a chance to open a Pandora's box of bioterror.

When they entered the main room again, they found Ray sitting in an oversized recliner and fidgeting with his cell phone. He looked up and smiled as the three of them entered.

"Well, glad you all could make it. One hour till go time, and we have a lot to cover." Derrick, Jessie, and Francine sat down on the couch. Ray was across from them in the recliner, and between them were neat bundles of weapons and gear. Ray began running down their plan. Derrick spoke up now and then, but he mostly let Ray run the show. Ray had been known as that rare operator who loved the planning and launching of a mission almost as much as the action itself.

After reviewing their plan, Derrick and Ray began sorting the weapons and electronic gear. They packed some of the heavier weapons and various gadgets in equipment bags. Ray began hauling this gear to the jeep while Derrick helped Francine organize the remaining equipment around the kitchen table. Jessie scrounged for another small table and some other odds and ends from Frank's utility room. Then she returned to the kitchen and helped Derrick and Francine set up the makeshift command post. Francine had brought along her laptop, and pretty soon she and Derrick had arranged a nest of electronic gear around her computer. As Derrick finished up, Francine began making coffee, and Jessie dragged in some more comfortable chairs.

"Quite the cozy command center," Jessie said as she took a seat at the table.

"Yeah," Francine said as she poured a cup of coffee, "I think two girls should be comfortable while they are locating targets and arranging missile strikes."

Derrick rolled his eyes. "Hey, you two—no missile strikes." Derrick pointed a screwdriver at Jessie. "Or heavy artillery or any other foolishness. Me and Ray will have enough to do without dodging ordnance."

"Oh, don't be such a party pooper, baby. Francine has been in the army a long time, and she has never once had a chance to rain down hellfire on someone. Isn't that right, Francine?"

"Not a single time. I feel incomplete somehow."

The three of them laughed, and for a moment it seemed like they were simply three friends gabbing while they installed a new kitchen appliance.

Just then Ray entered the front door and nodded toward Derrick. "We are set. You ready to roll?"

Derrick glanced at Jessie and Francine and then back down at the final connection he needed to make. "Almost. One more line."

Francine handed Ray a cup of coffee as he examined their kitchen table command post.

"Looks tight. Nice work. You two remember that we want to stay nice and quiet until we have our eyes on the target. No communication unless absolutely necessary, and then, Francine, remember to use the protocol we talked about."

"Will do. But, Ray—you remember that Jessie and I have you two on the clock. If we hit the deadline and you haven't checked in, then I will assume control of the operation from here and let the dogs loose."

"Roger that. But we'll make our target. You ready, Radar?"

Derrick stood up and stretched. "OK, command post is all set. Let's go, Ray."

Jessie followed Derrick to the door, and the two stood for a moment holding each other before she whispered in his ear. "If you don't come back to me in one piece, I will hunt you down in eternity."

"Understood. I love you too." Derrick winked at her as he headed out to the jeep. Over his shoulder the evening light was fading into night.

Jessie stood at the door and watched until the taillights of the jeep rounded the next wooded corner on the road north. Then she closed the door and took her seat beside Francine at the kitchen table.

Derrick had always felt a twinge of claustrophobia at dusk in the mountains. Maybe it was because he had grown up in wide-open spaces. There was something comforting about dusk on the high plains, with its razor-sharp line between earth and sky. He loved the mountains in the daytime. Their scale and beauty made him feel appropriately small and, at the same time, closer and more visible to heaven. But as daylight evaporated, the mountains grew dark and faceless. They seemed to close in around the jeep as it hummed along the two-lane highway. Derrick pulled on a field jacket and tried to focus on the flashes of deep forest and rocky terrain spotlighted by the jeep's headlights.

"Getting cooler," Ray said. "Looks like it will be a still night."

Derrick shook himself alert and looked at Ray. His brother was smiling and leaning forward to study the sky above the jeep. Ray had been so jumpy as a kid that his comments were usually running a beat behind his observations. He might mention that a cow looked sick after he had walked on from the cow and was staring at a plant he found fascinating. Derrick had long ago learned to follow these jerky monologues and so didn't bother to comment on the fact that Ray could not read the winds or temperature from studying the stars. What Derrick noticed instead was the ease and contentment on his brother's face. Ray was never more at peace with the world than when he was on a mission.

Derrick smiled to himself and began to catch up with Ray's observations. "Yeah, but cool weather works for me. I'm just glad the bad guys didn't decide to target a winter conference."

"Snow would be a pretty big problem for our team. Can you see the moon?" Ray turned his head and seemed to be trying to peer through the roof of the jeep.

Derrick laughed and shook his head. "Hey, Captain Old School, you heard of something called the Internet? I checked our period of darkness conditions when we were setting up at the house—crescent moon, calm with puffs out of the southwest, clear to partly cloudy, with a twenty percent chance of seeing Bigfoot."

"Already seen him when I was out on road-clearing crew: sort of a disappointment—big wimpy guy." Ray looped his arms over the steering wheel and smiled.

"Speaking of locating Bigfoot, we are about ten clicks from that elbow turn into the woods. Stop when you see the right place for us to start scouting our entry. I will be surprised if the Guardians aren't covering that elbow."

"Closest point of contact to a roadway—that is, if our hunches hold up."

Ray slowed the jeep as they entered a switchback turn. The jeep's headlights panned across a gashed and twisted guardrail. The middle section had been driven over the side of the ridge, and the headlights grazed over a section of empty sky.

"Must have been a gravel truck," Ray whispered absently.

"Didn't end well," Derrick added.

The jeep rounded the turns amid hulking fir and hemlock trees. They were close now, and Ray moved the jeep along at a quiet crawl. The wider shoulders of the road near Frank's house had narrowed to dirt ribbons on either side of the mountain road. They had not seen any signs of a spur or trail leading away from the road so far. According to Ray's topographical map, they should be closing to within a mile or two of the trailhead. Derrick spotted a wider space in the shoulder up ahead and tapped Ray on the shoulder. Ray slid the jeep into the space and cut the engine. The brothers sat still for a moment in the jeep, getting their bearings and listening for anything out of the ordinary.

The wind blew through the trees now and then like a raspy whisper. In the lulls came the thrumming of leopard frogs. A snowmelt creek was running some fifty yards below them. Now and then they could barely make out the distant yapping of coyotes. And then, as if on a single cue, the frogs stopped calling, and the night fell completely still. Ray and Derrick both strained to pick up anything unusual in the silence, but there was nothing. The breeze blew enough to rustle the nearby trees. A lone frog began to call, and shortly the chorus had returned.

Derrick and Ray rose from their seats and began silently taking gear and weapons from the jeep. Derrick motioned toward a small clearing in the trees about twenty yards from where the jeep was parked. They hauled a bag from the jeep and worked together to set up a small tent and arrange an ad hoc campsite. It might not fool a pro, but Derrick and Ray hoped their faux campsite would take care of the worries of any local passerby or law enforcement. Fishermen and hikers often parked their vehicles alongside backcountry roads during the day. But just in case someone was concerned enough to stop and check on a jeep parked way out here at night, Derrick and Ray hoped that the nearby campsite would fill in the picture and relieve their worries. They also hoped that in a pinch their ruse would slow down the Guardians a beat or two. Until they could locate the "campers," they would at least have to ponder the possibility that this was not a bluff.

The road took a meandering course alongside the mountain for the next few hundred yards. Derrick and Ray moved through the shadows along the side of the road that hugged the mountainside. The trees shrouded their movement from anyone who might be watching from above. Nevertheless, Ray stopped at breaks in the cover and carefully examined the higher terrain. Derrick kept a lookout ahead and over the downhill slope.

An owl suddenly began hooting from its lofty perch above where Ray was walking. Ray and Derrick both crouched into cover and froze. They waited for a return call or for any sign of movement along either side of the road. Nothing stirred, but the owl continued to hoot expectantly.

"Damn bird," Ray whispered.

"Just be glad it's really a bird. I see it up there, about fifty feet over your head."

Ray and Derrick scanned the terrain for another minute and then continued making their way along the road. The owl eventually gave up, and Derrick and Ray crept along in near silence. The wind picked up, and the night grew cooler as they made their way through two more switchbacks and out into a widening curve. The road flattened out and widened along this curve. Derrick and Ray were no longer picking their way through low shrubs and saplings. Instead they hugged the rocky breaks alongside the road and at times even risked walking in the shadows of an open stretch. The shoulders were a mix of fine gravel and loose rock.

Derrick began to feel the effect of his time in the hospital and recovering at home. Ray was a step lighter and faster, and Derrick hoped that as they slogged on into the backcountry he would be able to keep up and stay alert. He paused just long enough to pinch his legs hard in a couple of places. As a Ranger he had used pinches and slaps to keep himself going on long maneuvers. Sometimes even a knife prick was required, but he wasn't to that point yet.

"I see the trailhead." Ray crouched and turned back to face Derrick. "Maybe fifty yards ahead, the shoulder widens out to the right. See there?"

Derrick peered over Ray's shoulder. "Downhill side. I'm not sure, but that could be an old lumber company marker on the other side of the road."

"Roger that. We should probably cut through that heavier brush between here and there. I don't like the look of that exposed ground where the trail cuts off the road. They could be covering it from above and at road level."

Derrick and Ray made their way swiftly to the heavy cover and then began turning slowly downhill. The brush was thick, and in places it towered three or four feet above their heads. They were mostly enveloped in the dark brush. And as they wove their way downhill, Derrick could smell the sweet aroma of huckleberries. *We may not have to worry about the terrorists*, he thought to himself as he tried to pick a few huckleberries in the darkness. *The bear who rules this huckleberry patch may find us first.*

Suddenly Ray halted and held up his right hand. Derrick crouched and scanned the labyrinth of brambles and dark forest. At first Derrick saw nothing ahead but more tangle, outlined in places by a light dusting of moonlight. But gradually he saw what looked like an opening just ahead. There was a small seam in the trees, and the brush was not as tall. Their cut through the brush was coming to an end and they were about to join the trail. A mosquito buzzed near Ray's ear, and he cursed the bug's uncanny timing. It sounded to Ray as loud as a helicopter, but he knew that a swat would be the sound that caught attention. And so he ignored the buzzing and began making hand signals to Derrick. It took only a few quick signals to confirm that they were on the same page. This was the jumping-off point. Until now they had mostly been taking a nice little nighttime hike. But once they set foot on this trail, they were down range. If they were right about this base camp, and Ray thought the odds were pretty good, then their enemies would be found somewhere along this trail. Maybe the Guardians would expect them to follow the funnel to a trap they had laid. Or perhaps their leapfrog would catch the terrorists by surprise. In that happy event, they would hit hard and take Reuben and Frank before the Guardians knew what hit them. And they would coordinate with Francine and Jessie to bring hell down on the terrorist's plot.

Then again, the Guardians must know by now that this wasn't Ray and Derrick's first rodeo. What had appeared to the brothers as an obvious trap could also have been a more sophisticated version— the sort of trap that leads Special Forces troops to believe that they have spotted the cheese and outsmarted the cat. They would know soon if they were dodging a simple trap or walking headlong into a more sinister one.

Chapter 31

GHOST AND TUPE kept casting glances back over their shoulder toward the mountains—and toward Crowfoot. When they were sure they were out of earshot, they grumbled to one another about their situation. Each blamed the other for their current predicament. Finally they agreed that they would play this out for now. Sooner or later Crowfoot would make a mistake, and they would be off the hook. They had no intention of serving as his foot soldiers. When they could avoid it no longer without looking suspicious, both Tupe and Ghost ducked into the nearby forest and began searching for firewood.

Meanwhile Crowfoot approached the truck. So far everything was working according to his plan. Tupe and Ghost were dangerous. But to survive they must help him kill Nasim. And both of them were prepared to kill another in order to live. The giant Samoan had only hesitated regarding killing the old man and the boy because he was concerned about consequences in the spirit world. Tupe would have no such qualms about killing Nasim and his cold-blooded followers.

Crowfoot grabbed a water bottle from the cab of the truck and drank half in one long, hard swig. He poured the rest over his head and shoulders and shook like a dog that had just swum to shore. He studied the mountains for a moment through the prism of water droplets and then ran both hands over his head and face.

Time to check on the old man and the boy. Crowfoot walked to the tailgate and began working a knot loose in the corner of the tarp.

"How are you white Indians and that mangy dog getting along back here?" Crowfoot taunted. "Not sure which one of you would have more fleas." Crowfoot walked to the other side of the truck and loosened the knot on that corner. "What—cat got your tongues? Or maybe the dog got your tongues?" Crowfoot chuckled at his own joke and began lifting the edge of the tarp over his head. "What's going on under here?"

Before Crowfoot was able to step back or draw his own pistol, the huge hands were wrapped around his throat.

"Don't—be still or I will choke the life out of you," Frank whispered in Crowfoot's ear.

Crowfoot struggled to breathe and thrashed his hands behind him to try to reach his pistol.

Frank lifted Crowfoot effortlessly into the bed of the truck and onto his back.

"Move again like that, and it will all be over—right here, right now."

Reuben slipped a hand behind Crowfoot's back and took his pistol. He pointed it at Crowfoot's head and smiled. The struggle stopped. Frank eased his grip slightly and then moved his face to within inches of Crowfoot's face.

"Do not make a sound. If you do, we will shoot you—but only after we let the dog have a shot at you first." Reuben reached over and jangled the pin loosely hanging from Bear's cage. Bear's growl was a deep rumble, and his massive teeth were fully bared against the wire cage.

Frank gradually released his grip and tore two strips of his bloody shirt to use as a gag. Crowfoot heaved hard to catch his breath. He managed a raspy whisper to say, "You will never make it out of here alive. There are snipers on the ridge."

"I said no sound." Frank stuffed the gag in Crowfoot's mouth and wrapped the other strip around his head. Then Frank slipped another coil of rope from the tarp and used it to bind Crowfoot's feet.

"I doubt your sniper has x-ray vision, but I guess we are about to find out. You know it would be ironic if he shot you instead of one of us." Frank slid around Crowfoot's trussed-up body and to the back of the cab.

"You ready?" Frank asked Reuben.

"All set."

Frank ran his hands along the sliding window for a moment and then shoved his palms against the frame. The window popped out cleanly and fell onto the pickup seat. Then he reached around and pulled the larger window back out and into the bed of the truck. Frank held the tarp in position while Reuben slid through the open space and into the driver's seat. Whoever might be out there would certainly notice the difference in size between Crowfoot and Frank. But Reuben was just close enough that they might hesitate a second or two. And Frank was hoping that a few seconds was all that they would need.

Reuben tried to calm his pounding heart as he turned the key to start the pickup. The pickup rumbled to life. *Well, it's on now,* Reuben thought as he slid the truck into drive. He pulled away slowly at first, not wanting to rouse attention from any of Crowfoot's crew. But then he saw the Samoan in his rearview mirror, dropping an armful of firewood and running faster than Reuben thought any man that size should be able to run. Reuben stomped on the gas. The pickup slid sideways and launched gravel and dust in plumes. Reuben thought he heard a gunshot, but he couldn't be sure. The next time he looked back, the Samoan was farther away and slowing down. Just then a writhing bundle dropped from the bed of the truck and rolled toward Tupe and Ghost. Frank had given Crowfoot the boot, and he and Reuben were officially on the run. Another crack rang out, and this time Reuben knew it was a gunshot because the bullet crashed through the driver's side of the windshield. Reuben veered toward a stand of trees on one side of the old logging road. The ground was level here, and the truck gained speed. Soon Reuben felt confident enough to stop. Frank winced as he slid from the bed of the truck and then hustled to open the door. He let Bear in first and then piled in after him and slammed the passenger door. Reuben hit the gas again, and the three of them went flying down the backcountry road.

Nasim paced the hallway and checked his watch again. This time Crowfoot had crossed the line. His tough-guy routine and cavalier attitude was one thing, but now the head of security for the Guardians was compromising the mission.

At least Nasim had been given warning. He knew better than to fully trust Crowfoot. He had made a backup plan, a fallback created without Crowfoot's knowledge. He and the leader of their operational team had secretly agreed that if Crowfoot was late by more than one hour, the packet was to be transported without him. The Guardians would be prepared to strike, with or without Crowfoot.

Nasim relaxed for the first time that afternoon, smiling at the thought of Crowfoot missing his own show. In the next room and down the hallway, he could hear the sounds of his crew dismantling the laboratory. His life's work was coming to a brilliant close. They had said that prions were not subject to manipulation. *How could one turn something that was not quite alive into a biological weapon?* His colleagues in the movement had argued that he was wasting money and time. All of them believed that the *big fist* was to be found in the deadly bacteria or viruses. *The Black Plague*, they had declared, any number of times and often at the top of their voices, *we must create a modern and more deadly version of the Black Plague!*

Pigheadedness. These men had shown no creativity, no appreciation for the elegant solution. They would use a grenade to kill a mosquito.

Fortunately for Nasim, scientists in Europe and the United States had mostly followed the worn-out logic of the most vocal and pigheaded Guardians. They had focused their defenses on ancient plagues and fantasy superbugs. And so they were secure, perhaps many times over, against an outbreak of smallpox or a dust storm of supercharged anthrax.

But Nasim had cracked the code. He had remained diligent and undeterred. He had tolerated the doubters and outmaneuvered opponents. Even the mighty Crowfoot had only caused him mild irritation. His nervousness and pleading had mostly been an act, a persona that gave Crowfoot's inflated ego something distracting to push against. It had also allowed him to convince Crowfoot that he had more power with the other Guardians than was the case. Nasim as the agitated and furtive scientist was a foil that helped Nasim and the other true leaders reassure Crowfoot of his power in the organization.

Crowfoot had played his part brilliantly. Every organization of their type needed a charismatic and foolhardy figurehead—the supreme martyr.

Nasim's reverie was interrupted by the sounds of a centrifuge winding down. The whirring came from a room near his old office. It was the last room of the complex that was still in operation. And the slowing of the centrifuge marked the close of even this operation. This was the final packet.

Nasim checked his watch again and then began walking to the small room that contained the dying centrifuge. *Perhaps Crowfoot is already dead*, Nasim thought suddenly. He was surprised that the thought didn't please him. Certainly he had dreamed a thousand times about the moment when he would know that Crowfoot was dead. But that was it—he wanted to know. Learning that Crowfoot had been killed by one of their enemies or even by one of his ridiculous hired killers would not have the same satisfaction of Nasim's dreams. Crowfoot was seriously late now, and that might require Nasim to adjust some of his plans. But as he entered the small room and moved to the centrifuge, Nasim committed himself to seeing all of his dreams come true.

Chapter 32

JIM CROWFOOT LANDED hard on rocky ground and rolled over choking in the dust. The old man's grip had been more powerful than he could have imagined. Crowfoot wavered between seeing shooting stars and sensing a black shade coming down over him.

He could hear the truck roaring away and the idiotic shouting of Ghost and the Samoan. A shot rang out from the hillside. *Good*, Crowfoot thought. *Drill that old man. And then I want to personally deal with the boy and that mongrel dog.*

Crowfoot felt the Samoan's giant hands on his chest. Ghost was standing over him and smiling. "Well, well...," Ghost began and then was cut off by a barked order from someone else nearby.

"Get back, both of you! Hands where I can see them."

Crowfoot strained his neck and located the source of the orders. It was one of the Guardian scouts. Once the scout had backed Ghost and Tupe away, he moved to Crowfoot's side and drew a large hunting knife from its sheath. He quickly sliced through the ragged cloth and tattered rope and then stood and held his rifle level at Tupe and Ghost. The scout glanced back down where Crowfoot lay writhing on the ground.

"Jim, you OK?"

"Did you shoot them?" Crowfoot croaked.

"Not unless they were hit by ricochet. No clean shots."

Crowfoot stood slowly and coughed. He put his hands on his knees and breathed heavily.

"That old Indian has quite a grip. So you say that you didn't shoot him or the boy?"

"Jim, we were shooting through trees at the top of a moving—"

Crowfoot sprang so suddenly that the scout had no time to react. In one swift upward movement, he had taken the rifle, leaped back, and fired three times.

The scout fell where he stood, red stains over both lungs and his heart. A gasping moan rose along with the dust surrounding his body. And then everything was quiet and still.

Crowfoot was still heaving in breaths, but he was standing upright, and his face was hard and blank. He casually turned toward Tupe and Ghost.

The two stood frozen in place. Tupe was staring at the scout's body, watching the circle of red growing outward in the dust. Ghost was looking straight at Crowfoot. He smiled and spoke softly. "Nice shooting. No wasted rounds."

"Shut up!" Crowfoot gasped, loud enough that it surprised Ghost and Tupe.

Crowfoot seemed surprised at this own voice, and he wiped a hand across the dust and spittle on his face. His eyes narrowed, and he raised the rifle to his shoulder.

"You let them go, didn't you, Ghost! You and your big dumb buddy here decided to just let them go!"

Ghost held out one hand. "Whoa, Crowfoot, back up now. You have this all wrong. Why in the world would we do that? If you will recall, Tupe and I wanted to kill them all right here."

"Yeah, I do remember that. I had a different plan. So maybe you two geniuses decided not to go along with my plan. Maybe you had another plan of your own."

"Crowfoot, look at the dead man on the ground there. Before all the shooting started, you told me and Tupe that these hills were covered up with guys like him—snipers and scouts. Maybe you didn't get along with this one so much, but our impression was that you had your own little army out here. Tupe and I have been around some. We know the odds. We were following your lead here."

"And what if I don't believe you?"

Crowfoot's eyes were steady, but Ghost could see the faintest tremor of the rifle barrel. Ghost shook his head slowly and looked down at the body of the scout. He looked up slowly and met Crowfoot's gaze.

"Well, boss, nothing me and Tupe can do about that. But I don't think another burst of rifle fire is going to help your cause much. Whoever your remaining enemies might be, they should be on alert by now. So you can shoot us and go face them alone or put that rifle down and let the three of us get on with our business."

Tupe shifted his weight, and Crowfoot swung the rifle around to aim at his huge chest.

"Whoa, Crowfoot!" Tupe put his hands higher in the air. "Ghost is right. We aren't your enemy."

Crowfoot gradually lowered the rifle. Sweat was beading along his forehead and mingling with the dust on his face. Tupe watched in fascination as Crowfoot's face slipped back from extreme agitation to its usual stone-cold expression. The eyes that only seconds ago seemed to be burning coals were now flat and cold.

"Move the body to the woods over there and cover our tracks." Crowfoot cradled the rifle and pointed toward the tree line with his free hand. "But if I find out later that you double-crossed me on this, I will hunt you both down. You understand?"

Ghost smiled and motioned for Tupe as he began moving toward the scout's body. "I understand perfectly, Crowfoot. Hunting down an enemy is one thing that Tupe and I understand perfectly. Right, Tupe?"

"Yep." The Samoan scooped up the scout's body with one easy motion and heaved it over his shoulder.

Ghost gave Crowfoot a smile and a wink and then began working to cover their tracks.

Crowfoot understood the mercenary mind-set better than most men. But as he watched Ghost stomping dust into the pool of blood, he felt a shiver up his spine. He needed them to help him get this job done. But he would also need to keep a close eye on them every minute. They were an odd pair, this cold-blooded assassin and his giant sidekick. But they were also a dangerous pair. When Tupe returned from the woods, they began to make their way out of the clearing. As they walked together, Crowfoot wondered if he would soon regret his decision to lower the rifle instead of firing just two more shots.

They walked in silence until they reached a broken ridge that cut through the valley. On the other side lay deeper forest and the twisted and overgrown path to the laboratory. Crowfoot held a hand to his eyes and studied the fading light on the western horizon. He needed to get to the laboratory and make sure that Nasim did not spoil the glorious conclusion of his plan. But the old man and the boy were a more immediate concern. Those two had caused far too much trouble already, and as long as they were on the run, there was the risk that they could ruin everything. They had crossed the clearing and then taken an old overgrown logging track, barely visible before the truck roared back over it. The cover and closeness to the mountain face had saved them from the sniper and given them a running start. Had they driven straight ahead on the same track that had brought them to this point, they would never have made it out of the field. They were clever at times, his enemies. Of course, what the old man and the boy couldn't know was that the road that they had taken was a short one. A landslide had long ago severed the old timber road.

Heading north would lead them to the primitive footpath and on their way to the laboratory. But Crowfoot turned his gaze west and studied the broken rock and heavy brush leading back down near the valley floor. The old logging road was down there, hidden from his view by the taller brush and deepening shadows. They would need to cover rough ground to make it to the landslide before nightfall. And even in broad daylight, the rock pile and the brushy ground nearby would provide perfect cover for the old man and the boy.

"What are you looking for?" Tupe had taken a seat on a boulder nearby and was trying hard to catch his breath.

Ghost stood under a tree nearby, cupping his hands to light a cigarette. His breathing was steady and regular, and in the glow of the lighter, Crowfoot could see the usual crooked smile, like a man who knew the joke ahead of time.

"We need to take care of the old man and the boy before we go to the lab. They are down there somewhere, likely taking cover for the night."

Ghost blew smoke between pursed lips and walked over to study the area Crowfoot had just pointed out. He squinted and turned his head to study the ragged rocks and thick brush. "Looks like a great place to set an ambush."

"Yeah, I thought I would send you in first."

Ghost blew out smoke and smiled. "Why waste our time on those two anyway, Crowfoot? Leave them in that rock pile, and let's get on to that lab. The old man and the boy are no threat now. They can't drive that truck out of here without getting shot. Both of them are hurt, and it will take a day or two for them to make their way out this wilderness. They might even cooperate with us and die on their own before they make it out of here."

Tupe had caught his breath now, and he was leaning over with his elbows on his knees. His face was resolute and sullen. "I agree. And besides, I don't feel like huffing it over a bunch of rocks to hunt down an old man and a boy."

"We're going to split up," Crowfoot replied.

"What?" Ghost looked back down the ridge, as though he might find something there that would help him make sense of what Crowfoot had just said.

Crowfoot watched him scan the ground below for a second before he spoke again. "The old man and the boy know this country well. And, even though it is hard to tell sometimes, the two of them are still Nez Percé. They will not die in some hidey-hole. And we cannot leave them out here to cause us trouble."

"OK, but why split up?" Ghost had stopped scanning the terrain and had turned to face Crowfoot. "You apparently have other enemies in the area, including down there somewhere at this lab. We should stick together."

"No." Crowfoot motioned back over his shoulder toward Tupe. "The Samoan will sound like a buffalo coming down into that rock pile. You said yourself that it looks like a great place to set an ambush."

Ghost turned to look at Tupe. Tupe shrugged.

"All right, Crowfoot. So what's our play?"

"I will go after the old man and the boy. You two will begin making your way toward the lab. I will get you started along the route. Once I take care of those two troublemakers, we will meet up and move together on the lab."

"Won't your shots raise an alarm this close to that lab?" Tupe asked.

"I don't plan to fire any shots." Crowfoot tapped the sheath on his belt that held a long, black tactical knife.

Chapter 33

"Com check. This is Panther."

Jessie was relieved to hear Derrick's voice. She quickly clicked on her handset and responded. "Clear, Panther. This is Lightning."

"Roger, Lightning. Panther in-country and mobile."

Derrick signed off and then listened for a moment to the sounds of the forest around him. He was trained to hear nothing in particular but anything out of pattern. So far everything sounded just like a forest in the Idaho highlands on an early summer night.

Ray tapped him on the shoulder and motioned ahead. They were close now. If their hunch was a good one, the base camp should be just over the next rise. In any case they knew that this ridge was a high point. Assuming they could make their way to the ridgeline without interference, Ray and Derrick would have a good view of the small valley below.

But they expected interference. Ridgelines and rocky outcroppings surrounded the small valley. On a larger scale, it would be a tough place to defend. But a relatively small force could guard a camp set in this isolated little valley. Controlling a half dozen key points along the ring of high ridges and deep forests would give defenders excellent sight lines and firing lanes.

Suddenly Ray signaled Derrick to go to ground. Ahead and just to his left, Derrick could make out the sound of rustling in the thick brush. They were still in fairly deep cover and some fifty yards away from the ridge.

The sounds were coming from a dense tangle of cedars and high shrubs. Thick grass grew at the edges of the tangle, and it appeared to Derrick that this was a marshy spot, likely either a slight depression that was pooling snowmelt or one of the many small springs that dotted the mountains. He listened for the sound of water but heard none. It was tough to walk silently in water. But otherwise this marshy spot offered good cover. If they had already spooked a scout assigned to an observation point on the ridge, he might have retreated to this defensive cover.

Derrick watched over Ray's shoulder for any sign of movement in the dense brush. The wind rustled in the trees. But otherwise the hillside was quiet and still. Ray was just turning to signal that he was going to move in for a closer look when Derrick heard footsteps in the marshy patch. Ray heard them too, and he turned slowly back to his rifle sight. Whoever was now tromping through that wet ground had either failed to spot Derrick and Ray yet, or he had plenty of backup. Derrick slowly slid his safety mechanism and easily lined up his sights on the sound. This was far too early for a shootout. They had no idea if Frank or Reuben were anywhere around, and they hadn't even spotted the camp. Firing now would mean only one thing—a running gun battle to survive. They would be hotfooting it to the jeep without rescuing hostages or slowing down the terrorists. Alarm bells would ring, and the hounds would be set loose. Derrick slowed his breathing and prayed that this scout—perhaps a rookie—would miss two special ops guys hugging the ground within a stone's throw of his lookout post.

Suddenly the brush parted slightly, and Derrick caught a reflection in his scope. *Could be a watch on an arm*, Derrick thought, *or...*

the tip of a massive antler. As Ray eased away from his rifle, the bull moose shook his antlers through the brush and stepped into the open. Derrick almost laughed out loud but quickly choked the reflex. Their reaction to a moose could reveal them to a nearby scout. And they weren't exactly out of immediate danger. The bull was easily fifteen hundred pounds and in no hurry to leave his forage. Thankfully he hadn't sensed their presence. There was nothing to do but wait him out. After what seemed like an eternity, the old bull sniffed the air, snorted, and shuffled on down the hillside.

Derrick and Ray unfolded themselves from their frozen positions and began making their way silently uphill. The ground was rough and broken by patches of scree and thick brush. Derrick and Ray checked their footing before setting each step. They worked their way along the edges of the brush to avoid giving an outline to anyone who might be sweeping the area with binoculars. It was a slow and painstaking way to cover ground. Derrick thought of Jessie back at the makeshift command post and felt a clock ticking in his head. He knew that there was no other way to accomplish this mission than to move deliberately. But the sooner he was back home with Jessie, the better. They had both had more than their share of riding the rodeo over the past few months.

Out of the blue, Derrick heard a voice.

"Hill Nine, what's up?"

Derrick and Ray shared a puzzled look and then cocked their ear toward the sound of the voice near the crest of the ridge.

"You worry too much, Hill Nine. The trucks have already rolled. We are just killing time until the bosses pack their bags. Hey—you got any girls over there?"

Derrick and Ray had both fixed on the sound. The scout was leaning against a massive tree at the edge of a brushy pile. He was

291

sitting down on the other side of the tree trunk and facing the valley. The handset was in his right hand, and now and then Derrick could make out the tip of his elbow peeking out from behind the tree.

"I thought so! You dog...Hold on, Hill Nine, HQ."

"This is Hill Eleven. No, sir. Must be interference from a ranch in the area. Roger that, HQ. Radio silence. Fixed band."

Derrick noticed that Ray was pressing the record button on his handheld, capturing the scout's voice.

"All clear, HQ. Nothing to report from this post."

"Roger that. What's his ETA?"

"Understood. Will maintain lookout for Eagle One and notify immediately."

"Roger, HQ, over and out."

Derrick and Ray could make out that the scout was shifting his weight and fiddling with the settings on his handheld.

"Hill Nine, I'm back. Listen, my girl just showed up, so I better give her my undivided attention. We'll catch up more when we get back to The Six."

Ray and Derrick moved quietly to the brush line that ran to the big tree where the scout was seated. They crouched back to back and made visual sweeps for anyone else in the area. It appeared that the scout posted to guard duty on Hill 9 was alone.

Ray left the brush line and circled the tree on the clear side. He was on the scout before the man realized that anyone was nearby. A few quick blows, and the man toppled over. Derrick and Ray quietly dragged the unconscious scout into the brush and trussed him with zip lines and clear duct tape. They made a quick search of his pockets but found nothing but lint and old chewing gum. If this guy was a terrorist, he was certainly not a varsity player, more likely an expendable watchman.

The brief conversation that Derrick and Ray had heard between the two scouts indicated that the bioweapon had already rolled out and the camp would soon be abandoned. If the leaders of this outfit were worth their salt, Derrick felt certain that they would destroy their base camp on the way out. And likely the scouts on Hills 9 and 11 would never make it to the postgame party either.

"Ray, we may have gotten to this party a little late. That scout chatter sounded like their bioweapon is already on the move."

"Yeah, I caught that. What are you thinking?"

Derrick rubbed his chin and looked down toward the compound. "I'm working on it."

Ray worked the scout's handset while Derrick dusted the ground and took his first look at the valley below them. The valley was shaped like a bowl and only a few miles across at any one point. It was mostly carpeted by dense forest. Here and there rocky outcroppings broke through the forest. The western side of the valley was dotted with marshy ground. Sparkles of moonlight shone off the small pockets of water, slashed now and then by the vibrating reflections of reeds. The eastern side of the valley was more densely forested, carpeted by thick hemlock and towering Douglas fir trees.

Derrick's heart had sunk when he first swept the valley with his binoculars, and he almost missed the camp altogether. Only an odd bend in a roof line snagged his attention. Working from that point, he made his way along the contours of the building and surrounding compound. Whoever had designed and constructed this place was good at making large things invisible.

The building was set at a height to match the surrounding hemlocks, and its roof was sodded over. The builders had cut the main cover trees to perfect height and then filled in with live brush and shrubs. Derrick could only make out the faintest lines of spider netting from this distance. From the air even a search-plane crew might fly a dozen rounds over this valley without spotting any sign of a building.

Now that his eyes were adjusted to the contours of the place, Derrick could make out the rough poles of several animal pens. They were arranged to look like dead and falling trees, with brush woven through the spaces. At the front of the compound was a small open area, undoubtedly cleared for communication purposes. The front of the building was windowless and as black as ink. Derrick lowered the binoculars and studied the ground that dropped away from the ridge-line and down toward the compound. He was thankful for a slivered moon. But it was still going to be tough to make it down to the valley floor without being spotted. Satisfied that he had located the best available route, Derrick turned back to check in with his brother.

Ray was hunched over the headset with one hand cupped around his ear. He changed settings and then listened for a moment more.

"All good," Ray whispered. "I have this set to play 'Roger that' and 'All clear' a few times in response to any calls." Ray tapped a small device now attached to the scout's headset. "Ready to set him up?" Ray nodded toward the scout.

Derrick nodded.

Ray removed a syringe from a kit and slipped the needle into the scout's shoulder. The man's eyes opened wide, and he briefly struggled against his restraints. Ray put his forearm over the man's chest, and Derrick pinned his feet to the ground. In a few seconds, he fell limp, and Ray and Derrick released their grip. Ray closed his kit and checked the man's pulse. He gave Derrick a thumbs-up sign, and they slowly moved the man back to his original seated position in front of the huge tree. They taped the man's arm in a crooked position.

"I spotted our compound," Derrick whispered. "Check it out— bent roof line." Derrick handed Ray the binoculars and steered him to a starting point.

Ray whistled softly. "Nearly invisible. And rigged."

"Yep. Electronic trip lines maybe fifty feet out. One dead drop on this blind side. I imagine there is a matching one on the other side."

"We'll need to break their perimeter down before we take them offline. Otherwise we may get tied up in there and give them too much time to recover."

"Roger that."

Ray lowered the binoculars and handed them back to Derrick. He picked up the headset again and taped it in the scout's hand. "He looks good, don't you think?" Ray smiled.

"As good as when we found him."

Derrick pointed the way to his chosen route and took a step toward the shadows of the hillside.

"Derrick, wait." Ray grabbed his brother's arm. "Hold up a second."

"What's up?"

"I think we need to break this off and go after that convoy."

Derrick turned and sat on his haunches. "Ray, we do that, and we are leaving Reuben and Frank out here someplace with that maniac Crowfoot."

"Brother, listen. We only have time to do one thing. We either press on with this recon search-and-rescue mission, or we break off and go try to stop terrorists from launching a bioweapons attack. Doing one means not doing the other."

"What if the scout had it wrong? He wasn't much of a scout, so maybe he wasn't up to speed on the overall plan either. What if everything we are looking for is sitting down there in that compound? Hell, Frank and Reuben could be locked up down there for all we know."

"I think Ray is right."

Derrick and Ray froze. The deep bass voice was behind them—and unmistakable. *Frank*.

"Doesn't make sense wasting time helping two Nez Percé who don't need any help."

Derrick could just make out Frank's huge outline against the brush. He and Reuben crept over and knelt beside them. Derrick and Ray smiled and shook their heads.

"Where the hell have you two been, and how did you get away?"

Bear slunk out of the shadows and rumbled his low growl.

"Make that the *three* of you. Easy, boy." Ray held up both palms.

Frank whispered something to the big dog. Bear nosed Derrick and Ray suspiciously, including their gear. Satisfied for the moment, he lay down in front of them.

"Yeah, he seems to want to go wherever we are going. The whole thing is a long story," said Frank. "But what you need to know now is that we broke away from Crowfoot and his helpers a few miles southwest of here. We took his pickup. It gave us a head start, but we abandoned it where an old logging road was cut off by a landslide. We hid the truck and made some nice tracks down into the pile for Crowfoot and his pals to follow. Then we crossed your tracks and came here."

"Let me take a look at that." Derrick pointed to Frank's leg.

Ray motioned Reuben to show him his arm. Neither man protested as Derrick and Ray cleaned their wounds and secured them the best they could.

"You both need medical attention soon. But this should hold you tight so we can get out of here.," Ray said.

"Why didn't Crowfoot and his goons kill us right away?" Reuben asked. "What's he up to anyway?"

"That's a *really* long story," Ray replied. "We'll talk later. But now we better get moving before someone else picks up our trail. Frank, what about the dog? He could give us all away."

"He won't," Frank replied. "I will keep him with me."

Crowfoot couldn't believe his luck. He had intersected their tracks. Crowfoot was only a third of the way down into the rock pile when he noticed the broken twig. And just below the break was a track that looked like a set of nails had been driven into the ground. It was maybe the one spot within a hundred-foot circle where the big dog could have stepped down, and his nails made that impression. All around was hard rock and thick ground cover. But here, standing out like the glimmer of a gold nugget, was a clear track of a big dog.

The old man and the boy had been clever up to this point. They'd ditched the truck and then made a set of off-and-on tracks down into the rock pile. Their tracks downhill were just faint enough to be convincing and just obvious enough to not be missed. The old man must have hoped that Crowfoot would waste a good deal of time here, moving slow and watching for ambush. And while Crowfoot was creeping down the incline, the old man and the boy would be making their getaway.

But the tedious work of the old man and the boy was all undone now. They had covered their uphill tracks well, but the nail prints of that monster dog were deep and took time to cover completely. Crowfoot knelt and checked to make sure that the prints did not belong to a wild animal. He smiled as he examined the prints. Only the big dog could have made these tracks. Crowfoot was close to his quarry now. He still had time to scoop up these two strays on his way to deal with Nasim.

Crowfoot stood and began following the dusted remains of the trail. The dog's track had saved him a long and difficult scramble down into the valley and back up again. And although he would never have admitted it to Ghost or Tupe, Crowfoot had not been looking forward to that descent into darkness and heavy cover. It was just as he had told Ghost—the old man and the boy were Nez Percé. They were both known to be good hunters. And no doubt the old man had set his share of traps for criminals on the run. Crowfoot considered himself a master hunter. But in rough terrain and growing darkness, his odds of beating the old man's ambush were probably just about even.

Crowfoot turned and began following the tracks back to higher ground. They had left very little sign. But now that his eyes were conditioned to look for their pattern, Crowfoot could just make out enough to track their course. Now and then he lost them and had to circle back or crouch down and study the ground more carefully. It was more difficult to see in the dusky light. After he had made his way for what he guessed was a little over a mile, Crowfoot stopped suddenly. He could see fragments of boot prints in a bit of muddy ground at his feet—commando boots. It might be the tracks of hunters. Crowfoot knelt down to examine the tracks more carefully. The prints were made by military-issue boots, of the sort commonly worn by commandos for desert duty. They looked fresh, although he could not tell for sure. It was a long shot, but in his gut Crowfoot felt that it might be the tracks of those two cowboys that had interfered with his plans before.

The wind was picking up, and now it washed over him. She seemed to be calling to him, and Crowfoot could see her brushing a strand of her long black hair from her face and shielding her eyes to see a purple kite he had made for her. She was always amused by the sight of it dipping and soaring overhead and by the sight of her burly soldier manning the kite string. He could hear her laugh as she ran under the swooping kite.

Crowfoot opened his eyes suddenly and looked at the ground around him. They were all down this trail, not far from where he was standing. But the rescuers had not arrived here out of thin air. Their trail also went back. Behind him lay their trailhead and their point of entry. Crowfoot turned quickly and began working his way in a circle around the intersection. The cowboys must be heavily equipped, and they had made little effort to cover their tracks. Crowfoot easily picked up their trail and began following it back down the ridge and toward the rugged road on the other side.

Chapter 34

JESSIE GOT UP from the table and walked to the small kitchen for another cup of coffee. It had been two hours since that first communication check. She knew it would take time for Derrick and Ray to make their way into position. She had reminded herself any number of times that they were both experts, that they were highly trained and exceptionally good at this sort of work. She had tried to push out of her mind that they were approaching a terrorist base camp, that Derrick was maybe not yet back to full strength, that the two brothers had never actually worked together on such a mission.

Coffee would help. Jessie swatted her thigh as she strode to the kitchen, something she had done as a girl to give her courage for barrel racing. And something she still did on occasion just before treating a wild-eyed horse or restless bull. Many times the ritual had worked to give release to her anxiety, to redirect a stampede of fear into concerted action. It wasn't working so well now.

Jessie waited for Frank's old coffeepot to finish gurgling and hissing and then poured two cups of coffee. She returned to the command-post table and placed one of the cups in front of Francine. Francine looked up and mouthed her thanks and then quickly turned back to an ongoing phone conversation.

"Yes, I'm still here, sir. No, I'm sure I don't understand every-thing that would be involved on your end...Right, sure, I can see that..." Francine looked to Jessie and rolled her eyes.

Jessie smiled back and gave her an exaggerated thumbs-up.

"But this is one of those unusual situations, sir. This is one of those times when I simply have to ask you to trust me and take ac-tion...No, I really can't hold...Hello? Hello?" Francine chucked the cell phone down on the table and stretched her arms over her head.

Jessie took a sip of coffee. "Make a new friend?"

Francine brought her arms down and made a circle with her hands. "How many years do you think I would get for strangling that guy?"

Jessie laughed. For just a moment she could almost forget that they were hunkered down and in the fight of her life. They could be working on some interesting lab project, and Francine could be bark-ing at a lazy lab technician.

"Any luck on your end?"

"None. My contact with the Idaho Health Department is on vacation. The other people I spoke with weren't buying. It's a scary thought, but I think they were mostly afraid of passing on a crackpot to their bosses."

"I guess career risk is real. A bioterror attack sounds more like fiction."

"Until it's for real."

"No kidding." Francine gently set her coffee cup down on its saucer—or what she thought was a saucer. Jessie knew that Francine was more of a cup and saucer girl, so she had scrounged Frank's cup-board for a butter plate. Close enough to fool her for now.

"I'm thinking we may have to ratchet this thing up, Jessie. The state and local people are a washout."

"We agreed to wait on word from the guys. They should be calling soon."

"I'm not talking about letting the dogs loose. I just think it's time to make the sort of calls that get the engines warmed up and the people in position."

Jessie studied the surface of the coffee in her cup. The liquid was circling slowly. A thin curl of steam was rising off the surface and twisting into a ropy funnel cloud.

Nasim was securing his notes for transport when he heard a breathless scout come in the front door. Moments later his most trusted guard strode down the hall and stopped at his office door.

"Yes, what is it?"

"A scout just arrived from Sector Six. He says that he and another scout spotted activity at the old man's house—lights and movement."

"And nothing from Crowfoot?"

"No, sir, not since his last contact around oh nine hundred this morning."

"Well then, Captain, it appears we will have to clean up this mess ourselves. Gather a few good men from your unit and bring my truck around."

"Yes, Nasim." The captain gave a nod of respect and then turned and strode back down the hallway.

Nasim could hear his firm voice calling names and giving orders. Only a short time later, he heard the truck rumble by outside his office and grind the gravel as it came to a stop near the front door. Nasim slipped a pistol into his coat pocket and lifted an old leather satchel from its resting place behind his desk.

Nasim walked down the hallway and then came to a stop at a small office near the front door. A young man wearing wire-rimmed glasses was removing files from drawers and placing them in moving boxes. Nasim knocked twice on the doorframe, and the young man startled and wheeled around in his chair.

"Oh, Doctor, it is you."

"Sorry to have startled you, Raheem. I need you do something important for me."

"Of course, of course..." The young man nodded his hand and at the same time waved Nasim into his office.

Nasim stepped in and closed the office door.

Derrick led them by a different route back to the jeep. The path that he and Ray had taken into the forest was easier than this one. But Derrick wanted to make sure that they were not making it easy for any of the Guardian scouts to lay an ambush for their return. He could not assume that all of the scouts were as hapless as the one posted on Hill 9. Crowfoot and his gang might be out here somewhere as well, although Derrick guessed that he might have located his hidden truck by now and headed to the Guardians' base camp.

Ray and Derrick helped Frank and Reuben over some of the rougher and steeper ground, although both men displayed remarkable steadiness in spite of their injuries. It was slow going, and Derrick could see Ray fidgeting and grinding his chewing gum. His brother carried a tactical clock inside his head—a more sophisticated version of the eight-second countdown he had lived by as a bull rider—and Derrick could see that Ray was feeling behind schedule. They needed to get clear of the backcountry and catch up with Nasim before it was too late.

The small group finally closed on the roadside. Derrick stopped them just before the break in the trees. Ray scanned the forest behind them while Derrick slipped between trees and crouched in the shadows at the edge of the road. The road was still and quiet. Derrick didn't hear the tree frogs that he had noticed on their arrival. Then a lone frog cranked up a song and was answered by a few scattered individuals. A faint breeze stirred the tops of the trees now and then. Moonlight and shadows shifted with the breeze across the rock and gravel of the road. Derrick could just make out the jeep tucked in the shadows of some larger trees on the downslope side of the road. He could also make out the top edge of the tent in their decoy campsite. Derrick made one more complete scan and then turned and gave Ray the all-clear signal.

As Derrick had suspected, Ray was antsy. He nudged Reuben and Frank along and then loped over the rise and onto the road. Ray kept his assault rifle in front of him, sweeping the road as he walked toward the jeep. Frank and Reuben took time to catch their breath and stretch in the shadows near the road, while Derrick and Ray walked on ahead. Ray arrived at the jeep first. Following patterns ingrained in him by his time as a Delta operator, Ray circled the jeep and examined the surrounding ground. No prints. No signs of broken twigs or cigarette butts. Derrick stood guard on the road, glancing back toward Reuben and Frank as they made their way slowly toward the jeep and then shifting his gaze along the uphill side of the road.

Ray made his way down to their faux campsite and checked for signs of visitors. The only tracks were made be a raccoon. *He probably saw the tent and figured he would score an easy meal from a sleeping camper,* Ray thought and smiled to himself. Satisfied that the raccoon had been the only visitor, Ray quickly stowed the camp gear in a duffel and made his way back up to the roadside.

When he was within a few yards of the jeep, Ray set the duffel on the ground, crouched, and then dropped down to his hands and knees. He inspected the ground underneath the jeep, as well as the underside of the jeep itself: no signs of scuffled ground and no wires or other telltale signs of mischief. *All clear. Time to roll.*

Ray called softly to Derrick. "Firing her up; then we'll load up and head out."

"Roger that." Derrick walked up the road to accompany Reuben and Frank the short distance back to the jeep.

Ray opened the door of the jeep and was lowering himself to the driver's seat when something caught his eye. The spot was small, and anyone else would have missed it. But Ray's eyes were conditioned by combat, and the tiny smudge on the steering column jumped out to him as clearly as if a rattlesnake had been left coiled in the driver's seat. Ray sprang from the jeep and shouted for Derrick and the others to take cover.

Ray had just turned his back and taken his first running step when the jeep exploded and a fireball flew toward the tops of the fir trees.

"What the hell was that?" The sound was like a distant clap of thunder, but the reverberations had rattled her coffee cup.

Francine shook her head and listened for a second longer. "Sounded like a blast. Do they do mining out here?"

Jessie bolted out the front door. Francine followed. From Frank's small porch, the two of them scanned the mountains in the distance. They stood motionless and listening, but there was no other sound.

"Grab some binoculars please."

"Jessie, that was probably a mining blast or some road work." Silence. Francine darted back inside and returned with a pair of military binoculars.

"Really, Jessie, the guys would have radioed if there was trouble. I think that sound was something unrelated. We should get back inside."

"I see smoke."

"Where?"

"There." Jessie pointed with one hand and passed off the binoculars to Francine with the other.

"Maybe a lightning strike?" Francine strained to make out the contours of the smoke cloud, but they were tough to make out across the distance and the darkness. Then she realized she was standing on the porch alone.

"Jessie...Hey, Jessie..." Francine ducked back in the house through the open door. She walked through their makeshift command center and to a small back bedroom where she saw that a light had been switched on.

Jessie had dumped a shotgun on the bed alongside her purse. She looked up from searching a dresser top when Francine entered the room.

"Have you seen my keys?"

Francine tried a calming smile and reached out to the bed. "Hey, Jess, why don't we take a breath here and figure this out together."

"I'm going, Francine. Something's wrong out there."

"Whoa, Jessie, we don't know that. We don't know anything except that we heard a loud noise and saw some smoke."

"We don't have time to argue! You stay here and keep the fort. I've got to go to Derrick."

"That's *one* plan. Here's another one..." Francine knew that she could only stall Jessie so long before she would simply bull past her and head out into the night. "We have a radio. Let's call the guys and check on them."

Francine and Jessie returned to the front room and began trying to make contact with Derrick and Ray.

"Panther, this is Lightning. Come in, Panther." Francine repeated the call every few seconds, and she and Jessie listened intently in the spaces between. After a half dozen attempts, Jessie began to get up from her chair. Suddenly Francine caught her arm.

"I've got something, Jessie. It's faint."

Francine whispered, "Come in, Panther. This is Lightning. Do you copy?"

A hoarse voice whispered a reply. It was so hoarse and faint that Jessie could barely make out that it was Derrick. "Copy, Lightning. This is Panther."

"Panther, what is your status?" Francine asked.

There was a long pause and then some clicking and scraping noise.

"Packages secured. Mule disabled. On the road."

Then a final click and the radio went silent.

"Panther? Come in, Panther?"

Jessie stood up and resumed her initial plan. Francine knew it would be hard to stop her, but she had to try.

"Jessie, listen. Jessie? Hey—look. We made contact. And we received good news, right? Listen."

Francine tried to maneuver to maintain eye contact with Jessie, but Frank's room was small, and Jessie was on the warpath.

"The guys recovered Reuben and Frank! That's great news, right?"

"You heard him, Francine. Did Derrick sound right to you?"

"Yeah, he did as a matter of fact. Derrick and Ray are out there on recon. Maybe someone was nearby, and they didn't want to risk being overheard. They could have been walking along the road, and we caught them at a bad time. Maybe they were in the jeep and dealing with wind noise."

"That's not what it sounded like to me. It sounded like they were hurt or in trouble."

"With all due respect, Jessie, you are a veterinarian. You aren't exactly experienced at interpreting military radio communication."

"And you get a lot of practice with that working in your lab?" Jessie checked a pistol and then threw another small duffel bag filled with ammunition on the bed.

"OK, fair point. So I only have a smidge more experience than you. But better we wait and let the guys work through whatever is going on out there than the two of us go charging into the night."

"Only one of us. As the more experienced military person, you need to stay here on base."

"All right." Francine sighed and let her arms fall to her side. "So what is your plan?"

"I'm loading up and going to visit one of Frank's neighbors. You might have seen the place on the way in—elk antlers over the front door. I'm going to ask to borrow their Buick."

"Planning to go to the door wearing all your ammunition belts?"

"I'll ask nice."

"OK, and assuming Frank's neighbors don't shoot you first, what happens after you commandeer their Buick? Have you thought about how your arrival might impact things if, as I think is the case, Derrick and Ray are doing just fine on their own?"

"The mule is disabled," Jessie said.

"Excuse me? I lost you there."

"Do you know what Derrick meant when he said, 'The mule is disabled'?"

"No, I sort of let that one go because I heard that they had rescued Reuben and Frank and that they were on their way back here. What's the mystery with the mule?"

"I may not know all the military codes, but I do know that Derrick's nickname for a jeep is 'mule.' They are on foot, and I don't think that cloud of smoke we saw was caused by an overheated engine."

Francine was caught short. She was struggling to hold on to her initial sense of relief. Derrick's words sounded mostly reassuring. But she knew deep down that his voice had sounded strained. Derrick wouldn't tell them about any trouble they encountered unless he had very good reason. And now the only reason that made sense had come wandering along in Jessie's translation of "mule" to "jeep." This was the commando's version of *I'll be a little late getting home.* But even though Jessie was likely right that the guys were on foot now, Francine was equally convinced that the last thing Derrick would want was for Jessie to mount her own rescue in the neighbor's Buick. She had to try one last time.

"Any way I can keep you here?" Francine's voice was drained of all fight now, and she was looking at Jessie as she had so many times over a friendly cup of coffee.

"No."

Jessie gathered her gear and began heading to the front door. She smiled at Francine as she opened the door.

"Jessie, I'll be sitting on the radio. If you encounter trouble out there, don't try to take it on by yourself. Derrick will kill me if I let you go and something happens to you."

"I won't let anything happen. You'll be OK here?" Jessie hesitated.

"Safe and sound. Ray left me this armory." Francine nodded toward the array of guns and deadly gear spread across Frank's living-room floor. "Go now, and get back soon."

Francine closed the front door and leaned her head down to pray. After a few moments, she slipped over to a window and peeked out the curtain. Jessie was on the neighbor's porch, and from all Francine could make out, it looked like things were going well. She could see a large TV screen lighting up the curtains and sending shafts of light from the front door. Maybe Jessie caught them watching their favorite show. Perhaps it would be easier to give up your car keys if a charming and slightly intimidating woman showed up as you were just beginning to piece together the case on *Law and Order.*

Jessie disappeared inside for a few minutes. Francine had set a rough timetable for this part of Jessie's bizarre plan. If Jessie didn't reemerge from the house on schedule, Francine planned to strap on her own .45 and take a turn visiting the neighbors. But Jessie was only inside a few minutes before she stepped back out of the house and toward the cruiser-length old Buick. She looked back toward Frank's house for a split second, and Francine could only shake her head. Jessie retrieved her gear where she had hid near the neighbor's front porch and threw it in the passenger seat. Then she slid behind the wheel and started the engine. The Buick rumbled to life. Evidently Frank's neighbor liked some muscle in his old Buick cruisers. Jessie rolled out of the front yard and then gunned the car onto the main road.

Chapter 35

FRANCINE HAD TRIED at first to picture Jessie's progress along the route into the backcountry. But then she forced herself to concentrate on the tasks at hand. It was time to stop messing around with skeptical state and local bureaucrats. She had been left to run a command post. And she had a gnawing feeling that she was behind events. It was time to kick this operation into a higher gear. She would begin with people she knew and trusted. And she would include at least one or two individuals whose orders could move mountains. The first person she would call fit both of those categories.

Brigadier General Thomas Crocker had once been a senior scientist at the institute. A combat veteran, he had transferred back into command of a combat unit just prior to the first Gulf War. His Special Forces units had distinguished themselves across the first two wars in Iraq and more recent service in Afghanistan. Crocker's own career as a combat soldier was legendary, and he demanded the same uncompromising aggression and professionalism of the troops under his command. "Croc" rarely raised his voice and was a master of using silence and body language to communicate. Junior officers dreaded the "Croc stare"—a fixed glare over razor-sharp black reading glasses. The running joke was that if you served under Croc, you knew exactly how a deer felt when it looked up and saw those crocodile eyes just above the waterline. He was not as well loved in his old scientific circles, where some of Francine's colleagues felt that there was something diabolical about a crack scientist who preferred battlefield command. And in these circles, there were even occasional whispers that there was something more sinister underneath Crocker's vaunted combat aggression.

But Francine had gotten along well with Thomas Crocker, and besides, right now what she needed most was someone with a crocodile profile.

"General Crocker, good day, sir. I know this is out of the blue, but I need your help."

"Senior Scientist Booker, let me guess: you shot someone for incompetence. I was afraid someone would fail to meet our standards."

Francine smiled. "No, sir."

"OK, you shot someone for insubordination. I'm sure he deserved it. I will see that all charges are dropped and you receive a commendation."

"Not yet, sir. I've been tempted a few times."

"Me too. Well, then how are you doing, Booker? And what can I do for you?"

"Sir, I have a situation here…"

Francine tried to make the story sound as sensible as possible. At the same time, she didn't try to spin the unusual nature of her own involvement or the extent to which she had allowed herself to become involved in an "off the grid" operation. She knew that Croc was not one who would fall for spin anyway. They had earned one another's trust by shooting straight, and Francine figured she was in too deep at this point to worry about presenting herself in the most favorable light.

When she paused, Francine heard only silence for a few moments.

"General Crocker?"

After a few more beats, Crocker spoke. His voice was lower and gravelly, almost an intense whisper.

"*Damn it*, Booker."

"Yes, sir."

"You know the drill. I will need to authenticate. So in about five minutes, all hell will break loose."

"Yes, sir. Any chance we can make that only the parts of hell that will respond rapidly and effectively, sir?"

"Damn it, Booker."

"Yes, sir."

Francine could hear Crocker's slow breathing.

"Senior Scientist, authentication process to follow. Prepare to receive instructions. And, Booker?"

"Yes, sir?"

Suddenly the front door of Frank's house flew open, and two of Nasim's guards stormed inside. Francine had reached for her .45 and begun spinning up out of her chair when the first blow came. The guard's baton struck her in the jaw and sent her reeling onto the table. The guard relaxed and began to move forward to put restraints on her wrists. Francine surprised him by wheeling and firing. Addled by the blow to the jaw, she had misjudged where the guard was standing. The round meant for his heart instead grazed his side. But it was enough to take him out of the fight. He clutched his side and fell back toward Frank's couch.

Francine heard a sickening click. The other guard had stepped to her side and now held a pistol only a few feet from her head.

"Drop the weapon, Dr. Booker." The voice came from a man hovering in the shadows of the doorway. "Please, no more unpleasantness."

Francine held fast to the .45 and slowly moved her arm to point it at the man in the doorway. "Your man can kill me but not before I shoot you dead."

Francine could feel a rivulet of blood making its way down her neck. She worked to slow her breathing so that she could think more clearly and, if it came to it, make that one last shot.

A voice suddenly broke the silence. It was muffled and coming from the floor. Francine's cell phone had flown out of her hand and landed on the floor near the couch. She could just make out General Crocker's voice. The wounded guard tracked the sound, stood, and stomped the cell phone into pieces.

Francine saw the man in the doorway motion with one hand. She could hear the shuffle of feet on the porch.

"Don't move!" Francine barked and shook the pistol at the man in the doorway.

"Easy, Dr. Booker." The man held his hands out with palms up. "I was simply letting my men know that we are having a conversation. You do know that I have other several other men out here, correct?"

"Move forward out of that doorway—into the light."

Nasim removed his fedora and stepped forward. He was wearing a leather jacket over light blue hospital scrubs. Francine thought the outfit would have looked comical in any other setting, but as the wardrobe of a bioterrorist, it appeared about as funny as those clown outfits in the horror movies. Francine had a sudden urge to pull the trigger, to make sure that whatever happened, this real life monster did not leave Frank's house alive. But then she was gripped by a sudden realization that she could not fire her weapon. This man was a scientist. And for all appearances, he was maybe the senior scientist— Nasim. This man knew dark and deadly secrets. And he must be taken alive. If Francine shot him, she might also be killing any chance of stopping a pandemic.

Suddenly Francine felt woozy, and the room seemed to be moving in waves. She was running out of time. The guard managed to get his hand on her pistol just before Francine struck him hard in the throat. The last thing she remembered, she and the guard were falling together toward the floor.

When Francine regained consciousness, she found that she was tied to one of Frank's dining-room chairs. Her head was pounding, and one eye was beginning to swell closed. She tested the restraints but found that she was bound tight.

"Well, hello there, Dr. Booker." The man in the leather-and-scrubs outfit was seated in front of her, studying her face as though he might draw her portrait.

"We were not properly introduced earlier. I am Dr. Abdul Nasim. I believe that you and I share a number of professional interests."

Francine tried to speak, but her face muscles seemed sluggish and uncooperative.

"Ah, I imagine it is difficult to respond due to your injuries."

He leaned in close and studied her face. She could smell tobacco smoke and laboratory chemicals.

"Yes, you put up quite a fight, Dr. Booker. I believe my men assumed that a lab worker like yourself would cause them no trouble."

He chuckled to himself, and Francine could see that his teeth were yellowed at the edges. Perhaps in the early days, he had been forced to be his own test subject.

Nasim reached into a coat pocket and drew out a cigarette. He tapped it absently on one knee before lighting it with a flourish. He blew the smoke upward and continued to study Francine's face.

"Like any good doctor, I have brought my kit with me. Let us take care of those injuries of yours."

Nasim smiled at her and lifted a leather satchel off the floor beside his chair. He nodded at one of his guards, and the man brought over a small table. Nasim slowly lifted two black metal boxes from the satchel and placed them on the small table. Each box was about the size of a paperback book. He also lifted out some packages of gauze and tubes of what appeared to be antibiotic ointment. Nasim opened one of the tubes, slathered the gauze from its contents, and then began to clean the wounds on Francine's jaw and forehead. He daubed at her wounds gently, almost tentatively. When he was satisfied, he placed butterfly bandages over the cuts and leaned back to study his work.

"A temporary solution. We must not invite infection."

Again that creepy yellow smile. Francine felt nauseated.

"They are coming for you," Francine said.

Nasim cocked his head to one side and smiled.

"I'm sorry, Dr. Booker. You are slurring your speech a bit. Did you say that someone is coming for me? And who might that be?"

Nasim made a show of looking about the room and checking the door. The guard at the door snickered.

"All of them," Francine said slowly, "I sent out a marine dog whistle."

The guard's face fell. But Nasim only widened his smile.

"Well, well, Dr. Booker. So you have called nine-one-one, eh? You are a long way from help, I am afraid. And by the time anyone arrives at this miserable little cabin, my friends and I will be long gone. You see, our plans have already been set in motion. And there is nothing that a battalion of your marines can do about it now."

He leaned back for a moment and took another drag on his cigarette. Francine could not be sure, but she thought he was listening for the sound of a drone or a helicopter. He might sound confident, but she was pretty sure that Nasim was a bit less confident than when he strode through the cabin door. He shifted his weight forward and snuffed out his cigarette on the cabin floor.

"Now then, Dr. Booker, let us get down to business. I am going to ask you a series of questions. You are going to provide me with answers."

Nasim unlatched one of the boxes and opened it wide. It contained a syringe.

Francine's stomach tightened into a knot.

"If you provide me with satisfactory answers to my questions, you will receive this welcome shot of morphine—not a heavy dose, mind you, but just something to ease your pain until you can return home."

Nasim unlatched the second box and opened it wide. It too contained a syringe, but the syringe contained a yellowish-white liquid, and the inside of the box was framed with writing in Arabic.

"Now, this box, Dr. Booker...This box contains a very special solution. In another setting I would very much enjoy talking with you about how I developed this solution. It is an amazing story. Unfortunately today I must simply tell you that you do not want me to inject you with this solution. I'm afraid it will greatly increase your pain. Over time your physical pain will be matched by mental deterioration. You will lose your ability to think clearly or control your actions. I have carefully documented the stages just before death, and they are quite remarkable—something one cannot believe unless he has seen it for himself. So, if you don't honestly answer my questions, Dr. Booker, you will live out your worst nightmares. Do we understand one another?"

Francine wasn't sure that she could speak anymore. But she tested her jaw and found that she had just enough strength to reply to Nasim.

"You...go straight to hell."

Chapter 36

THE BLAST HAD slammed Ray with a hurricane wind and blanketed the area around the jeep in a deafening cloud of shrapnel and debris.

The skeleton of the jeep landed at a crazy angle in the crook of a gnarled tree overhanging the hillside. It crackled and snapped as the fire gutted its engine and blew over the packs of ammunition and gear. Fire burned in the surrounding trees, and bits of burning debris littered the road.

Ray had been blown to the other side of the road and lay crumpled against a pile of loose rocks. Derrick and the others had been blown off their feet and back down the road. They lay in the road with arms outstretched, like toy soldiers toppled by an angry child.

Derrick had rallied enough to answer the radio but then slumped back into the fog. He awoke with a start because someone was tapping his shoulder. It was Reuben.

"You OK?"

Reuben's words seemed to be coming from somewhere far away. As he saw the blast debris around him, Derrick realized that the blast had affected his hearing. He concentrated on reading Reuben's lips and on responding quietly.

"Yeah, I'm good. Where's your grandfather?"

Reuben nodded toward the other side of the road.

"Helping Ray."

Derrick shook himself to his feet and stumbled in the direction that Reuben had indicated. His legs weren't quite steady, and Reuben came alongside to lend support. By the time the two of them reached the side of the road, Ray was shooing Frank away and attempting to stand. As Derrick closed in, he could see that Ray had an ugly bruise on the side of his head. His shirt was torn on one side from the shoulder to middle of his forearm, and the ragged material was bloodstained. Frank had been trying to work on a long gash in Ray's shoulder and shrugged at Derrick as he and Reuben approached. Ray had taken the worst of the blast. Derrick knew that they needed to get somewhere safe, shake off the cobwebs, and regroup. Ray was in that furious state where he didn't always think straight.

"Ray, listen to me," Derrick said slowly and carefully.

It was hard to get the right pitch and volume when he could only faintly hear his own voice.

"See that hollow in the side of the mountain up there. We need some cover while we regroup."

"Fine, you go ahead. I'm going to take that rifle over there and go down to that little compound in the valley. Be back with scalps by dinner."

Frank laughed out loud, and then the four of them froze and scanned the smoky forest surrounding them.

"Sorry," Frank whispered. "Indian thing."

Derrick studied Frank for a moment before resuming his plea to Ray.

"We have one chance here, Ray. Crowfoot probably thinks we are all dead. We have one chance to use that to our advantage. If you go playing cowboy right now, you will blow that chance—and likely get killed in the bargain."

"Derrick, I'm not going to stand by and—"

Suddenly Ray heard the rumble of an engine on the road. By the look in Derrick's eyes, Ray knew that he had heard it too.

"Quick, get to that cover!" Derrick whispered as he began trotting toward the dark gash in the side of the mountain. The others followed as quickly as they could, moving along the shadows of the roadside and through pockets of brush. They finally made it to the narrow cave and ducked inside just as headlights rounded the last bend in the road before their hideaway. Whoever was coming must know the backcountry road well or else be drunk. They could hear the big vehicle fishtail as it rounded the hairpin curve. It came to a sliding stop just twenty feet from the mouth of the cave. The headlights panned down the road toward the blast site.

For a moment dust clouded the view between the cave and the big car. And then the haze began to clear, and Frank stood up and began walking out of the cave.

"Frank, what are you doing?" Derrick whispered.

Without responding Frank stepped out onto the road and called softly toward the car. "John, is that you? John Warhorse?"

Derrick moved near the cave and pointed his pistol at the driver's door. The car door opened slowly at first and then in a rush. A woman came tumbling out. She was armed with a shotgun and moving in a familiar way. Now it was Derrick who stepped out of the cave.

"Jessie, is that you?"

"Derrick!" Jessie lowered the shotgun and swept past a puzzled Frank and into Derrick's arms.

Derrick held her tight for a moment and reassured her that he was OK. When he could recover his voice, he spoke in a whisper. "What are you doing out here? Where is Francine?"

"And what you are doing with John Warhorse's car?" Frank mumbled as he stared at the big Buick.

"I figured something bad had happened—like maybe a jeep had blown up or something." Jessie nodded toward the blast site.

"Yeah, that was a pretty close call. But Ray spotted it in time for everyone to walk away." As Derrick was speaking, Ray appeared ghostlike from the entrance of the cave.

"Hey, Sis. It's all Derrick's fault." Ray smiled, but weakly.

Reuben and Derrick gathered what gear they could quickly salvage from the debris, and then the five of them piled into the big Buick. Derrick's stomach clenched in as Jessie made a U-turn that barely cleared the edge of the drop off, and then they were headed back down the backcountry road they had used to locate the terrorist base camp.

In spite of his objections, Jessie pulled over under a lighted ranch gate and examined the gash in Ray's shoulder. It was a deep wound. She removed a few small pieces of shrapnel and gave the wound an initial cleaning. After covering it with a temporary bandage, she looked Ray directly in the eyes.

"This will need more serious attention and stitch work later tonight."

"Yes, Doc. Now, can we go?"

Frank was still waiting for an explanation. "So did you steal John Warhorse's car? He's very protective of this car."

Once they were back in the car and headed to his house, Jessie told Frank the story about going to his neighbor's house and asking to borrow his car. Frank asked for a description, and Jessie told him that the old man was a bit stoop-shouldered and thin. His hair was mostly gray but shot through with strands of coal black and tied in two long braids. And he was wearing a Seattle Seahawks cap.

"That's him. That's John Warhorse," Frank said, shaking his head and elbowing Reuben. "Can't believe he let you take his Buick."

Once Frank was satisfied, Jessie was anxious to know how they had found each other and if they had located the terrorist base camp. Ray was accustomed to debriefings. In spite of suffering the most direct force from the blast, he was able to walk Jessie through the key points. Reuben and Frank smiled at each other when Ray reached the part about "locating" them.

As Ray continued to recount the steps leading up to the blast, Derrick's mind drifted into a review of their current situation. Reuben and Frank were safe, if a little worse for wear. Derrick and Ray were both hurt, but neither seriously. Their jeep and a load of valuable gear had been lost. They could replenish most of that from their cache at Frank's house. They had found what appeared to be the terrorist base camp, but they hadn't confirmed it. If that scout had been right and the attack was already launched, they were seriously behind and still mostly working in the dark. He was thankful that they weren't on foot, but the five of them were still rolling along in the backcountry in a borrowed Buick Electra. Perhaps Francine would have good news for them when they arrived at Frank's house. If the state or local authorities had kicked into gear, they might just have enough time to head off a disaster.

Nasim checked the room one last time and then closed the front door to the small house. He had hoped to capture the old man and his grandson and to use the two hostages to further humiliate Crowfoot. But the scientist was an unexpected coup. Despite her lack of cooperation, she would still serve Nasim's purposes. They had also been fortunate to intercept such an impressive collection of weapons and communication equipment.

Nasim was now more convinced than ever that Crowfoot had made a mess of security. He would have to pay. Nasim turned from the door and scanned the road beyond the cabin. Just past the nearest neighbor's house, he saw a small animal ducking back into the brush alongside the road. Its white tail rose like a flag and then disappeared. Nasim thought it might be a fox, but it was hard to say from this distance. In any case, it was the only thing moving. Everything else was quiet and in perfect order. As he took his seat in the truck, Nasim could only hope that he and his men had arrived before Dr. Booker had time to cause them significant trouble. The soldiers were missing, along with the old man and the boy.

The truck eased quietly away from the little house, and Nasim watched as the second truck pulled out to follow them back to the laboratory. Hopefully the Guardians responsible for the final stages of his project could deal with any contingencies that might arise. In the meantime, Nasim would return to his lab and settle accounts with Crowfoot. They had only been on the backcountry road for ten minutes or so when Nasim noticed headlights coming in the opposite direction. For a split second, the car crossed the centerline, and Nasim's driver swerved to avoid a collision. But then the other driver corrected his course. *Likely some local drunk*, Nasim thought to himself, *driving with one hand and opening his beer with another.* His driver cursed quietly and then resettled himself in the seat.

Nasim looked out his window at the sliver of moon. Although it was a warm night, he felt a familiar shiver. He pondered its meaning for only a moment and then spoke over the seat to his driver.

"Hasim, a change of plans. We will not return to the laboratory. Instead take the route north, the one we took to enter this country."

"Yes, sir, but what about the final arrangements at the laboratory?" The driver leaned back to one side to catch Nasim's response.

"I left Raheem instructions. He can take care of the final arrangements. Notify Mustafah of the change in plans."

"Yes, sir, right away." The driver picked up his cell phone and called the Guardian who was driving the second truck.

There was a small pause, which Nasim knew was the driver's shock. Everyone expected a showdown tonight. But Mustafah was loyal, if rather dull. He would follow orders. And with that Nasim responded to the whispers of the night, and his team headed north toward the Canadian wilderness.

Jessie caught the wheel and crossed back into her lane. "Whoa! My bad."

Derrick startled at the jerk and Ray winced.

Frank chuckled. "Warhorse likes his steering nice and loose. Calls this his sailboat."

Jessie could see Frank's house in the distance. The lights were on, and nothing looked out of order. She had nearly forgotten Francine in her rush to locate Derrick, but now she felt desperate to reach the small house. Jessie gripped the steering wheel tightly and used her foot to tap the lights to bright. She pressed the accelerator, and the big car glided smoothly toward home.

The distance was deceptive, and it seemed to take forever to reach Frank's house. But finally Jessie eased the big car into the drive and killed the engine. Jessie was about to bound from the car and call Francine's name when Derrick caught her shoulder.

"Just in case, Jessie, let me and Ray go in first."

Jessie's heart raced, but she nodded, and Derrick and Ray began making their way slowly to the front porch. They had pistols drawn and pointed at the door, although Derrick considered it merely precaution. There were no signs that anyone else had been here since they'd left the house. Ray was the first to reach the front door. He signaled back to Derrick and then slipped a key into the lock.

"Francine?"

Ray slipped into the door and swept the room with his pistol.

"Derrick, get in here!"

Derrick bounded through the doorway as Ray slipped back down the hall to sweep the house. Immediately Derrick's eyes fell on Francine. She was bound to a chair in the center of the floor. Her face was swollen and bloody and tilted to one side. Derrick checked her pulse. Her heart was beating, but weakly.

Ray called, "*All clear!*" and then reappeared at Derrick's side.

"Is she alive?"

"Yeah, but in bad shape. Get Jessie in here."

Just as the words came out of Derrick's mouth, Jessie came rushing into the room.

"Francine!" Jessie lunged past Ray and knelt at Francine's side.

"She's alive, Jess, but her heartbeat seems weak and irregular to me. See what you can do, and then we will get her to a hospital."

Jessie placed an ear to Francine's chest and then began trying to rouse her. Francine's eyes would slide open briefly and seem to fix on Jessie. Jessie would see the familiar glimmer. And then Francine's eyes would cloud over, and she seemed to slip under the surface of consciousness.

"Those bastards drugged her—needle mark on her left arm. She's also taken a serious beating. That eye doesn't look good, and she has a broken jaw." Jessie looked into Derrick's eyes with a fierce desperation and determination. At that moment he wanted to move heaven and earth to rouse Francine.

"Francine," Jessie called more softly. "Hey, it's Jessie. I'm here. You've been knocked around, and they've given you something. I need you to dig down deep and wake up enough to tell me what they gave you." Francine's head lolled back against Jessie's hand, and her eyes fluttered.

"That's it, army girl! Come on now, wake up and help me out here, Francine."

Suddenly Francine's eyes opened wide and locked on Jessie's face.

"Homemade," Francine whispered. She shuddered and then closed her eyes again.

Jessie again leaned her ear to Francine's chest and then rose up quickly.

"Derrick, we have to move. She's slipping in and out here."

Ray and Derrick swiftly cut through the remaining restraints, and Derrick gently lifted Francine from the chair. They hustled out to the Buick, and Derrick laid Francine in the back seat.

Frank and Reuben retrieved Bear from where they had tied him to a tree near the car. They watched quietly as Derrick loaded Francine. Then Frank called out to Ray.

"Ray, I've called ahead to Saint Alphonsus and alerted state patrol to pick you up on your route to the hospital."

"Thanks, Frank. And you'll let—" Ray seemed suddenly confused.

"Warhorse? Yes, I'll let him know that we still need his Buick."

Ray moved a bit closer to Frank and lowered his voice. "Listen, Frank, whoever did this to Francine is still out there. You two keep a close eye out, and we will get back here as soon as we can."

"Don't worry about us," Frank responded. "Just make sure you stop him."

Chapter 37

CROWFOOT HAD MOVED down the ridge after rigging the jeep and then stopped on a little bluff about halfway to Nasim's lab. He felt a need to press on, but at the same time he couldn't resist seeing the show. It would be like Fourth of July fireworks, only with a more patriotic purpose.

He had taken up position on a flat rock behind a thin screen of young cedar trees. A slight breeze was blowing, and the night was turning out cooler than he had expected. Crowfoot took out a pair of night-vision goggles and scanned the upper tree line. He didn't see any movement. The old man and the boy were wounded. It would take time for them to make their way up the steep slope to the road. Crowfoot pushed the stem of his watch and checked the glowing dial. It was taking longer than he had expected. He swatted at a mosquito and checked the tree line again. This time he thought he caught movement at the side of the road. It shouldn't be long now. Crowfoot stretched his legs out on the rock and settled his vision on the dark line of the road where it bisected the mountain. Tree frogs began to sing nearby, and he found himself rocking to the pulse of their song.

Crowfoot had almost closed his eyes when the blast erupted on the mountain road. Flames backlit the tree line and shot skyward against the rocky cliff on the other side of the road. Burning shrapnel and debris flew to the tops of the largest fir trees lining the downslope side of the road. Crowfoot sat mesmerized by the sights and sounds. It reminded him of a volcanic eruption he had seen once in Hawaii. The explosion lit up both the mountainside and the billowing smoke above. When he scanned with his binoculars, Crowfoot could see the husk of the jeep lodged in the crook of a big tree.

He watched the burning debris until the mosquitos returned to interrupt his reverie. He had eliminated any chance of interference from those two white Indians and their cowboy soldier sidekicks. Now it was time for the main event.

Crowfoot turned away from the blast and let his eyes adjust to the darkness around him. Then he crept down from the rocks and began making his way through the forest. He had to tell himself to keep a sharp eye out for scouts that might be loyal to Nasim. A burden had been lifted from his shoulders as he watched that blast. Crowfoot felt like breaking into a run and laughing out loud. The world was about to change. The tribes were about to rise up. And he was coming to be their leader.

"What the hell?" Tupe turned toward the sound of the blast and saw a shower of sparks and flaming debris against the night sky. He turned back toward Ghost, who was huddled against the trunk of a large pine. Ghost's face was hard and menacing.

"Crowfoot," Ghost whispered.

"What did he do?" Tupe asked.

"Either he changed his mind about using that knife, or the old man outfoxed him. Either way we better go check it out."

Tupe and Ghost had gone far when they met up with Crowfoot. When Ghost spotted him, Crowfoot had a crazed smile on his face. Something about that look sent a chill up Ghost's spine. But when Crowfoot saw Ghost and Tupe making their way toward him, Crowfoot's smile quickly disappeared.

"You two are supposed to be watching the lab."

"Yeah, well, we were a bit distracted by the fireworks show. You lose your knife on the hike down?" Ghost studied Crowfoot's face.

Crowfoot raised his chin in the direction of the explosion. "That blast took care of all our loose ends at one time," Crowfoot replied. "Now let's get back down there to that lab."

"Sure," Tupe muttered, "now that whoever is down there has been given a nice big warning and some time to collect their ammunition."

While Crowfoot was making his way through the forest to the laboratory, Raheem was sitting in his office with a pair of headphones on his head. He was listening to a recording of Dr. Nasim's directions. It had taken a long time for Raheem to persuade Dr. Nasim to allow him to make these recordings. Although the two men were from the same village and had known each other since Raheem was a boy, Nasim had been slow to accept Raheem's claim that he needed the recordings in order to correctly follow his orders. He had even taken the unusual step of asking Crowfoot to thoroughly vet Raheem's condition and the need for the recordings.

Raheem thought that his scars should be enough to convince anyone that his mind did not work as it had before the injury.

He had only just turned fourteen when the accident happened. Raheem had been recruited by a local Taliban leader to plant explosive devices along roadways frequented by US troops. He had been afraid at first and trembled each time he held one of the fearsome devices. But over time he had become more confident—and more careless. One day he and a friend had spotted an American convoy and decided to risk planting an explosive just ahead of them. Raheem's friend had hung back too long trying to ensure a perfect camouflage. Raheem was already running for cover when he turned back one last time to wave his friend to safety. His friend was looking at him and smiling when the device exploded. His friend was killed instantly, and Raheem was struck in the head by a dagger-shaped piece of shrapnel. Three Taliban fighters were killed in the ensuing firefight. A Taliban fighter finally dragged Raheem to safety as the US troops raced to the scene.

The Taliban were able to keep Raheem alive, but they could do nothing about the ragged scar that ran from the middle of his left cheek to the top of his head. And they could do nothing about the occasional blackouts or the times when his memory failed him. On the surface he was treated as an honored soldier, but as one whose mind was no longer reliable. His friends moved up the ranks and began leading raids. Raheem made tea for the other soldiers and helped with equipment. In despair he had volunteered for duty as a suicide bomber. But his request was rejected out of fear that he might botch the attack.

He had met Crowfoot not long after the drone attack on the village. Although he had known Nasim since childhood, Raheem had not known that the man was working in the struggle. Crowfoot made it all clear to him and met with him and Dr. Nasim. And when the time came to move their operation, Raheem made his way with a few others on the long and circuitous journey from Afghanistan to the United States.

Dr. Nasim had treated Raheem differently than the other leaders in their movement. He often spoke to him in their local dialect, sometimes sharing jokes with the boy or, more often, sarcastic comments about Crowfoot and other Westerners. The man who was so cool and aloof to others in the laboratory could be warm and relaxed toward Raheem. Nasim seemed oddly comforted by Raheem's scar and his occasional lapses. Raheem felt that he knew Nasim better than anyone in the laboratory. He knew that Nasim saw enemies and threats everywhere he looked. But Raheem sensed that Nasim considered him safe. He was never sure how much of Nasim's trust was given him because of their shared heritage and hometown, and how much was due to his disability. But he suspected that Nasim saw him first as a simpleton, an intellectual eunuch who could be trusted in the palace of the Scientist-King. *No matter*, Raheem thought. *He trusts me, and that is all that matters.*

Raheem pushed rewind and began listening again to Dr. Nasim's instructions. He wanted to make certain that he was prepared for Crowfoot's arrival and that all went according to plan.

Frank's friends in the state patrol had linked up to provide escort for Warhorse's car on the highway south of Cascade. The entourage flew down the road as Francine drifted in and out of consciousness. Jessie lay down on the vast floorboard and held her friend's hand. She tried to distract herself with checking vitals and attempting to rouse Francine. Jessie tried to push away the thought that her friend was dying. But they were nearing Boise, and they needed to know what Francine had been given and how to counteract it. She feared that Nasim had given Francine a shot of his deadly prion cocktail. How would she explain that one to a trauma physician? What could they do to counteract it anyway?

Jessie tried to reassure herself with what she had learned from Francine about recent attempts to manipulate prions. Known prion illnesses were all slow burners. In many cases it took months or even years for symptoms to develop. Whatever was attacking Francine was no slow burn. It was hitting hard and fast, more like a toxic drug or a bacterial illness. Jessie pressed the back of her hand to Francine's forehead. Her temperature was elevated, probably over a hundred degrees Fahrenheit.

Ray began braking, and Jessie could see brighter lights outside the car.

"Here we go, Francine. We are at the hospital. You hold on. We are going to beat this thing together."

When Ray stopped the car, there was a flurry of activity as the trauma team removed Francine from the car to a gurney and whisked her into the trauma department. Jessie stuck close to Francine's side and disappeared inside. Ray and Derrick moved more slowly and made their way to some seats in the waiting area.

A nurse approached the two of them, and her eyes widened. "What happened to you?"

At first Ray and Derrick were confused by her question. They were focused on Francine, and Derrick tried to explain that they had driven a friend who was very sick.

"Did you have a wreck on the way here?"

At that point Derrick and Ray both paused and looked at one another. Their clothes were burned in places and torn ragged in others. Ray's shirt was blood soaked on one side, and his hair was singed in spikes around his head. Derrick's forehead was still dripping blood, and he was covered in dirt from the road and the debris. They looked like two castaways washed up on the shore of a Boise hospital.

Derrick told the nurse that they had left their insurance information in their vehicle and that they would return shortly. Then he and Ray slipped back out to the Buick and drove to a nearby store. Derrick looked most presentable, so he went in and bought each of them a change of simple clothes, some soap, towels, and a few gallons of water. They drove the Buick into a nearby closed car wash and cleaned up the best that they could. They scrubbed their wounds quickly, dried off, and then hustled into the new pair of work pants and shirts. Within minutes they were back in the hospital parking lot and waiting for word from Jessie.

Meanwhile Jessie was trying to walk a tightrope. She needed to give the trauma team any and all information that would help them save Francine's life. But if she provided *too much* information—especially about prions and bioweapons—she risked being written off as the delusional friend of a likely case of drug overdose.

Fortunately the lead trauma nurse was sympathetic, and she promised Jessie that she would ask the lead physician to come out and speak with her as soon as possible. Jessie had been pacing the hallway for an agonizing ten minutes when a grizzled doctor emerged from the trauma room and dropped his mask.

"I'm told you are a veterinarian and friend of Dr. Booker's."

"Yes, that's right."

"I'm Dr. Jacobs. And right now I'm confused about what is going on with your friend. Her vitals are all over the place. Is this a drug overdose?"

"No, at least not in the usual sense."

"Come again? Listen, Dr...."

"Anderson, Jessie Anderson."

"Dr. Anderson, I need to know what I am up against."

Jessie paused and studied the old doctor's eyes for a moment. It was a big risk. But his eyes seemed honest and clear. Jessie knew it was now or never.

"Dr. Jacobs, we may not have much time. So I'm just going to tell you what I know. It will sound crazy, but I believe with all my heart that Francine's life depends on you hearing me and trying hard to believe me."

Now it was Dr. Jacob's turn to study Jessie's face. He raised his chin and squinted, his gray eyes alight beneath bushy salt-and-pepper eyebrows.

"I'm all ears," Dr. Jacobs responded.

After she unloaded her best version of the facts on Dr. Jacobs, Jessie headed back down the hallway to update Ray and Derrick. The last report was not encouraging. Dr. Jacobs had been called away just as Jessie was completing her account. A nurse had reassured her that Francine was hanging in there, but barely.

Jessie slipped past the automatic doors and out into the scattered chairs of the waiting room. She didn't see Derrick or Ray, which for a split second caused her heart to race. But then she remembered their dislike for all things medical, and walked past the waiting room and through the exit.

Warhorse's car was easy enough to locate. But Jessie had to look twice to convince herself that the two men inside were her husband and his brother. They looked more like freshly scrubbed—if a bit battered—maintenance men showing up for the night shift. Jessie climbed in the back and scooted far across the seat to avoid the blood stains where only moments before Francine had been resting her head. She fought twin urges to cry and to be sick.

Derrick turned back to her and held out his hand. "You OK?"

"No, but I will be when Francine comes walking out of there."

"Copy that," Ray said softly.

Jessie updated them on her talk with Dr. Jacobs and on the latest word on Francine's condition.

"Some general had alerted Dr. Jacobs, which helped him to believe our crazy story. Either of you know a General Crocker?"

"Croc." Ray leaned his head back against the seat and smiled. He tilted his head back toward Jessie. "That doctor better believe him, or General Crocodile will come through the phone line and take his head off."

"Well, whatever helps at this point," Jessie replied. She turned and looked toward the bright lights of the emergency-room entrance.

"Sis, do you think Francine's been infected?"

A tear rolled down Jessie's cheek. "I don't know, Ray. I don't think so. This thing she has is moving awfully fast, and known prion diseases don't work that way. But we also know that this madman was working to manipulate prions." She paused and brushed the tears from her face.

"Dr. Jacobs has a hunch that he is working—and it's not related to prions. I just pray that he's right and my gut is wrong."

Jessie leaned her head back down on her hands. The three of them sat in silence for a time. Most of their state trooper entourage had left shortly after Francine was admitted to the ER. Now a pair of troopers exited the hospital and headed to the lone cruiser parked near the door. Jessie sat up suddenly.

"I need to get back to Francine. And you two need to do me a favor."

"Anything," Derrick replied.

"Go find these monsters. And stop them." Jessie looked into the rearview mirror and directly into Derrick's gaze. He knew that she had planned only that last deep look before she tore out of the car, but Derrick jumped out first and caught her up in a bear hug midstride.

"Francine is going to make it. You are each strong enough to hold the rope for the other."

Jessie buried her face in Derrick's chest. She rested there for a moment and then reached up to whisper in his ear. "Nice shirt."

Derrick looked down to see that she was smiling through her tears—tough as nails. "Yeah, the crew shirts were on sale." Derrick brushed a tear from her cheek. "You take care of Francine. Call us if there is any change."

"Don't be too proud to accept help."

"Yeah, I know. I imagine this General Crocker is already sending out the cavalry."

Ray had slipped out of the other side of the car and was leaning on the roof with his head on his hands. "Um…Speaking of cavalry, we better get going."

"Shut up, Ray." Jessie hugged Derrick one more time and smiled at Ray over his shoulder.

"Roger that." Ray winked and slid back into the passenger seat.

Derrick stood for a moment and watched Jessie stride back toward the hospital. Then he climbed back into the Buick and fired up the engine. There was nothing more that they could do for Francine. *She is in God's hands and Jessie's care. You can't do any better than that,* Derrick thought as he steered the big car out of the parking lot and headed east.

Chapter 38

CROWFOOT PAUSED AT the final line of brush in front of the laboratory. Nasim's scouts seemed to have pulled back. Or maybe they had run away. Nasim had never been very good at selecting the best and brightest. Crowfoot checked the building perimeter carefully. Nasim was not a great leader, but he was ruthless and clever. He was the sort of man to leave a booby trap just outside a front door.

Once he had checked for anything out of the ordinary, Crowfoot signaled to Ghost and Tupe, and the three men moved out of the brush and covered the final open stretch to the laboratory. He pointed out a trip line near the door, and Ghost and Tupe stepped high over the wire. When they reached the entrance, Crowfoot swung open the front door of the lab and entered with his arms outstretched and pistol in hand.

Raheem came out of his office and then jumped at the sight of Crowfoot's pistol aimed at his face. His thin arms shot into the air.

"Crowfoot, you startled me. It's me, Raheem."

"Yes, Raheem, I can see that it is you. Who else is here?"

"No one, Crowfoot—just me."

"And Dr. Nasim?"

"He is on the road somewhere, taking care of some operational issue."

Tupe and Ghost stepped through the door and stood flanking Crowfoot.

"And who is this?" Raheem asked.

"Fellow soldiers. Put your hands down, Raheem, and let us make an inspection." Crowfoot turned to Ghost. "You two stay here. Raheem and I will be right back."

Raheem realized as he lowered his hands that they were shaking. His head was beginning to pound, the onset of one of his headaches. But he braced himself and began to walk ahead of Crowfoot through each of the rooms in the building. Crowfoot held the pistol aimed at Raheem's back as he paused at each room and checked the space. After the two of them had made a complete circuit, Raheem paused at a small office just down the hallway from Dr. Nasim's office.

"Dr. Nasim was expecting you, sir. This was the office where he told me to have you wait for him."

Crowfoot scanned the office. It was barely bigger than a supply closet and contained only a single metal chair and a small desk.

"I would not wait in such a place."

"Yes, sir."

"I would wait in Dr. Nasim's office. I would put my feet up on his desk and smoke one of his prized cigars."

"Yes, sir."

Crowfoot nudged Raheem with the pistol, and the two of them made their way back to where they'd begun their tour, just outside Raheem's tiny office. Crowfoot waved Raheem in, and Raheem took a seat behind his desk. Crowfoot took the seat opposite. He waved Ghost and Tupe into chairs nearby. Crowfoot laid the pistol on the table in front of him and crossed his arms. He studied Raheem for a moment. Crowfoot felt comfortable here. The space reminded him of the interrogation room back on the reservation. The rez police called it "the box," and someone who was adept with interrogation was known as a "boxer." Crowfoot was considered a heavyweight champ.

"So, my friend Raheem, let us talk. It has been some time since we were able to sit down and have a conversation."

"Too long, sir."

"You and I go way back. Of course, you have been working closely with Dr. Nasim as well."

"Yes."

"This was necessary, and I am sure that you have been a great help to our cause."

"I like to think so, sir."

"You do not need to address me formally, Raheem. We are old friends. 'Crowfoot' will be fine."

"Yes, Crowfoot."

"Nasim recruited you, did he not?"

"Yes."

"Took you into his full confidence, correct?"

"Yes."

"Excellent. But here is the crucial question my friend—have you remained loyal to the pledge you made to me back in Afghanistan?"

"Yes, sir...um, Crowfoot. I made a blood oath, and I have kept it."

"All right then, you have protected your life and your honor. Just as I had hoped that you would do." Crowfoot picked up the pistol and began unloading each chamber and slipping the rounds into a pocket.

"So, Raheem, how was it to be done? What plan did Dr. Nasim share with you for killing your old friend Crowfoot?"

"He tainted his old office with P15—the weapon. He told me to ask you to wait in the small office, knowing that you would refuse and occupy his office. The cigars, the coffee cup—everything was tainted."

Raheem reached into his pocket and retrieved his small recording device. "I recorded it all—just as you asked."

Crowfoot took the device and slipped it into his pocket.

"Excellent. I will listen to it as I hunt down our enemies. Now, did you remember to take care of Dr. Nasim's vehicles?"

"Yes, I attached the devices to their vehicles, just like you instructed me. But now there are problems."

"What sort of problems?" Crowfoot stiffened in his chair.

"The devices have a limited range. I was waiting for you to arrive, as you asked. But in the meantime, the vehicles have driven out of range for detonation."

Crowfoot rubbed his forehead for a few seconds and then slammed a fist down on the small table. The pistol bounced, and Raheem jumped in his chair.

"Damn it! Where? Where were they heading?"

"North. And there is one more thing: they stopped at some point along the way north. After that the tracking device stopped working. I don't know if they removed it or it simply failed, but I lost track of them."

Crowfoot rubbed his chin and pondered Raheem's report. It was possible that the young man had made mistakes in setting the devices. He had taken a calculated risk in giving such an important assignment to Raheem. But the man's shortcomings were the very things that placed him close to Nasim. Nasim trusted Raheem, in part because he assumed the man incapable of taking initiative. Crowfoot also considered the possibility that Raheem was more capable of initiative than even he had suspected. Was it possible that Raheem had double-crossed him?

Crowfoot drew one of the bullets from his pocket and casually slipped it into the chamber of the pistol. He pointed the loaded pistol at Raheem's face. The young man recoiled in terror.

"Crowfoot, what are you doing? I have done what you asked. I promise."

"I hope so, my friend. I hope so. Now tell me something. The attack is to take place in Sun Valley. But you say that Dr. Nasim and his men headed north. What was it that spooked them? Why did they not stick to the plan?"

"I don't know—I swear to you. All I know is that they took off in a hurry to deal with some problem in Sector Six. That is south of here, as you know."

"Sector Six? What happened? Why were they going there?"

"Let me see…um…I am trying. Please be patient. Sometimes I cannot remember when I am under pressure."

"Relax, Raheem. Think. It is very important."

"Old man!" Raheem blurted. "They said something about going to the house of an old man. Lights were on at that house, and the scouts were not expecting anyone to be home."

"And they stopped there? How long?"

Raheem signaled that he wanted to check on his laptop, and Crowfoot waved him on.

"Thirty-five minutes—they were stopped in Sector Six for thirty-five minutes."

"And when they left this house, then they headed north?"

"Yes, Crowfoot, then they headed north."

Crowfoot clicked the safety on the pistol and stood up. Raheem fell back into the chair and rubbed the side of his head.

"You believe me now, Crowfoot?"

"Yes, my friend, I believe you. It sounds just like Nasim. When his so-called scouts alerted him, Nasim dashed off to the old man's house. He would love to take care of a problem that I had overlooked. But he ran to a false alarm. I took care of the old man and the boy on the way here. I don't know what those idiots did for thirty-five minutes at that house—probably argued with one another. Anyway, at some point they decided to run away. No matter. I will take care of those cowards later."

Crowfoot paused for a moment. He seemed to be deep in thought.

"The trucks, Raheem. You followed my instructions regarding the trucks?"

"Yes, Dr. Nasim believed that the trucks that left here earlier were loaded with the weapon. But they were loaded with harmless material loaded in Nasim's boxes. The weapon is loaded on trucks that are parked now at the staging area. They will only move out on your direct orders."

"Good, then it is time for me to go there and give them their orders. Call Hassan and tell him to pick me up at the road."

Crowfoot began walking out of Raheem's office and toward the front door of the laboratory.

"What about me, Crowfoot? Should I come with you?"

"No, Raheem, I would like you to stay here and take care of our two guests. I promised these soldiers that they would be paid when they had helped me secure this laboratory. You still have access to the safe?"

"Yes, Crowfoot, I know the code to the safe."

Ghost smiled at Tupe and then at Raheem. He had been prepared to kill everyone in sight, including Crowfoot, in order to take what was owed to him and Tupe. But now it appeared that Crowfoot was following through on his promise. *Once in a while*, Ghost mused, *a miserable job pays off in the end.*

"Excellent, my friend," Crowfoot replied, "I believe your memory is improving. Now, I am going to write down an amount and—"

Tupe rose suddenly from his chair, moving much faster than Crowfoot had thought possible. He grabbed Crowfoot's arm and held it pinned to Raheem's desk.

"I want to see the amount you write. I want to know that Ghost and me are getting paid what you promised. You and this office boy aren't going to cheat us out of our pay."

Crowfoot's face hardened for a moment but then relaxed into a menacing smile. "Ghost, please tell your partner to let go of my arm before I shatter his thick skull."

Ghost leaned back in his chair. "Oh, I don't know, Crowfoot. I sort of agree with Tupe here. No particular reason for us to trust you and your little buddy Raheem. So how about you write out your instructions for all of us to see?"

Raheem's head was pounding now. He wanted this to be over.

"Crowfoot, sir," Raheem said, "I will be happy to record your instructions. These men can listen if you agree that this is appropriate."

Crowfoot studied Tupe's hand for a moment. The giant paw covered half of his forearm. The pistol was pinned to the desk. No matter. Crowfoot could kill this giant before he had time to react. A hard strike to the eyes, and the big hand would release its grip long enough for Crowfoot to deliver a bullet to the big man's brain.

But Ghost was coiled up behind him, and Crowfoot knew that he could strike with lightning speed. He would never be able to take them both, and in this particular situation, he knew that Raheem would be unable to help. Crowfoot relaxed and nodded.

"Yes, Raheem, I think that is an excellent idea. I will dictate my instructions to you, and our guests can follow along."

Tupe released his grip and dropped back into his chair. Crowfoot studied the deep handprint left on his arm for a moment and then turned back to face Raheem. He began dictating dollar amounts and instructions for shutting down the laboratory. It was good that Crowfoot had worked with Raheem recently to ensure that he remembered the old Afghan code. For now as he listened to ordinary instructions for closing down the laboratory, Raheem also heard his orders for taking care of Crowfoot's two guests. When he was finished dictating, Crowfoot stood and reloaded his pistol.

"Raheem, did you make copies of Nasim's laboratory notes as I instructed you?"

"Yes, I have them here."

Raheem ducked down for a moment and then lifted a file box. He handed the box to Crowfoot.

"All right then, Raheem, once you have followed my instructions and sent our guests on their way, you are to take one of the scout's horses and ride to the place we met before. I will meet you there tomorrow, and then we will head north together. Understand?"

"Yes, pay your guests and feed them a meal. Then after they have departed, ride a scout's horse to our meeting site. You will meet me there tomorrow."

"Good, Raheem, if scouts show up, just tell them that you are acting on Nasim's orders."

Crowfoot turned and faced Ghost. "Raheem will take care of you from here on. I have other business to attend to."

Crowfoot turned and began heading toward the door.

Raheem smiled at Ghost and nodded toward Tupe. "Gentlemen, if you will follow me." Raheem began walking back toward the hallway that led to Dr. Nasim's office.

"No, wait," Ghost replied.

Crowfoot turned around. "Now what?"

"Tupe and me aren't walking into some trap that you two have set. Crowfoot, you wait here while your errand boy retrieves our money. Once we have our pay, you can go."

Crowfoot's eyes narrowed. He stared at Ghost for a moment and then turned to Raheem and nodded. Raheem picked up a small recorder off the desk and then slipped away down the hallway.

"Who's back there, Crowfoot? One or two of those scouts?"

"Tupe, your partner is seriously paranoid." Crowfoot leaned back against the doorframe and studied Ghost's face. "You look a little pale, Ghost. Are you really afraid of Raheem? He is the only one here. And, as I would think even you two idiots could see, Raheem is no threat."

"Uh-huh, you just relax there until we get our money. And then we will leave together."

Raheem returned carrying a briefcase. "Open it," he said to Raheem.

Raheem slipped a key into the lock and then snapped open the case. When he lifted the lid, Ghost whistled and then smiled back at Tupe. He picked up a stack of bills and began counting. Tupe nodded along to Ghost's monotone counting of the cash.

After he had checked a number of the bundles, Ghost took the key from Raheem and closed the briefcase.

"All right, Crowfoot, the money seems to be in order. Tupe and me are satisfied. We will be on our way now."

"Remember," Crowfoot replied, "you were never here, and you know nothing about me or the Guardians. If one of you talks to anyone, I will know about it. And you will be hunted down wherever you go. Clear?"

"Perfectly clear," Ghost replied. "And just remember that if you try to double-cross us, you are not the only one with dangerous friends."

Crowfoot nodded and opened the front door to the laboratory. "See that our friends get on their way safely, Raheem."

"Yes, Crowfoot, I will see to it. And I will meet you tomorrow as we discussed."

Crowfoot nodded and headed out the door. He glanced back over his shoulder in time to see Ghost lighting a cigar and elbowing Tupe. The Samoan was laughing and trying at the same time to finish a swig of water. *Birds of a feather,* Crowfoot thought to himself. He couldn't be more relieved to be parting ways. Crowfoot holstered his pistol and began making his way to the road. Finally it was time to strike.

Chapter 39

DERRICK AND RAY had been pulled over by the state police a few miles from the hospital. It seemed that John Warhorse wanted his car back. But Frank had worked his magic again. One of the two detectives that pulled them over took the keys to Warhorse's pride and joy and exchanged them for the keys to an unmarked Dodge Charger.

Ray headed for the driver's side while Derrick was thanking the detectives, who seemed baffled by the entire enterprise.

"Now the Anderson boys are in business." Derrick had just settled in on the passenger side when his brother turned and and smiled at him. He had his aviator sunglasses pulled down on his nose. Derrick shook his head. Ray had a superpower. He could turn into his eighteen-year-old self at the drop of a hat.

"Let's wait to pull out until the detectives are on their way—what do you say?" Derrick said as he buckled up.

"Party pooper."

"You think those detectives suspect that Frank is in the Mafia?"

"Hell, at this point I suspect that Frank is in some sort of Mafia," Ray replied.

"Well, try not to wreck this hot rod. I'm not sure who we would owe, but I have a feeling the bill would be more than we can pay."

The detectives quickly made their way off the curb and cut their lights. They turned a corner and disappeared into traffic. Ray gunned the Charger once for effect and then eased the car out onto the thoroughfare. They headed southeast on Highway 20.

As they rounded the bend at Mountain Home and began running due east, Ray and Derrick passed an old fuel depot tucked in a scattered grove of hardwoods. The paint was peeling off the Sinclair signpost out front, and rust streaks scarred the sign's face. The pavement leading up to the sign was cracked and badly potted. Grass grew thick along the fissures, and clumps of maidenhair and blanketflower had taken root around the edges of the broken pavement. The truck sheds had been buffeted by windstorms, and a few of them hung at a crazy angle. Everywhere the metal roofs were rusted and streaked to a grayish red that blended in with the surrounding terrain.

Intent on reaching Sun Valley, Ray and Derrick streaked past the abandoned depot. Neither gave it a glance. But even if Derrick and Ray had been searching for a roadside crew, they might have been forgiven for missing them. Crowfoot's men were pros at using the local terrain to their advantage, and the trucks were perfectly screened behind the tangle of old metal and the broken brush.

The men waiting in the trucks paid no notice to the black Charger either. They had been told to report a vintage Buick Electra, but otherwise they were to lie low and wait on their leader.

Crowfoot was running late. A few men kept guard behind the light camo screen they had earlier woven into the brush and the ruins of the depot. One of them leaned against the dark brown side of one of the trucks, one foot propped on a back tire. Another sat on a running board and leaned against the driver's door. Behind him, a dignified coat of arms and the words "King's Catering" were painted on the door in a rich wheat color. "King's Catering" was also printed on the side of the truck in the same color, along with a sham address and a phone number answered by one of Crowfoot's men. One of the guards swatted at a biting fly and said something in Farsi to his fellow guard. The other guard nodded and softly repeated the curse.

And then the guards' radios crackled briefly to life. They both looked down and recognized the code. Hassan had only touched his radio to send a burst of static. He and Crowfoot were close. Both men jumped to their feet and banged hard on the side of the trucks. Inside they could hear the men fumbling awake and cursing. Before the truck made the last rise ahead of the depot, all the men had poured from the trucks and arranged themselves in vigilant poses.

Hassan nosed the dark brown SUV off the road quickly and ducked in behind the cover to park alongside the two larger catering trucks. The SUV was also marked as belonging to Knight's Catering but with some additional script on the door and tailgate that suggested that this was a vehicle driven by the owner. In fact, it was. Hassan had been a chef before joining the cause, and before that he had been the manager of a high-end catering business. For today he was taking up his old identity and acting as chief of Knight's Catering.

Crowfoot stepped down from the truck and studied his men. "You have been napping." Crowfoot smiled.

His men stiffened and held their breaths.

"Just as well. We will be going without sleep for a while." Crowfoot paused and kicked at a piece of tin lying at his feet.

"The path ahead is clear now. Nasim has done his part and withdrawn. Those who have attempted to interfere with our plan have all been destroyed. These trucks are loaded with justice for tribal people everywhere. You and I are going to unleash that justice. It is going to fall on their best and brightest, on the pride of their nation. And when it does, tribal people everywhere will know that we are their Guardians. We are their future."

Crowfoot paused and scanned the men's faces. They were fully awake now and fully prepared. He could see the determination and hate on each of their faces.

"You are here tonight as the warriors representing all our people. Concentrate on striking the blow and nothing else. If a child wanders into your path, show no pity. If a woman tries to hold you back from your duty, strike her down. Enjoy killing any man who dares to get in your way. The only thing that matters now is that we strike this blow. Anyone who isn't prepared to do that should leave us now. The most honorable way to do that would be to walk back into that grove of trees and put a bullet in your brain."

Crowfoot paced back and forth for a moment. "Anyone?"

None of the men moved. Some nodded and others checked their weapons.

Crowfoot stopped pacing and turned to Hassan. "Good, we are ready then, Hassan."

Hassan stepped forward and began reviewing the details of the plot. Crowfoot stepped back and leaned against one of the catering trucks. As he listened to Hassan's review, Crowfoot looked past him to the line of mountains in the distance. He had dreamed of this day for a long, long time. It would not erase her memory. Nothing could do that. But in his heart he would be able to lay her to rest after this mission. Sun Valley would be her memorial—and an arrow driven into the heart of his enemies.

As Hassan briefed Crowfoot's men, the kitchen crew at the Sun Valley Resort was moving into high gear. The first major event was only six hours away, and the chefs were still on edge. The détente negotiated the previous day by Sophia DeClair had mostly held over the course of the past twenty-four hours. But as their first big test loomed, the chefs could feel tensions rising among the various kitchen factions.

As executive chef, Amelio knew that he must keep a close eye on his staff and encourage everyone in the kitchen to focus on the work in front of them. A pastry chef who became idle for even a moment was likely to allow her mind to slip away from pastry and back to some past grievance. Amelio could bark as loudly and colorfully as any successful executive chef, but he preferred to encourage and inspire. Their trial preparations had been well received by several members of the resort's staff and most importantly by Sophia DeClair, the executive responsible for coordinating major events like the Allen Conference.

But preliminary tests were one thing, and live events quite another. Amelio knew that he would need to keep his staff upbeat and flexible. Such a large conference as this one never came off without a few changes and surprises along the way. Head counts were rarely on target, and any number of guests would make last-minute requests or demand alternations to his carefully crafted cuisine. Staff in other areas of the resort could be counted upon to create stress in the kitchen, often by breezily suggesting to a guest that kitchen staff could surely "whip up" (Amelio's least favorite expression) some hopelessly exotic and troublesome item. And as the conference wore on, Amelio knew that it would be harder to maintain esprit de corps in his kitchen. He must do what he could now to lift their spirits and tamp down tensions.

And this was why Amelio thought that the last thing he needed right now was to visit with yet another contractor. He had never heard of the man in the first place, and in the second place, ice was the least of his worries at the moment. But Sophia seemed enamored of Mr. DeAngelo Jackson for whatever reason. She had insisted that Amelio take five minutes to talk ice with him and then to allow him to check the facilities for whatever it was that ice contractors checked. *Two minutes*, Amelio, thought to himself. *Two minutes is more than enough time to discuss everything I have to discuss with a man who provides ice for a living.*

Amelio couldn't know that Deacon Henderson didn't know enough about ice to talk for two minutes. But in his role as DeAngelo Jackson, he had boned up on the ice trade enough to get by Sofia DeClair. The executive chef might turn out to be detail oriented, but Deacon was betting that today he would have other things on his mind besides ice.

As the black Dodge Charger rumbled into the outer ring of estates near Ketchum, Derrick decided it was time to risk making contact with Deacon. He hadn't talked to Deacon since before the search for Frank and Reuben. Derrick could only hope that by now Deacon had managed to work his way inside the Sun Valley Resort. They could use some eyes and ears on the inside.

Deacon was just telling Amelio how he could influence melt rates when his cell phone buzzed. He intended to wave the call off but then recognized the number. He held up a finger in a faint apology as Amelio glared at him.

"Deacon, it's Ray."

"Yes, Mr. Jones, thank you for calling me back. I was hoping we could help you with ice service for Cindy's wedding and reception."

"Are you inside?"

"Yes, that's right. I'm visiting with the Sun Valley Resort folks right now. Can I call you back in five?"

Deacon hung up and tried to pick up where he left off. But Amelio's patience had run out. He waved off the ice expert with a towel and told him to stay out of the way of his staff. Deacon knelt down near an ice maker and appeared to check his iPad. When he was sure that the executive chef was on the other side of the kitchen, Deacon made his way out to a small hallway.

Meanwhile, Ray slowed the Charger and worked his way through Ketchum summer traffic.

"So Deacon's in position?" Derrick asked..

"Sounds like he's at least in the ballpark. I wish we knew more about how the terrorists plan to deliver this stuff."

Ray's phone rang, and Deacon was back on the line.

"OK, cowboy, I'm in a private spot now. But I can't talk long."

"Roger that. How much access do you have?"

"Wide open, as long as I stay close enough to ice cubes or machines that make them. Probably won't last long though—too many cooks in the kitchen already."

"Me and Derrick are in Ketchum and on our way there. Any sign of trouble so far?"

"Not yet, but I better go see what's cooking. Watch your back."

"You too. I will text you an ice order when we are onsite."

Ray parked the Charger a block away from the Sun Valley Resort. *We'll need at least a block to come up with a plan*, Ray thought as he killed the engine.

"So, big brother, what's our play here?"

"Call General Crocker."

"What?"

"Look, Ray, for all we know, Crocker has a plan going. If we go marching in there without some coordination, we could blow it."

"If Crocker had sent a team in there, we would know by now. Deacon would have recognized operators."

"Maybe, or maybe Deacon is working for Crocker. He *was* CIA you know."

"OK, but suppose Crocker isn't running ahead of us. Suppose we are the point of the arrow here. If we call Crocker now, then we are officially notifying him. And a brigadier general can officially call us to a halt. How long do you think it will take Crocker to get a team out here, huh? Hours? A day maybe? It could be too late. I say we go now and ask for forgiveness later."

"And what if Crocker knows what we are looking for? What if Francine gave him key information before she was drugged? Ray, right now we are groping around in the dark."

They both fell silent. Derrick stared out the window at the Sun Valley Resort. Ray studied the steering wheel and tapped along to an unheard beat. When Derrick finally spoke, his voice was more quiet and determined.

"Ray, you trust this guy Crocker, right? I mean, if he sent you down range on something, you would be good to go?"

"Yes, but I would also trust him to throw a couple of mavericks like us in the brig—or just shoot us if that was more convenient."

Ray stopped tapping on the wheel and looked down the road to the Sun Valley Resort. "But you are right about one thing for sure. We are blind at the moment. And blind is not good. I'm willing to roll the dice on going to Leavenworth if you are." Ray shook his head and held his hands up.

Derrick began dialing his cell phone. Ray climbed out of the Charger and paced alongside the car while Derrick worked on reaching the general. Ray could hear Derrick's voice rise when he finally connected with General Crocker.

Now we've ripped it, Ray thought. *They don't call him the Crocodile for nothing.*

But Derrick's voice maintained an even tone. Ray heard no signs of argument or pleading. That wasn't a sure sign, since Derrick could remain dead calm while being screamed at by an enraged ironworker. Ray had always been the one to throw the first punch in an argument. So even though it was his own career that hung in the balance on this conversation, Ray was glad that Derrick was on the phone. Maybe two crocodiles could reach an understanding.

Ray bent over to look inside. Derrick was concentrating hard and scribbling notes. Ray leaned against the car and studied the front of the Sun Valley Resort. The place was a beehive of activity. Guests dressed in the latest summer casual fashions were arriving in a stream of limousines and rented SUVs. Flitting around them were resort staff, some dressed in the formal attire of greeters and drivers, and others in the service workers' crisp sky-blue uniforms. Ray could pick out private security types now and then. Some of them were casually dressed and doing their best to blend in. Others were playing their part to the hilt—including aviator shades and flashy holsters under their dark sports coats.

Delivery vans and trucks were lined up at the entrance in back. A driver from Madison's Flower Service appeared to be in an argument with a member of the hotel staff directing the flow of traffic at the service entrance. Stress levels were probably running pretty high at this point, Ray thought as he watched the hotel staff member wave the florist's van to move up for unloading. A chocolate-colored SUV with gold lettering took its place, followed by a couple of delivery trucks that appeared to be from the same business: Knight's Catering. Ray's mouth watered. They just looked like the sort of trucks to deliver great chocolate dishes. For a moment he wondered what it was like to attend the Allen Conference. *Must be nice*, Ray thought, *at least, as long as no one slips something into your food.*

Ray's reverie was broken by the opening of the passenger car door. Derrick stood and looked across the top of the car at his brother.

"We are on. Croc knows everything, and he's good with us on point. Other assets are in place. I'll fill you in on the way, but we need to get moving."

Derrick and Ray began walking down the sidewalk alongside Saddle Road. They cut left at Sun Valley Road and began making their way to the entrance of the lodge. As Derrick and Ray made their way toward the lodge entrance, the service manager at the rear of the hotel cleared the next vehicle and motioned it forward. The Knight's Catering truck eased forward toward the open delivery bay.

Chapter 40

FRANCINE MOANED AND pushed her head back into the pillow. Her eyes were closed, and any other time it might appear that she was simply having a bad dream. But Francine was still roaming in and out of consciousness, and her nightmare was real. The trauma team had done all that they could do. Now it was up to Dr. Adler.

He had used some bluff and bluster to transfer Francine to this small room in the trauma unit. It had originally been set up to deal with the Ebola scare back in 2014. It was probably an overreaction, but Saint Alphonsus had been designated as the northwestern US center for receiving Ebola patients. The room had never been used, but it was designed to perform double duty. Adler had never expected to receive an Ebola patient, but some other sensitive scenarios—like smallpox or anthrax—weren't beyond the realm of possibilities. He had only needed to convince a few key staff members that Francine's case was one of a "sensitive" nature, while at the same time dancing around a specific diagnosis and dodging their calls to follow the protocol that required notifying the CDC. *"I will notify them personally,"* he had told them, *"just as soon as I have the results of a few key tests."* He didn't like to lie, and he was not good at it. So he was pretty sure that his staff had simply gone along with his story and assumed that he must have good reasons to mislead them. At most, this charade would probably buy him twenty-four hours.

Dr. Adler studied the screens above Francine's bed. She was fighting hard, just as General Crocker had said to expect. But Adler just didn't know how long her body could keep up this fight. Her temperature was rising again, to 104 degrees now, in spite of all their efforts to keep it under control. Her brain and spine were inflamed as though she had meningitis. But he had ordered the tests, and they had all come back negative. Dr. Booker's heart was strong. After some wavering in the early stages of the trauma, it had returned to a steady rhythm and an impressive fifty-eight beats per minute. *What was her resting heart rate when her body* wasn't *under stress?* Adler wondered. Of course a strong heart could be both a blessing and a curse. They needed to get ahead of this strange inflammation so that Dr. Booker's heart would have great reasons to keep on beating.

General Crocker had told Adler what he knew about the prion research, and Jessie Anderson had filled in the recent history of their exposure. Adler was a trauma physician, not a medical researcher. So what he knew about prions was very little beyond what he had read in medical journals. But if this was a prion illness, it was certainly a terrifying new form. All the Creutzfeldt-Jakob–type diseases were stealthy killers. Even kuru began with diffuse neurological symptoms—occasional loss of balance, emotional swings, and depression. Only toward the end stages did prion diseases blanket their victims with disability and mental breakdown.

Adler considered it a cruel irony. Dr. Booker's research had advanced understanding of the most fearsome diseases in the world, the same black plagues that terrorists were so anxious to harness for their own purposes. And now she was battling for her life against one of those same plagues.

Francine turned her head on the pillow. Adler watched as she slowly opened her eyes and looked around the room. Or at least she seemed to be looking around the room. Adler had seen neuro patients appear to be conscious when they were still deep underwater.

"Dr. Booker, can you hear me?"

Francine's eyes turned to the pillow and then back to the ceiling.

"Dr. Booker?"

"Jess?"

It was barely a whisper, but Adler recognized it as a name. She was awake. "Dr. Booker, this is Dr. Adler. Do you know where you are?"

"West...Sun Valley," Francine whispered, as her vision seemed to focus on his face.

"It's a start. Dr. Booker, the man who injected you—do you remember anything he said, anything that might help us know what was in that syringe?"

Francine's eyes closed. Adler thought she was fading again. He looked at the screens. Her heart and respiration were rising. Maybe she was trying to swim to the surface. Although not known as a comforter, he reached out a calloused hand and patted the back of Francine's hand.

"Silver spoon." Francine gasped, and her eyes opened wide.

"I'm sorry. What was that?"

"Sun Valley." Francine's head rocked back into the pillow, and her neck stiffened. Her eyes fluttered, and she began seizing.

"Nurse!" Dr. Adler called out.

Francine's hand shot from under the sheet and grabbed Adler's forearm in a vicelike grip.

"My institute," Francine hissed, her eyes open wide and focused on Dr. Adler's face. For a split second, she seemed to have broken the surface. Her face was fraught but alert, almost normal. And then her eyes rolled back, and her hand lost its grip on Adler's arm. Francine fell back, and her body began to stiffen and shake.

A trauma nurse and a technician hustled into the room at that point to assist Adler. The seizure was not long but violent. When it was over, Adler felt drained. He left Francine with the trauma nurse and walked out to the hallway. He swept his paper head covering off in one motion and fell into a hallway chair. Jessie was seated across from him. She waited a second for him to catch his breath.

"Dr. Adler, how is Francine?"

"About the same. Pretty bad seizure just now. But otherwise about the same." Adler studied his hands for a moment.

It seemed to Jessie that he was trying to make up his mind about something. "Is there some treatment that you are considering?" Jessie asked, leaning forward in her chair to make eye contact.

Adler sat back and returned Jessie's hopeful gaze. "No, I'm sorry, but no breakthrough on that front. But Dr. Booker did mumble a few words just now. They made no sense to me, but I was just thinking..."

"What did Francine say?"

"Well, it's probably nothing. You have to understand that she has a fever of a hundred and four and has been drifting in and out of consciousness. But just now, before the seizure anyway, she seemed to be working hard to tell me something. Her vitals ticked up, and she seemed fully conscious. And she said what sounded like 'silver spoon.' She also said, 'Sun Valley.' And then as she was seizing, she seemed especially intent and said, 'My institute.' Any of those things mean anything to you?"

"Silver spoon?" Jessie couldn't help smiling. "I've teased her any number of times about being born with a silver spoon in her mouth."

Dr. Adler sighed. "That's probably it then. You brought her here, and in a fevered state she may just be connecting various dots."

Adler started to get up from his chair. He felt the sudden need for strong coffee.

Jessie jumped out of her chair first. "Wait—Francine said, 'My institute'?"

"Yes, she works at the army lab, right? Don't they call the place 'the institute'?"

"Yes, but never 'my institute.' She must have been working on something there that is somehow connected to what is going on here. She's trying to tell us something that connects the dots."

"Whoa, whoa, Dr. Anderson." Adler began waving his hand back and forth and standing up at the same time. "I'm following you, and we are guessing in the same direction. But I'm not sure how much this helps us. Dr. Booker may be trying to tell us something important, or she may simply be talking out of her mind right now. We should follow up on these breadcrumbs. But I don't want you to let your hopes run ahead of reality here."

"I understand. But you should understand something too. Francine is army to the core—even more than my husband or his brother, if that's possible. She may not be so clear right now, but trust me that she is trying to communicate whatever she might know about this plot. That would be her mission right now."

"Yes, General Crocker said the same thing. So…Did Dr. Booker share any notes with you about what she's been up to lately? Or would someone at the army lab know more about her recent work? We need everything we can get our hands on—and fast."

"I'm on it." Jessie began digging around in her purse. Adler thought maybe she had lost her keys, but Jessie was searching for Francine's journal. Francine had asked her to put it in her purse for safekeeping when the two of them were at the cabin.

Adler sensed the coming of a headache and began making his way down the hallway toward the break room. After he had taken several steps, he paused and turned back to Jessie.

"Oh, one more thing, Dr. Anderson: when Dr. Booker first regained consciousness, I asked her if she knew where she was, and she said 'west' and then 'Sun Valley'? That's a hopeful sign—that she knew where she was, I mean—didn't say 'Boise,' but in a way 'west of Sun Valley' is more impressive. She knew her location."

"Thanks, Dr. Adler. I know you are doing all you can."

Jessie wiped away tears and then turned her attention back to exploring the recesses of her purse.

Adler turned and shuffled down the hallway to the coffee room. The coffee room was too noisy and far away for Dr. Adler to hear the commotion when Jessie gasped and dropped her purse.

Sofia DeClair accompanied Crowfoot and Hassan to the grand dining room. As they walked she reviewed the schedule and interjected notes of history about the lodge and Sun Valley. Crowfoot listened only enough to nod or smile at the right moments. Otherwise he was preoccupied with the daydream of Sofia DeClair losing her mind and drooling on her fashionable business suit.

"And here we are, gentlemen, the grand dining room. You are responsible for setting table and providing backfill for our kitchen. I know that our executive chef provided you with the menu back in April, and he can update you regarding any details or last-minute adjustments."

"Do we have firm numbers at this point?" Hassan asked.

"Numbers for this conference are notoriously difficult to firm up," Sofia said and then, dropping into a conspiratorial whisper, added, "but you didn't hear that from me."

She smiled and winked at Hassan. Hassan fought to keep a charming smile on his face, mostly by imagining that he was breaking this woman's elegant neck.

"We have made arrangements here for a seating of five hundred, but you should be prepared to flex by thirty or so—fifty in a pinch."

"This is a wide range," Hassan commented, scanning the dining room.

"First time for your firm?"

"Pardon?" Hassan tilted his head as if listening more intently. Crowfoot stiffened.

"Sorry, I mean first time for your firm to cover the Allen Conference. No matter how many other gatherings a company has served, this one stands out. It is the greatest test of the ability to respond on the fly—and to do so with outstanding service. The Allen guests are the most discriminating in the world, and at the same time, they think nothing of making last-minute changes. Maybe it has something to do with their experiences in technology. At any rate, other questions?"

Hassan followed up with a few questions while Crowfoot meandered around the bare tables. He could see that Sofia DeClair was impressed with the chief of his catering company and that she enjoyed his company. *Hassan was the perfect choice*, Crowfoot thought as he heard Sofia thanking Hassan for his attention to detail. As he walked by each table, Crowfoot pictured them set with china plates, sparkling silverware, and delicate glassware. The food would be the very best and freshest available, a cuisine fit for kings and queens. And he could see them now, smiling and tipping their wine glasses. In the relaxed setting of Sun Valley, these kings and queens could unwind and lower their guard. They could talk freely about the *future*, that kingdom which they ruled together. There were no outsiders here to consider, no guests whose stake lay entirely in the decaying land of the *present*.

Crowfoot paused at the last table and smiled. This would be the last meal for the royal court. The *future* was about to be overthrown.

"Mr. Knight?"

Crowfoot tapped the table and then turned around to answer Sofia DeClair. "Sorry, Ms. DeClair, I was just picturing how beautiful it is all going to be."

"Yes, with your help it's going to be amazing."

Crowfoot returned Sofia's beaming smile as he made his way back across the large hall.

"Well, gentlemen, it has been a pleasure. And thank you again for helping out with the place settings. Not many catering companies are so agreeable when it comes to that sort of work. But every detail is crucial here."

"We could not agree more," Hassan said and took her extended hand. He bowed his head slightly as he shook her hand, and Crowfoot thought he caught the faint signs of a blush on Sofia's face.

"Mr. Knight."

Crowfoot nodded and shook Sofia's hand. As soon as Crowfoot released her hand, Sofia turned and hustled off to her other duties. Crowfoot smiled at Hassan as they stood for a moment in the silence of the great hall.

Aaron Thompson was making the final rounds before giving the all clear to Leonard Davis. His billionaire boss had begun to take him more seriously about the risks of wandering the Sun Valley Resort on his own. Tonight was the big kickoff dinner. So now Aaron was walking the route they would take to the dining room. He would also make a pass near the kitchen just to see if anything seemed odd or out of place.

The last thing he was expecting to see as he rounded the corner near the kitchen was an old friend from his military days.

"Deacon Henderson, what are you doing here?"

Aaron regretted calling him out just as soon as he saw Deacon's face. He looked like he had been shot, or as if he might be in the next second. Why hadn't Aaron considered the fact that Deacon might be on the job? He had let his mouth run ahead of his brain.

"Sorry, sir, but you must have me mistaken for someone else. I'm DeAngelo Jackson, of Jackson Service Company."

"Oh yes, now I see. For a moment there I thought you were someone I once knew in the hotel business. My mistake."

Aaron kept moving and scanned the area to see if anyone had seen him talking to Deacon. There were a few women sitting at a table nearby and sipping cocktails, but they seemed absorbed in conversation. A waiter was cleaning another table a bit farther away. He hadn't looked up since Aaron had passed him on his way to the kitchen. There was only light guest traffic in the area nearest the kitchen, and everyone seemed to be otherwise occupied. *That was close,* Aaron thought as he completed his sweep of the kitchen and began walking down the hallway to the great dining hall.

Aaron spotted an exit door about midway down the hallway. He stepped outside to get a sense of the area. Aaron was just about to step back inside when a powerful hand gripped his forearm and pulled him outside. He was just about to land his first blow when he came face-to-face with Deacon. Deacon put a finger to his lips and then motioned for Aaron to follow him. They walked to a narrow space near some air-conditioning equipment. Deacon stopped at a spot that was screened by the building on one side and neatly manicured shrubs on the other.

"You trying to get me killed back there?"

"Sorry, Deacon, I was glad to see you. Just blurted out your name before I thought. What the hell are you doing here anyway?"

"I might ask you the same question."

"Private security for Leonard Davis. You?"

"Helping a friend…off the books."

"Anything I need to know?"

"If I come across something, I'll be in touch. Meantime keep your eyes and ears open—and, of course, your mouth shut."

Deacon looked fearsome for a moment and then broke into a big grin.

"Roger that. I'll keep my mouth shut, and you keep your big paws off me."

"Deal."

Aaron walked out from behind the shrubs first, looking as though he had lost something on the ground. He slipped back in the doorway and continued his sweep of the hallway and dining hall. Deacon waited a minute and then exited himself, typing on his iPad as he walked back inside.

Deacon hadn't noticed the kitchen staff member who had slipped out a nearby door to drop off some garbage in the bins on the other side of the building. Before the man went back inside he slipped out a cell phone and dialed Crowfoot's number.

"We have a problem," the man said in an Arabic that was thick with Chechen accent.

After Aaron had completed his walk-through of the large dining hall, he returned to Leonard Davis's room and notified him that everything was clear. Then he crossed the hall to his own room and threw his coat on a chair. He had maybe an hour to kill before the dinner. Aaron turned on the television and began surfing channels. He usually relished this kind of downtime, a chance to let his mind relax before going back on full alert. But now he was having trouble relaxing.

Before the Sun Goes Down

What is Deacon Henderson doing here? Aaron had heard that Deacon had left the agency some time back and was maybe doing some freelance work. Of course, the government might have rung his number to provide covert security at the Allen Conference. That was the good-news scenario, the one that made Aaron feel better about the situation. Having Deacon here was another powerful layer of security. But it was all the other possible scenarios that kept Aaron from relaxing. Deacon could usually be found where there was trouble. He was a sort of ghost's ghost, the kind of operator whose presence alone was a warning that something big might be afoot.

Aaron couldn't relax. He decided to take a walk.

Jessie couldn't understand all the notes. Francine had used a code that was several generations ahead of the ones Jessie had learned when she worked at the institute. But what she could make out had caused her to tremble with both fear and hope.

Francine had been working on a special project. Her notes indicated that this project, code-named Viper, was not reported through the usual chain of command. Instead Francine was working solo on the Viper project and reporting the results directly to a single person. Jessie hadn't been able to decipher the person's code name so far, but she could tell from the notes that this was someone far up the chain of command. This mystery person might know something that would help them save Francine's life.

Jessie's phone rang, and she almost jumped out of the chair. She didn't recognize the number.

"Hello, this is Dr. Jessie Anderson."

"Jessie, it's Frank—Frank Higheagle."

"Yes, Frank, hello. How are you and Reuben doing?"

367

"We are fine. Sorry to call under the circumstances. But I may have some information that could help the doctors treat your friend Francine."

"What? Oh, that's great news."

"Our dog, Bear, began acting funny and then came down sick."

"Frank, I'm so sorry."

"Thank you. I think Bear will be OK. I'm going to let you talk to our veterinarian now. Hopefully he can explain it to you."

"Hello, this is Dr. Paul Simpson. I understand you are a veterinarian."

"Yes, that's right. Dr. Jessie Anderson."

"As Frank was telling you just now, they brought Bear in to see me. He's a Neapolitan mastiff. Apparently Bear managed to wander around the crime scene at the cabin before the police were able to shoo him away. A few hours later, he became wobbly. Stumbled into furniture. Frank noticed that he was feverish and brought him to me. I've run some tests—the basic canine assay for this type of case."

"Dr. Simpson, I'm sorry to interrupt. But do you think there is some connection between Bear's case and Francine's? I don't see how that could be the case."

"Right. When Frank told me about your friend, I didn't see how the two might be linked either. But I think you should at least be aware of my test results."

"Sure, yes, I'm listening."

"Bear isn't nearly as ill as your friend. But he has some inflammation of the brain and spinal cord. Many of the illnesses that could cause his symptoms are slower burn, and he might have contracted them prior to his contact with the crime scene. But I've ruled all those out."

"What about poisoning?"

"I would suspect it, but Bear doesn't have any of the usual symptoms of poisoning, no frothing or vomiting. In fact, he's pretty calm about the whole thing. My next hunch was that maybe he and your friend were given some exotic neurotoxin—venom of some kind perhaps. But that was before I took a spinal sample from Bear."

"And...?" Jessie stood up and held her breath.

"Viral meningitis."

Jessie's heart sank. "Oh, that's not good. I'm sure they would have recognized viral meningitis in Francine's case."

"Maybe not, Dr. Anderson, this is a pretty weird form of viral meningitis. Do you have a smartphone?"

Within seconds Jessie's phone screen was covered with purplish viruses. A few looked almost like the classic viral meningitis, with only a slight tail on one end. But most carried a twisting tail that ran one-third of their length. These were not classic viruses. And they were not typical of anything seen in dogs.

Jessie gathered her things and headed down the hall to find Dr. Adler. She wanted to be thrilled that maybe Francine had dodged one bullet. Nasim hadn't wanted to release his primary bioweapon before their attack in Sun Valley. He must have known that any preview, even a brief one, might give doctors a chance to develop some sort of protection or treatment.

But as Jessie hurried down the hallway the word *meningitis* kept ringing in her brain. She knew that her friend might have simply dodged the first bullet, only to be killed by the second.

Chapter 41

DERRICK AND RAY took some time to loiter in the lobby and get their bearings. Lines were forming at the bar, and the buzz in the lobby was growing louder all the time. The dinner tonight would formally kick off the conference. But for now the guests and their staffs were mixing and mingling. So that they didn't stand out from the crowd, Derrick and Ray stood close together and posed as tech buddies catching up with one another. In between cover chatter, Derrick was able to catch Ray up on his call with Crocker.

From Crocker Derrick had learned that there was at least one Guardian working in the kitchen and possibly others. The plan was simple at this point. Track the Guardians to the bioweapon, and stop the plotters before they had a chance to attack.

Derrick sent a text to Deacon ordering a truckload of ice. Deacon replied, "Order confirmed for Rose Garden party."

Derrick made his way outside and began wandering the gardens. Ray stayed in the lobby and pretended to be fascinated by his cell phone. It took some time for Derrick to locate the small bed of roses near a fountain, but he hadn't been there long when Deacon arrived.

The two men scanned the grounds before speaking to one another.

"There is a rat in the kitchen," Derrick said, "at least one anyway."

"I sort of figured that, cowboy. Any idea who our rat might be?"

"No, but finding the rat is our only chance at finding the cheese. Anyone look good to you while you were checking the ice?"

"Mixed bag. One Greek dude looked shady to me—prison tat on his left forearm. But he stayed at his station the whole time, talked to people as they came by like he was good with the crew. That's a pretty tense group in there, so hard to spot someone who might be more uptight than average."

"Can you get back in there?"

"Yeah, but I'm running out of time. They are revving up for the big dinner, and I was told to make my business quick. If anyone in a chef hat spots me, I'm sure they will delight in kicking my butt out of their precious kitchen."

"OK, so make the time count. Me and Ray are going to mingle and see if we can spot any of Crowfoot's crew."

At first Aaron had walked around the lobby and the bar. But the crowd was growing, and he needed some fresh air. He found the nearest exit and began walking the grounds.

It was cooling off now, after a warm afternoon. A few stray fishhook clouds were draped across the growing sunset. Purple and orange light reflected off the thin clouds and lit up the peaks and ridges of the mountain range to the east. The grounds were beginning to break into pools of light and shadow. Massive fir trees stood guard over the gardens in places, and Aaron paused before one of them to study the setting sun. Because he had a habit of keeping track of such things, Aaron knew that tonight would be a crescent moon. The resort used tasteful lighting, of the sort that security men like Aaron disliked—not enough to see by, but just enough to throw off a person's natural night vision.

Aaron drew in a deep breath of mountain air and then continued his walk. He decided to finish up by making a lap around the outside of the kitchen. The delivery area off the back of the kitchen was the one place he hadn't visited earlier in the day. Not likely to be a hot spot, but he wasn't ready to go back inside. Aaron began walking back down the path, nodding to the occasional guest that he met along the way.

As he rounded the corner where he had earlier met with Deacon, Aaron realized that he had picked up a tail. At first he thought it might be someone from resort security, a guard simply making sure that Aaron wasn't up to any mischief. But when he took a quick glance at the ground and then back behind him, Aaron saw military-issue boots and jeans. His tail was either an oddly curious tech guy or a more serious player. Aaron kept his measured pace and moved around the corner to the sidewalk that led to the delivery area. The place was calmer than earlier in the day, but one truck was still unloading, and a few dockhands were milling around here and there. Aaron paused to listen. His shadow had been well trained, and Aaron heard nothing but the snippets of distant conversation.

It was time to make a call. He could continue his walk and wait for his escort to make his move. The man would be exposed to lights and other people pretty soon. Aaron would have the drop on him, but he might have to shoot first and ask questions later. And the man might not take the bait. If he disappeared now, Aaron would have no chance to find out why he was being followed. And he would leave a potentially dangerous asset roaming the property just before he was to escort Leonard Davis to the big gala. Pretty easy decision.

Aaron made the motions of hunching over to light a cigarette. He didn't smoke, but his spook probably didn't know that. As he heard the man step forward, Aaron dropped low and launched himself at the man's legs. His kick made contact, and Aaron felt the man's knee crack and buckle. The man muffled a scream and swung a knife down hard toward Aaron's shoulder. Aaron turned just in time to avoid a fatal stab, but the blade sliced through his coat and cut a long glancing streak along his back. Aaron caught the man's arm in a judo hold and drove him into the nearby wall. He felt the man's arm give way and heard the tactical knife hit the sidewalk. It was over. He had the upper hand.

Aaron lifted the man from the sidewalk and pushed him back into the shadows. He pressed him against a wall and drew his pistol. The man held his palms out, and Aaron stepped back and aimed the pistol at his chest.

"Who are you? Why are you following me?"

The man heaved and winced in pain.

"Talk!" Aaron hissed.

"I was hired by your employer, Mr. Leonard Davis. He thought perhaps you were slipping. He sent me to make sure that you are doing your job."

"You're lying."

"And now I can report to him that you are fulfilling your duties quite well." The man tried a smile but was met with Aaron's cold gaze.

"What is the name of Mr. Leonard Davis's assistant?"

The man's face hardened, and he stared straight into Aaron's eyes.

Aaron tightened his grip. "Yeah, I didn't think so. Now, let's try this again. You tell me the truth, and you get away with a bad knee and a sore arm. You lie to me again, and you die tonight. Who are you, and why are you following me?"

The man's eyes lit up, and he began to smile again.

"I am your worst nightmare."

Aaron never saw the man behind him. He had only begun to turn his head when the blow came crashing down from behind him.

Deacon watched from the shadows as the man struck Aaron with the business end of a police flashlight. The man was dressed like a cop but was clearly not on the job. Deacon had decided that he would break into the open if the man drew his gun, but he figured Aaron could take one more knock to the head. Besides, Deacon wasn't sure who was on what team just yet. This could be a spat between terrorist types.

In any case, he had located a couple of prospects for Derrick and Ray. They had rats to follow now. They would be tracking them, and if Aaron turned out to be righteous, Deacon could always scoop him up later.

Deacon texted Derrick and then watched as the two men lifted Aaron and loaded him into the back seat of a black SUV marked "Mountain Produce."

Chapter 42

JESSIE HAD ALMOST run over Adler. He shifted his coffee to his left hand and wrung the searing coffee from his right.

"Sorry, Dr. Adler. Meningitis."

"No, just a coffee burn, but I'll be OK."

"*Francine* has meningitis."

Adler rubbed his free hand on his lab coat and took another sip of coffee. "I ordered a lumbar puncture early on, Dr. Anderson. We tested for meningitis, and the test came back negative."

"You didn't test for *this* meningitis." Jessie held up her phone to Adler's face. Purplish viruses reflected in his reading glasses.

"What the heck? Where did you get that?"

"Long story that I will tell you sometime later. Right now we need to contact your lab."

As he walked to the hospital laboratory, Adler had tried a couple of times to explain to Jessie that hospital policy did not allow her to accompany him to the lab. So she could just head back up to the waiting area, Adler had suggested, and he would meet her there as soon as he had the results. Jessie hadn't argued with him, but she also hadn't stopped marching alongside him as he made his way to the lab. And a last appeal at the door had no effect either. Soon Jessie was hovering over Adler's shoulder as he adjusted a scope and as other lab employees scurried away from the scene of the crime.

Finally Adler stood up and released the scope to Jessie. And there it was—the wiggly meningitis virus that had shown up in Bear's spinal fluid.

"It beat our test," Adler mumbled. "How did it beat our test?"

"No time to explain," Jessie said as she stood up from the lab stool.

"I'll order the proper supportive care. But as you well know, Dr. Anderson, changing one thing about this virus may change twenty other things. It beat our test."

"I understand."

Adler's team began with some of the standard protocols for treating viral meningitis and then began tweaking care as he could see the mutant strain responding. It was like hunting some new and dangerous beast, trying to draw it out into the open and to better understand its predatory pattern. But with patient steps Adler managed to bring Francine's fever down to 101. The seizures grew lighter and then faded away altogether. Dr. Adler was ready to declare that Francine had turned the corner.

And then she crashed.

From out of nowhere, Francine's body seemed to be struck a dozen blows. The screens around her bed flashed, and Adler's team responded to multiple warning sirens. They struggled to identify the source of the downturn, but it only seemed that everything was going wrong at once.

Adler stepped out of the fray just long enough to update Jessie. It didn't look good. Francine was failing fast, and they didn't know why. Maybe her body was responding poorly to the drugs or an interaction of the drugs. It was also possible, Adler said, that this mutant strain of meningitis was unbeatable. At that point Jessie had pounded Adler's chest with her fists and cried on his shoulder.

No, she demanded, they had to hold on to her. Francine would come through. Adler did his best to comfort her. He felt miserable himself. Dr. Booker was so young and bright. And he and his new tough-as-nails veterinarian partner had been so close to whipping this ugly bug. Jessie collected herself and apologized for the beating. Adler apologized for the news and slipped back through the double doors. It seemed like a long walk to Francine's room.

Hassan watched as his team put the finishing touches on the place settings. He was always struck by the magical transformation of bare tables to sparkling works of art. And this was art in its highest form. The deep green tablecloths formed a stunning background for bone china and silverware. At times like this, Hassan missed his old life as a master of this glittering domain. But this was a final gift, an opportunity to join the two passions in his life.

He began walking around the hall and making sure that each table was properly set. The guests would be arriving soon, and they would only have this one opportunity to set things right.

Suddenly his final check was interrupted by Crowfoot's voice in his earbud.

"Two of our men neutralized a security man who came too close to the trucks. All clear now and proceeding as planned."

"Excellent, sir," Hassan responded. "All is set and ready inside."

Crowfoot signaled to his men, and they radioed the driver of the Mountain Produce delivery truck to pull into the delivery area.

The manager of deliveries for the lodge was puzzled by the arrival of the truck. Mountain Produce wasn't on his list of scheduled deliveries. He signaled to a member of his security team, and the two of them met the truck at the entrance.

Just as the two were about to confront the driver, two of Crowfoot's men slipped up behind them and knocked them out. Both men were quickly relieved of their radios and uniforms, drugged, and shoved into the SUV with the unconscious security man.

Crowfoot's driver eased forward and parked the truck in position for unloading. Another Guardian unlocked the truck's back door and lifted the sliding door. He checked his watch to confirm that they were on schedule and then signaled for a crew of Guardians to begin unloading their cargo and moving into position.

Leonard Davis was more irritated than usual. It was time to go down for dinner. But now his security man was running late. This was one dinner that he looked forward to every year. It was an opportunity to talk about what mattered most to him, and with people who understood what mattered. It was also an evening when the clubby lodge atmosphere lulled many attendees to drink too much and talk more freely. Leonard had picked up a few of his better ideas by listening closely and pretending to drink heavily.

"Ms. Elliott! Have you located that idiot yet?"

Nancy Elliott covered her cell phone with her free hand and replied, "Not yet, sir. Not answering his phone and no luck with hotel staff."

"To hell with him, I'm not waiting around. Get my coat. I'm going down to dinner."

"But, sir, the whole point of bringing personal security—"

"The whole point of Mr. Thompson's security so far is to be a royal pain in my neck. I think he creates these risks of his out of an overactive imagination—and then charges me a fortune for protection." Davis paused and gave Elliott an icy stare. "*Where is my coat!*"

Ms. Elliott hung up her call and brought Davis his coat. She tried one more appeal.

"Sir, just give me ten minutes to see if I can locate him. I'm sure that he's here at the resort."

"And I'm just as sure that he's walked off his post. He's unreliable, Ms. Elliott."

Davis put on his coat. He checked a mirror and smoothed his lapel.

"I'm not going to be late to this dinner. If Mr. Thompson is located, please let him know that he is fired. You are not as good at firing people as I am, but I believe you may enjoy conducting this termination."

With that, Leonard Davis walked out of his suite and headed down to the great dining hall. Thompson's ineptitude had almost upset his evening, but as Davis got closer to the dining hall, his mood brightened again. It was a relief really, to finally be shed of that pesky security man. *Enough with all those boogie-man stories and breathless warnings.* He was free to enjoy himself again. And now all that Leonard Davis needed was a drink in his hand and an opportunity to make good on some boozy tech talk.

Ray and Derrick had made their way through most of the crowd before they received Deacon's text. In another social setting like this one, it might have been tough to appear distracted at just the right moments, to avoid being trapped in some sort of conversation that would blow their thin cover. But in a lodge full of technology types and politicians, it was the most natural thing in the world to respond suddenly to one's cell phone. And if it meant completely ignoring one or more people you were approaching, the move was even more authentic. And so the brothers had found it pretty easy to work this room from one end to the other. They had even had an opportunity to take a look in the great dining hall. The conference was not seating guests yet, but the place was decked out for royalty. Ray and Derrick had both worked security for a few high-level dinners. This one took the cake.

But no obvious rats, or at least ones they could readily identify. They were relieved to get the message that Deacon's hunt was going better.

They gradually worked their way to nearby exits and soon were alongside Deacon in a wooded rise that offered a view of the delivery area. Deacon handed Derrick a pair of binoculars and then turned to Ray.

"These rats are not shy. Since they knocked out that former operator I was telling you about, they've clocked the delivery manager and his security sidekick, stowing all their hostages in that black SUV over there."

"Mountain Produce," Derrick said, "any scoop on them?"

"Nope, but I'm guessing they aren't farmers."

"They are sure out in the open here. What are they unloading?"

"Lettuce," Derrick said. "Take a look."

"Where is hotel security?" Ray asked as he took the binoculars and focused on the unloading dock.

"My guess is that these guys aren't in the hostage business," Deacon replied. "I think they only knocked heads earlier because they were concerned about noise. Now it looks like they are in full control of the place."

"Well, for a few more minutes anyway." Derrick took out his cell phone.

"Who are you calling?" Deacon asked.

"Cavalry. Time to close this down."

Ray looked up from the binoculars.

"Wait, Brother—are you sure that's the weapon down there? I thought Francine and Jessie said this thing was found in meat."

"*Developed* in cows, but once it's been weaponized, they could use anything. Meat probably seemed a little obvious, so they spray some lettuce—same results."

Ray glanced through the binoculars again. "Those workers aren't wearing any protective masks or gloves."

"Those dudes are dead men walking, Ray," Deacon said and nodded toward the delivery area. "And I'm pretty sure they know it. Or maybe Crowfoot waved some money around at some guys who aren't that bright. Anyway, if this stuff is as bad as you all seem to think it is, I can't imagine anything short of walking around in spacesuits would keep them safe."

"Good talk," Derrick said. "Now I'm calling the cavalry."

Hassan watched from the kitchen door as the guests began filing in and taking their seats. All of the background players had cleared the hall now, and Sun Valley Resort staff had taken their places. They were excellent hosts, Hassan noted, as he watched the resort staff members greet their guests and graciously direct traffic. It took training and some talent to herd people without making them aware that they were being herded. Especially powerful people, Hassan thought, who were more sensitive than most to being directed.

Hassan's earbud crackled, and then Crowfoot's voice returned.

"Phase two is beginning shortly. All our people are in place."

"Excellent, sir. The guests are taking their seats, and service will begin with salads in ten minutes."

Hassan took one last look at the dining hall. Many of the guests were seated now and engaging one another in introductions and small talk. The other guests were moving toward their tables in good order. Many of them were carrying drinks from the bar. Hassan had a talent for reading crowds. It was one of the things that had made him such a good caterer. He had known when something was going wrong, often before a complaint was heard. And now he could see that this crowd was relaxed and comfortable. They were among their own people, and they were looking forward to a wonderful meal. Hassan must not disappoint them. He turned away from the door and headed back through the kitchen. It was time to put the finishing touches on the first course that the attentive resort staff would serve to their expectant guests.

Crowfoot and two of his men slipped out the unlit back door from a kitchen storage room and into a waiting black sedan. The driver pulled away from the curb and headed away from Sun Valley Resort. They drove south to the small town of Hailey. Many of Hailey's residents worked at the various resorts and restaurants in the valley. The little town was quiet. Only a few lights shone in houses and small stores. No one in town noticed as a black sedan pulled off the main road and came to a stop on the side of the road behind a black Hummer. And no one saw the three men exit the sedan and enter the Hummer. The two drivers nodded at one another as the Hummer headed south on Highway 75. The black sedan eased away from the curb and headed north.

Crowfoot settled back into his seat and gazed out the window at the night sky. There were no more commands to give now. The years of preparation and planning were over, and the attack was underway. He took a deep breath and allowed himself a moment of quiet satisfaction. A thin veil of cloud was slipping across the crescent moon. Crowfoot could see her face again, and she was smiling. Everything was in Hassan's hands now. And as the Hummer rumbled south, Crowfoot thought how appropriate it was that on this night when everything turned on one soldier doing his duty, that this soldier was her brother—Hassan. Just as Crowfoot would give everything for this cause, he knew that Hassan would lay down his life as well. Crowfoot had wanted to stay and to sacrifice himself with the others. But Hassan had convinced him that this was a better plan. Their enemies knew Crowfoot, and if they spotted him at the last moment, it might compromise all their plans. Besides, Hassan had argued, the movement needed a powerful leader to take full advantage of this attack, to build upon their initial success. And so Crowfoot had slipped away to fight another day. All he could do tonight was wait. Crowfoot leaned back and closed his eyes.

As Crowfoot and his men were slipping out of town, an Army Special Forces unit and a Homeland Security counterterrorism team were descending on the delivery area of the Sun Valley Resort.

Derrick, Ray, and Deacon stood and began walking toward the delivery area. The place was now swarming with special ops soldiers and agents in FBI and Homeland Security jackets. The soldiers had quickly overwhelmed Crowfoot's men, and the entire place had been subdued without the firing of a single shot. Derrick thought that they must have caught Crowfoot and his men completely by surprise. Even at that, he considered it a lucky break that there hadn't been some sort of gunfight.

Just as the three of them arrived at the sidewalk alongside the delivery area, a burly man in a leather coat stepped into their path. General Crocker looked even more formidable in person than Ray remembered. He had saluted before he realized what he was doing.

"General Crocker, sir."

"At ease, CI Anderson. Derrick, how are you doing these days?"

"Fine, sir. Do you know Deacon Henderson?"

"Oh my word—the Deacon! I didn't recognize you at first."

"Yes, sir, playing the part of a contractor. Dressing less cool than usual."

Crocker laughed and his eyes glittered. Laughing or scowling, Derrick thought, the nickname fit that face.

Crocker took them over and introduced them to the senior Homeland Security official. He debriefed Derrick and Ray about the prion theory and about the intelligence they had gathered so far on the Guardians. He seemed to know most of the story, and Derrick figured that they had already gotten most of what they needed from General Crocker and maybe from talking to Jessie or Francine. Derrick only hoped that Francine had recovered enough to answer questions.

The bioweapons specialists had cleared the truck and delivery area. Unlike the unprotected dockworkers they had watched earlier, these workers were covered from head to toe. A few of the team in hazmat suits were setting up a temporary quarantine for the dockworkers and hotel personnel who might have been compromised. The others descended on the delivery truck armed with every manner of testing device. A field lab was set to one side of the delivery area.

"General Crocker," Deacon said, "they took a few hostages, sir. Loaded them in that SUV over there, the one marked 'Mountain Produce.' Three individuals: two hotel personnel and a private security contractor."

"Any reason to think any one of those three might be hostiles?"

"They took hard cracks over the head, sir, but I couldn't say for sure. My impression was that they are friendlies who were in the wrong place at the wrong time."

Crocker called over one of his team leaders and gave him orders to clear the truck. They watched the team gather and head toward the vehicle, and then Derrick turned back to General Crocker.

"What are they telling the people at the dinner, sir, the conference guests?"

"Telling them to enjoy their drinks for now," Crocker replied. "If this pans out the way I expect it to, we'll have to shut down the festivities. But I've already been told several times, that won't go over well. So I want to hear what our bug crew says first."

The senior team leader was walking back in their direction. His team was following, guns down and smiles all around. Something was off.

"General Crocker, no hostiles in that truck—no friendlies either."

"What?"

"Truck was empty, sir. No blood, no signs of struggle. Single Diet Coke in the cup holder."

"Deacon, I thought you said you saw hostages taken—three men whacked on the head and loaded into the truck."

"General, I don't know what is going on here. But I did see those men get whacked and loaded into that truck—the one your men just searched. Mind if I take a look?"

"Be my guest." Crocker shook his head and dismissed the special-operations team.

"Ray, what the hell is going on here? Tell me you guys haven't been drinking or making up ghost stories!"

"No, sir, General Crocker, I'm sure there is an explanation. It may be that the hostiles were able to move those men while our attention was on the delivery truck."

"Of all the people on this planet, Anderson, you three should not to fall for some sleight-of-hand distraction."

"Yes, sir."

Crocker drew a cigar from the coat of his leather pocket and bit off the tip as he stormed off to check in with the head of the Homeland Security team. Meanwhile, Deacon took a stroll over to the Mountain Produce truck and began his own search of the vehicle. It was like the team leader had said. The truck was clean—no sign of hostages. Deacon made his way to the spot where he had seen the Guardians overcome the two hotel staff members. He found a few spots of blood, but he knew that was too little to go on. He wasn't about to try another round with Croc. This would surely sort itself out soon.

Deacon began making his way back to where he had left Ray and Derrick. And then he wished he wasn't walking in that direction. Crocker stormed back from the delivery area and seemed ready to light Ray and Derrick on fire—or maybe arrange an impromptu firing squad. The general's arms were flailing in all directions, pointing one second at the delivery truck and then at the truck and finally at Ray and Derrick. Croc wasn't known for yelling, and he wasn't yelling now. But the words that Deacon could make out were spoken with a chilling tone. As he approached the unhappy gathering, Deacon was sorry for once that he was the sort of soldier who never left fellow soldiers behind.

"Ah, Deacon, find anything?" Crocker growled between clenched teeth.

"No, sir, not a thing."

"Funny—*us either*!"

"What?" Deacon was beginning to think he was stuck in some bad dream.

"No bugs. Well, maybe I'm being unfair." Crocker's growl now turned sarcastic. "I'm sure if these gentlemen keep looking, they could find a cutworm or a sow bug. But what they aren't finding, CI Anderson and sidekicks, is any damn sign of a bioweapon!"

Crocker puffed on his cigar and then put a hand to his forehead. Deacon wasn't sure if the storm was over or if Crocker was just gathering his strength. It wasn't over.

"Do you have any idea how much this little exercise cost taxpayers!" Crocker waved his cigar around in a sweeping gesture. "And do you have any idea how much egg I now have on my face because I came out here on this Wild West excursion!"

Crocker began pacing the sidewalk as the Homeland Security team started packing up their gear. Deacon could see the soldiers hustling to pack their kits as well. Some high-level folks had been embarrassed here tonight. This ground had some bad juju, and everyone wanted to pack up and get as far away as possible. But here he was, the Master of Motown, stuck to the sidewalk with his two discredited cowboy friends.

"General," Derrick said, "whatever else is going on here tonight, I know a few things for certain. A group calling themselves the Guardians were working out of a terrorist base camp in the wilderness north of here. They were using that base to produce bioweapons. Ray and I have been tracking them, and everything leads to this place and this gathering. They are going to strike, sir. I don't know what we are missing here, but we are missing something."

"Ray, Deacon—what do you think? Do you agree with Derrick?"

Deacon felt himself going over a waterfall. "Yes, sir, I agree with Derrick about this group and their intentions. I can't explain what is happening right at this moment. But I don't think we should let this go."

Ray crossed his arms and tapped his finger on one forearm. "General Crocker, the two leaders of this group are a bad combination of mad scientist and special operator turned psycho terrorist leader. I'm sorry that we missed bagging them tonight, but I don't believe this was a snipe hunt."

Ray uncrossed his arms and pointed in the direction of the dining hall. They couldn't see faces, but from here they could hear faint music and the drone of dinner conversation.

"Sir, do you really think any one of the three of us would have brought you into this unless we were thoroughly convinced that an attack was coming tonight and that it was aimed at those people inside?"

General Crocker snuffed out his cigar on the bottom of his shoe and put his hands on his hips. He glanced toward the dining hall and then looked down at the sidewalk in front of him.

"I'm not sure what to think." Crocker sighed.

"Hold your teams here, General," Derrick said. "Pull them back out of sight maybe, but hold them in position until this conference is over. We missed something on the timing tonight, but I still believe this conference is the target."

"I have no basis to hold my troops here. Homeland Security found nothing to keep their team around."

"But, General, if we are wrong and they *are* attacking this conference...From what Jessie and Francine tell us, this mad cow thing would be a nightmare."

"No disrespect to Drs. Booker or Anderson, Derrick, but I'm skeptical on their prion theory."

"Then why did you come, General? That was the basis of our call to you."

"Hell, I came because of *who* was calling me. Dr. Booker's the best we've got in this bug warfare business. You and Ray—throw in Deacon for good measure—are top-notch operators. Best in the business. I just thought the prion angle was terrorist chatter, maybe even a screen for smallpox or some other horror show. Cracking a prion is like cracking a steel ball bearing. Even if this Guardian scientist was skilled enough to crack one, I don't believe he would be able to change the internal clock on prions. What terrorist group wants to wait around ten or twenty years for their victims to begin showing symptoms?"

Crocker straightened and looked up at the starry sky. Except for the stiffness of his shoulders, he looked as if he was searching for a favorite constellation. After a few moments of silent searching, he turned and extended his hand to Derrick.

"Derrick, tell Dr. Booker that she is to recover fully—and that's an order. I'll visit her then. Tell the other Dr. Anderson hello for me."

"Yes, sir."

General Crocker turned to level his gaze at Ray. "CI Anderson, keep me posted. I mean it. After I finish dealing with my own blowback, I will do what I can to cover your ass on the CI side of things."

"Thank you, sir."

"Deacon—I didn't see you, and you didn't see me." Crocker winked and shook Deacon's huge hand.

"Copy that, sir."

"OK, you three, I would say, 'Stay out of trouble,' but it's a little late for that. I'm going to leave a number that Ray can call if you need backup. It is not my number, and I'll deny that I gave this one to Ray. But a team will be under my standing orders to deploy here within ten minutes of receiving that call."

"Thank you, General," Derrick replied.

Crocker nodded and walked briskly away. His SUV was the last to leave the delivery area. Derrick, Ray, and Deacon stood for a moment and surveyed the area around them. Only an hour ago, it had been the scene of a full-on counterterrorism operation. Now it was an ordinary resort delivery operation, quickly humming back to life. Homeland Security had whisked away a handful of workers that they could not immediately authenticate, but otherwise everything looked as it had before Derrick called in the strike.

"Well, that was fun," Ray said. "Maybe we can set each other on fire next."

Chapter 43

DR. ADLER HAD been on his feet for sixteen hours straight. He could feel himself starting to fade, but he also knew that he needed to force himself to push through the exhaustion. Francine Booker had been hovering between life and death for the past three hours. In fact, it was more accurate to say that his patient had been swinging violently from one state to the other. He had never seen a body's processes swing so abruptly from recovery to near collapse. Meningitis could be volatile, but its course tended to follow one of a few patterns. And it was not known to cause lightning strikes of dysfunction outside the central nervous system. This illness, on the other hand, was more like the work of a raging arsonist who started a new fire just as Dr. Adler and his team had tamped down the last one. It was a maddening cycle, and Adler felt the anger building inside him. It was as if this demonic illness were not only trying to destroy Francine Booker, but also to set ablaze Dr. Adler and the others who were fighting to save her life.

And then it was over. Just as quickly as the firestorm had started, it burned itself out. A trauma nurse was the first to recognize it. Adler had been conferring with a colleague about the latest flurry of symptoms when the nurse came over and directed his attention to one of the screens. Her fever was dropping. Within minutes other vital signs began to stabilize and then to show the first flickers of improvement.

Adler had seen false recoveries and predeath rallies too many times to be fooled. So he had waited and watched. And the recovery continued. Finally satisfied, at least that they had reached some temporary beachhead, Adler hurried from Francine's room and found Jessie slumped in the hallway chair, asleep. He tapped her shoulder and gave her the good news.

As Francine's fever was breaking and her recovery beginning, Derrick, Ray, and Deacon were milling around the delivery area in back of the Sun Valley Resort and trying to get their bearings. The last few hours had been completely disorienting. Derrick knew that it was possible that they had gone off the trail somewhere. But it was also possible that the Guardians had intended to throw them off balance at this point and that this was the very moment they needed to be most alert. As he was retracing their earlier steps, Derrick's cell phone buzzed.

"Derrick, it's Jessie. Great news—Francine is doing much better."

"Oh wow, that is great news!"

"Dr. Adler is cautious, but he thinks that the worst of the meningitis may be over. He is hopeful that she can make a full recovery."

"Meningitis?"

"Oh yeah, sorry, it's been a whirlwind. Yeah, long story, I'll tell you later. How is it going there?"

"Not so good." Derrick did his best to explain recent events.

"Maybe we were wrong, Derrick. Maybe the terrorists faked us out. It's not a bad ending, you know: Francine recovers, and the people attending the Allen Conference are safe. I want Nasim and Crowfoot to pay for what they've done, but that will happen. They won't get far. I'm just ready to be home again."

"Yeah, that sounds good right now. But I can't get all the puzzle pieces to lie down just yet."

"I know. Dr. Adler and I were playing charades with Francine for a while, and I was wishing in the worst way that you were here. You know I'm terrible at that game."

"Charades?"

"Well, of a sort: Francine was in and out of consciousness and in quarantine. So all this came to me through Dr. Adler. But Francine woke up once during the worst stretch and said a few words. We were trying to make them out, hoping that they might help us diagnose her case."

"What did she say?"

"Well, she gave a clever answer to the basic question about where she was. Francine said, 'West...Sun Valley.' For Boise I guess—west of Sun Valley. She also repeated what she had said at the cabin, the word 'homemade.' That was useful, along with some other clues that helped us identify what that creep Nasim had injected."

"She mentioned Sun Valley?"

"Yeah, smart gal. Oh, and then she said one other thing that was either pure delirium or a dig at me."

"What was that?"

"Silver spoon—kind of an odd joke really, since it was always her that I considered linked to the silver-spoon crowd."

"Jessie, I love you."

"I love you more. Guess you need to go?"

"Yep. Give Francine a hug for me."

Derrick hung up as calmly as he could and then grabbed his brother's arm.

"Call that number Crocker gave you."

Ray looked at Deacon, who took the signal to step in next.

"Say, sheriff, that number was only for go time. You know, evidence jumping up in our face, terrorists pulling guns sort of thing. All I hear stirring is that hoot owl in the woods over there."

"The Guardians are using the table setting," Derrick replied.

Now it was Ray's turn. "Brother, you aren't making sense. And I'm with Deacon on using that number. Maybe if the angel Gabriel appears and—"

Derrick grabbed Ray by the shoulders.

"Listen—Francine was sick, but she was trying to tell us something she picked up from Nasim's crew. They probably thought she was unconscious at the time. Anyway, she said 'silver spoons.' Think about it! Dose the salad and some people may skip it. Doctor the dessert and half the crowd is on a diet. But coat the silverware…No one in that room will eat a bite without using a spoon or a fork."

Deacon stopped shaking his head suddenly and picked up Derrick's train of thought.

"And no one out here—including that crack bug crew from Homeland Security—would examine the china or the silverware. They would be focusing on the food."

Derrick released his grip on Ray's shoulders, and the three men stood in silence for a moment. Deacon took a deep breath and shoved his hands deep in the pockets of his black cargo pants.

"All right, cowboys, so what now?"

Ray turned to look toward the lights glowing inside the huge dining room. He blew out a breath and looked directly at Derrick.

"We can't call Crock. Not enough to go on."

"Ray, those people are—"

Ray held up his hands and nodded.

"Hold up, hold up. Let me finish. We can't call Crocker because we don't have solid intel. Derrick, what we have is a tip—a possible signal. I agree with you. I think Francine is pointing us in the right direction. But imagine reporting our tip to Crock. 'General Crocker, while suffering from a high fever and a nasty concussion, Francine said something about 'silver spoon.'"

Derrick sighed and looked up at the sky. A cloud was moving across the quarter moon.

"See?" Ray continued. "We don't have enough to make that call."

Derrick nodded. "So what are you thinking?"

"Well, first I'm thinking that we have to keep those people out of that dining room."

"How do we do that without tipping off the Guardians?" Deacon asked. "Only thing worse than calling General Crocker with another false alarm might be starting a fight with a kitchen full of terrorists, especially if it was a fight we couldn't win."

Derrick had begun kicking at a tuft of grass growing through a crack in the pavement. He stopped kicking and looked up at Ray. "Maybe it's time for us to go from white hats to black hats."

Ray's face was expressionless at first, but then he broke into a wide grin.

Deacon looked from Derrick to Ray and then shook his head. "You cowboys want to let a Motown man in on your little joke?"

"Deacon," Ray replied, "you think you and Batman could work up a little diversion that would give a couple of cowboy-terrorists time to set up a counterassault on a highly trained kitchen staff?"

"In English please," Deacon sighed.

"What my brother is saying is we need you and Batman to make all of those guests forget about their dinner and focus instead on their dearly beloved technology. And it wouldn't hurt if you spiced it up a little with the possibility of a couple of terrorists roaming the resort. You know...black hat types."

Deacon shook his head. "I don't know if I should be more worried about what you two are thinking or the fact that I am beginning to understand what you two are thinking."

"We need to get you a cowboy hat," Ray replied.

Deacon made his way back to the rose garden where he had met Derrick earlier in the night. It seemed like a week had passed since then, Deacon thought as he retrieved a burner phone from a pocket and called Batman.

The hack would have taken longer, but when he was making his rounds of the ice machines, Deacon had seen one of the chef's log in to the resort network. So now he was able to work from the inside while Batman worked his magic from the outside.

It was not their most sophisticated work, and anyone investigating this later would have no trouble picking up their trail. But there was no time for making themselves invisible. Guests were beginning to crowd the lobby and hallways of the resort, talking and laughing as they gradually moved toward the great dining hall.

"Deacon, are you sure you want me to include this bit about bad guys onsite? It might set off a panic that would compromise what you guys are doing there."

"Risk we need to take. Just a sprinkle though—you know, conversation starter. I think these tech folks are more likely to panic over their cell phones acting up than they are over the Taliban crashing their dinner party."

"Got it," Batman replied. "I sure hope you guys know what you are doing. Otherwise we may be cellmates at Leavenworth."

"I get the top bunk. How's it coming with that dark cloud?"

"ETA of five minutes. First attack will be a scattering of cell phones, followed quickly by an attack on the resort server. You picked a tough crowd—encryption, firewalls, redundancies...oh yeah, and some of the best computer minds in the world."

"Just need to punch them in the face, Batman. Don't need to knock them out."

"Roger that. Punch in the face on its way. Good luck, Deacon."

As Deacon hung up and began moving into position, Raheem was checking to make sure that he had followed Crowfoot's instructions. The two men called Ghost and Tupe had left some time ago, drunk with newfound wealth and ringed by cigar smoke. Raheem had watched them carefully for a time, using the binoculars to trace their path away from the laboratory. He would need to report all this to Crowfoot when he met up with him later. When the two men staggered from view, Raheem turned back to his checklist. He needed to close down the laboratory, including destroying the animals in the pens out back. Then he needed to set the explosives and make sure that he destroyed the laboratory completely.

Raheem did not like killing animals. He had kept various pets when he was a boy—a stray dog, a ground squirrel, a crippled goat. The Taliban considered any sign of sympathy, even for an oddly tame ground squirrel, as a sign of weakness. He had seen them toughen some of their young soldiers by having them take in a stray dog and then, when the boy had grown fond of the animal, commanding him to slit its throat and watch it die. And so Raheem had kept his own pets in secret. He would shelter them in some abandoned shed or junkyard and bring them food whenever he could steal away from his handlers.

Crowfoot's instruction regarding the animals was unfortunately simple and clear. *"Kill all the remaining animals. Tear down the pens before setting your charges."* Crowfoot expected him to destroy any sign of the animals and their role in the development of the weapon.

Raheem walked around the pens and counted the animals: six cows. Raheem went back inside and located his rifle and a box of ammunition. He returned to the pens and loaded the weapon. Raheem tried not to look at the animals. One of the cows began mooing softly, its head outstretched toward him. He shivered and tried to distract himself by clicking the gun's safety mechanism off and then on again.

But he couldn't hold his gaze and ended up staring at the bellowing cow. Her brown eyes were wide and framed by white. Raheem could not tell if she was merely curious or afraid. He had intentionally avoided contact with the cattle over the time that he had worked in the lab. He did not want to know how they felt or what they saw.

And now he forced himself to look away and to focus on sighting in the weapon. He must make sure that he used as few shots as possible. He panned the area through the rifle sights. He paused a moment when he sighted one of the cremating ovens. Then Raheem leaned the rifle against a rail and checked Crowfoot's instructions again. No, he had not mentioned the cremating ovens. Raheem thought that this might be a problem. The charges he had been instructed to set were not powerful enough to ensure the destruction of these blocky ovens. They might be a clue left behind. But then again, Raheem assured himself, Crowfoot must know something that he did not know. Crowfoot was careful, and he was able to think clearly. Raheem had long ago accepted that his own brain could not be fully trusted. Raheem shook his head and willed himself to focus. He must complete his checklist and proceed to the meeting place.

Just as Raheem was lifting the rifle from its resting place, he heard a strange sound from inside the laboratory. He froze for a moment and listened. The wind was picking up, and it rattled a loose corner of the tin roof. One of the cows shuffled against the fence.

Raheem lifted the rifle and began walking toward the nearest cow. The noise hadn't been real. It was his mind misfiring again. There was no more time to waste. Raheem shouldered the rifle and took aim at the cow.

Then he heard a moan from inside the laboratory. This time it was clear and real—a human sound, like a cry. Raheem checked again that the rifle was loaded and the safety was off. Then he made his way back inside the laboratory.

The door from the animal pens led directly into the secure testing area. It was another of those areas that Raheem had avoided. He had only been inside this area once, when the laboratory first opened and before Dr. Nasim began his experiments. The hallway was pitch-dark except for two tiny lights near the far end from where Raheem stood holding the rifle. As his eyes gradually adjusted to the low light, Raheem could make out the rows of small rooms running the length of the hallway. A metal wall ran along the bottom half of each row of rooms, and above this wall only clear glass or plastic. Raheem could see that the windows were thick, and some were smeared on the inside. On the other side of the windows, he could see a hospital bed in each room, and above the beds were several computer screens. Strands of wire ran like thin white tree branches from the bed to the various computer screens. The screens were dark, and the beds were empty. Raheem could hear his own breathing and, again, that moan. It came from one of the rooms at the other end of the hallway, near the faint lights. Raheem gripped the rifle and began making his way toward the light.

The two rooms on each side of him were dark and empty. As he made his way to each one, Raheem swept them with the rifle and then examined them again over the rifle sight. Here and there the beds were covered with dark stains. The glass in some rooms was more smeared and splattered, as if some drunken painter had been let loose in them. A few wires were dangling loose. Raheem's shoes made a tiny squeaking sound on the tile. He had seen Dr. Nasim come out of this area wearing paper booties. He must have hated the noise that was made by shoes on this tile.

Finally Raheem reached the faintly lit room. He swung the rifle around and made a quick sweep of the faintly lit room. It contained the same hospital bed and nest of computer screens. But otherwise it was empty. The glass was clearer than in some of the other rooms. Raheem moved to the middle of the glass and made a careful examination of the room from floor to ceiling—nothing. And then, from just behind him and to his right...

"Please...shoot me."

Raheem wheeled and pointed the rifle in the direction of the faint voice. A young woman was huddled in the corner of the hallway. She was wearing a hospital gown, and her feet were curled up under the gown. Raheem could barely make out her face. She was thin, and her head seemed to be floating just above the stained hospital gown.

"Who are you? What are you doing here?" Raheem shouted.

"Sara Kaufman...I am one of your laboratory rats. But you know all this! Now get it over with please—shoot me and get it over with!"

The woman's face seemed to break into pieces as she sobbed and shouted at Raheem. He had only seen such a face at funerals in his hometown—the tortured face of a woman in mourning. Raheem lowered the rifle. His head was pounding. This was not on Crowfoot's list. He had no instructions.

"Sara Kellum—"

"Kaufman!"

"Sara Kaufman, you should not be here. You are not supposed to be here."

"Right, that's what I'm saying." Her body heaved in a loud sob, and she brushed back a strand of blond hair from her face. "You all have done your best to kill me with the shots, but for some reason I've been a little slow to die. So now...What was your name?

"Raheem."

"So now, Raheem, I need you to shoot me before the worst of it hits."

"The worst of what?"

"Is part of the torture you appearing ignorant! The *worst* of it—the worst of *that*!" She flung out a rail-thin arm and pointed to the other rooms down the hallway.

Raheem jumped back at the sight of her ghostlike arm. And then he looked back over his shoulder at the dark and empty rooms.

"Dr. Nasim tested the materials on animals," Raheem said. "He identified certain persons to be his first human subjects, but they have only recently been infected."

"You are more ignorant than I thought. Do you know how to fire that weapon?"

"Yes."

"Then quit lying to me, and shoot me before it's too late."

"You are crazy."

"No doubt. So were the others before they died."

Raheem stood and began walking back down the hallway.

"Where are you going? Raheem, don't leave me here!"

Raheem fumbled in his jacket and brought out a lighter. He had often used it to light Dr. Nasim's cigar. Raheem opened the lighter and walked back down the hallway. He stopped and studied the inside of the rooms carefully.

"Raheem?"

The woman had lowered her voice. And she had stopped sobbing. She was growing resolute, ready to die. Raheem had seen this transition before. Some individuals had begged for their lives to the very last. But others had fallen silent before their Taliban tormentors. They had taken the last few moments to release their grip on life and to greet what lay beyond.

Raheem studied the rooms now in a different light. He could see that these rooms had been places of torment and struggle. Desperate hands and angry fists had made the smears on the windows of these rooms. This was not a place of testing cows or other animals. These

Before the Sun Goes Down

were rooms for human subjects. Raheem moved to the next room and saw that the sheets in this room were twisted and bloodstained. One of the bed's side rails was bent, just at the point of a bloody hand-print. It would require great strength to bend metal like that, strength born of terror and rage. Raheem turned and walked back to where the woman lay. He knelt down.

"You must go. You should not be here."

"No."

"Why not? Don't you understand? I am setting you free. I want you to leave this place and go back to wherever you came from."

"I can't do that. I'm infected."

"No! That is not possible."

The woman shifted her weight and pushed herself up against the wall. Raheem could now see her face more clearly. She was a young woman and pretty.

"Raheem, you may be right that I am going crazy. And that is probably why I am giving you the benefit of the doubt. So working on the assumption that you don't know what I'm talking about...here goes. The so-called doctor—"

"Nasim," Raheem said.

"Right, *Dr.* Death. These rooms were used for his insane human experiments. He had people captured and placed in one of these rooms. Then he injected us with some sort of nightmare drug or something. It causes horrible things—unspeakable things. I was only here a couple of days, but I heard sounds that I've never heard before in my life. The screams—they were not like any other screams I have ever heard. I'm sure they were all restrained to the bed like I was. But some of them must have broken loose from their restraints. I heard them hitting the walls with such force I thought they would break through and come running into my room. They beat against the windows and threw things until someone would come and stop all the commotion. And at night this place was like a jungle—all manner of cries and growls and whimpers.

"Then one of the loud ones would fall quiet. Guys in hazmat suits would come and bag the body and load it on a cart. I've heard eight of those carts go by in the two days that I've been here."

Raheem looked down at her stained gown. "And you were given these injections?"

"Yes."

"But you are not screaming and running into walls."

"No, not yet, but it will begin soon. And that is why I am begging you to pick up that rifle and make sure that I don't end up that way."

Raheem looked intently at the woman's eyes. She had stopped crying. Her green eyes were both intense and sad. Her face was thin, her skin clear and smooth. She seemed less desperate now, more resigned.

Raheem stood up suddenly and grabbed the rifle. He turned away from the woman and began walking back down the hallway.

"Raheem, please don't leave me here!" the woman called after him.

But Raheem ignored her cries and strode down the hallway and back out into the main laboratory building.

Sara Kaufman hung her head and slumped back against the wall. The symptoms would surely start soon. And now her one chance for help was gone.

But then she heard footsteps. He was coming back. Maybe he had found his courage.

And then Raheem appeared out of the gloom of the hallway, carrying a carved walking stick and an old backpack. The rifle was strapped over his shoulder.

"Stand up," Raheem ordered.

"I can't."

"Yes, you can. Now stand up!"

Sara clung to the wall and slowly rose from the floor. She turned to face him and brushed her hair from her face.

"I suppose we are going outside. That makes sense. I don't want to make this any harder than it has to be."

"Shut up!" Raheem shouted. His shout echoed down the hallway. He and the woman both fell silent and stared into the darkness. It was as if they expected his shout to rouse some sleeping beast.

Raheem held his hand to his temple for a moment, waiting for the burst of pain to subside. When he spoke again, his voice was quiet and firm.

"You are not going to die, and you are not going to suffer like the others. I did not know it at the time, but I filed the charts that were used to time the effects of these experiments. You have been here two days, yes?"

"Yes, that's right."

"And you were injected when you first arrived in this room, on the first day, correct?

"Yes."

"Then you were not injected with…what the others received."

"How do you know?"

"The charts—by the times recorded in the charts, you would have begun experiencing symptoms on the first day. And your time in the experiment would have ended by now."

"I would be dead by now—I mean, by the schedule?"

"Yes, and you are not dead. And so you must go."

"Are you sure?"

"I don't remember some things so well. Other things I remember perfectly. Charts are one of the things I remember perfectly. You are alive because you did not receive the experimental injection. Now you must go quickly. I am already far behind schedule. There is food and clothing in the backpack. My coat is hanging near the front door. Take it, and use the walking stick to help you make it uphill. If you head straight uphill when you leave this place, you will climb a few hundred meters until you reach a road. There is not much traffic but enough that someone will come by soon."

Raheem turned and walked down the hallway and out the door near the animal pens. Raheem walked toward the animal pens and swung the rifle over his shoulder. He studied the cows for a moment. They were huddled together against one side of the pen, with the laboratory building forming a windbreak and shielding them from the snow. A fresh gust of wind blew snow around Raheem's head and shoulders. He shivered. And then he set the rifle on the ground and strode quickly to the gate. He pulled the pin and opened it and swung the metal gate outward. The cows remained bunched in the corner. Raheem walked around to the back of the pen and waved his arms at the cows. It took a bit of coaxing to move them from their shelter, but eventually they broke for the gate and ran through the gate. They kicked up dirt as they ran, and Raheem watched until they had run into the forest. He closed the gates to the empty pens and then began walking around to the front of the laboratory.

Before he reentered the lab, Raheem scanned the ground that rose steeply toward the road. He could just make out the tiny bundled figure working her way up the rocky ground. *Sara Kaufman.* Raheem was frightened to realize that he had remembered her name.

Chapter 44

THE HALLWAY FROM the delivery area to the kitchen was quiet. Derrick and Ray had expected to encounter a few workers. They figured their first challenge would be identifying any Guardians mixed in among hotel staff. But the hall was empty, and the two brothers moved quickly toward the kitchen. The back entrance to the kitchen was a set of swinging doors with metal kick plates at the bottom and small windows at eye level. The glass was not the best quality, maybe the only glass in this place that was below par. And years of kitchen steam and a collection of scratches made it tough to see clearly.

Derrick could just make out the various stations in the kitchen and the workers manning each station. Some things in the kitchen looked normal. A few workers were cutting vegetables and stirring dishes as they simmered on the huge stoves. Others were taking trays from one location to another and dropping off various items on the large metal cutting surfaces.

But as their eyes adjusted, Derrick and Ray could easily see the signs of the impending attack. A Mac automatic pistol was partially covered by a towel and lying within the easy reach of a man cutting carrots. A burly man stood stirring a pot of soup and at the same time wiping his brow. Now and then he peered at the pot of soup as though it might burst into flames. It was hard to tell if any of the men and women in the kitchen were cooks or compromised members of the resort staff. But it was easy for Derrick and Ray to see that most of these individuals were about as comfortable in a kitchen as they might be tending a preschool classroom full of two-year-olds. Ray picked up a bit of conversation coming from the man cutting carrots and another man who was not visible through the glass. He couldn't be positive, but it sounded to Ray like the men were conversing in Chechen, or in one of the other tribal languages spoken along Russia's southern borderlands.

Derrick and Ray slid away from the door and took several steps back down the deserted hallway. They huddled in a corner near the back door, out of sight from the kitchen entrance. Ray checked his watch: two minutes to go time. He and Derrick checked their weapons and burner phones. If everything worked the way they had planned, every other phone in the resort would soon be taken hostage—that is, every phone except three. As Derrick checked his weapons, he prayed that Deacon and Batman had managed to quickly thread this needle. If they couldn't maintain contact with Deacon, then the three of them would likely lose one another in their own communications fog.

After the time had passed, Derrick nodded to Ray. They began moving back down the hallway toward the kitchen doors. They were only a few feet from the doors when suddenly a cart began rolling their way and then banged into the double doors. There was no place to hide in the brightly lit hallway, and Ray and Derrick instinctively jumped against opposite walls and slid behind the swinging doors. Their moves were sudden and hardly agile, but the cart was noisy, and they could only hope that the person pushing it had not heard them. The doors swung farther outward, and the cart rolled into view, followed closely by one of the Chechen men Ray had seen through the kitchen door. The man was whistling as he pushed the cart and its load through the double doors. Ray could see earbuds dangling from the man's ears. They had been lucky. Ray held his pistol tight until the Chechen had pushed his cart through the exterior door and headed outside.

Deacon was making his way across the lobby when he heard the first reaction. A woman in a black evening dress turned to a man standing near her.

"What is this all about?" the woman asked.

The man adjusted his tortoise-shell readers and examined her screen.

"Must be a hoax or something. What site are you on?" The man slipped his own iPhone from his pocket, typed to log on, and then wrinkled his brow at the results. He turned away from the woman to examine the crowd behind him, craning his neck and looking around those standing closest to him. "Oh, there he is. Hang on a second, babe; I'm going to slip over and catch Zach. See what's up with all this." He held up his phone for a second and then began moving through the crowd and calling his friend's name.

About the same time Deacon noticed a few other heads bobbing up from the crowd and a few couples huddling over a cell-phone screen. Batman's fog had begun to make its way through the crowd.

Deacon moved back to a hallway off the main lobby and tried to tuck himself out of the way. He pretended to study his own cell phone, all the while keeping one eye on the movements of the crowd in the resort lobby.

At first it seemed to Deacon that their plan wasn't working. The crowd was milling around for sure, and now and then he picked up tense bits of conversation. They weren't mixing and mingling in the same way as they had a few minutes earlier. But they weren't heading for the exits either. Maybe the resort had better cybersecurity than they had thought. Was it possible that Batman's assault had only struck a glancing blow? This group would brush off one or two odd reports or a short-lived network malfunction.

This is not good, Deacon thought. Their plan to move the crowd didn't seem to be working. And now he was across the resort from Derrick and Ray. He had to stop Derrick and Ray from making their move. Deacon quit pretending and started to type out a text to Derrick and Ray. He was about to hit send when his message disappeared and his phone screen went blank.

"Great," Deacon whispered to himself, "that's just great." He slipped his phone in his pocket and reached for the pistol tucked in his jacket. *Time for plan B.*

And then the crowd began moving. Deacon had been just about to push away from his hideout and head through the crowd when they began chattering loudly and moving in pairs and small groups away from the great dining hall and back out into the main lobby. They were not moving as one, but the momentum seemed to be shifting. Deacon thought of all the times when he had seen mobs in the street. There was almost always a critical moment of hesitation among crowds, a quiet pause when it could go either way. Some crowds lost their common energy in this critical moment. It was like watching sleepwalkers wake up all at once, dazed and wondering what they were doing in the middle of a crowded street.

But others crossed over that threshold into a shared hypnosis. Once that happened a crowd was no longer made up of individuals but of the coordinated cells of a single body. Deacon could see that starting to happen now in this crowd. They were a mix of loners and skeptics and geniuses, this bunch, and so not easy to turn. But Batman's technological version of a shark sighting was beginning to take hold, and the techies were beginning to turn from the water and head for the beach.

The couple passed near the hallway where Deacon was standing, their friend Zach and his escort in tow.

"Likely someone's bad idea of a joke. But can't hurt to take precautions," the man named Zach was saying to the others as they passed by.

The woman who had first spotted the problem with her cell phone didn't seem convinced. She was clearly giving her date a private earful about missing the dinner. But he wasn't hearing her. His face was a mask that Deacon knew well, the look of a man who was terrified and at the same time trying hard not to let his face show the fear.

Following this couple was another clutch of four well-dressed guests. Two private security guards flanked them on either side. They hadn't drawn their weapons yet, but both men's neck muscles were as tight as piano wires. Deacon could see that these men were only one click away from their active combat mode.

After the mass of the crowd had moved by him, Deacon pushed away from the hallway wall and checked his cell phone again—still dead. The only thing to do now was to head back toward the kitchen and hope that he could meet up with Derrick and Ray. The three of them would need to coordinate in the dark.

At least they had got that crowd moving, Deacon thought. They wouldn't have to sort out the Guardians from that mixed crowd of security and techie types. He slipped his useless cell phone back into his pocket and turned to go. Deacon never heard the man slip up behind him, only the whoosh of air just before the blow.

Two Guardians caught Deacon as he began to collapse and then struggled to drag him quietly down the hallway toward an open door.

Ray and Derrick had begun moving on schedule. But it seemed to Derrick that something wasn't right. He had expected to hear more sounds of confusion and movement by now. Instead what he heard so far were the sounds of a fine gala. An orchestra was playing classic music, and threaded through the music were bits of conversation and foot traffic. Most of the sound was coming from the lobby, but it had been getting near them as he and Ray made their way to the rendez-vous point. He had expected to hear the sounds of the crowd moving away from them by now.

It had probably been too much to ask. Batman and Deacon were pros, but this resort might have state-of-the-art systems. They hadn't had time to check that out. The Sun Valley Resort was a rustic lodge in the mountains. But it also happened to be a rustic lodge that hosted one of the world's most elite technology conferences.

Derrick turned to Ray, cupped a hand to his ear, and pointed down the hallway and toward the great dining hall. Ray nodded and then shrugged. He pointed to his watch and held up two fingers. Derrick nodded. They would hold up for two more minutes. Maybe by then they would hear the crowd turn. In the meantime they would need to sit tight and hope that no one came their way.

For once in her life, Sofia DeClair hadn't gotten the memo. She had been sending a staff member on an errand when her phone went dark. Her next stop was the kitchen, and she had been on the move before her guests turned course and began moving away from the great din-ing hall. And so she had ended up here, in the hallway near the back of the kitchen, just as the Guardians were realizing that something was going wrong with their carefully crafted plan.

She knew it would only last a few seconds, but Sofia savored the quiet of the back room's hallway. The only sound was her heels click-ing on the well-polished floor and the low hum of kitchen sounds on the other side of the wall. The meeting was going well. No crises that she had not been able to resolve. And so far not a single guest had stormed out over one or another tiny inconvenience. If this amazing streak held, it would be a first. Sofia allowed herself the first relaxed smile of the past week. This dinner was the big event, the crescendo of a finely played symphony of coordination. After this evening, Sofia could see smooth downhill sledding toward a weeklong vacation on an isolated beach with no cell-phone service.

Ray spotted the attractive woman making her way down the hall but a second too late. A side door of the kitchen opened just ahead of her, a burly hand shot out to cover her mouth, and then she was gone—whisked inside the kitchen before she could make a sound. A slip of paper she had been holding in one hand skated along the floor in the breeze of the closing door.

Ray started for the kitchen door, but Derrick stepped out into the hallway to stop him. Derrick knew it was risky to whisper, but he also knew that Ray would charge ahead unless he could convince him otherwise in about three seconds.

"We can't go off half-cocked, Ray."

"They'll kill her."

"Focus, Brother. We are up against pros here. Every move has to be tight."

Ray nodded and turned his gaze away from the kitchen door. "Right, but I'm gonna bust up that kitchen crew."

"Roger that." Derrick smiled. "Soon."

Inside the kitchen Hassan was receiving troubling news. A Guardian named Amir had captured a man working to interfere with their plans.

"Hassan, this man was talking to someone outside. They must have sent some message and frightened our targets. All of the dinner guests are moving away from the dining room."

Hassan turned to several men standing nearby.

"You men, establish a tight perimeter around this building. Do not fire a shot. Use your hands and your knives but no gunshots. Do you understand?

"The rest of you," Hassan called out to the other Guardians working in the kitchen, "secure the dining hall, and make sure that no one compromises our preparations. Do not draw attention. Cell phones are compromised, so use the walkie-talkies. For now we will stick to our original mission. If it becomes necessary, I will notify you to move out and employ our backup plan. Do you understand?"

The Guardians posing as kitchen staff all nodded, and Hassan turned back to the Guardian who had sounded the alarm.

"Come, take me to this man."

As Hassan was about to leave the kitchen, one of the Chechen men spoke up.

"And what about this one?" Hassan looked back and saw the man standing over the woman. Her white blouse was spattered with blood, and one eye was beginning to swell closed. The Chechen was smiling, and Hassan was surprised at how unnerved he was by that smile. Hassan had been a warrior in the highlands of Afghanistan. He had known plenty of dark souls. But these two Chechens were perhaps the blackest souls he had ever met.

"You will not lay one hand on her until I return. If you do, I will gouge out your eyes myself. Do you understand?"

The Chechen smiled. "I will eagerly await your return, Hassan," he replied, his black eyes appearing to look through Hassan.

Deacon was just beginning to see light in the distance, as though it were coming through a tunnel. And then he felt a hard slap. He couldn't see who hit him, but he was grateful for the slap. It helped him swim up out of the darkness toward full alert.

"Wake up, you black dog!" the man shouted, spit flying into Deacon's face.

Now Deacon was really waking up.

"Back off, little man," Deacon said softly.

The man slapped him again, as Deacon knew he would. The blood rushed to his face, and Deacon's combat senses returned. His head throbbed, but otherwise he felt intact. Tied to this chair, but not by an expert. His tormenter was pacing in front of him now. He was trying to maintain an air of calm control. But Deacon heard a bit of tremor in the man's voice, and the pacing was a sign that he was struggling against anxiety and fear. The man stopped suddenly and bent low to look directly at Deacon.

"You have made a grave mistake, black dog—a *fatal* mistake." The man was smiling broadly and leaning close to Deacon. "The only question now is whether you will die quickly and painlessly or slowly and in unimaginable pain."

Deacon studied the man close up. He was dressed in a senior chef's outfit, and it seemed to fit him more than some of the other terrorists manning the resort's kitchen. He was probably the one responsible for setting up the whole terrorists-as-kitchen-crew cover. Deacon picked up a Pashtun accent. But the man had spent time abroad and seemed like someone who might have been born to an important family. His face was lean and earnest, and his beard trimmed short and precise. He seemed accustomed to looking down his nose at most people, including, at the moment, Deacon. A high-born guy who expected other people to defer to him. *Maybe start with that,* Deacon thought. He stared directly into the chef's eyes.

"Did your papa let you herd the goats on your own, or was he afraid that you might wet your pants if a wolf came around?"

The supply closet was filled with handy instruments, and Hassan selected a wooden-handled cleaning brush and swung it hard into Deacon's ribs. Perhaps a cracked rib or two would teach this black infidel some respect.

Deacon flinched at the blow but made no sound. He slowly adjusted as best he could in the restraints to sit straight up.

Hassan could see that the man's face was calm and hard. Hassan was shocked, and he looked at the Guardian scout who had taken Deacon hostage. He only hoped the scout had secured this man's restraints.

"You trying to tickle me, goat herder? 'Cause I'm not really ticklish." Deacon looked up and locked eyes on Hassan. It was the look he gave new recruits at Ranger school just before he taught them what it was like to confront death.

"Shut up!" Hassan hissed. "You will listen to me now. We have captured your friends. You have interfered where you do not belong. And now if you do not follow my instructions, you will watch your friends die a slow and painful death. And then it will be your turn."

Deacon studied the man's face. "You're bluffing, goat herder. You wouldn't be alive right now if you had run into any of my friends from Detroit."

The man standing behind Deacon struck him in the back with the butt of his assault rifle.

Deacon heaved and then gathered himself again and stared at Hassan.

"You will address me as 'Hassan.' Now, your friends are suffering as we speak. You must get to work if you want to save them in exchange for your own life. I am going to dial the last number of the person you were speaking with earlier. Batman, wasn't it? And you are going to tell this man to repair the damage and send an all-clear message. We will know if you try any tricks."

Deacon looked intently at Hassan as he spoke, all the while flexing the muscles in his upper arm. The man behind him must have turned the rifle butt in an attempt to miss Deacon's restraints. But he had grazed one of the ropes. Deacon could feel maybe an inch of looseness in his restraints. It wasn't much, but maybe it was enough. Deacon nodded.

Hassan held up Deacon's cell phone and began to redial Batman. As Deacon listened for the first ring, he turned his right arm just enough to get a firm grip on one of the chair's back spindles.

"Batman. Hey, brother. Yeah, it's Deacon. All good here, so how about you restart the network and send an all clear to some of the guests...That's right...Run it in reverse. Got it? OK, Batman, and please hurry."

Hassan ended the call and slipped the cell phone back in his pocket. The man standing behind Deacon started to pull a large knife from a sheath at his waist, but Hassan waved him off.

"I am going to walk to the lobby and see about the effect of this phone call. You two stay with him until I return."

Hassan turned to open the door of the supply closet and headed out toward the lobby. He didn't turn back, and so he never saw the smile on Deacon's face.

Zach Tetrov had been stargazing when the first cell phones came back to life. It was an odd cacophony of jingles and buzzes and snippets of the latest dance tunes. His own phone buzzed in his pocket, and Zach turned from the stars to examining his cell-phone screen.

"A message from Sun Valley Resort: The network has been restored. Earlier messages a prank. Our security team has issued an ALL CLEAR."

Zach slid his phone back into his pocket and took his girlfriend's hand. He began walking toward the valet station. She seemed poised to object but then dropped her head and began to walk with him. He was relieved to see that she knew him well enough to know that he would not change his mind. Zach had grown up a diplomat's son, moving from one dangerous part of the world to another. One of his best friends had died in a terrorist attack on an embassy. And so Zach knew enough to know that "all clear" was often the last message that victims of such attacks received, the words that caused the targets to relax and move away from shelter. Zach did not intend to wait around to see what happened next. While he waited on the car, Zach sent an urgent warning text to his friends attending the conference. He knew from hard experience that many of them would wave off his warning. But he did not have time to track them down and make a personal appeal, not if a clock was ticking somewhere inside that building. A text was the best he could do at this point.

He handed the attendant a twenty-dollar bill and slid behind the wheel of the Porsche 911. Once the two of them were safely in the car, Zach took a last look back toward the resort. Here and there some of the guests were peeling off and heading for the exits. Some had, no doubt, learned from hard experiences elsewhere, and others were hustled off without question by their security details. But most of the crowd, likely including at least a few of Zach's good friends and many of his business associates, were turning and strolling back inside the resort. Some were laughing, and others were jostling one another like school kids returning from a routine fire drill.

Zach shivered. *God, I pray there is no fire tonight,* he thought. Then he gunned the Porsche out of the parking lot and away from Sun Valley Resort.

Two Guardians were just coming out of the woods near the exit road when the black Porsche roared by them. One of the men turned to the other with a shocked expression on his face.

"They are escaping! We had orders to stop them."

The man looked ready to run down the road in a hopeless attempt to catch up with the speeding car. But his companion grabbed his arm and smiled.

"Do not concern yourself, Ahim. They will not get far. Come, we must see to the others."

Hassan was relieved to see that most of the guests were filing back into the Sun Valley Resort. But some remained outside, clustered in small groups and huddling around the light of their cell-phone screens. Hassan walked out the front door and pretended to be looking for someone. He did not like what he saw in those standing outside. Here and there individuals were smiling or talking, but most of those huddled outside appeared blanketed in a common anxiety. They were not panicked, but neither were they reassured.

The all clear had only been partially successful. Hassan swept the crowd for the security personnel, and they were not at all difficult to spot. None of them were smiling, and few of them were paying any attention at all to cell phones—theirs or the ones that their clients were holding up for them to examine. Those earlier messages had alerted the security professionals to the possibility of danger. Once alerted, these watchdogs tended to stay on alert. Now their faces were set, and their eyes were continually scanning the area surrounding their clients. *Situational awareness*, Hassan thought to himself. The entire operation now teetered in the balance. He had to tip the scale in their favor—and fast. He retrieved the small walkie-talkie from his pocket and began to make his way back inside.

Chapter 45

SOFIA DECLAIR COULD only see well through her left eye, which she kept glued to the kitchen worker who was standing guard over her. Shortly after Hassan had left, he had tied her to one of the metal poles that ran floor to ceiling in the kitchen. It was so obvious to her now that her guard was not a real cook. His hands were scarred and heavily calloused, and a smeary tattoo ran across one set of knuckles. He was thick bodied and heavy browed—a thug, only now dressed up in kitchen garb and tormenting her in her own kitchen. Another of the men in the kitchen had recommended tying her to a chair from the head chef's station. But her guard had taken the extra time required to tie her up in a standing position. He seemed to prefer harassing her from all angles and at eye level. He had begun drinking as soon as Hassan left the kitchen, but so far he had heeded the warning not to harm her any more. She was thankful, because the one time he hit her in the hallway had closed her right eye and left her woozy. Of course, Hassan's warning did nothing to stop his leers and threats.

"You think I am afraid of Hassan, eh? You think that is why I am not hurting you?" His face was only inches from hers, and the smell of vodka and sweat was overpowering. "I will cut out Hassan's heart anytime I choose. No, I am not afraid. I am taking my time. Ya?" He was smiling, and she could see that some of his teeth were broken off.

An ugly scar ran from the corner of his mouth to the middle of one cheek. He began to laugh, staggered back away from her, and took another swig of vodka.

"Ya, I am taking my time with you. My friend Dmitri is always telling me that I should slow down and enjoy life more. Isn't that right, Dmitri?"

Another kitchen worker ambled over and took the vodka bottle from her guard. He took a deep swig and studied Sofia for a moment. If anything, Sofia thought he was more terrifying than her guard. He was handsome, with fine features and a carefully groomed beard. But his face seemed absent of any emotion or sympathy, and his light blue eyes as cold as any she had ever seen.

"Yes, comrade, you are always in such a rush. I tell you that it is good to stop and smell the roses."

The man stared at her for a few seconds. She tried to hold his gaze, but she felt a shiver and lowered her head. Dmitri smiled and turned back to share another drink and some whispered conversation with her guard in their own language. They were laughing together now and seemed to be lost in their own private revelry. So neither of them noticed when Sofia managed to wriggle one hand free of her restraints and slip it into her skirt pocket. Her hand had automatically gone to her pocket when the man grabbed her, and her phone was still there. She pressed buttons by memory, and managed to tap out 911 just before the main door burst open and Hassan strode back into the kitchen.

Hassan walked directly up to where Sofia was tied to the pole, withdrew a large tactical knife, and begun cutting her loose.

"You, Dmitri, bring me that chair."

Dmitri gave Hassan a sullen look, shot Sofia an icy glance, and then walked over and retrieved the chair. Hassan removed the rest of her restraints and motioned for her to take a seat.

"I have removed your restraints. Do not move or make a sound, and you will be fine. If you disobey me, you will die along with your entire staff. Understand?"

Sofia nodded. Hassan stepped away from her and then strode to the center of the kitchen.

"The infidels managed to scramble communications and send a warning. We captured one of them and forced him to undo this damage and to issue a message of reassurance to our targets. Many of our targets are returning to the lobby. But the security personnel are causing problems, and it is clear that they will turn their masters away from us. So we must act quickly now. It is time to for us to *become like the night.* Move out and execute precisely as we trained."

The kitchen workers began scattering away from Hassan and toward the kitchen exits. Derrick and Ray heard the commotion only just in time to duck inside a nearby custodian's closet. They listened as several of the Guardians hustled out of the kitchen and down the hallway to the back exit.

Dmitri and Sofia's guard had not moved when the others began to leave the kitchen. Sofia wondered if they had understood what Hassan had just said. Dmitri was casually drawing a cigarette from his pocket. He placed the cigarette between his lips and fished in his pocket for a lighter. Her guard stood with his arms folded across his chest and his eyes blazing at Hassan. Dmitri lit his cigarette and then snapped his lighter closed with a flourish.

"We will take the woman with us," Dmitri said.

Hassan drew a pistol from inside his chef's uniform and pointed it at Dmitri's face.

"You and your ignorant friend will proceed to your station and follow your orders. The woman is not your concern."

"Ah, but she is our concern, comrade," Sofia's guard growled. "You see, I captured her, and I consider it my duty to guard her to the last."

Hassan made the slightest nod. And before either of the Chechens could react, two other Guardians struck from behind. They clubbed the two Chechen's with their rifle butts, and both men dropped in a heap at their feet. The two Chechens had been going for their weapons when they were struck, and a large tactical knife clattered across the kitchen floor in Hassan's direction. Hassan studied the knife for a moment and then turned back to the Guardians standing over the two unconscious men.

"Chechen mongrels," Hassan hissed. "Take them away, and make sure they cause us no more interference." Immediately the two Guardians began dragging the unconscious men out of the kitchen and toward the back exit from the resort.

Hassan picked up the Chechen's tactical knife and secured it under his kitchen jacket. He walked slowly around to stand in front of Sofia. Then he bent down and studied her face. She could hardly believe that man was the leader of this gang of thugs. She had considered Hassan so refined and charming when she had met him for that initial tour of the resort. She was embarrassed now to recall that she had spent more time with him in that meeting than absolutely required, that she had been witless enough to have been taken in by his charm and his good looks. *Flirting with a psychopath gang leader,* Sofia thought to herself as Hassan looked into her one good eye, *this must be marked as a new low with respect to meeting the right man.*

Hassan turned and walked to a freezer nearby. He returned with ice wrapped in a fresh kitchen towel and applied it gently to her throbbing injured eye. Sofia tried not to wince, but her good eye began to water in response to the pain. Hassan lifted the compress for a second and brushed the tears from her cheek and then returned the compress to her eye.

"Here," he said as he nodded to the compress, "hold this in place."

Sofia's hand brushed Hassan's as she took the compress from him and held it to her eye. He seemed puzzled for a moment or confused. She could not quite tell, and she couldn't trust her blurry vision. In any case his odd expression lasted only a moment before the cold calm returned. He straightened up and smoothed his jacket.

"I am leaving you here now. Do you have a cell phone?"

Sofia's good eye must have looked suddenly terror stricken. She had only begun to speak when he interrupted her.

"Give it to me please."

Sofia's hand shook as she reached into her skirt pocket and retrieved her phone. She had felt a surge of hope when he had said he was going to leave her here. But now all her hope evaporated. She clutched the cell phone and held it out to him. All that it would take now is for him to glance at her recent calls. And then it would all be over.

Hassan took the cell phone from her trembling hand. He dropped it as though the phone were a hot dish that might burn his hand if he held it any longer. And then he stomped it under his heel. The phone shattered, and pieces of metal and glass skittered across the kitchen floor.

"Now," Hassan continued, "you will stay here. If you leave this chair, you will die. But if you stay seated in this chair, I will send someone back for you later, someone who will release you safely. You will carry away from this place a message from our organization. Do you understand, Sofia?"

She shivered at the sound of him saying her name. "Yes, I understand. I will stay here."

Hassan walked to the freezer and came back to her with a tray of ice. He searched the area near her chair for a moment as if he were looking for something he might have left behind. And then, without a word, Hassan walked out of the kitchen and left Sofia alone.

Deacon wasn't answering his phone. Derrick looked at Ray and nodded. It was time to move. From here on they would have to play this by ear. They began moving down the hallway and had just reached the door back out to the main lobby when the first Guardian appeared. He was still wearing his chef's hat but otherwise not making any pretense at working in the kitchen. In his hand he was carrying a nine-millimeter pistol fitted with a silencer. Ray heard the suppressed fire just as the first bullet whizzed near his chest and struck the wall behind him. He was just about to fire his own weapon when he saw the knife hit the Guardian in the chest. The man looked down at the big tactical knife, puzzled, and then slumped to the floor. Ray looked over at Derrick and nodded. Derrick put his index finger to his lips and then motioned toward the door and bent his hand in a right-hand turn. Derrick had just delivered a fatal knife strike from fifteen feet away. But his face was calm as still water and trained on the door just ahead. For a fleeting second, Ray saw Derrick not as his big brother, but as a professional warrior. If they hadn't been brothers, Ray would choose Derrick above any man he knew to be beside him in a fight. And the fact that they *were* brothers only made Derrick more ferocious in Ray's defense. *Look out whoever is on the other side of that door,* Ray thought as he moved to follow Derrick through the hallway door.

And on the other side of the door were four Guardians moving out of the kitchen toward the dining room. All four were dressed as chefs but at the same time clearly armed and moving with some urgency. The Guardians were caught off balance by the

sudden appearance of two heavily armed men in the doorway behind them. Two of them turned and began firing from pistols with
silencers, as the other two used the covering fire to move farther
into the lobby. Ray and Derrick fired at the same time, and one of
the Guardians fell hard to the floor. The other shooter grabbed at
his abdomen and then tried to move to one side for cover. But Ray
fired again, and the man went down.

Before the shooting started, Ray had noticed a stream of guests
moving back into the resort dining room. Derrick's knife trick and
the Guardian's use of silencers had made the confrontation a quiet
one at first. But now Ray and Derrick were banging away, and the
guests were beginning to respond. The lobby that a few seconds before had been humming with conversation and background music
was now roaring with the sound of screams and panicked footsteps.
Derrick tried to focus on the two Guardians that moved quickly toward the lobby, but he lost sight of them in the whirling currents of
the crowded lobby. Security men were racing forward to cover possible entrances and exits. Guests were scattering in every direction,
colliding into one another, running over one another.

Derrick caught sight of one of the Guardians moving through
the crowd, but he could not get a clear shot. Then he heard Ray fire,
and the man dropped beneath the streaming crowd. Derrick moved
beside Ray and pointed toward the front doors of the resort. They
needed to make their way forward and try to get control of the chaos.
Ray had just begun to move forward when their path was blocked by
a half dozen thickly built security professionals. They were wearing
the standard-issue dark clothing of soldiers-turned-bodyguards. Two
were trying their best to be discreet while at the same time holding
assault rifles, while the other four were brandishing state-of-the-art
pistols. All six seemed planted to the floor and focused on what they
considered to be the source of all the trouble—Derrick and Ray.

Ray tried to shout out their case—"We are on your side!"—but the bodyguards were having none of it. In desperation Ray pulled up his sleeve to show them the Rangers tattoo on his forearm. Derrick thought it looked like a good idea, but apparently the mercenaries didn't agree. The six men surrounded Derrick and Ray and began shoving them toward a conference room off the main lobby. The only way to avoid being herded into the room was to make an aggressive move. But Derrick knew that these guys were only doing their job. He would have done the same if he had been in their shoes. He only hoped that Ray didn't fire on them. His brother was not always so willing to play along.

As one of his captors was closing the conference room door, Derrick could see the white coats of Guardians here and there in the crowd, guiding guests and acting as if they were assisting them to safety. Derrick had no idea how he would explain this situation to their captors. But he needed to make friends fast, and they needed to use their combined force to prevent a disaster.

While Ray and Derrick were being forced into the conference room, Guardians were weaving their way through the panicked guests and trying to reassure them that the situation was under control. Hassan had used the walkie-talkies to coordinate the message that there had been a disturbance by antitechnology activists but that security had now captured the perpetrators. His men were busy trying to persuade the harried crowd that the earlier cell-phone problems had been caused by these same activists and that, failing that attack, a few desperate members of this group had fired some shots in the air in an effort to create panic. These individuals were now under arrest, and all was well. The Sun Valley Resort security force had joined the attempts at restoring calm, although not with the same enthusiasm as Hassan's crew.

Bill Sanders, Sun Valley Resort's head of security, was only sure of one thing—something weird was going on. He didn't buy the account of the earlier hack as the work of antitech activists. He might not be in the league of the technology gurus attending this conference, but Bill Sanders had once been the head of a computer security firm. He knew a thing or two about networks, and he knew that punk amateurs could not break the Sun Valley Resort system. That network attack had been military grade.

He wasn't sure about the source of that gunfire. He had been working his way in that direction when he had encountered the first of the kitchen crew members working to restore calm. He was glad to see that sort of team spirit and a bit surprised that it would bubble up from the usually fractious group in the kitchen. But right now Bill would take whatever help he could get. They needed to restore calm. A few guests had already been injured in the stampede. More panic would not help the situation. As he worked his way across the lobby, Bill tried to calm the crowd and encourage the kitchen help. Now and then he encountered the professional security types, many of whom he knew personally. They were surfing the same balance as Bill—encouraging calm while at the same time hunting for the truth in a fluid situation. When he was about halfway across the lobby, he ran into an old friend in the business.

At five feet five and probably a hundred pounds, Carly Thomas had always reminded Bill of a Doberman. She was sleek, attractive, rather fidgety, and deadly. Carly was a mixed-martial-arts expert before there was such a thing. No person in his right mind would have entered a cage with her.

"Hey, Bill! A couple of the guys captured two of the shooters. They are holding them over there." Carly pointed toward the conference room. "I'm going to get my people out of here. No offense, Bill, but I just have a bad feeling."

"None taken. I think we will get a handle on this soon, but I understand that you have to make the call for your people. Take care, Carly."

The crowd was beginning to calm but also to thin out. Bill could sense that the resort was losing its hold on its most prized guests. He wished that he had pressed Sofia harder for a larger staff this time around. He needed more help if he was to have any chance to recover from this lousy situation. Hopefully he would catch a break when he reached that conference room.

But just as it seemed his path was clearing, Bill encountered a serious roadblock.

"Bill Sanders! Just the man I am looking for. What the hell is going on here, Bill?"

Nancy Elliott. Maybe not his worst nightmare at the moment—those might include encountering her boss, Leonard Davis, and an unscheduled meeting with the devil—but Nancy Elliott was high on the list.

"Ms. Elliott, as you can see, we have a situation on our hands here. But I am—"

Elliott cut him off. "Leonard Davis is missing."

"What?"

"That's right, Bill. Leonard Davis is missing, along with his head of security, Aaron Thompson. And you need to find them right now!"

"Nancy, we will locate them right away. I promise you. But first I have to get control of this situation. Mr. Davis and his bodyguard could be here in the lobby for all we know right now. Before we can find them, I need to restore some order."

"Bill, what you need to do is find my billionaire boss. This chaos was started by someone who wanted to get to Leonard Davis, and you and your team have played right into their hands."

"Nancy, we can't know that. Anyway I don't have time to debate with you right now. I have to go do my job."

He pushed around Elliott and hustled through the crowd to the conference room. He figured she might find a way to get the last word, and sure enough as he was moving through the crowd, Bill heard Nancy Elliott call out that she was holding him personally responsible. *Tell me something I don't know*, Bill thought as he reached the conference room door.

Hassan had managed to reach the dining hall a few minutes before the shots rang out. In those few moments, Hassan had thought that their original plan was going to succeed, in spite of the interference from their enemies. Perhaps a quarter of the guests had already been seated at their tables, and a steady stream of others were joining them and taking their seats. They had been laughing, if a bit nervously, and talking about the disruption and false alarm. He had been relieved to see that Leonard Davis was already seated, along with many other prominent targets. Hassan was just about to make contact and retrieve the kitchen staff when he heard the first shot. For a split second, Hassan thought about running to investigate. Perhaps he had mistaken the sound for a bottle of champagne. But such false hope did not last long. Two more shots rang out. The guests had already been made restless and fearful by the earlier disruptions. Now it was clear that the sound of gunfire was the last straw. Hassan turned aside as guests stood and began bolting from the dining hall. He called the Guardians and called on them to continue the struggle.

Deacon decided not to wait for the man in charge to come back with his report from the lobby. His two guards were young and nervous. It was only a matter of time before they broke discipline and took matters into their own hands. Besides, their leader might return with a bad report. Batman had worked wonders the first time around, but Deacon knew that even Batman might have found it impossible to get the genie back in the bottle.

"You boys seen any good movies lately?" Deacon asked, shifting one foot to gain maximum leverage.

"Silence!"

"You fellas probably assume that I'm a big fan of Denzel's. And I like Denzel—don't get me wrong—but I'm more into the classics. Either of you guys see Richard Roundtree in the movie *Shaft*? No? What about John Wayne in *The Green Berets*?"

The guard stepped from the side to confront Deacon directly. He drew his tactical knife and brandished it only inches from Deacon's face. It was just the move that Deacon had been hoping one of them would make.

A minute later Deacon was holding the door to the room open a crack and checking the lobby. The lobby was more crowded than before and moving in the general direction of the dining hall. He didn't see the man who had been interrogating him earlier, the one who had introduced himself as Hassan. But here and there he could pick out Guardians mingling among the guests. It appeared that they had left the kitchen along with the guests and now were returning with them. Deacon took a last look back at the small room where he had been held hostage. Pieces of the chair were scattered around the room, and his restraints were now securely tied around one of his former guards. The man's face was bloody, and one eye was swelling closed. He lay on the floor by the other guard, who was in worse shape and unconscious. Deacon walked back and checked both men's pockets again—nothing but the usual pocket trash. *These Guardians had to be communicating with one another in real time.* But Deacon had searched them twice now without locating a cell phone.

Just as he was about to give up and move on, Deacon saw a black object on the floor near the door. It was a small walkie-talkie. *Old school*, Deacon thought, *and outside Batman's reach.*

Deacon was holding the small device to one ear when he heard the first shot. It had come from the lobby and was quickly followed by a couple more rounds. Deacon pocketed the walkie-talkie and bolted through the door and into the resort lobby.

The sound of gunfire had triggered another wave of pandemonium. Security pros were hustling their clients toward exits. Guests were shouting to make contact with friends and spouses. A few were screaming, and many others crying. There were signs of panic here and there. Some individuals were shoving and elbowing their way through the current. Deacon saw a woman trip, and at first the crowd surged over her. A thickset security man bulled his way to the woman and scooped her up before she was trampled.

Above the din Deacon heard an unfamiliar buzz. It took a second for him to realize that it was the device in his pocket. He quickly retrieved it and pressed it to one ear. He covered his other ear and realized that he recognized the voice. He could only make out bits and pieces of what he heard, and it was tough to translate amid all the mayhem. But he recognized this voice. And then he saw the man behind the voice. Hassan was making his way out of the dining hall and into the crowded lobby. Deacon joined the crowd's main current as it jostled toward the front doors of the Sun Valley Resort. At the same time, he began edging his way across the current, searching for Hassan and hoping that he could stop him and the other Guardians before it was too late.

Just as Deacon was trying to make his way across the lobby, Derrick and Ray were reaching the breaking point in their negotiations with the security team that had trapped them in the resort's conference room.

"Do you hear that?" Ray's voice was level and menacing. "That's the sound of people who need our help. For the last time, the guys we shot were terrorists. We all need to get out there now and stop them before they kill a lobby full of innocent people!"

"And yet you two have no ID and no means of verifying your identity."

Derrick held out his right arm in a blocking move. It was pure reflex, because Ray hadn't moved. Derrick knew that time was running out for a friendly solution.

"OK, guys, listen. We are undercover. I can't say with what group, but we are US operators. We've been tracking this terrorist group—they call themselves the Guardians. They are attacking this conference as we speak, and we need your help to stop them. That's the full story, or as much of it as we have time for right now."

Bill Sanders studied Derrick's face for what seemed like a full minute. Ray began to pick out his first target and to plan the series of moves that might do the least damage to these hardheads while at the same time getting him and Derrick through that conference-room door as quickly as possible.

A woman's scream coming from the lobby seemed to break the stalemate.

"All right, you two," Bill said, "we are going to follow your lead. But I am also keeping a red dot on your backs just in case. We clear?"

Ray and Derrick nodded and headed for the door. The security men followed them. They hadn't taken three steps before Ray heard the first zip from a silenced pistol. The bullet ricocheted from a nearby doorframe and clipped Ray's elbow. Derrick returned fire and dropped the Guardian shooter at the edge of the whirling crowd in the lobby.

"You OK?" Derrick shouted.

"Yeah, just a scratch. We need to be there." Ray pointed to a long reception counter that flanked one wall of the lobby. Derrick nodded, and they started to run for cover. Ray heard a groan behind him and then a thud. One of the security men had been hit. Ray looked over his shoulder to see another member of his team going back for him and then going down in a spray of fire. There was no helping them now. The other men were returning fire, crouching low and running forward. Derrick and Ray led the way and dove behind the reception counter. Two Guardians were crouched behind the long counter when they arrived, but neither man had time to turn before Derrick and Ray had opened fire on them. The guests who remained in the lobby were either running for the exits or hiding behind small features in the lobby. Some Guardians were also hiding in place, but the rest seemed to have vanished. Derrick wondered if they were holding hostages in the dining hall.

"Ray, I'm going to make my way to the dining hall and check that situation. Cover me." Derrick darted from behind the counter and made his way to the hallway near the dining hall. He tried once to make his way to the dining-hall entrance but was met by a burst of gunfire. Two Guardians were positioned behind a fountain across the lobby. They had perfect cover and a clear sight line. Just as Derrick was pondering his next move, he heard a call for help. It was a woman's voice, and it was coming from the kitchen. Derrick peeled back away from the dining hall and ran down the hallway toward the kitchen.

He and Ray had seen Sofia DeClair taken hostage at this door. Derrick knew that her calls might be a trap and that the others couldn't afford for him to fall for the bait. He crept low and checked the clearance under the side door. Derrick could see the wheels on carts and a few bits of kitchen debris. Otherwise the kitchen floor looked clear. He could not see Sofia, but he could hear her calling out and sobbing. She was somewhere in the middle of the kitchen. It was the location Derrick would expect if the Guardians were laying a trap for him. No matter where Derrick entered the kitchen, reaching Sofia would require him to cross the same no-man's-land. Derrick circled to the back door of the kitchen. He checked for Guardians and then risked a peek through the clouded kitchen door windows.

The kitchen appeared empty and still. Pots and pans were sitting on stoves unattended. Knives lay on counters next to half-chopped celery stalks and mounds of broccoli. Sprayer arms hung limp from their metal catches. He could hear a faint clicking noise coming from somewhere near the large ovens. Otherwise it was quiet and appeared abandoned.

Derrick crouched and slid through the back door of the kitchen. He made his way past the big ovens and around one of the counters where utensils and stray vegetables lay scattered. Something scraped along the floor, and Derrick froze. The counter was poor cover, but he made himself as small behind it as possible and waited. The scraping noise came again—this time more distinct. A woman's shoe on the floor. Derrick peeked over the counter and deeper into the kitchen. No sign of anyone—at least no one who was standing up. The sound was coming from the center of the kitchen. She must be seated in a chair, and her heels were now and then sliding on the tile floor. Derrick heard a burst of gunfire from the lobby. He couldn't afford to wait any longer. Time to make a move.

"Sofia?" Derrick called.

"Hassan? I'm still here, sitting in the chair like you said."

Derrick recognized the voice. It was definitely Sofia DeClair. So why was she calling out for Hassan? Could she be one of them? It was too late for him to turn back now. Derrick stood up and walked toward the sound of her voice. As he neared the center of the kitchen, he found her beside a pole and seated in an office chair. He was surprised to find that she wasn't bound, but she was clearly in bad shape. Her eyes were full of terror and confusion, and she seemed disoriented.

"Who are you?" she asked and recoiled against the back of the chair.

"Listen, Sofia, I am Derrick. My wife and I met you earlier, but you may not remember. Anyway you are safe now."

"You aren't with them? Where is Hassan?"

"No, I'm not with them. Hassan is gone. Listen, I want you to sit tight in that chair for just a second while I check things out. Then we are going to get out of here. OK?"

Sofia's eyes looked glazed and vacant. She started to rock forward in the chair.

"No!" Derrick shouted and then held out a hand toward her. "Be still, OK? Don't move."

Sofia froze. "Hassan said that too. He said stay in this chair," Sofia said, her voice hollow and mechanical.

Derrick quickly surveyed the floor around the chair and then knelt down to check the chair bottom—nothing out of the ordinary. He surveyed the pole and the counter behind the chair but found nothing. Derrick was just about to conclude that Hassan had indeed left her here without any sort of guard when he spotted the thin wire running along a rack of pans opposite the chair. He followed the wire and quickly discovered that Hassan had not left his hostage uncovered after all. Derrick motioned again for Sofia to remain still and then searched among some pots and pans hanging from a nearby rack. He chose a heavy bake pan and returned to kneel down beside Sofia.

"Listen carefully, Sofia. I am going to count to three. On the count of three, I want you fall out of this chair to the right. Go fast and hit the floor. Do you understand?"

"Yes."

Derrick positioned the baking pan in front of Sofia and then began counting. When he reached three, Sofia dropped out of the chair onto the kitchen floor. As she left the chair, there was a whooshing sound and then the pinging sound of metal striking metal. Derrick reached out a hand and lifted Sofia up from the kitchen floor. On the floor lay the dart that had struck the baking pan. The tip was bent, and the shaft was maybe a bit longer than typical, but otherwise the dart looked like one that might have been lost from a pub's dartboard.

"A toy dart?" Sofia asked, looking up to Derrick.

Derrick helped Sofia to regain her balance and then knelt down to study the dart.

"No toy," Derrick said as he stood up and took her arm, "more like the dart from hell. But you are safe now. Let's get moving."

The two of them retraced his steps back out of the kitchen and down the hallway toward the lobby. Bullets whipped by them as they darted back behind the reception counter. When Derrick landed behind the counter, he ran into something hard. He was shocked to turn and discover that he had plowed into Deacon.

"Deacon, thank God!"

"Hey, cowboy. You OK? Who is this?"

"Sofia DeClair. Guardians were holding her hostage in the kitchen. She's with the resort."

"Anyone else in the kitchen or that dining hall?"

"Couldn't get to the dining hall. Too much covering fire. But the kitchen was empty." Derrick held up his cell phone. "We lost contact with you."

"Yeah, I got held up. But I traded in my phone for this model." Deacon held up the walkie-talkie.

Ray slid down from where he had been covering the far end of the counter and joined Derrick and Deacon. Sofia slumped against the counter nearby.

"Where did you get that?" Ray asked Deacon.

"Long story. But it belonged to a Guardian. I borrowed it." Deacon smiled.

"Pick up anything yet?" Derrick asked.

"Chatter about the time the shooting broke out, but it was hard to make out for all the commotion. Best I can tell these guys are shifting tactics, and they said something about the wind."

"The wind?" Ray asked.

"Yep."

"Deacon, what do you think it means?" Derrick asked.

"Well, obvious thing would be something airborne. Or it might be code."

Derrick turned back to Sofia. "Sofia, where are the main HVAC controls for this building?"

"What?"

"Heating and air conditioning—where is the control center for that sort of thing?"

"Utility basement. There's a set of stairs at the end of the hallway that runs by my office. Do you know where that is?"

"Yes."

"You'll need this." Sofia reached into her suit pocket and withdrew her employee badge. "There's a swipe pad beside the door at the bottom of the stairs."

Ray and Deacon covered Derrick as he darted from behind the counter and made his way back down the hallway and past the conference room where he and Ray had earlier been held hostage. The hallway lights had been shot out, and Derrick had to move slowly at first to adjust to the low light. But once he opened the stairwell door at the end of the hall, he heard the stairwell lights buzz to life.

Derrick checked the hallway behind him one more time before darting into the stairwell. No one was following, and the hallway looked more eerie for being empty. *Where are they all?* Derrick thought as he turned and began making his way down the concrete stairway.

Deacon had also borrowed a few weapons and ammo from his earlier captors. As Derrick headed off to shut down the ventilation system, Deacon and Ray took turns firing at the handful of Guardians remaining in the resort lobby. For determined terrorists Deacon thought that those firing back at them now seemed pretty listless. They were sheltering in place and only now and then moving to get a better sight line. None of them seemed to be moving to any particular spot. And strangest of all, they didn't seem to be targeting the guests. Deacon had seen at least a dozen people cross the lobby since he'd left his supply-closet confinement, and all of them had made it safely across the lobby and out one of the exit doors. Better terrorists would have already turned this situation into a massacre. These guys seemed determined only to kill the security guards, not the people they were guarding. Maybe they had lost their nerve, or maybe their leadership had been taken out. He hadn't seen Hassan since their earlier encounter.

Or maybe..., Deacon thought as he ducked behind the counter and grabbed Ray's arm.

"Is Derrick back yet?"

"No, why?"

"Because the fight has gone outside for some reason. Take a look around: these guys are just pinning us down. And they are letting the guests run out the exits."

Ray poked his head above the counter and fired a few rounds, at the same time surveying the lobby. It was almost empty of guests. A few people were pinned down here and there. Ray saw a man who had been hiding behind a decorative plant run for a nearby exit. Bullets whizzed behind him, but to Ray they looked like intentional misses.

The Guardians firing on the man had ditched their white kitchen garb, but they were easy to recognize and still in the same positions they had occupied so far.

"They aren't moving, and their aim is worse than yours. Think they've lost their nerve?"

"Doubt it," Deacon replied. "I think they are taking the fight outside."

"Outside?"

"Yeah, like where the *wind* blows. We need to find Derrick and get moving before it's too late. You bring her." Deacon nodded toward Sofia, who sat motionless against the wall. "I'll meet you out front." Deacon started to head away and then turned back. "Keep an eye on the sky, Ray. I'm afraid these guys have drones."

Ray started to say something, but before he could speak, Deacon had hustled down the counter and around the corner. He was always amazed that for such a big man Deacon could move with the gliding agility of a cat.

"Drones?" Sofia asked in a whisper as Ray turned back to her.

"Right, not great news…But hey, we've made it so far, right?"

Sofia nodded slightly. Her face was a mask, but a few tears were beginning to leak from the corners of her eyes and run down her cheeks.

Ray moved close to her and placed his hands on her shoulders. She was trembling. Ray looked straight into her face for a moment. And even though she was clearly traumatized, he could see strength and perhaps even the first glimmers of anger. It would have to be enough.

"Listen, Sofia. You are alive. And you are going to beat these scumbags by staying alive. Now, I'm going to make sure that we get out of this lobby. All that you have to do is follow me closely and do exactly what I tell you to do. Do you understand?"

"Yes." Sofia blinked and then raised her hands to clear away the tears from her cheeks.

"I need you to walk, and when I tell you to, I need you to run. Can you do that?"

"Yes." Her voice was a bit stronger this time. "But just one thing."

"What's that?" Ray asked.

"What's your name?"

The question caught him off guard, and Ray couldn't help breaking out in his biggest cowboy grin. It was faint, but Ray thought he caught the beginning of a smile on her face.

"I'm Ray."

"All right, Ray, I'm ready to go."

Deacon had just slipped through the door to the basement stairs when he heard one or two soft footfalls ahead of him. Derrick had been away long enough to finish his work down here, but he would be coming up the stairs. Whoever was just ahead of Deacon was heading down toward the basement. When he hadn't found a light switch at the top of the stairs, Deacon had expected automatic lights to come on when the door was opened. But either these lights were the slowest of those environmentally friendly bulbs, or someone had already made sure that this stairway remained dark.

The man on the stairs hadn't moved. Deacon had been silhouetted against doorway when he had entered the stairway. Why hadn't the man fired at him? Whatever the reason, Deacon remained still and used the time to allow his eyes to adjust to the darkness. He had his pistol drawn, but Deacon didn't want to fire down the stairs unless it was his only option. It could still be Derrick down there. He might not have seen Deacon enter the stairway.

Seconds passed. Deacon's vision was clearing enough that he could make out the figure on the stairwell. He was just about to risk taking a step down toward the figure when suddenly a commotion broke out on the stairwell. He could hear the blows and the groans. Two men were clearly locked in combat just below him, but Deacon could not make out their identities, and he didn't dare risk a shot.

Deacon heard a loud thud. One of the two men had just landed hard at the bottom of the stairwell. It was too late to play it subtle now. Deacon launched himself down the stairs. But he had only made it a few steps when he crashed into another man coming the other direction.

"Deacon, it's me!" Derrick yelled in Deacon's ear as he grabbed his friend's shoulder to avoid falling backward down the concrete stairs.

"Derrick, you OK?" Deacon could barely make out Derrick's face even though they were only inches apart.

"Yeah, all good, HVAC is shut down."

"Was that a Guardian goon I heard hitting the deck down there?"

"Yeah, he's shut down too."

"All right then, let's get going. Looks like the Guardians were playing for time in the lobby. They are drawing everyone outside."

"Outside? But…"

"No time to explain, Derrick. I'll catch you up outside."

Derrick and Deacon headed up the stairs and burst out of the stairwell and into the lobby. A Guardian was patrolling the hallway and wheeled around to face them. But before the man could fire on them, he was hit from the side and went down. Ray emerged from behind the counter just behind the crumpled Guardian. He spotted Deacon and Derrick in the hallway and waved them on as he provided covering fire. Derrick and Deacon raced up to join Ray and Sofia, and then the four of them raced out the front door just as a hail of bullets shattered glass behind them. Ray steered Sofia around a corner of the building and behind the trunk of a large fir tree. Deacon and Derrick followed and took refuge behind a low stone wall.

It was chaos outside, a replay of the earlier commotion inside but with the added features of room to run and many options for escape. Some guests were fleeing toward their cars. Others were running across the grounds of the resort in all directions. Some were hiding behind trees and other points of refuge. And a few, apparently short-circuited by the successive waves of fear and relief, wandered aimlessly out in the open. One man carrying a few wildflowers was walking in front of the stone wall where Deacon and Derrick were hiding when Deacon reached out and hauled the man to safety.

Ray surveyed the scene from under the cover of the big fir tree. Although the Guardians had left their kitchen garb behind, they were not that difficult to spot. There were more beards among the Guardians than among the fleeing technology tycoons. And, unlike their comrades in the lobby, the Guardians outside the resort were moving with purpose and with a clear direction in mind.

The Guardians had set up a loose perimeter, probably in the earlier stages of the chaos inside. Scanning in all directions, he could spot nests of them here and there along tree lines and near major points of exit. Several were posted along the exit road. Many others were covering the footpaths that radiated away from the Sun Valley Resort. Normally used by vacationers and casual hikers, these routes would naturally catch the eye of the panicked guests now fleeing the resort. They didn't have enough men to make a tight circle. And if they were only playing a ground game, it was clear to Ray that the Guardians would not be able to contain their targets. But air support would change everything. And Ray thought he could see the launch point for the Guardians' air assault. He had seen several Guardians who were not on the perimeter entering at the same point of a pocket of deep woods about fifty yards away, on the western side of the exit road. The trees and underbrush were thick along this stretch of road, but behind them Ray could see a rise of land and a clearing. That bald patch of high ground would give the terrorists a clear view of the entire resort compound, as well as a blocking presence along the main artery of escape. Any car attempting to exit the resort would need to drive some two hundred yards within sight and close range of the Guardians' launch point.

After instructing Sofia to stay put, Ray raced the short distance to Derrick and Deacon's position.

"They are heading up there. See, the deep cover and then that clear high ground behind it." The three of them peeked over the top of the wall, and Ray pointed toward the woods alongside the exit road. Just then another Guardian ducked into the cover and disappeared.

They ran to the tree and collected Sofia, and then the four of them sprinted from cover to cover until they reached the head of the trail into the woods. Bullets zipped through the air around them, but the firing was less heavy than Ray had expected. The Guardians must be sinking back into position and preparing to launch their air assault.

Derrick could hear voices and movement up ahead as they neared the end of the deep pocket of forest. He signaled for the others to slow down and use cover. Within a dozen yards of the break into open ground, he called a halt, and the four of them crouched close together.

"Ray, you stay with Sofia at the edge of this cover. We'll need you to provide fire for us as we come and go along the edge of the clearing. Did you make the call to the SpecOps team?"

"On their way."

"Good, all we need to do is disrupt them. Keep those birds out of the air until the cavalry can get here."

"Uh, we might be a little late with that." Ray was looking through a patch of woods at the sky over Derrick's head.

Derrick turned, and the four of them watched as a tiny drone rose from the clearing and then began streaking toward the resort.

"So much for the element of surprise." Deacon drew the .45 pistol he had taken from one of his Guardian captors and aimed through a break in the trees. He fired four times before he hit the speeding drone, and it was not a direct hit. The drone spun and hissed but only gradually lost altitude as it headed toward the resort. Deacon could see what looked like a smoke trail but was actually a faint stream of powder or dust trailing the damaged drone.

"It was loaded: chemical or bugs. Something spraying out of it as it comes down. "

"Are we OK here?" Ray asked.

"Yeah, that's the good news," Deacon replied. "Bad news is the wind is blowing toward the resort."

A bullet zipped through the brush and hit a tree near where Deacon was standing. The four of them ducked down and moved deeper into the bush as bullets began hitting limbs and ricocheting all around them. Derrick returned fire and urged the others toward a boulder at the base of a large pine tree. The fire was more dispersed now, as the Guardians were guessing their location. Ray recognized a voice calling out above the gunfire and ordering several men to charge their position in the woods. It was Hassan. He was alive and directing traffic. Ray looked around the boulder and saw four of the small drones lifting off from the clearing. At the same time, a half dozen Guardians armed with automatic rifles were running their way. And then a larger drone lifted off and, flying lower than the others, bolted toward their position in the forest.

"Time to choose targets, cowboys," Deacon said in a whisper. "Drones or bad guys with guns?"

"Drones," Derrick answered. Ray turned back to face Sofia.

"Sofia, I want you to run. *Now!* Head back down this trail and wait for us at the edge of the forest. Don't go back to the resort, and don't get in any car. Understand? Now *go!*"

The blank stare was gone now, and her eyes were clear and focused. "But what about..."

Ray could hear the buzz of the larger drone closing fast. "No time to explain—just run!"

Sofia turned and raced down the trail, pushing aside limbs and flying through the brush. She had disappeared into the forest by the time Ray heard the missile zipping through the trees.

A tree behind them exploded into a million pieces, and burning shrapnel whistled all around them. Deacon screamed a curse and then opened fire on the bigger drone. Derrick also opened fire. A second missile zipped away from the drone, but it flew wide and cut a burning swath through the forest about ten yards away. Then the drone wobbled, pitched, and plowed through the forest and into the ground. Burning limbs and brush rained down on their position, and small fires were beginning to catch all around them.

"Deacon, you hit?" Derrick called.

"Yeah, but still standing."

Ray could see a gaping wound in Deacon's back. An ugly piece of shrapnel had torn into the middle of his back and driven a deep furrow to the top of his shoulder. The metal edge was pocking through just above his collarbone, and a faint smoke trail was still visible above it.

Ray pushed forward and joined Derrick and Deacon as they fired on the remaining drones. It took most of their ammo to hit two of them, but the other two escaped unharmed and zipped over their heads in the direction of the resort. Just then the Guardians closed on their position and began to lay down a withering barrage of automatic gunfire. Deacon was fading fast and nearly out of ammunition, and Ray knew that he and Derrick could not possibly hold off six men with assault rifles. It was time to leave cover and try to outflank Hassan's main crew in the clearing. It was a desperation move, and Ray wasn't sure Deacon was up to making a run for it. But maybe at least one of them could reach the flank of that hill and do enough damage to stop the drone attack.

Ray tapped Derrick on the shoulder and motioned for Deacon. He took the covering position and trailed the other two as they began making their move. The Guardians were nearing the edge of the clearing now. Bullets were pouring into the edge of the forest now, shredding limbs and breaking off rock shrapnel from the boulder where they had been hidden.

A bullet tore through Ray's forearm and spun him to the ground. As he landed in a blanket of pine needles and rotting leaves, Ray could hear bullets buzzing overhead like an entire hive of angry bees. Bits of limb and leaves showered down on him. Ray crawled behind the trunk of a nearby tree and regained his footing. He was just about to run after Deacon and Derrick when he heard the pounding of boots. They were on him. Ray turned to see three of the Guardians closing fast. They were only yards away now and slowing down for the kill. Ray could see that the man in the lead was smiling. Although it was futile now, Ray raised his pistol and pointed it at the smiling Guardian.

And then the man stopped smiling and dropped in a heap. The two other Guardians turned back toward the clearing and then shook violently as though they had been stung all over. They dropped beside their companion. Ray stared at his pistol. It took him a second to realize that he hadn't fired and that the Guardians had been shot by someone in the clearing.

Just then a special ops soldier ran into the forest and paused near the dead Guardians. He kept his weapon trained on Ray, and the two studied each other for a moment.

Then the soldier called out for him to drop his weapon, and Ray surrendered. Derrick and Deacon came walking back toward him, accompanied by their own pair of special ops soldiers from General Crocker's unit. It took a moment to establish their identity, but then the soldiers let them walk out to the clearing and see the rest of the operation. A dozen or so of Crocker's men were surrounding Hassan and his remaining men, who were seated on the ground, their hands and feet bound by zip ties.

The rest of Crocker's soldiers were fanning out through the woods and making their way toward Sun Valley Resort. There were shouts now and then and occasional gunfire, as they captured or killed the remaining Guardians. Crocker's team had shot down the drones before they could reach the resort, although they could do nothing about the white powder that had leaked out of them. By the time they walked out of the forest at the edge of the resort, hazmat soldiers in full bug suits were setting up a perimeter and beginning their work.

Sofia was crouched low near a fallen log at the edge of the forest. Ray knelt down beside her. "You OK, Sofia?"

"Yes, but you are hurt." She pointed at Ray's bloodied arm.

"Yeah, could have been a lot worse. Here, let me help you up." Ray extended his uninjured arm, and Sofia took his hand.

The two of them walked back to join Deacon, Derrick, and the other special ops soldiers. They stood in silence for a moment, surveying the scene in front of them. The hazmat soldiers had cleared the survivors out to the parking lot. They sat in small groups huddled under blankets. On any other night in Sun Valley, they might have been waiting for the start of a summer concert. But on this night, they were sitting in shock as EMTs moved among them and treated their wounds. The normally pristine grounds of the resort looked like a war zone. Smoke drifted, and the air was tinged with the smell of gunpowder. Chef's coats lay on the ground haphazardly like sleeping ghosts. Shattered glass was scattered in a wide arc around the front of the lodge, and long shards of glass hung like loose teeth in the huge window frames. Crouching soldiers scurried across the open lawn and along the edges of the forest, moonlight glinting off their rifles and gear.

"Any idea if the people are safe? Do we know if we stopped it yet?" Derrick asked a soldier nearby.

"No, sir, no idea. The signs are good so far. All the casualties I've seen are gunshot wounds, and there are fewer of those than we expected."

Medics arrived to treat Deacon's and Ray's wounds. Derrick tried to encourage Sofia to let them check her out, but she would only accept a blanket and take a seat nearby. He stood by long enough to make sure that neither Deacon nor his brother would skip any steps or wave off treatment, and then Derrick sat down and leaned back against the trunk of a spruce tree.

The fatigue of combat washed over him as he studied the small bits of debris that littered the ground around him. The air seemed heavier now and the mountains closer. The crazy blend of smells in the alpine air took him back for a fleeting second to Afghanistan. He had never thought the mountain breezes around Sun Valley would carry that complex aroma of a battlefield amid an alpine forest. Derrick stood up suddenly and shook himself alert. He studied the scene around him one more time, this time taking a few snapshots in his mind. He felt a rising panic—an intense need to remember that it had really happened here, in Sun Valley. Derrick wanted to remember the sights and sounds and smells of this particular battlefield. Crowfoot and the Guardians had brought this battle to Derrick's doorstep. This was personal now. And as Derrick walked back to join the others he knew that whether he wanted it or not, the fight was now his.

Epilogue

ACCORDING TO ARMY protocol, the ceremony should have taken place in Washington or perhaps at the institute. But General Crocker had been known to break with protocol when it served what he considered a higher purpose.

And so on a crisp fall day, a small group began gathering at Derrick and Jessie's ranch house. Ray had come early and planned to stay late. He seemed to enjoy time at the ranch more than ever. Deacon wasn't supposed to attend, but he had charmed doctors and nurses alike.

"It's just hard for them to resist the appeal of a Detroit man," he told Jessie when he responded to her invitation.

Frank and Reuben had driven down from Cascade. They had been doing more camping and fishing over the summer, and both of them looked to be in fine form. And they brought Bear along. Like Deacon and Francine, the mastiff was still on some medical restrictions. He wasn't supposed to tear through doors or windows anytime soon, and the big dog was supposed to take it easy on the chow until he fully recovered. Reuben had given him half rations this morning, just in case Bear managed to sneak some party food.

A few other guests were there from the institute and army CI, as well as some of the special-operations soldiers who had helped in the mop-up operation against the Guardians.

Jessie and General Crocker had conspired to keep the guest of honor in the dark about today's gathering. Francine had been told only that she should wear her dress uniform because Jessie wanted to get some pictures.

Francine was surprised and embarrassed at the attention. But she was gratified by the main surprise of the day. General Crocker presented her with an Army Commendation Medal. Francine and her team had been working all along on a preventative vaccine in the event that the Guardians were able to perfect their prion bioweapon. A few of those who had been infected in the Sun Valley attack were spared an agonizing death by the swift application of this experimental vaccine. As she recovered, she hoped to work on strengthening defenses against both prion-related illnesses and the new strain of meningitis with which she herself had been infected.

After receiving her commendation, Francine learned that she would be working on these new projects in a new location. General Crocker had consulted with leaders of the institute and the Pentagon about establishing a new army laboratory. He had lobbied successfully for Francine to be promoted and given command over the new lab, which would be based just outside Boise, Idaho. After the ceremony and official announcements were completed, the little group began celebrating. Everyone was relieved to hear good news, to know that they were recovering together, and to look forward to good days ahead.

"Hey, city girl," Jessie said, "time for you to learn to ride Western."

"Do I at least get a horse, or am I stuck with mules?"

Frank looked up from his punch. "Hey, my mules are better than any horse." He winked at Francine.

"Oh, I almost forgot…" Jessie disappeared into the kitchen for a moment and then returned bearing a small and simply decorated cake.

"For Bear," she announced and made a grand show of serving the big dog. Bear sniffed at the cake for a moment and then looked up at Frank.

"Go ahead, big dog; she's the host of this party." And with that Bear dug in and made short work of Jessie's miniature chicken and carrot cake with yogurt and peanut-butter icing. When Bear finally lifted his massive head, it was covered with icing and crumbs. Even General Crocker laughed.

Derrick caught his brother's eye for a moment, and Ray tipped his glass in Derrick's direction. In spite of the celebration around him he found himself wishing that he could wake up and shake all this off as a bad dream. Derrick gazed out the window. Jessie's horse Pocco was grazing in the nearby pasture, the sun bathing her sleek back. A part of him would give anything to go back in time. He wanted to be back in his office at the university or sitting beside Jessie in their porch swing at the ranch. But another part of him knew that there was no going back now. The thugs who called themselves Guardians had invaded his homeland. They had hurt people he loved. A line had been crossed. He took a second longer to grieve what he was leaving behind. And then Derrick opened his eyes and took the first steps of his life on the other side of that line.

A week later Francine was moving to Idaho and working to establish the new laboratory. Meanwhile Derrick and Ray were asked to come to Washington for debriefing sessions. There had been some mistakes along the way, including falling for that head fake at the delivery area. And there had been more than a few breaks in protocol.

"Going off the reservation," as General Crocker had said, although he seemed to be the only one in the room who failed to catch the dark irony of that worn-out phrase. It was true. They had broken rules and sidestepped procedures. Deacon was labeled a rogue operator along with Derrick and Ray, even though he maintained his "just a private security man" persona to the end.

In the plus column, they had blocked the worst of a major terrorist attack and saved the lives of many victims. The only victims of their bioweapon had been those infected in the dining hall, among them the billionaire Leonard Davis. His death had been agonizing, and his estate had filed lawsuits in all directions. The drone assault had been unsuccessful, although bioweapons experts who reviewed the case were concerned that a future assault might prove more deadly. Ten individuals had died in the attack. All but three of the victims had died from gunfire. Seventeen terrorists had been killed and eight others captured.

The attack had spurred biodefense efforts, and the new lab in Boise was expected to further advance the science. From a counterterrorism perspective, Derrick, Ray, and Deacon had shed light on a terrorist network that had been functioning for years under the radar.

But there was unfinished business. Crowfoot was still out there. Rasheem had left the lab intact, and it had been captured along with a treasure trove of information about the Guardians' bioterror program. Two contract assassins known as Tupe and Ghost had been found dead in the forest about five miles from the laboratory. Both had been infected by the weaponized prions and died of the illness. Dr. Nasim was also a victim of his own cronies. Homeland Security investigators found him dead at a picnic area along a forlorn stretch of Idaho highway. He had apparently been trying to make his way to Canada at the time. He was brutally murdered at the picnic stop, and all the signs pointed to Jim Crowfoot as his killer. Crowfoot had headed north toward the Canadian border, but investigators lost his trail not far from the Nasim murder.

So the Guardians had been bloodied but not destroyed. Francine had fought back hard against their monster diseases, including the one that almost took her own life. Derrick and Ray had done their best to defend those who had gathered at Sun Valley. But it seemed likely that the Guardians would be back. Jim Crowfoot was a determined and vicious enemy. And as much as he wanted to believe otherwise, Derrick left the briefing knowing that this fight was far from over.

The End

Acknowledgments

I WOULD FIRST like to thank my parents, Charles and Maxine Petty, who placed a high value on reading and storytelling. It has taken me longer than I expected to write this first novel, but I am happy to complete it as my father celebrates his ninetieth birthday. Thank you for your endless encouragement and love.

Idaho is the setting for this novel. I am grateful to my nephew Justin for introducing me to this beautiful state. Our visits to his home in Bonner's Ferry, and later, to Justin and Lynea's home in Hailey, Idaho, started me daydreaming about the place. At first I daydreamed about moving to Idaho, but for now I have had to satisfy myself with visiting through the writing of this book. Visiting Idaho in one's mind is not quite the same as being there, but it is still a fine journey.

Thanks to friends Brian and Gwynda Allen for reading earlier drafts of this book. Your encouragement and feedback helped me to keep going, particularly in the tougher stretches. I would also like to thank our son Connor and daughter-in-law Charley for reading and reacting to earlier drafts of this manuscript.

Our daughter, Makayla, helped at points with research, particularly related to bovine diseases. She also put up with me in those times when I was in the writing zone. Thanks for your patient help and even more for being an amazing daughter. Our son, Hudson, is an excellent writer, and I appreciate him sharing his ideas and perspective. I hope that in our writing conversations I am able to at least partially return the favor. Thank you, Hudson, and all the best with your book.

Finally, I want to thank my wife, Joan. I could not imagine writing this book without Joan's help. She was first of all an insightful reader and encouraging editor. But beyond this, Joan gave me her wholehearted support. Writing a book is a long journey, and I cannot imagine going it alone. Joan made this journey a pleasant one, and I look forward to our next one together.

72580929R00276

Made in the USA
Columbia, SC
21 June 2017